By the same author

RETURN JOURNEY

R. F. Delderfield

SIMON AND SCHUSTER · NEW YORK

Published by Simon and Schuster
Rockefeller Center, 630 Fifth Avenue
New York, New York 10020

SBN 671-21786-0
Library of Congress Catalog Card Number: 73-21471
Designed by Edith Fowler
Manufactured in the United States of America

2 3 4 5 6 7 8 9 10

Every character in this book is fictitious. None are intended to represent persons living or dead.

RECONNAISSANCE

I stopped the car at the top of the hill and looked down the broad cleft to the sea. I braked without knowing why, obeying a kind of reflex, so that it took me a moment or two to recall that this was the exact spot I had stopped for a last look back on the way out of Redcliffe Bay, more than thirty years ago. I was twenty then and travelling hopefully if desperately: I was over fifty now and pretty much resigned to rootlessness and loneliness. All the same, it cost me a moment of desolation to come to terms with the grinding passage of the years.

I knew then, looking down into the bay, that I had made a mistake coming here at all. There was little likelihood that anyone down there would remember me, or that I should recognise a single Redcliffian who had his being there in the late nineteen-twenties and early nineteen-thirties. Too much time had passed, too much had happened, and I had left it far too late. Yet curiosity nagged at me; curiosity and the strong tug of nostalgia. I didn't want to reintroduce myself to anyone—I had made up my mind about this—but I did want to potter round the old town, and smell the weed that used to pile up under the breakwaters. I wanted to watch the sun set on the red, slabsided face of Mitre Head, the western promontory. I wanted to feel the uneven surface of the promenade tarmac under my feet. I wanted to make some kind of assessment of what I had missed; if anything.

The place was all but unrecognizable and I realised this as soon as I dropped down the long slope to the heart of the town. Every house and every shop looked raw, like the buildings in one of the towns in northern France over which two wars have rolled in one generation. I knew that Redcliffe Bay had been the target of any number of hit-and-run raiders between 1940 and 1943, but I hadn't bargained for change on this scale. All the old High Street shops, that had once looked like illustrations in a book of fairy tales, had been replaced with glass and chromium showcases and most of them displayed names you could see in any High Street anywhere in Britain. There was a busy roundabout at the entrance of the old town, and then three or four sets of traffic lights. There was a huge black and white sign reading "REDCLIFFE BAY WELCOMES CAREFUL DRIVERS" that would have made any original Redcliffian gape with amazement. In the old days we didn't give a damn how visitors drove just so long as they crowded into the boardinghouses during the all-too-short summer season. In any case, in those days very few of them did drive. They arrived by train from the junction, clutching strapped suitcases and looking wan, hunted and bewildered.

The railways did not seem to be handling much holiday traffic today. Every street was jam-packed with cars, honking and writhing and daring one another. The atmosphere reeked with exhaust fumes. I found a car park in what had once been the yard of Trumper's Auction Mart and walked through a side lane I didn't remember into Stump Enclosure and here at least I recognised something. The Stump was still there at the apex of a triangle of green, checkered with rectangular flower beds, shaded by about a dozen horse chestnuts. The Stump, crowned by a bronze lifeboatman, commemorated the loss of the Redcliffe Bay lifeboat crew, in 1871. It was Redcliffe's sole claim on posterity and in my day the square and its enclosure used to do duty for a village green. In the nine out-of-season months groups of youths and girls gathered here of an early evening, passing and repassing each other, and scuffling and skylarking, as they did around the bandstand in high summer. Old men used to come out here too, staking a claim on one or other of the elm seats, each marked "R.B.U.D.C." to establish Council ownership. In a way the Stump, east and west, was the heart of the town between late September and early June, and a number of Redcliffe

Bay's most prominent citizens had their place of business here.

The Stump itself hadn't changed at all but it looked very incongruous indeed among so many new buildings. I remember we used to joke about the memorial, asking each other what the sou'-westered lifeboatman on the top of the column expected to see under the palm raised to shield his eyes from the glare of the sun. When the memorial was built in the late seventies it was then assumed he was looking at the wreck in the bay, but the facetious would argue that wrecks never occurred under conditions of strong sunshine, so, being level with first-story windows, he might have been playing Peeping Tom to pass the time. The Tivoli Cinema, at the top of East Stump, was now a Bingo Hall, and where Gloria Swanson had displayed her curves was a shocking-pink poster announcing that fortunes could be won inside three times a week. Scatty Wallace's ironmongery store, a few shops down from the Tivoli, was gone and in its place was a clinical-looking supermarket. Noting this I wondered what had happened to Scatty, his indomitable wife and four daughters, especially Esta Wallace, his youngest, who had played such a major role in promoting my exit back in 1932.

Over on West Stump there were more startling changes. A block of flats occupied the site of Myfanwy Pritchard's Gift Shop and the Church School, and this recalled to me the marriage of Myfanwy and Owen Rees, the headmaster, soon after Myfanwy had rescued his aged mother from a fire when Owen was away conducting a school glee chorus in the Albert Hall.

I felt more at home down here but much more nostalgic. It was like returning from the dead after a couple of centuries. Every step I took as I circled the Stump raised another ghost. Barclays Bank was still there and I remembered the peppery little manager of my day, who was also the tyrant of the Redcliffe Bay Operatic and Dramatic Society. On the East Stump, close to the junction of Frog Terrace, there was still a Congregational Church but it was not the building I recalled where the pastor, the Reverend Rex Sweetland, once laid siege to his deaconness–organist but sent her packing when he realized we had our eye on him, and became reconciled with his wife, Alison. Nearby, Hansen's music shop was gone and I wondered what had become of Ken Pigeon, who looked like a cheerful rook and had married Hansen's solemn daughter, Greta. The Rainbow Café was gone too, so that one could no longer peer through its misted windows on winter nights and watch the elegant Dora Gorman mince to and fro with plates of hake and plaice, while her husband sliced away at the chip machine in the corner. Suddenly I became greedy for memories and walked on down Frog Terrace (so named because the French *émigrés* had lived there when Redcliffe Bay was still a fishing village) towards the sea front, in my day a half-mile strip dignified by the name "Esplanade."

I thought changes would be less obvious here but I was wrong. It wasn't my sea front any more but a broad, featureless mile, with chalets and beach huts on one side and a new sea wall on the other. Heavy concrete groynes had replaced the old wooden breakwaters and there was a swimming bath, paddling pool and parking ground where the captured German guns had stood. There was no capstan or coastguard station and where the lifeboat house had stood was a snack bar, its entrance hung around with rubber floats and strings of postcards. The postcards were views. There were no comic ones featuring red-nosed husbands, irate wives and blonde sirens with jutting breasts and mountainous behinds. The old golf links had been built upon and all the shanties had been cleared from the dock area. The beach itself was crammed with sunbathers, some displaying braces, others nearly all they had to show. The racket down here was terrifying. An endless stream of cars rolled back and forth along the lanes, an aimless, prowling, tooting avalanche of chromium and cellulose, and the people sitting in them looked neither happy nor unhappy but just blank, as though they were awaiting a climax to this business of patrolling, a tidal wave perhaps, or an invasion from the sea.

I decided that the Stump area was the best of a bad job and retraced my steps there, returning via the shrubbery that ran under Frog Terrace and passing recesses with Council seats in them where, on the way home from the band enclosure on summer nights, I had embraced most of Redcliffe Bay's flappers at one time or another. Recalling some of them, their little artifices and high spirits, and recalling too how young and hopeful everybody was in those days, my disappointment ebbed a little and when I was back on Stump, and sitting under a chestnut tree within yards of where my old studio had stood, I began to get the feel of the old town again. Not as it was, that was beyond me, but how it used to be.

It always strikes me as odd that successive generations create tinsel legends about decades that are passed but close enough to be recalled in detail by the living. When I was a boy people used to talk about the Gay Nineties and the Edwardian Afternoon, and recently there has been a cult of the twenties. But it has no real affinity with the twenties as I recall them, or not as they were lived out in a place like Redcliffe Bay. Anyone relying upon television for a picture of what it was like to be young in those days could be forgiven for supposing we were all caught up in a nonstop orgy, stamping our way through endless sessions of the Black Bottom and Charleston in our Oxford bags and waistless dance frocks. People behaved like that and dressed like that in musical comedies but that was about all. We locals danced the Charleston now and again at Church Hall hops, and I tried (and failed) to learn to play the ukulele, but as I recall it most of us were primarily occupied earning anything up to thirty shillings a week. Money was scarce everywhere, particularly among dwellers in small towns who lived by taking in one another's washing. What the popular conception misses, I think, was the self-containment of those days, and the sense of belonging that has gone forever from Western Europeans. The twenties was not really a period of great change. Most of the conventions and traditions of Victorian and Edwardian England survived the war and people not only knew their place but accepted it without bellyaching. In places like Redcliffe Bay there was still a carefully-graded social scale but the restrictions it imposed didn't bother anybody but a few eccentrics. At the top of the scale was the so-called gentry, mostly professional people and retired service families who lived in what we called "The Valley," under the western slopes of Coastguard Hill, the eastern buttress of the town. Nearer the sea front, and in and about the High Street and the Stump, lived the tradesmen, who were largely responsible for administrating and diverting the community. Down near the tiny dock were the dozen or so rows of redbrick terrace houses named after Boer War battles and these gimcrack terraces sheltered the artisans and their families, all of whom left school at fourteen and went to work the next day if they could find anything to do. The three grades intermingled very freely, the Valley folk extending patronage and the terrace-house families paying them deference but not too much of it. Everybody seemed instinctively to know where to draw the line and the tradesmen, some of whom were comfortably off, acted as a kind of buffer between the two extremes, so that it was possible for people in all income groups to work together in harmony, particularly on behalf of a locally-inspired event, like the annual Water Carnival.

I said we were self-contained but we were more than that really. We were like a big, tumbling family, feuding and fraternizing as the fancy took us, and we paid very little heed to what went on up or down the coast, or more than a few miles inland. Perhaps communities like ours still exist in isolated areas of the country but I hardly think so. The telly and the transistor, the small car and the tourist agencies, have seen to that. Not one per cent of the original Redcliffians I knew had traveled abroad if one excepts war service, and in the late nineteen-twenties a man who owned any kind of car was automatically upgraded. I'm not blowing a horn for those days. All I'm saying is that the era is as far removed from today as we were from the mid-nineteenth century or before that. There were injustices, plenty of them. Most people were grossly underpaid and underprivileged. Three spectres haunted all of us—Unemployment, Sickness and Old Age—each spelled out in capital letters, but in spite of this most people, especially young people, were both gayer and more tranquil than they are today. They seemed so anyhow because so few of them expected much. I was the local exception and that was my misfortune or otherwise, whichever way you care to look at it.

I sat under the chestnut a long time lighting one cigarette from another, reflecting on some of the folk who had once lived around here and, in the process, trying to decide whether I had won or lost by acting the way I did. I suppose I was one of the very few of my generation in Redcliffe Bay who had actually achieved what I had in mind at that time, namely to make money, to go places, and to be someone if, in fact, anyone is anyone when the books are balanced. I began as apprentice to a seedy, small-town photographer, and had finally made the top league, photographing international clowns like Hitler and national institutions like Churchill. The middle-aged men I had known when I was a boy in Redcliffe Bay had served in one war but I had had a ringside seat at a dozen, without having to live in a ditch on plum and apple jam. A few of the Redcliffians in those days had had a quick glimpse of one sovereign but my work had taken me into the presence of every important head of state in a generation. There was hardly a country I hadn't visited and my personal experiences were, by Redcliffe Bay standards, immensely rich and varied. I had earned and spent a lot of money and failed in marriage. I had a good many expensive possessions but no home to put them in. I had no children and no one who cared a damn what happened to me when I began to run down. Sitting here under the big chestnut tree, where it had all begun so long ago, I realized that I had been searching for something a good deal more elusive than I had found during this thirty-year traipse. I wasn't sure, even now, what that something was, unless it was some kind of human relationship that I could have had for the asking, without setting foot outside the town, and this set me pondering about something else. What, precisely, were the factors that had launched me into space? I had always supposed that I knew them but now I saw that I did not, or not with any kind of certainty. Yet I wanted very much to know, and that was why I sat here such a long time, poking among forgotten scenes and circumstances as a man rummages a pile of dead leaves with a stick.

CHAPTER ONE

The atmosphere of the town, greatly changed as it was, worked upon the memory like a powerful stimulant so that faces and voices left behind over the years began to catch up, like stragglers who sense that something important is happening ahead of the line of march.

Staring up at the bronze lifeboatman on the Stump, for instance, I suddenly recalled the day the rhythm of my life in this place faltered. I even remembered the date, January 6th, 1932, within about a month of my twentieth birthday. That was the day Esta Wallace and I came to our understanding; it was also the day I met Lorna Morney-Sutcliffe. If I was really looking for a starting point here it was.

By then I had the business pretty well under my hand, for Birdie Boxall, founder and proprietor of the Grosvenor Studios on West Stump, was beginning to fail and sometimes didn't show up for days on end. He said it was his bronchitis but I knew better. He had been putting it back for years and was no longer fit for anything but routine work and not too much of that. I didn't resent his withdrawal, in fact I welcomed it, because some of the mothers who came in to have their cherubs photographed objected to Birdie's beery breath and his fumbling preliminaries with the lights. As to outside work, taking the kind of pictures we sold to the *County Press* and the *Messenger*, our local paper, he was past that altogether. You would ask him to get a shot of a breached sea wall after a gale and he would come home with a close-up of a gull on a lamp-standard and an angled smudge of cotton wool sea in the bottom right-hand corner.

I had worked with Birdie getting on for six years then, first as his clerk and errand boy, then as his apprentice, latterly as his factotum. Before he began drinking heavily he was a very good photographer, with plenty of energy and original ideas, but after his wife died he went to pieces. He taught me everything I knew about studio photography and getting newspaper pictures under difficult lighting conditions, and he was only just in time because if I hadn't been interested enough to stay on he would have had to close up altogether when the lease ran out on the studio two years after I joined him straight from school. As it was, old Rufus Trumper, who owned a lot of the property in and around the Stump, renewed his lease on a yearly basis and we not only kept going but increased our turnover. There was no other photographer for miles around and in the summer season we developed thousands of Kodak snaps for the visitors. Winter business was quieter but more interesting. We photographed every wedding group in the area, scores of family album subjects and also grossed about five pounds a week taking half-guinea pictures for newspapers. On the rare occasions when anything sensational happened, a wreck, a bad fire, a landslide, or anything of that kind, we acted as local agents for the daily papers and were paid on results.

I liked Birdie and I liked the job and it was just as well I did, for there wasn't much in the way of alternatives in those days. My father had been killed on the Somme, and my mother died soon afterwards so that when I was five, or thereabouts, I had been sent down to Redcliffe Bay to make a home with some of my mother's cousins who fed and clothed me on the small army pension my mother had been allotted. They were kind, unremarkable people called Frisby, who lived in one of the older Jubilee terraces behind the railway goods yard. Fred Frisby worked in the local timber yard for sixty shillings a week and his wife, Meg, earned extra money as a daily woman at one of the big houses in the Avenue. They don't come into the story because I moved in with Birdie the week after his wife died and he found a woman to cook and clean for us. He paid me fifty shillings a week and keep, which was reckoned generous in those days, and it was understood that when he died, or retired, the business would pass to me.

I was happy enough with these arrangements, happier than I

have ever been since, and I think this was partly because, even then, I regarded Redcliffe Bay and Birdie's Studio as a jumping-off place, the starting point of a brilliant career I would launch myself upon as soon as I had two or three hundred pounds in the Post Office Savings Bank. I had no clear idea where I would go or what I would do, apart from qualifying as an ace photographer and graciously consenting to hire myself to a daily newspaper, but I didn't think of the future consciously. You don't when you are twenty, well fed and living inside a friendly circle.

Birdie was an exceptionally easygoing boss and I knew everyone in town, many of them by their Christian names. We youngsters, boys and girls, had all attended the same Secondary School and in those days the classes were co-ed so that most of us succeeded in bypassing the awkwardness and shyness between the sexes that stems from segregated education after kindergarten days. By the standards of the day, I suppose, we were precocious but not by today's standards. There was a great deal of flirting, and squeals in the map cupboard, but it seems to me that the local girls had more sense and the boys more scruples than have the average teenagers today. The girls set certain limits and the boys accepted them without much resentment. When a girl did find herself pregnant, as happened less often than it does today, there was a family row, a two-family conference, a registry office wedding, then all parties were more or less satisfied. There were several marriages of this kind among the Secondary School set but they worked out pretty well, without benefit of welfare officers, magistrates, clergymen and marriage guidance counsellors. Premarital sex is the subject of any number of tedious discussions in the press and on television today, but we didn't talk about it much. If there was a prospect of marriage we practiced it and if there wasn't we usually didn't, because neither boy nor girl cared to run the risks involved. We certainly took sex for granted in a way that not even the Archbishop of Canterbury is prepared to do today and if we, as youngsters, had made an issue of it, no one would have taken us seriously.

Birdie Boxall was an old-type photographer, a leftover from the Watch-the-Birdie era, hence his local nickname. He was lean, windblown and jocular, with a shock of iron-gray hair and a twinkle in his eye. He had practiced in the very early days of studio photography, when every client was carefully posed beside a potted palm or under a rustic arch, wearing a glassy smile and looking damnably uncomfortable in his Sunday best. Birdie's imagination, however, came into play during freelance work and in his day he had captured some impressive shots of the bay, the shores east and west of the town, the deep woods that covered the further slopes of Mitre Head and the miles of heather and pine country between the extreme limits of the town and the road leading to Paxtonbury, our nearest city nearly twenty miles away. He was good at photographing antiques for auction catalogues and old buildings for house agents' advertisements. Taken all round, Redcliffe Bay was lucky to have him until he began to soak it up in the Lamb and Flag, Redcliffe Bay's most popular pub at our end of town.

That day, January 6th, began like any other day.

Birdie called me into his bedroom and said his bronchitis was frightened of the east wind, already chasing the dead leaves round the Stump, and I assured him that I could easily cope with the day's commitments entered in the diary by Beryl, our pound-a-week cashier–receptionist. It looked like a full but routine day and the first job was to execute a commission for Messrs. Duckworth's, who had at last got a footing in the town by buying George Wayland's Penny Bazaar from his widow, Olga Wayland. The sale had caused a considerable stir in the town because the local tradesmen walked in fear of company shops and had closed their ranks against infiltration, despite the comparatively high prices offered for premises that became vacant. Wayland's Penny Bazaar was the very first to go on our side of the town and neighbors of Olga Wayland had sent a deputation to her, begging her not to sell. The deputation came away with a swarm of fleas about their ears, for Olga was a plain-speaking woman and George hadn't left much money. Local loyalties, if she had ever had any, were certainly not strong enough to reject an offer of four thousand and the deal was about to be completed. Duckworth's intended to extend the premises and were sending in a building firm but they wanted a record of the old building before the demolition team went to work.

I went out across the enclosure, turning up my collar to the keen wind. The sun was very bright but there was no warmth in it and I could see, looking southwest, that it was going to cloud over pretty soon and probably come on to blow hard. All our gales came in from the southwest but we were accustomed to them and much preferred them to snow. With a southwesterly the temperatures always rose and something told you winter hibernation was more than halfway through and that daffodils and narcissi would soon be showing in the beds of the Stump enclosure. That meant that summer wasn't all that far away and with it the bustle and variety of the holiday season. We Redcliffians always looked forward to the holiday-makers' arrival but we were just as glad to see them go.

I took a spread of pictures in and about the Penny Bazaar and on the way back along East Stump I ran into Ben Dagmar, editor and owner of the local paper, the *Redcliffe Bay Messenger*, that came out every Friday. He and I were on good terms and he had always helped and encouraged me, suggesting pictures I might take and hawk around the county if he didn't want them. This time he told me about Scatty Wallace's whistling kettle and advised me to call on Scatty and get a picture of it.

"You never know," he said gravely, "the kettle might amount to something and if he gets it patented a picture of the original, and the workshop he made it in, would be saleable to a technical paper. Supposing someone had had a chance of photographing Stephenson's Rocket!"

I wasn't much impressed. I had photographed a good many of Scatty's inventions and the only one to show a profit was the pressure cooker that blew up and set fire to his out-buildings. Scatty was Redcliffe Bay's most popular eccentric. He was an ironmonger by trade, whose premises were about halfway along East Stump and always decorated with strings of pots, pans, fireguards and other hardware. But Scatty took no interest whatever in his shop, leaving its administration to his hard-pressed wife and daughters. He regarded himself as an inventor and had worked on a variety of gadgets, mostly kitchen gadgets, one of which was always going to set the family up and enable Mrs. Wallace to buy a boardinghouse and dower her four daughters. He never patented any, of course, but he went right on trying and fires and explosions were routine in his workshop. Mrs. Wallace did not resent her husband's dedication to science. In fact she was the one person in Redcliffe Bay who took him seriously and behaved as if she considered it a privilege to serve a genius in the shop, the kitchen and in bed. Her daughters were unremarkable girls, at least, three of them were, and they were still unmarried and thus a source of some anxiety to their mother, whose second priority (after nurturing her husband's genius) was to get them off her hands. She showed a certain ingenuity in her efforts, organizing a string of parties to which all Redcliffe Bay's eligible young men were invited and her front room, back room and kitchen were at the disposal of any regularly-employed young male at all hours of the night. After a dance at the Church Hall you could always be sure of coffee, buns and privacy at the Wallaces', so long as you observed the protocol based on the seniority of the girls. Myrtle, the eldest, entertained in the parlor and Nancy, the next eldest, had the run of the dining room. If you had a fancy for Jonquil, the third girl, you had to make do with the kitchen, where the love-seat was a bagged-out horsehair sofa. I passed several hours in the kitchen with Jonquil, who was fair and forthcoming, but that sofa encouraged me to transfer my affections elsewhere. It had a glacial surface and no matter how you arranged yourself on it you kept sliding off onto the floor. It was cold too, for Mrs. Wallace allowed the use of the gas fire in the parlor but drew the kitchen stove before she went up to bed to listen to Scatty's recital of the day's progress in the workshop. Neither of them bothered about their daughters' virtue once the lights were out. It was often after three A.M. before things settled down at the Wallaces' place.

The fourth daughter, Esther (she preferred to spell her name

"Esta" and we always thought of it as that), was different. She had almost nothing in common with her sisters and very little, I would say, with either parent. She was slightly below medium height and very small-boned but her figure was neat and nicely proportioned, suggesting not only energy and agility but latent strength, at all events strength of will.

She was a person you had to know to appreciate, and I don't mean solely as regards her character. Esta's figure had a kind of uniform shapeliness that only registered after you had come to terms with its neatness and symmetry. It was the same with her general appearance. She wasn't pretty, yet her face grew on you once you had learned to evaluate her features individually and discovered that they added up to something pleasing, original and elusive. Her hair was very dark and plentiful, her skin clear and pale, but whenever she was pleased or excited two bright spots of color glowed on her prominent cheekbones. She had big brown eyes and a generous mouth that was very pleasant to kiss because it was soft and more submissive than most. Her chin was small but resolute, rather too resolute for a person with so much femininity. It gave a false impression of obstinacy but Esta Wallace was not obstinate; she was just steadfast and exceptionally self-contained.

Perhaps it was the quality of self-containment that misled people, especially boys on the make. She wasn't as popular as her extrovert sisters, Myrtle, Nancy and Jonquil, and some would have said that she was either shy or slightly aloof when, in fact, she was neither to any marked degree. In those days, when I still had a great deal to learn about lighting and posing, I devised my own method of getting "through" to the character of a sitter and tried to slot each of them into a specific period, even seeking some kind of help in this artificial attempt to settle an approach by consulting the reproductions of famous paintings in a set of volumes Birdie had brought home from an auction sale. I think Esta was the first person on whom I practiced this haphazard technique. I always saw her as an early Victorian, the kind of girl to be found on the edge of a crowded canvas by a painter such as Frith. She had that kind of innocence and honesty but also, held in check, a certain promise. When I got to know her well I never revised this assessment. She was innocent and she was honest. She had promise too but it wasn't the kind that encouraged you to push beyond the point where you had to begin thinking of mothers-in-law, rate demands and a perambulator under the stairs.

Esta Wallace was not very popular with the boys but there was one who singled her out and pursued her with a stolidity and singlemindedness that often embarrassed her. This was Cecil Trumper, the lumpish son of Rufus Trumper, the local auctioneer, and the nephew of Alfie Trumper, the local bookmaker. Cecil, at school and afterwards, was always a bit of a butt. He was ungainly, slovenly and afflicted by a slight stutter. Notwithstanding this he would have been regarded as a good catch by local mammas had he been able to exploit either of the commercial possibilities open to him as the only son of an auctioneer and the nephew of a bachelor bookmaker. His handicap prevented this. It would have taken him about ten minutes to dispose of one lot in his father's mart, and by the time he had accepted and repeated a bet over the telephone the result of the race would have been broadcast throughout the country. Poor old Cecil. I can see him now, mooning about his father's Fore Street premises, getting by with a little clerical work and a certain amount of van-loading, but all the time, year in year out, feeding upon his yearning for Esta Wallace like a man living on his own fat. Esta was gentle towards him, as she was to almost everybody, but she wasn't at all interested in his suit.

There wasn't much for girls leaving school in Redcliffe Bay in the year 1932. The shops paid miserly wages and only those living in the terraces beyond the railway yard could think of seeking the slightly higher weekly rate paid to domestic servants. Esta went off on a furrow of her own and decided to train as a nurse, getting a post as probationer at the Cottage Hospital, at the far end of the Valley. At the time of which I write she was about halfway through her three-year apprenticeship, working ten hours a day, six days a week, for forty pounds a year. It was hard and exacting work but she stuck at it. She stuck at most things, having her father's belief that one day something splendid would happen, providing she went her own way at her own pace. In a way, I suppose, she was rather old-fashioned. I remember standing beside her and her sister Myrtle at a Church Institute hop when Cecil Trumper had been more than usually persistent and hearing Myrtle say, "Why on earth don't you put Cecil out of his misery, Esta? He's got money coming to him, hasn't he, and that's more than you can say of most of the boys round here!" Esta had replied with an edge to her voice, "When I marry it won't be to put anyone out of their misery and it won't be for money either!" Myrtle could be obtuse and failed to take the hint. She said, "Well, I'd snap him up I can tell you, if he was mooning after me!" "I'm sure you would," Esta said, snappily for her, "but then, neither you, Nancy or Jonquil minds who puts their hand down your neck. I suppose I'm just that much more fussy!"

Myrtle was naturally annoyed that she said a thing like that in front of me and would probably have clouted her if I hadn't stepped up and whisked Esta onto the floor, but neither of us referred to the conversation during our dance. I remember I thought at the time that her attitude to her sisters was a little priggish but now I see that it about sums Esta up. As I was to discover shortly after the incident, she was very far from being a prude but she was unique among the Wallaces and all the other girls in Redcliffe Bay.

On this particular morning I was on the point of leaving Scatty Wallace's workshop in the yard behind the shop when Esta called from a second-story window at the rear of the house. I knew it was the bedroom she shared with her sister Jonquil, and also that she was probably going to bed because she had been doing a spell of night duty at the hospital. She looked very chirpy as she shouted, "Come on up, Pip! It's my birthday!"

I was glad to see her, not because she attracted me more than any other girl in town but because she had always interested me as a person. I know that, like me, she had ambition, because we had talked about the subject at a recent dance in the Church Hall. I had seen her home that night but, as all the courting space at the Wallaces' was already occupied by her sisters, we had said goodnight in the porch, which was open to the punishing east wind. We hadn't stayed out there long but long enough, I recalled, to catch colds after sweating it out at the dance.

I went through the kitchen where Mrs. Wallace was busy over the stove and all she said was "Go and wish Esta many happy returns! She's eighteen today, Pip!" I said I was on my way to do just that and halfway up the dark stairway I had an idea.

The week before I had completed a photographic record of old Mrs. Snell's collection of porcelain, ivories and miniatures and the old lady, who was very kind-hearted, had handed me a little gift to mark her appreciation of the trouble I took on her behalf. She gave me a little gold locket, containing a portrait of her grandmother painted in the early nineteenth century. It was an odd present to give to a boy but she said, with a laugh, that it would save me buying a Christmas present for my best girl. I kept it handy, meaning to exchange it for cash at Myfanwy Pritchard's gift shop, but now, without in the least knowing why, I made up my mind to give it to Esta, although there was no question of her being more than a convenient dancing partner.

I was right about her coming off night duty. She was already in her nightdress and dressing gown and combing out her dark hair and very pretty she looked, I thought, with her back to the light and winter sunshine flooding the little room. I said, "Many Happy Returns, Esta!" and leaned over the back of the chair and kissed her and then I put the locket down on the homemade dressing table that she and Jonquil used and it was fun watching her reflection in the swing mirror. She picked it up and examined it very carefully, releasing the little spring and studying the portrait inside.

"It's absolutely beautiful!" she said at length. "It's the nicest present anyone has ever given me, Pip!" and suddenly she jumped up and threw her arms round me, kissing me in a way she hadn't kissed me in the porch or at any of the parties we had attended together since we were kids.

I was flattered, particularly as her dressing gown wasn't sashed and her artificial silk nightie was thin. It seemed to me that the locket was paying a dividend in record time and we held each other for about a minute before she disengaged herself and examined the locket again. She said, giving me a sharp, sidelong glance, "What made you give it to me? You didn't know it was my birthday, and anyway, where and when did you buy it?"

"I didn't buy it," I admitted, "it was given to me 'for my best girl' by old Mother Snell. She was pleased with some pictures I took of her china and made me a present of it as I was leaving!"

"It's eighteen-carat gold; did you know that?"

"Yes," I said, although I hadn't been sure.

"And we're not even going together, are we?" "Going together" was current slang in Redcliffe Bay for a semipermanent but unprejudiced arrangement between old friends.

"Well no, I suppose not," I said, "but we've got to start some time, haven't we?"

I have no idea why I said that, unless it was prompted by the pleasure I had derived from the embrace. I'm not sure even now that it was so. It might have been no more than an expression of high spirits, or a simple desire to please. At all events I was taken aback by her reaction for she said, quietly and with obvious sincerity, "I've never been the least interested in anyone else about here, Pip. But you know that I suppose?"

No, I told her, I hadn't known it. She had not seemed all that much interested in me on previous occasions when we had met and danced and kissed. But she said this was because she didn't approve of the chop-and-change techniques of her sisters, or their theory that the only way to get a husband in a dead-and-alive place like Redcliffe Bay was to egg a man on until he was safely hooked. "Most of the girls around here do that," she added, "even if they don't realize what a dirty trick it is!"

This time she did sound priggish and I laughed, but she didn't qualify her opinion in any way but gave me another of her level, disconcerting glances, saying, "It's not so funny, not when your own mother encourages it!"

"How does your mother encourage it?"

"By looking the other way. Why else do you think she gives every boy with a steady job the run of the house after dark?"

I must have been a good deal more naïve than I thought myself. Up to that moment I had never considered this as an explanation of Mrs. Wallace's excessive tolerance but now that I did it seemed reasonable. Mrs. Wallace had an inventor husband and four daughters to house and feed out of a small-town iron-mongery business, and no one could blame her for doing her best to insure against the future. I said, "You could marry Cecil Trumper tomorrow, Esta. That would be one daughter off her hands!"

It wasn't a very tactful remark and if it had not been for the locket it would have been my exit speech. She threw up her head and looked as angry as I had ever seen her look but then, quite suddenly, the sparkle left her eyes and she seemed tired and defeated. She sat on the bed, leaned back on her hands and said, slowly, "Can you imagine me spending my life with Cecil? Don't remind me he's a good match. Mother's always telling me so and I daresay he is, for girls like Jonquil and the majority of our crowd. But I'm not that hard up, Pip. I want a man with a bit of go in him, someone who doesn't just accept the prospect of getting a living wage, and living and dying in Redcliffe Bay. I want someone I could look up to and maybe help a bit. That, and someone I enjoyed going to bed with!"

I was more interested in her assessment of Redcliffe Bay than in the implied compliment. "I never realized you were that much fed up with living here," I said. "I remember telling you last time we met I hoped to make the break sooner or later but I got the impression you were keen on nursing for its own sake."

"Nursing is a means to an end as far as I'm concerned," she said, surprisingly, and then, with obvious deliberation, she changed the subject abruptly, adding, "I suppose you'll be going to the Hospital Ball tonight, Pip?"

I said I would, everyone was going, and Birdie had been commissioned by Doctor Morney-Sutcliffe to take some lime-light pictures of the event. We did this every year and I sometimes wondered what he did with them afterwards. Probably he pasted them in an album entitled "The Miraculous Achievements of the Emperor of Redcliffe Bay," for that was how Morney-Sutcliffe thought of himself and how most locals thought of him. He was one of those men who get a more-than-alcoholic kick out of subservience, who was not merely a big fish in a small pond but a bloody great pike enjoying every moment of his isolation in a tank stocked with minnows.

Esta said, resignedly, "I can't go. Almost all the hospital staff will be there, but I'm only halfway through my night-duty spell." Then, eagerly, "Look Pip, it goes on until two A.M., and Matron and Sister won't be back until about two-thirty. Couldn't you slip out half an hour before it's over and come up to the hospital? I get a supper break about then and well . . . you could tell me about it! I wouldn't feel so left out. Will you do that, seeing it's my birthday?"

I said I should be very glad to and I was telling the truth. This casual encounter with Esta had made a powerful impact on me and I began to think of her as a cut above every other girl in town. I wanted to kiss her again too, and maybe adventure a little further. I had a conviction that she wouldn't object and it would be something to look forward to, especially if the dance was as stuffy as it usually was, with Morney-Sutcliffe's insistence on boiled shirts and all the Valley girls dancing with our sort as though they were carrying ashcans round the hall. I said I would be at the hospital about one-thirty-five and that if I could slip into the refreshment room on the pretext of filling my camera I would steal one of the half-bottles of champagne Morney-Sutcliffe put aside for the organizing committee. She laughed at that. As a probationer who had had more than her ration of Morney-Sutcliffe's pomposity it must have seemed a good opportunity to score over him. Very few of us townsfolk liked him but the younger nurses hated his guts.

"I'd better get tucked in now," she said, picking up her locket. "I've been on duty since six o'clock last night and it gets too noisy to sleep when the girls troop up here and Mother begins her lunch-time clatter underneath."

She slipped out of her dressing gown and climbed into bed, snuggling down like a cat and looking as if she could purr like one. She put the locket under her pillow. "It's nice," she said, smiling up at me, "wish you were here!"

"So do I, by God!" I said, and I meant it. Although I had known her since we were ten-year-olds I was seeing her now for the first time, not simply as a girl who was desirable but as a person of quite extraordinary coziness, someone who could offer, in addition to sex, any amount of warmth and understanding, someone who it would always be fun to have along, who would grow on you a little every day.

"Do you know about the old-time custom of bundling?" she said, "when the man does his courting sitting beside the girl's bed?"

"Yes," I said, "but it never seemed much to write home about. They sew up the girl in a damned great bag, don't they?"

"I'm not sewn up!" she said.

I slipped her nightdress from one shoulder and stroked her small breast. This was Licence Number One in Redcliffe Bay at that time and I had done it before but this time it was different. Then I kissed her breasts, both of them, without hurry or fuss. It was one of those moments that can be isolated and rescued from the flux of time, held up, looked at and put by for a rainy day. Such moments are not common; you can only catch them by the tail once or twice a year.

I looked at her carefully and it struck me, quite suddenly, that she was prettier than her sisters, prettier than any girl in town. Her dark hair, spread across the pillow, had a deep, satisfying sheen and in her brown eyes there was laughter and mischief too, of a special kind. I replaced her shoulder strap and kissed her mouth and as her hand emerged from the bedclothes to stroke the back of my head she said, lazily, "What a lovely thing to happen on a birthday! Suddenly I mean, right out of the blue!"

Ordinarily, I suppose, a remark like that, made in those circumstances, would have put me on my guard, but this time it didn't. I went out of there understanding that something important had happened. Important, exciting and different into the bargain.

CHAPTER TWO

[1]

The local magistrates wouldn't ordinarily have granted a drinking license for a Church Hall dance and very few promoters got an extension until two A.M., but Morney-Sutcliffe was a J.P. and there wasn't anyone big enough to stand up to him on the Bench. That was why the Hospital Ball was reckoned the most important of the year. Admission tickets were five shillings and there was a buffet supper for an extra half-crown. I went in on a press card, having arranged to write a paragraph or two of copy to go with my pictures for the *Messenger*.

It was never any good attending a local dance until round about ten-thirty, so as soon as I had got into my dinner jacket (most of the locals wore tails at this ball but I didn't own a set) I went across to the Lamb and Flag to get steamed up, and as soon as I entered the public bar I realized that something unusual was afoot. It was crowded and very noisy and there was a general air of expectancy among the regulars and the landlord and his wife, Dick and Mabel Bannister. It didn't take me long to find out what was due to take place. They were all preparing to play a practical joke on the new police chief, Inspector Crisp, who only that week had replaced the tolerant Inspector Baxter.

It seems that Crisp was wielding an officiously new broom and had promised himself the pleasure of pouncing on the regulars in the sawdust bar for taking gross liberties with the licensing hours. They had posted sentries at each end of the Stump and were all set to create a terrific hullaballoo at about a minute to ten, which was closing time during out-of-season months. Then, when Crisp showed up, they planned to make a mass exit through the kitchen and over the yard wall into the railway goods siding. They assumed that Crisp would look and feel an idiot when he found the bar empty at two minutes past ten and that it would stop him getting too uppity and encourage him to turn a blind eye to minor infringements in the future.

I thought I would wait around a little and see the fun and it worked out exactly as they planned. At five minutes to ten the uproar issuing from the public bar could have been heard at the top of High Street, where the police station was situated, but the moment Dudley Snell, the solicitor's clerk, popped in to announce that Crisp and the Sergeant were converging on the pub from either end of the Stump, the place emptied in a matter of seconds. Everyone rushed into the yard and climbed over the siding wall so that when the Inspector marched in there was nobody there but me and Mabel Bannister, the landlady. She said, with gravel in her voice, "I'm afraid I can't serve you, Inspector! It's gone time you know!" I thought she was asking for trouble because Crisp was liable to be calling the tune around Redcliffe Bay for the next five years but I daresay she knew her business. Crisp was a snappish, good-looking man about forty, a great contrast in appearance and manner to the leisurely, pot-bellied, ex-Bow Street runner who had been with us ever since I could remember. He asked me if I had been drinking and I told him no, I was there to take a picture and I took one to prove it, which seemed to amuse Mabel Bannister. He went out then without a word and Sergeant Wright winked at us behind his back.

I said goodnight to Mabel and went out and along West Stump towards High Street. The Rainbow Café was doing a brisk trade and Dora Gorman was there as usual, sweating it out in a cloud of steam but still managing to look like the proprietress of a Cathedral Close teashop who had lost her bearings. She was untypical of our part of the world and looked, I always thought, half Italian or Sicilian. She had calm, classical features and a very stately way of walking. Nobody could ever understand how she came to marry Syd Gorman, a pallid, diffident man, with no eyelashes. Dora brought a good deal of trade into the Rainbow. She never flirted with customers but the men liked to study her figure while they were waiting for their piece of hake and three-pennyworth of chips. Dudley Snell, who coined or relayed most of Redcliffe Bay's salty stories, admired her and used to raise a laugh in the bar of the Lamb and Flag by pretending to be revolted by the notion of Syd Gorman making love to the stately Dora when the blinds were down and the smell of frying fat hung over the bed. "Ugh!" he used to say, "it's sacrilege, my friends! Beauty and the Beast; and the Beast with grease on his fishy paws!" Personally I don't think it was like that at all. Dora was the kind of woman who was married to the till-roll.

The wind had dropped but there was a moderate frost and sounds carried a long way in the deserted streets. I could hear the orchestra beating it up in the Church Hall, which stood at the junction of High Street and Old Fore Street, a very large building for a town like ours and having an excellent pine floor capable of accommodating three hundred couples at a pinch. I even remember what they were playing, a new and popular song called *Auf Wiedersehen* with a haunting lilt and false rhymes in the lyric. It was one of the tunes that was to have significance for me all my life.

I had a job to do in there but I didn't intend to stay long because it wasn't my kind of dance. The majority of people attending it would be middle aged and there was sure to be a depressingly high proportion of dances like the Valeta, the Boston Two-Step and Paul Jones, where you were likely to find yourself prancing round with a succession of corsetted old trouts. I thought I would take my pictures, have a word with the M.C. for caption material, then walk up the valley to the Cottage Hospital. If Matron and Sister were safely out of the way I would have the run of the place and the bright stars overhead made me think pleasantly of Esta.

The stage had been very attractively decorated with ferns, potted plants and great bronze chrysanthemums, and Ned Willis's Dance Eight were providing the music. The Eight was a Paxtonbury team and very expensive. We didn't get them down here more than twice a year and all the younger set admired Ned's saxophonist, who would have earned big money nowadays but was then a musician by night and a garage assistant by day.

I took my pictures, had a dance or two and then went into the buffet bar to reconnoitre the half-bottle of champagne that I had promised Esta. It was there all right, sitting in a crate beyond the ice-cream tub and I edged along the trestle table awaiting my chance to grab it. I almost had my hand on the crate when a fruity voice at my elbow said, "Ah! Young Stuart isn't it? Just the man! Oblige me by giving my wife a turn or two, young feller-me-lad! She hasn't danced with anyone under fifty all evening and is threatening to go home!"

It was Doctor Morney-Sutcliffe himself, huge, baby-faced and hectoring. He talked to everyone as though they were five years old and getting under his feet. I never once heard him say "please" or "thank you." Somehow I don't think he knew the words.

His wife was standing beside him in a dance frock of green brocaded silk that didn't come from a local shop and would have attracted a window-shopping crowd in Paxtonbury Close. It was obviously my day for reassessing the local talent. She looked beautiful, with her red-gold hair cut in the then fashionable long bob and curled under, and as I glanced at her I remembered her as a person who was very seldom seen at local functions and was said to regard the whole lot of us, including Morney-Sutcliffe, as a rabble of chawbacons. I recalled also that she was reported to have been "discovered" by the Doctor on the Left Bank of the Seine, and brought home in modest triumph to live in the largest and best-appointed house in the Valley, a place standing in two acres of ground and called, for some inscrutable reason, "Heatherdene." There were all kinds of vague rumors about her, some of which were hard to believe, seeing that presumably she had married the Emperor of Redcliffe Bay of her own free will. Some said she had been a painter, others a fan dancer at the *Folies Bergère*. She was also said to have married the Doctor for his money, which was probably true, and also that she had been down to her last five-franc piece when they met, which seemed to me very unlikely. She was English—I knew that because I had once talked to her on the telephone—but her voice didn't match her hauteur or, for that matter, the Valley in which she lived. Almost all the women in the Valley either honked at you or spoke as though they were balancing plumstones on their tongues. The Anglo-Indians did the honking and the people who had made small fortunes out of the war did the plumstone-balancing. Mrs. Morney-Sutcliffe's voice was pleasantly pitched but direct, telling you that she wasn't interested in anything you had to say but was prepared to be reasonably polite for five minutes. She said, with a bleak glance at her husband, "Why the hell should a boy his age want to dance with me? There aren't so many young men here but there are plenty of pretty girls!" And then, to me, "Don't let him bully you into wasting your time, Mr. Stuart. People your age ought to enjoy themselves, even at a grisly wake like this!"

The doctor was not in the least offended by this declaration of independence. One of his strongest characteristics was an armor-plated skin and you couldn't insult him or upset him under any circumstances because he never listened to anything anyone said except "Yes, Doctor!" or "Certainly, Doctor!" All he replied now was, "Well, hustle along, the pair of you! I've got to arrange the draw and I'll come for you when it's time for you to pick the winners, Lorna!" And then he was gone and she lifted her shoulders, expressing the impossibility of coping with his elephantine lack of tact.

I would never have asked Lorna Morney-Sutcliffe for a dance. At previous dances of this kind I had sometimes drawn a Valley daughter, or a Valley matron in a Paul Jones and it was never any good trying to make polite conversation with them. Sometimes they replied to your remarks in brusque monosyllables but more often they didn't answer you at all. Apart from that they held themselves stiffly, so that your points of contact with them were restricted to one hand on the shoulder and the other enclosing the tips of their fingers. For all that I was glad the Doctor had singled me out for the honor. She was by far the most attractive woman in the room and now that I looked at her closely I realized that she was younger than I had imagined when I had seen her driving her red sports car along Stump, or passing in and out of Barclays Bank in the mornings. I judged her to be about twenty-eight, or maybe a year younger, and she had a full but nicely-proportioned figure, with a very shapely bust and a neat little bottom. Her features were small but very regular, with a short, straight nose, a full and rather discontented mouth and hazel eyes with flecks in them. Like Esta, her best feature, however, was her hair, which really was red-gold and changed color under differing degrees of light. Out here, under the supper-bar strip lighting, it was almost blonde but in the softer light of the hall a much darker tint crept into it and it glowed like the coals of a fire that someone has forgotten to stir. She was using a perfume that was new to me and was as exclusive as her gown. Round her wrist she had a diamond bracelet and the sapphire ring on her fourth finger was the size of a pea and must have cost Morney-Sutcliffe the equivalent of several appendix removals, with any number of half-guinea visits thrown in.

She said, as soon as he was out of earshot, "You don't *have* to dance, you know! We could sit out and have a drink. Would you like a drink? They're on the house for me!"

I said I would prefer to dance if she didn't mind, so we moved out onto the floor, where I discovered that she was a supple partner and far more easily led than any of the local girls. She made me feel that I was a good deal more expert than I was and we fox-trotted round for five minutes or so without saying anything. She didn't have to talk as far as I was concerned for her perfume was poetry enough.

When the drums rattled to a finish she said, "Thank you, that was nice! I should have been permanently crippled if I had danced with any more of those councillors. Would it be asking too much for you to stay around until it's time for the draw? I think they're beginning again!"

They were, a blues number called *Muddy Water*, and it turned out to be a limelight dance for soon the main lights were dimmed and the suspended kaleidoscope went into action. It was a slow number but movement in any case was difficult because by now the floor was crowded, the half-light tempting all the bad dancers to bestir themselves. We shuffled round and as we passed within close range of the band she said, clearly and distinctly, "You can loosen up a little, Mr. Stuart, I won't break!" which I took to be an invitation to hold her a little closer.

It was a long time since I had enjoyed a dance as much as I enjoyed that one, but the bonus was still to come. When the number ended, and the final flourish was in progress, they seemed to have a little trouble restoring the lights and she pressed her thighs against me in a way that made me tremble. At first I was so astonished that I assumed the movement was accidental and that she was being projected towards me by jostling couples behind her but it wasn't so. It was quite deliberate and once I had recovered from the shock I felt drunk with triumph. From that moment, and it was no more than a moment, stemmed all the false surmises I was to make and harbor about Lorna Morney-Sutcliffe.

The lights went up just in time. I couldn't have stood there indefinitely without indicating the extreme pleasure she was giving me and, even as it was, she was by no means unaware of the effect she was producing because she laughed and said, "I think you could do with a drink now, couldn't you Mr. Stuart?" and led the way back to the supper bar where we found a table under one of the rustic arches they had erected for the occasion. She bought two double whiskies and two ices, getting served ahead of the queue. I didn't drink whisky then and I had already had two pints of bitter in the Lamb and Flag but I pretended to like it and it certainly helped to steady me.

"I don't think we have met before, have we?" she began and I said we hadn't but that I knew all about her, as everyone living in Redcliffe Bay did.

"I'm not sure I like that one!" she replied, smiling. "What do they know exactly?"

I said that it was common knowledge that she had lived in Paris and had been a painter there, and that the doctor had met and married her some years ago and this had surprised everyone in town because it had been taken for granted he would always remain a bachelor.

She laughed again, saying, "Well, they're on the right track. I wasn't a painter but my father was. As a young man he hobnobbed with some of the Impressionists and even tried to be one, so I imagine that would rule him out as an artist in the eyes of Redcliffe Bay. The final word in painting around here is Holman Hunt's *Light of the World,* isn't it, Mr. Stuart?"

I was interested in the sneer for it proved that the local rumormongers had one thing right. Mrs. Morney-Sutcliffe obviously did regard everyone in town as a lout, with mud on his boots and a pig under his arm.

"Don't keep calling me 'Mr. Stuart,'" I protested. "No one does around here. I'm generally called 'Pip.'"

"'Pip'?" She said it as though I ought to apologize for it rather than proclaim it and this was the first time her bitchiness put me on the defensive. There were to be countless such occasions in the future.

"It's just a nickname," I mumbled. "A lot of people about here have nicknames."

"They do in all farmyards," she said, "but why 'Pip'? It's a diminutive isn't it?"

I wasn't at all sure what a diminutive was, so I told her that my mother's cousins had given me the name of the hero in *Great Expectations* because, having no parents, I had come to Redcliffe Bay to be cared for as a kid.

"Have you any expectations?" she asked.

"No," I said, "not in the general way, but when Birdie—Mr. Boxall that is—retires he's promised to give me the business."

"What business is that?"

"The photographer's studio on West Stump, the Grosvenor Studios."

She wasn't as impressed as I had hoped but seemed to ponder my prospects while taking minute sips of her whisky and soda. Finally she said, "You mean you've settled for that? At your age?"

I knew what she meant but I played stupid and asked her to elaborate. She said, looking me straight in the eye, that I had disappointed her because she found it difficult to believe that anyone my age could be content to stay on in a place like Redcliffe Bay and think of a small business here as an end in itself. "If I was in your shoes," she said, "I would be out of here like greased lightning, expectations or no expectations! You may make a living here but there's more to being alive than that, isn't there? This is the kind of place older people come to die when they're old and tired. It's no place for anyone under sixty!"

I stayed on the defensive although, in a sense, I enjoyed being goaded by her and found it flattering, especially after that thigh pressure of hers when the limelight had lingered. I said that Redcliffe Bay was a good deal livelier than some seaside towns I knew. There were plenty of young people around and anyway, jobs were not all that easy to get without a specialist training of some kind.

"But you've got a specialist training, haven't you? How old are you, Pip?"

I told her I would be twenty in a month's time and she seemed to think this over, the way she pondered most of my replies.

"Have you got a girl?"

I told her I hadn't and it wasn't a conscious lie. Since dancing with her the memory of Esta, smiling up at me from her bed that morning, had receded.

"Now why is that?" she asked gaily. "You're a husky lad, not bad looking and a very good dancer for Redcliffe Bay."

I must have looked confused for she smiled again, this time in a friendly fashion, saying, "Look, don't take a damned bit of notice of me! I'm on edge tonight and I know why. It's having to be here, as if it wasn't enough to spend one's life in the place without going on show every now and again!"

The Doctor bustled in just then and said, in his en-route-to-the-operating-theatre manner, "Stir your stumps! The draw is about to take place on stage! Don't forget to pick three green tickets and three red, my dear!"

He didn't so much as glance at me but she took her time about getting up and then turned to me very deliberately, keeping him hovering with one foot in the arbor and the other in the buffet bar. I had never noticed what small feet he had for a man of his stature. Their smallness and neatness must have been responsible for his curious bobbing walk, as though, at any moment, he was going to overbalance and fall flat on his baby face. She said slowly, "Thank you for the dances, Pip. They were a very pleasant experience after all I've suffered tonight. I'll keep my promise about the Ladies' Invitation after the interval."

Then they were gone, the pair of them, and I sat on with my mouth agape, wondering if he had heard and if he had what he would make of an underage tradesman trying to make a pass at his wife in public. Then I thought, Damn it, it was the Doctor who dragged me into this by the scruff of the neck, so what the hell does it matter what he thinks? And I felt more devil-may-care than at any moment of my life and more expectant too, although concerning what I couldn't have said.

I heard the M.C. calling the names of the winners as Lorna pulled the tickets from the drum, and then the buffet became very crowded with everyone coming in for cold supper, so I went back into the hall and collected my caption material, enough to make a quarter-column in Friday's *Messenger*. After all, I was here on a press pass and I owed old Ben Dagmar his dues.

I checked with the saxophonist and learned that the Ladies' Invitation was down on the programme as the last dance but one. That would make it about one-thirty so that if I stayed on I would have to give the hospital a miss. Esta wouldn't be available once Matron and Sister got back. There was no question in my mind of going, however. I could see Esta Wallace any old time and a chance of dancing with Lorna Morney-Sutcliffe wouldn't come around again until next year, and possibly not even then if she gave expression to her obvious hatred of small-town life. I filled in the time dancing with one or two of the local girls, including Jonquil, Esta's sister, who tried to pump me on my relationship with her roommate. Then the Ladies' Invitation was announced and I positioned myself prominently in front of the central balcony pillar. Jonquil at once crossed over and asked me to dance but I said, "Morney-Sutcliffe asked me to dance this one with his wife!" She looked astonished, as well she might, and moved in under the balcony to camouflage what must have looked like a brush-off. Then Lorna moved round from the buffet entrance and claimed me and we moved around the crowded floor slowly and silently to the beat of *Carolina Moon*. It was a four-year-old tune then but still popular. Tunes had much longer lives in those days.

When it was over, and during the brief lull before the final dance was announced, Lorna said: "The Doctor had to go. It was a confinement over in Colony beyond the railway. I've got my own car here, would you like me to run you home?"

I was astonished for three reasons. In the first place by the Doctor's disappearance, in the second place by her offer, but more, I think, by her casual use of the local term for the rows of terrace houses west of the town, where I had grown up. We always called these terraces "The Colony," as though they housed coolies, and somehow the term seemed very odd on her lips, like a bishop admitting to familiarity with a string of local pubs. It was odd too to be taken home by a woman, and such a woman. I must have attended two hundred or more dances in that hall but it was always I who did the seeing home. Perhaps, because of this, I didn't answer her directly but said, "I'd like to ride in that car of yours, the red sports!" and she said it was parked on the far side of the parking lot and I could go there now because she was going to skip the last dance, promised to the Chairman of the Council. "He bounces so," she said, by way of extenuation. "I think he regards every dance as a Crimean polka."

I collected my coat and scarf and went out into the frosty night. It was colder than ever but the moon had risen over Mitre Head. I had a good look at the car while I was waiting. It was a new M.G. with a long, strapped-down bonnet, and any number of fancy gadgets on the dashboard. The car was far better known in Redcliffe Bay than its owner.

She came out in a few minutes, a fox fur over her shoulders, and I opened the tiny door for her to climb in. It wasn't the easiest kind of vehicle to drive in a tight dance frock and she displayed about eight inches of thigh in the process of settling herself. She started the engine and it shattered the silence of Old Fore Street. Then we were off, driving up to about fifty in as many yards and before I realized it we had shot round the Stump and skidded to a halt outside the studio. The old place looked so shabby in the bright moonlight that I felt ashamed of it and even more ashamed of the flyblown wedding pictures and coy portraits in the window.

"The Grosvenor Studios," she said, with easy contempt. "Why 'Grosvenor' and why plural? Are there more than one?"

"Birdie Boxall called it that when he opened it forty years ago," I told her gruffly, "I suppose he thought it sounded classy. It's a dump all right but we don't pay much in rent."

"And it's going to be yours one day?"

"The business, not the premises."

Suddenly I wanted to get away from the place and plant her somewhere where she wouldn't feel obliged to make any more gibes at my prospects. Inexplicably I saw the place as gimcrack and desperately provincial, and seeing it so I hated it. I said, "Let's go along the front and up Links Road to the Valley. I don't mind walking home, in fact I'd like to walk home. I don't feel like going to bed and it's a wonderful night. You can drop me off at the foot of your drive, Mrs. Morney-Sutcliffe."

"Very well," she said, "but if you're 'Pip' I'm 'Lorna.' 'Sutcliffe' isn't so bad but that 'Morney' nonsense irritates me every time anyone says it! I always thought of hyphenated names as damned pretentious. I never imagined I should be stuck with one. I don't much care for 'Pip' either. Haven't you got a real name?"

"Yes," I told her, "but it's just as pretentious as 'Morney.' It's 'Kent.' "

She was in the act of slamming the car in gear but stopped, turning towards me.

"*Kent?* Why Kent?"

"I was born in Kent and I suppose my mother thought it distinctive."

"So it is," she said, "and somehow it suits you. Do you remember your parents?"

"My mother, vaguely, but let's get going before we wake everybody up. People go to bed early round here."

She laughed and engaged the clutch. We moved down Frog Terrace at a moderate pace and turned onto the sea front, coasting along it at a speed of no more than twenty miles per hour. The bay looked beautiful under a flood of white moonlight and the sea was very still, with tiny wavelets sucking at the pebbles. I think the scene impressed even her because she didn't say another word until we had climbed the ascent of Links Road and swung right into the valley. Every twig was silhouetted against the sky and all the big houses were dark and silent at the end of their gravelled drives. She stopped just short of the white gate of "Heatherdene" and switched off the engine.

"Well, Kent," she said cheerfully, "here's your starting point. What will you think about while you're walking the two miles home?"

"About dancing with you," I admitted, knowing that was what she wanted me to say.

"Ah, it's nice to be twenty," she said unexpectedly. "When I was your age I used to like walking home after a night out but there was more to see on the banks of the Seine than on your sea front. I don't suppose you have ever been to Paris, have you, Kent?"

"No," I said, "I haven't even crossed the Channel."

"Then you've got it all ahead of you."

"Don't talk as if you were my grandmother," I said. "We all know how old you are."

"You do?" She seemed genuinely surprised, so I told her that Redcliffe Bay had been caught off balance by the Doctor's return from the Continent as a married man and had done its own investigating. Within days it had got around that he was old enough to be her father.

"He would have had to be a very enterprising boy of fourteen," she said and left me to work that one out. I wasn't absolutely sure of his age but I knew he was around forty-two so my original guess had been right. I said, "Well, goodnight Mrs. . . . Lorna, and thank you for a marvellous evening," and I put my hand on the catch of the door.

"Wait a moment," she said, and then, shooting her legs deeper under the dashboard, "Isn't it *de rigueur* in Redcliffe Bay to kiss the lady goodnight when you see her home? It always was in my day."

I was glad we were in the deep shadow of the hydrangeas growing beside the gate. It gave me a moment or so to get over my fright, and it was fright, stirring under elation. It simply had not occurred to me that she would let me kiss her, or would think of me as anything but a callow ass if I had attempted to kiss her. Once I had come to terms with the invitation, however, I took advantage of it and I kissed her in the way we thought of as conventional, having learned it from the close-ups at the Tivoli. I put one hand behind her head and another round her shoulders and I suppose I expected her to react in precisely the same way as Esta Wallace, Jonquil and all the other girls reacted, that is, to close her eyes and exert a little gentle pressure with her lips.

She obviously hadn't seen the same films. She relaxed her whole body and opened her mouth, searching for my tongue with hers, and I wasn't at all sure I welcomed the innovation. I had read about kissing in that style but had never experienced it, or expected to in Redcliffe Bay. I said, hastily, "Goodnight, Lorna!" and was surprised at my own hoarseness. As I climbed out of the car I thought I heard her chuckle but I couldn't be sure and I didn't stop to find out. I went down the broad avenue with long strides and did not slacken my pace until I got to the junction of the Links Road.

It was here, as I dropped down to the level of the sea front, that it caught up with me, not just the kiss, and the provocative way she had pressed her body against me when we were dancing, but the entire encounter, which seemed to me about as improbable as a night in bed with Janet Gaynor, Jeanette Macdonald or any of the other current reigning goddesses who smiled down on Stump from hoardings outside the Tivoli. I was immensely flattered, of course, but I was not quite such a fool as to assume that there was anything special about me as a target for a married woman's lust. I thought of myself as more than eligible for a girl like Esta Wallace, or any other tradesman's daughter in town, but this was a long way short of possessing the charm, masculinity or sophistication to qualify me as the lover of a woman as unattainable as Lorna Morney-Sutcliffe. It did occur to me then that the whole thing was a kind of lucky accident, that she was unutterably bored, had had a row with the Doctor about attending the ball, and had used me to assert herself and maybe diminish him in the way I had planned to do when I went looking for his champagne. But then I put this idea aside. There were young men of her own class present at the dance, young officers home on Christmas leave, whose parents were her neighbors in the Valley. She could have indulged in a mild flirtation with any one of them had she been so inclined. She was using me, but not, somehow, in that sense.

It occurred to me that she might have had a drop too much to drink. I had only seen her swallow a double whisky but she might have had any number before my arrival, and although she had appeared sober, with women like her it is sometimes difficult to tell. There was far more to it than that, however, and another thought I had was that the busy Doctor, rushing about town day and night in pursuit of his professional and civic duties, had grossly neglected her and she was clearly a sensual woman who needed a man more urgently than most Redcliffe wives. I pondered the pros and cons all the way home and I didn't get very far towards sorting them out. All I could be sure of was that the pass she made at me had something to do with her hatred of small-town life, a kind of macabre joke she was playing on the Doctor and, to an extent, upon herself. For all that, I had a much more balanced picture of Lorna Morney-Sutcliffe that night than I was able to establish in my mind later on, that is, I think I came closer to recognizing her for what she was, an oversexed and bitterly frustrated woman who saw her youth slipping away in a backwater and her looks wasted on a small-town sawdust Caesar. At least I understood enough about her to recognize danger and all manner of unpleasant eventualities for anyone in my position who tangled with her but in spite of that I entered the studio feeling several inches taller than when I had left it five hours earlier.

I didn't go straight to bed. There was something I had to do first, and I went into the storeroom where we kept our files and negatives and took down one of Birdie Boxall's massively-bound art encyclopaedias, slumping into the mock-antique sitter's chair in the studio and thumbing through the illustrations to check on an idea that had been taking shape in my mind ever since the Doctor had pushed me forward to dance with his wife. Just as I saw Esta Wallace as a Victorian Miss in poke bonnet and mittens, so I saw Lorna as a woman half a century earlier and her face, figure and general bearing struck a chord in my memory, as though I had not only seen her but actually studied her at close quarters a long time ago. I thought at first that she conjured up one of Lely's beauties, all ringlets and brocade, with a roundish face, prominent eyes and slightly sausagy fingers but it was not so. There was a page of Restoration girls there, Nell Gwyn, the Countess of Lennox, Lady Castlemaine and others, but they rang no bells so I turned the pages to the Gainsborough section. Then I saw it and I was so pleased with myself that I exclaimed aloud.

The picture was a full-page illustration of Gainsborough's *Mrs. Graham* and they were as alike, I thought, as sisters, far more alike than, say, Esta and Jonquil Wallace. Not only were they very similar in their features, and the way they stood looking over the right shoulder, but they had the identical expression of polite disdain, a compound of extreme vanity and boredom. I remembered Lorna's lower lip, full and flowing, and Mrs. Graham's mouth conveyed the same hint of petulance and sensuality. There was the same obstinate set of the chin and the same length of neck. It was difficult to compare their figures for Lady Graham's draperies were too extensive but I judged them to be about the same height and build.

I sat looking at the picture a long time and when I heard All Souls' Church clock strike three I marked the page, returned the book to the shelf and went up to bed. I didn't give Esta another thought until I ran into her walking up East Stump about tea time the next day. By that time I had got my encounter with Lorna Morney-Sutcliffe into a more rational perspective and in a way Esta derived benefit from this because the scent of Lorna's perfume, and the predatory thrust of her little tongue, had made me more urgently aware of what women had to offer than in the carefree period leading up to the occasion.

[2]

I greeted her a little uncertainly, aware that I had let her down and not knowing what her sister Jonquil might have told her about the dance but I needn't have bothered. She was still under the spell of the gold locket and the subtle change in our relationship that had occurred the previous morning. She greeted me gaily enough, saying, "What happened? I hung about the out-patients' ward for nearly an hour and then Matron and Sister came back and I had to skip back to the wards. Jonquil said you were cutting quite a dash with the Doctor's wife. Jonquil is a spiteful little beast sometimes and said you made her look an absolute fool when she asked for a dance."

"She knows perfectly well why I couldn't dance with her," I said, taking the cue offered. "Morney-Sutcliffe bullied me into dancing with his wife and once I was stuck with her there was nothing I could do about it. She was fed up with having her toes crushed by the councillors and Hospital Committee members and clung to me like a limpet. She even ran me back here in her M.G."

"*She* ran you back? Mrs. Morney-Sutcliffe did?"

"Yes, and I know why. She felt apologetic about the way the Doctor had monopolized me and even said as much. She's not a bad sort, Esta, nothing like as stuck up as he is."

"She's good-looking and she wears very expensive clothes. They say she costs him a packet, what with that car and her jaunts to the Continent. How many times did you dance with her?"

"Three," I said, and not wishing to invite further cross-examination added, "It was just as stuffy as ever. I don't think any of our set had much of a time. Are you going on duty again?"

"No," she said, "Matron gave the night staff an evening off for holding the fort last night. I'm not due on until ten-thirty. I thought about going to the pictures. I usually do the matinée but a matinée isn't the same, somehow."

I swallowed the bait contentedly enough. "What's on? Isn't it that gangster, with Edward G. Robinson?"

"That's right," she said, "and I don't like them awfully. There's a double-feature though, slapstick and Pathé Gazette. You can sit right through the program for ninepence."

"We'll go in the one-and-sixes," I said, and it was fun to see her face light up. "And if we don't like it we needn't watch in the back row. Afterwards I'll buy you a port and lemon and walk you up to the hospital."

"Pip!" she said, "you're very sweet and I won't say another word about you standing me up last night! I've just got a bit of shopping to do for mother and I'll meet you there when the second-house begins at ten past seven. I know you'll like the gangster, men always do when there's plenty of killing!" and she gave me a peck on the cheek that was something she had never done before in public.

I could see that she had gone to a great deal of trouble to doll herself up as soon as I watched her making her way up the steps to the foyer an hour or so later. She had dressed her hair differently, with a slanting fringe on the forehead and a dark curl under the left ear outside the tilted grey beret she was wearing. She had on her Sunday coat, with its imitation fur collar and high-heeled shoes that made her look taller and slimmer. I felt warm and safe about her. She was "me" and she was Redcliffe Bay; we had the same problems and the same prospects, and if the former were trivial and the latter unexciting it made for companionship that one might look for in vain with a married woman living in the Valley.

We knew Ruth Foster, the usherette, and she gave us two corner seats in the back row of the stalls. The Tivoli wasn't much of a picture house. The seats needed respringing and the cleaning fluid they used had a sickly smell that reminded one of boiled sweets abandoned in a stopperless jar, but we were accustomed to the Tivoli's limitations, in fact the place meant a lot to us.

I ought to say something more about that cinema, if only because it was the trend-setter of those days, filling the vacuum in our lives that television fills today. It lifted a red and gold curtain on another world, and although we were never more than half-fooled by the alternative values offered, it still exerted a very considerable influence on how we talked, how we dressed, and even how we made love. The girls followed the hairstyles of stars like Clara Bow, the "It" girl, and the boys played it tough, like the district attorneys and the cowboys. It converted us to the habit of gum-chewing and to phrases like "So what?" and "Oh yeah?" and "Okay by me." Apart from that it was the only place to go on a winter's night if you were bent on courting, and we valued the belt of darkness under the balcony, reserved for the more sedate patrons who paid one-and-six or two-and-three. The Tivoli was owned and managed by a dour, middle-aged man called Bruce Brayley who, a year or so before the time of which I write, had mortgaged everything he possessed to switch from silent films to talkies. In his own way Bruce was a good showman, appearing each night in a dinner jacket to greet incoming patrons as though they were crowned heads and he was running a plushy theater instead of a converted Baptist Chapel, which was how the Tivoli had started out in life. He enjoyed the same monopoly in films as Birdie enjoyed in photography and the London distributors recognized a salesman when they saw one. We had the new films a week or so after they were seen in the big cities.

Esta was right about me liking the gangster film. It was one of those pseudo-Chicago epics, where terse dialogue gave way to bursts of sub-machine-gun fire every other reel, and informers slumped to their death in bullet-shattered telephone kiosks. Touring cars, crammed with mean-faced bootleggers, cruised to and fro across the screen, and long-legged girls hung on the trigger hands of lovers and brothers caught up in the swirl of violence. Esta didn't take it very seriously but I did; it made me add Chicago to my secret visiting list.

During the second feature we indulged in the light petting that was obligatory if you took a girl to the Tivoli and sat in the one-and-sixes, and I enjoyed it the more because I felt safe and settled in there, with Esta's head on my shoulder. I had not yet shed the feeling that I would experience a sudden tap on the shoulder and look round into the infuriated baby face of Doctor Morney-Sutcliffe. When the lights went up, however, it was not the Doctor who was there, a seat or two nearer the screen, but poor old Cecil Trumper, who had been mooning after Esta ever since he was in short pants. He looked across at us like the lone survivor of an abandoned ship who sees his last two comrades making off in the last lifeboat. Esta smiled at him and I waved my hand, almost apologetically, and then, flushed into the open by his stricken face, we left and crossed over to the Lamb and Flag, where I bought Esta her first legal drink, an eightpenny port and lemon. To get it I had to explain to Mabel Bannister that Esta had celebrated her eighteenth birthday the previous day and I added, facetiously, that she had her birth certificate in her handbag.

The port made Esta the tiniest bit giggly but when we began our walk up to the Cottage Hospital she became thoughtful and silent, hesitating just a moment when I suggested we go via Vicarage Lane which cut behind the hill, joined up with the head of the Valley and ended at a stile at the highest point of the links where you could look down on the town and also eastward across the sweep of the cliffs beyond the Coastguard Station. The hospital was just over the brow of the rise and from here you could see its lights twinkling.

At the end of Vicarage Lane some thoughtful person had rolled an elm log against the bank and here we sat down, with the little town spread below like a copse composed of Christmas trees. We had both sat on that log before but not in each other's company. There was a splatter of rain and the wind was still very keen but who cares about that at twenty and eighteen? I slipped my hand inside her coat and over her breast but to my surprise she seemed unresponsive, so that after a moment or two I asked her what was the matter. She said, quietly and reasonably, "Nothing's the matter, Pip, except that I'd like to be quite sure of something. I'm not sure, you know, in spite of this evening. I'd like to be but I'm not." Then, less resolutely, she went on, "I didn't mean to say what I said when you gave me that locket yesterday. It just slipped out because I was . . . well, surprised and pleased! I mean about not being interested in anyone else in the town. I thought you knew that but . . . well . . . obviously you didn't, and now that I've had time to think about it I'd rather know your side of it and not let things drag along, if you see what I mean. That's the best way I can put it but I haven't expressed myself very well, have I?"

I thought she had but if she needed help I had none to spare. It looked to me as if this was as close a proposal as she could make without scaring me into the sea. I was off course, however, as I soon realized when she made another and even more forlorn attempt to say what she had in mind. It wasn't marriage she was proposing, or not directly, but a kind of partnership, pending a readjustment of our lives. I wanted to be sure, however, so I made no comment except to ask her to try and say precisely what she was getting at. In the event I got a great deal more than I had bargained for.

"I knew you were different from the other boys as soon as I moved up into 2A at school," she said. "There you were, stuck at the bottom of the class, not because you hadn't got brains or liked playing the fool, but because—well—because, even then, you didn't take any of us very seriously!"

"You mean you thought of me as a misfit?"

"Oh no, not that!" She sounded pained at being so hopelessly misunderstood. "No, you weren't a misfit, but you didn't belong with people like my sisters and Cecil Trumper and all the other locals and not because you weren't born here, and didn't speak Devon, but because you were different *inside*. How can I make you see what I mean?"

I appreciate her difficulties more clearly now than I did then. Freud, and all the other headshrinkers, didn't have so many disciples in those days. We had heard of Freud but only in the sense that we knew about George Stephenson and Madame Curie. We didn't pretend to know, as most people do nowadays, what made us tick. Mostly we ticked by instinct so that it must have been difficult for her to find the vocabulary to explain why she had set her cap at me and thought of me as a person with some kind of potential. She went right on trying, however.

"What I really mean is this," she said. "You hadn't settled for what you were and *where* you were! I didn't fall for you in the physical sense, or not then. I think I was a bit afraid of you in that way and maybe I still am but that isn't your fault, it's just that I'm odd that way. I don't mean I'm prissy and touch-me-nottish but—well—I couldn't bear to be messed about or even kissed by someone I didn't like and admire as a person. What I mean is, it would have to be something more than just sex. Does that sound as stuffy to you as it does to me?"

"No," I said, guardedly, "but there has to be an adjustment in that respect with everyone I imagine. You don't just make up your mind and grab, do you?"

"Well, I suppose I did as regards you," she admitted reluctantly, and my laugh made her feel more relaxed so that she went on, "I used to look across at you during those droning lessons and think, 'He's miles away, even now, and when he grows up he'll go chasing after his dreams!' And then I'd find myself thinking, 'Wouldn't it be marvellous if I could go along with him?' *Now* do you understand what made me throw myself at you the first time you gave me the slightest encouragement, like yesterday?"

I understood but it didn't boost my ego in the way her bedroom declaration had boosted it and I realized why before she had finished speaking. She was investing me with a separateness and a resolution and self-confidence that I hadn't got, so that I began to feel a bit of a humbug. At the same time I wasn't going to disillusion her, or diminish myself in her eyes. At nineteen it is comforting to have someone believe in you to that extent. What bothered me, I think, was her astounding honesty that seemed to cry out for equal honesty from me for it was clear that she had spent a great deal more time getting to know herself than I had, or anyone I knew had, and this certainly made me want to play for time. In a sense this was what I continued to do all the time we spent together. I never once faced the issues as frankly and courageously as she faced them from the beginning.

"I don't see what our feeling for one another has to do with leaving town," I said, at length. "That's something that would need money and planning. What I mean is, we couldn't just go and chance our luck. I know I couldn't, with jobs as hard to get as they are today, and I don't think you could either. I don't have to tell you what you can do on the wage they pay nurses."

She considered this for a long moment. Then she said, "I'll tell you the whole truth, Pip, but for heaven's sake don't regard it as another attempt on my part to take too much for granted."

"Well?"

"I could settle for staying right here if you did, if we were together for good, but I know you couldn't. You'd get more and more restless and grumpy as time went by, and then you'd start resenting me as the reason you had got stuck in Redcliffe Bay. I've seen that happen to young men here and so have you, and now that I think about it I suppose that's the real reason why I'm taking such a chance by talking like this the first moment you have given me any reason to suppose I mean more to you than any other girl in the place."

Suddenly the alarm bells stopped ringing and I felt easy and comfortable again. Esta was growing on me every hour I spent in her company and this was not because I now found her pretty, and far more intelligent than any of her contemporaries, but because she had somehow mastered the technique of welcoming a man without trying to trap him at the same time. She would be there every time I needed her but the price of limited access wouldn't include rates, taxes, electric light bills, nagging fidelity and the perambulator under the stairs of a semidetached. This was what was so special about her and I could have almost proposed to her on the spot on those terms.

"Esta," I said, and at the time I really meant it, "I'll tell you what I'll do the first chance I get. I'll have it out with Birdie Boxall about the future I've got down there. I'm twenty next month and that should be a good enough excuse to bring it up. He's always promised me the business but now I come to think of it I'm not so sure I want the crumby old place. I could improve it, and bring it up to date, but even so there's no real future in a place like that and I don't think there ever will be. When do you sit your exams for a staff nurse?"

"In just under a year from now," she said, happily, and then, glancing at the luminous dial of her little wrist watch, "My God! It's twenty-three minutes past and I'm on duty at half past! I'll have to run all the way down the hill!"

We ran together, hand in hand, arriving in the courtyard laughing and breathless. She shot in through the out-patients' entrance and I walked slowly back up the hill and down the Avenue. On the way I passed "Heatherdene" and glanced at it coolly. The spectre of the Doctor didn't seem frightening any more and as for Lorna, and all her thigh-nudging and French kissing, she seemed close to a figure of fun.

CHAPTER THREE

[1]

I had thought of Esta's doubts regarding the limitations of small-town life, and what it had to offer to anyone with a spark of ambition, as being similar to those expressed by Lorna Morney-Sutcliffe. I had assumed, and who can blame me, that they shared views as regards the essential sameness of the rhythm and that their disdain extended to everyone who submitted tamely to being fenced in by Mitre Head and Coastguard Hill. In this respect I was about as wrong as I could be and it didn't take me long to find this out.

Esta had no illusions about Redcliffe Bay but she had a deep and genuine affection for it as a community, so that she thought of everyone within shouting distance of Stump with tolerance and compassion, as was soon demonstrated by her involvement in their lives and in her almost frantic attempt to involve me. Somehow this concern, this involvement, aged her in my eyes, so that I saw her during the next few months not as an eighteen-year-old in love but more as a slightly exasperated mother, saddled with a brood of children often in need of help and advice.

This had two direct effects upon me. It enlarged her enormously as a person and it also encouraged me to do something I had never previously done, namely to probe under the surface of local affairs and take a closer look at my friends and neighbors. Up to then I had assumed that I knew Redcliffe Bay and Redcliffians, that their motives and characters were obvious to the point of tedium. It was Esta who demonstrated the falsity of this assumption.

To begin with, she was far better informed than I. The Cottage Hospital was a clearing house of local gossip and the Wallaces were a talkative, uninhibited family, with one daughter working at Colette's, the local hairdressing salon, and another handling the small-advertisement column in the office of the *Messenger*. One way and another the Wallace family were very advantageously placed for sifting local information and as, in succeeding weeks, I spent a great deal of time in their house, I shared in the steady stream of local currency that flowed through their letter-box. I discovered, for instance, how much had been paid by Duckworth's for the Penny Bazaar on East Stump and how the widow of old George Wayland proposed to spend her windfall. I discovered how much Bruce Brayley, the owner of the Tivoli Cinema, was in debt to Barclays Bank, and how important it was to him to attract good audiences. But money did not greatly interest the Wallace family. They had been living in a financial straitjacket all their lives, owing to Scatty's preoccupation with his inventions, and what intrigued them far more than their neighbors' credit were their neighbors' romances. Esta told me, for example, that the spinster Myfanwy Pritchard was hopelessly in love with her Welsh compatriot, one-armed Owen Rees, headmaster of the Church School adjoining her premises on West Stump, and that Owen returned her devotion but could do little about it owing to the tiresome longevity of his crotchety old mother, who shared his rooms in the schoolhouse, just across the asphalt playground. She told me too of Ken Pigeon's frustrated ambitions regarding his employer's music shop, on East Stump, and his longing to convert it into an up-to-date enterprise, selling popular records instead of the kind of sheet music that could have been found in the parlor of any Edwardian family that went in for evening soirées. Ken, she said, had any number of breezy ideas but old Olaf Hansen, the Dane who owned the shop, was very set in his ways and the fragile bridge between them was Greta, Olaf's only child, who was prey of divided loyalties. On a somewhat spicier level she told me details of the curious relationship between Him-and-Her, the local designation of Bill Belcher, the East Stump pork butcher, and Nell Scotcher, his mistress, an association that would have scandalized the neighborhood had it not been hallowed by time and circumstance. Both were about forty years of age, Bill, a strapping, jovial, back-slapping man; Nell, a comely, matter-of-fact country woman from a village inland, who had managed the shop very successfully when Bill's father died while his son was away at the war. Esta said Bill had been courting an anemic-looking girl whose parents ran one of the private hotels on Frog Terrace, but had ditched her as soon as it was made clear to him that marriage would cost him the services of the efficient and muscular Nell. So their association in shop and cold storage basement soon mellowed and it was now generally accepted that they slept together as well as worked together. Nobody minded this because it was understood they would marry whenever they could take time off from making and selling sausages. Belcher's pork sausages were reckoned the best in the West and satisfied customers were more interested in their flavor than in the proprieties of the man who provided them.

All this emerged piecemeal from casual conversations we had during the humdrum weeks that followed the Hospital Ball. I became a regular visitor at the tall, narrow house behind the ironmongery store and on fairly intimate terms with the family, but Esta and I still had to accept the hazards of the slippery horsehair couch in the kitchen because two of her sisters were still hard at work trying to bring respective boy friends up to scratch in parlor and dining room. We didn't mind all that much because we soon learned to relight the stove and anyway, ours was a more tranquil association. I daresay, even then, our half-formed plans for leaving Redcliffe Bay helped us to keep our relationship at an even temperature and we didn't spend all our time perfecting techniques learned at the Tivoli. We often discussed general subjects and pronounced opinions on them with the pathetic arrogance of the young. Esta told me that she suspected Myrtle and Nancy were no longer virgins (she wasn't sure about Jonquil) and sometimes a conversation like this would encourage us to play about a little but it was always artlessly, as though each of us wanted to avoid the kind of committal her sisters were seeking in the rooms close by. Besides, whenever we did seem like shedding the last of our inhibitions, we always slid off that damned couch and that made us laugh and broke the spell for the time being.

It was a little different on the odd occasion when we were alone in the studio, with Birdie Boxall asleep upstairs. The studio wasn't any more conducive to lovemaking but now and again we came very close to staking a claim on that perambulator under the stairs and only applied the brakes at the last moment. We were, of course, nothing like as sophisticated in this field as are the youngsters of today, knowing little or nothing of the mechanics of family planning, but there was a good deal more to the caution we exercised than the purely practical aspect. As I say, people of our age and milieu were always aware of the risks, the obligations attending them and, if I am to be quite honest, the responsibilities towards one another than is usual nowadays. If this sounds unpleasantly priggish I can't help it, it was a fact. Prigs of one sort or another were thick on the ground in places like Redcliffe Bay a generation ago and I don't suppose Esta and I were different in that respect from any other Redcliffian. I know that we could on occasion sound as pompous as the best of them. It was something along these lines that caused the first rift in our relationship up to that time.

We had come home early from an ill-attended and rather dreary Institute dance and, because it was the eve of my twentieth birthday, we called in at the studio to collect a bottle of vintage champagne Birdie Boxall had given me in a moment of expansion. We had the use of Esta's big living room that night and settled there about midnight.

I can see that room now, with its large bay window looking down on Stump, its heavy lace curtains and solid Edwardian furniture, and its mantelshelf loaded with pop-eyed Staffordshire dogs that Mrs. Wallace seemed to accumulate in vast quantities. The gas fire had a low song that we called "rustle of spring" and there was a brightly-patterned Turkey carpet covering the entire floor. The Wallaces never had much money and even less taste but they believed in warmth and comfort.

We emptied the bottle of champagne, which was excellent, and then Esta, who had no head at all for liquor, became tearfully sentimental about my birthday, coiling herself close to me and apologizing for the fourth time that evening for her inability to buy me a present.

"I've been saving," she said, "but I haven't got nearly enough yet. You'll have to wait for the flat season. I'll put everything I've got on a double and buy you something really nice on the proceeds!"

She was every bit a Wallace in that respect, quite unable to contemplate the prospect of losing a wager, and as her adoring swain, Cecil Trumper, was the bookmaker's nephew, she occasionally got inside information. I knew that her pocket money amounted to about seven-and-six a week, and any kind of gift would have embarrassed me, so I said, half jokingly, "I don't want a present, I'll settle for you right now!"

I think I would have made good the boast. She seemed to me to have been growing more desirable every day throughout the last few weeks and tonight the champagne, or the rare comfort of the room, had given her an additional sparkle. Instead of laughing or provoking me in any way, however, she astounded me by appearing to take umbrage at the invitation. She sat bolt upright, looked hard at me with unblinking brown eyes, and said, snappishly, "You don't mean that, Pip, so why the hell say it? You want to be careful, or you'll be falling behind with your insurance premiums!"

It was a kind of sneer and I accepted it as such. She was as good as telling me that the restraint we had practiced, and its relation to our half-formed plan to seek our fortune outside Redcliffe Bay, only continued to govern our approach to one another as far as I was concerned, and that, for her part, she was ready to let go and settle for domesticity. At least, that was how I saw it and I don't think I was wrong. In a way I was as glad to be done with it all as she evidently was for I wasn't entirely unaffected by Birdie's vintage champagne and I couldn't see us walking the tightrope indefinitely. She had obviously made up her mind, and the fact that I hadn't caused her a certain amount of humiliation. And yet, one doesn't make love coolly and cold-bloodedly at the age of twenty, and I couldn't help feeling I should make some attempt to justify myself in her eyes. I said, "Don't think there haven't been times when I've wanted you like hell, but you know and I know that once we start we'll go on and before either of us knows it we'll be making the kind of plans most couples make around here sooner or later! Do you really want that?"

She thought about this and I could see from her worried expression that it made sense to her. Finally she said, in a very level and reasonable tone, "I love you, Pip. I'm quite sure about that and I think you're sure of it! But what neither of us is sure about is you! Now don't start protesting. I'm not quarrelling with you in that respect because I don't think I have a right to. After all, it was me who started us off by saying what I said that time you gave me the locket on my birthday. I oughtn't to have prompted you, I ought to have waited for it to come from you if it was coming. So this is something for you to decide, not me, and anyway, you've had more experience. You can't keep secrets in Redcliffe Bay and you aren't going to tell me you're still a virgin!"

As a matter of fact I was in all but the technical sense. I had tried my luck, like most of the young men about town, but the few attempts I had made to prove myself had been botched or incomplete in one way or another. Her remark, however, seemed to me a challenge, so that suddenly I felt it was high time I grew up and to hell with the consequences. I pulled her round facing me and kissed her the way Lorna Morney-Sutcliffe had taught me to kiss and if I hadn't been so preoccupied with the thought of what would happen in a moment or two I would have laughed at her astonishment. She responded eagerly enough but only for a few seconds; then, as I tugged at her skimpy little dance frock, she fought free and stood up, looking down at me with a rueful and half-aggravated expression.

"No!" she said. "You're absolutely right, and thank God you've got more sense than me! Let's make some coffee and cool off a bit! I almost went back on everything then and I should have felt pretty sorry for myself afterwards!"

It was now my turn to feel frustrated and I sulked to myself while she was out making the coffee but when she came back, and seated herself at a safe distance, I was sufficiently curious to ask her what made her change her mind so abruptly. She said, stirring her coffee as though she were mixing concrete, "I've told you why, again and again! I think that way of getting a man is contemptible. I always have and I always will. Think of all the girls round here who go bleating to their fathers about "being betrayed" and put in the family way! As though somebody had raped them on the golf-course and they had played a passive part in what had happened! There was Beryl Lingshaft and Edith Nesbitt, they both got their husbands that way, and there was that waitress at the Rainbow Café, the one who took Jerry Bradshawe to court and came out waving her affiliation order as if it was a V.C.! God, they make me sick! I'd sooner have a string of illegitimate babies than behave like that and if it ever happened between you and me I hope I'd still want you to *feel* free. I'd hate you or anyone else to marry me out of pity, or because somebody had bullied you into it! Will you remember that, Pip?"

I don't think what she said would have impressed me much if it had come from anyone else, a girl like her sister Jonquil for instance, but I knew by now that there wasn't a tittle of humbug about Esta Wallace. Maybe this was why I said, "We can't keep this up indefinitely, Esta. Sometimes I feel like getting married now and making Birdie keep his promise about that partnership. We could live over the shop, providing you didn't mind him hanging about when he was sober."

Even at this distance I can't be certain how sincerely I meant what I said, or what I would have done if she had taken me up on it there and then. She didn't, however, and I imagine her rejection of the idea cost her a great deal for, God knows, she had never made any secret about loving me and needing me but she had herself well in hand by now and the skirmish had strengthened her resolve to hold fast to her old-fashioned set of values regarding the general dignity of women, and the demands they were entitled to make upon men. She advertised this by going on to make another of her half-articulate attempts to justify herself.

"What's so important to a man isn't necessarily so to a girl," she said. "It's unfair but that's how it is, and that's how it will always be, no matter how much people pretend otherwise. I don't mean all that trash about a man thinking less of a girl the minute she gives in. It's not a question of 'giving in' because, right now for instance, I'd get as much pleasure as I gave and maybe that much more and I can tell you why. I'd feel I belonged but that isn't the point; it isn't the point at all, Pip!"

She was so earnest and emphatic that she got up and began walking about the room as though she was debating with herself. She always fascinated me when she talked like this. Most of what she said and thought was immature, even to me, but that didn't matter in the least because it was a completely honest projection of Esta Wallace, the odd girl out in the Stump ironmongery family. Because of this, I imagine, her outlook had, or seemed to have, great originality. Indeed, compared with most of the fatuous, pompous and smutty pronouncements on sex I heard from other people all the time I was growing up in Redcliffe Bay what she said sounded sane and wise. She went on, still pacing about, "A few minutes and it's over and done with as far as a man's concerned but don't think I hold that against them! It's the way they're made and you can't blame any one of them for trying! But for most girls—certainly for me—it's a lot more, and I don't have to experience it to find out. I feel it every time you touch me, and have done from that first time you came up to my room on my birthday!"

She stopped suddenly and looked at me with her occasional expression of comic exasperation. "What an idiot you must think me! And a bore too, I wouldn't wonder. All this because of a bit of all-in wrestling on the settee!"

"You don't have to apologize," I said, "I like listening to you when you get steamed up. It's better than the Tivoli!"

"Then you do think I'm a fool! All right, go ahead, but I can't help it because the only thing I know for certain is that I love you and want you but if I can't have you on my terms then I'll settle for being an old maid!"

"I've never really understood what those terms are," I said, and I suppose this was as near I ever came to reciprocating her honesty.

"Well, at least I can tell you that without blushing!" she said.

"I want you as a person, as someone to look up to and help and be with for the rest of my life. I want to sleep with you and if I ever have any kids I want them to be yours, but here's the important part—only if you want the same! I'm not risking becoming a habit, which is what happens to most marriages I've seen as soon as the gilt wears off! You'd better go now. Even talking to you like this makes me feel I can't wait until you've made up your mind!"

"I made up my mind months ago," I said and I didn't think I was fooling myself, but she was a good deal sharper than I and said quietly, "No, you haven't, Pip. It's just the champagne!" and she put up her face to be kissed. I left it at that. As always, when we had one of these encounters, I couldn't match her frankness or the accuracy of her assessments, and needed more time to think. For all that I left with a light heart. She seemed to me, at that moment, to be worth all the people in that town lumped together.

I didn't expect to see her again until she came off duty about nine the following evening, when we had arranged to meet some of our friends in the Lamb and Flag. She telephoned from the hospital soon after lunch, however, asking if I would be in the studio about five, and when I said I would she seemed pleased and excited, saying she had something very important to do that evening and would appreciate my help and advice. Would it be possible for me to wriggle out of the party at the Lamb and Flag? I said I could do this easily enough, and asked for details, but she wouldn't say any more on the phone and rang off abruptly. I guessed that the Sister had shown up and quoted the rule against nurses making private telephone calls.

She came to the studio sharp on time and said she had swapped duties and had a free evening. She waited for me to close shop and as soon as Beryl, the receptionist, had gone she said with suppressed excitement, "It's something that just has to be done, Pip, but there's absolutely no obligation for you to join in! I'll do it myself if you don't care to involve yourself and after all, why should you? Alison Sweetland is nothing to you, is she?"

Alison Sweetland was nothing to me, and very little to Esta I would have thought. She was the self-effacing, slightly mousey little wife of the Reverend Rex Sweetland, Redcliffe Bay's chief exponent of what was then known as Muscular Christianity. He was pastor of the Congregational Church on East Stump and almost as big an extrovert as Doctor Morney-Sutcliffe, although his was the professionally jovial technique. He was always beaming, he walked with long strides, ran boys' clubs, produced missionary plays in which blacking-covered Sunday School scholars were allowed to play with real assagais, and was an acknowledged minor chieftain in the community. His wife usually went unnoticed. She was very shy and an easy prey to the heavyweights of the Ladies' Sewing Circle, who had been heard to tut-tut over her inadequacies as a fit mate for the pastor. Now that I thought about her I would have judged her age to be about thirty-four and she was rather pretty in a shrinking-violet way. She had soft brown hair that was neither bobbed nor shingled but worn in coiled plaits then known as "earphones" and considered old-fashioned after four-valve radio sets had replaced crystal sets in all Redcliffe Bay's living rooms. She had mild blue eyes and very neat hands and feet but her overall impression was one of complete withdrawal.

I said, "What the devil has to be done about Alison Sweetland? She isn't in any kind of trouble, is she?"

"She's in terrible trouble," Esta said smugly. "She's a damsel in distress if ever I saw one and I've made up my mind to help her! Are you interested or aren't you?"

I said that I was interested. Anyone would be interested in a parson's wife in trouble. It had a *News of the World* slant and, as far as I could recall, Redcliffe Bay had never yet made the Sunday papers.

"The Reverend is having an affair with his deaconess," said Esta, watching my recoil. "At least, Mrs. Sweetland thinks he is, and it's killing her, poor lamb. If somebody doesn't do something about it soon she'll probably gas herself."

I was suitably shocked and more than a little concerned. I knew the deaconess, a bossy woman called Angela Tapper, who had been called in about a year ago to help Rex Sweetland cope with his expanding flock and to play the organ on Sundays. She was a kind of substitute for a curate, a busy, bustling young woman, reputedly a great help to the overworked pastor. In the main, ours was a Free Church community and he had more to occupy him than had the local rector, who spent most of his time gardening and bee-keeping.

"How do you know this isn't just talk?" I demanded. "It sounds to me the kind of tittle-tattle your sister Myrtle would mop up while she was coping with one of the old trouts under the hair dryer."

"I know it isn't just talk, I've discussed it with Alison."

"*She* told you about it?"

"We're friends and have been ever since the Sweetlands settled in here. After all, we're next-door neighbors and although I don't like him I think she's sweet and could be very attractive if she made the effort or had the incentive."

"And suppose it's true. What on earth can you do about it? Tell Rex Sweetland to play his own organ?"

"I don't think that's funny," she said. "Listen Pip, I'm serious! I really am anxious to help her and you don't have to join in if you'd rather not. It's just that I've got a plan and I'm going to put it into action, in about two hours or so. Well?"

I was far too intrigued to back out but what ensured my active interest in the affair was not the scandalous element but Esta's earnestness. It struck me then that she had so much generosity that it welled out of her every now and again and this was why she was constantly involving herself in other people's concerns. She wanted my encouragement but it wasn't essential to her. She would have gone right ahead on her own if necessary and then looked around for another worthy cause.

I said, "You'd better brief me but stick to the facts and skip the suppositions."

"It's been going on for months and getting warmer all the time," she said. "That woman Angela is quite ruthless and she's really got him hooked. He isn't a bad sort, once you make allowances for his hearty-heartiness, but he's weak! All those kind of men are weak. That 'let's-get-started' technique is just a smoke screen. He knows he's largely ineffectual and is simply trying to cover up all the time. She—Alison that is—knows this, but Angela Tapper is the stronger character, and she's been hard at work on him ever since she came here. Haven't you noticed her clothes and hairstyle?"

"No," I admitted, "I haven't but I've noticed her figure. She's a bit hour-glassy for my taste but some men go for that."

"That's exactly what I mean," Esta went on eagerly. "When she came here she was far dowdier than Mrs. Sweetland but now—well, just watch her teetering in and out of that schoolroom adjoining the church. She walks like a tart, with her bottom jigging left-right, left-right, and he's noticed all right! They spend almost every evening in the schoolroom rehearsing for the missionary play, or so they say. Mrs. Sweetland hears the piano going, sometimes until after ten o'clock, and when he finally comes up he's overanxious to please and Alison says that's a guilty conscience!"

"It probably is," I said, "but if a whoring parson can't have a guilty conscience, who can?"

"It's not *funny*," repeated Esta, "or not to that wretched little woman, and certainly not to me! It's a tragedy, happening right under our noses, and the terrible thing is that a single push in the right direction could put everything right, don't you see that?"

"No, I'm damned if I do," I said. "Granted it's pretty hard luck on Alison but surely it's something they'll have to work out among themselves. Is Rex Sweetland actually sleeping with Angela Tapper, or is it just slap-and-tickle?"

"Mrs. Sweetland doesn't know. If she did I think she would tell the deacons and make Angela leave overnight. She's tried to make herself go through the side door that leads from the house to the schoolroom, and creep up to the little gallery where she could look down on them, but she hasn't the guts to do it so I said I would, tonight! I think if they knew the cat was loose it would all die a natural death. Fear of exposure would bring a man like Rex Sweetland to his senses at once but I don't think his wife is the person to challenge them. She'd win all right, and Angela Tapper would be sent packing, but there would always be shame on his part and resentment on hers and who wants to live the rest of one's life in that kind of atmosphere? Besides, she's madly in love with him and always has been."

"They haven't got any kids."

"No, and that's part of the trouble. They're both amateurs when it comes to making love—after all, she was a parson's daughter, and she told me that when she married she hadn't a clue about anything. You'd never believe the extent of her ignorance, Pip."

I said I probably would and was going to ask for details but Esta said impatiently, "If she could have a child it would solve itself, of course, but there's not much hope of that, especially now. He hasn't made love to her for two months and she thinks that has to do with his guilt as well."

"She seems to have confided in you pretty thoroughly," I said, but it didn't surprise me. Esta was the kind of person in whom most women would confide if they were given the chance. She wasn't only what the Italians call *simpatico* but she was also a nurse and therefore, in their eyes, half a doctor. I asked her about her plan and she said it was only an outline. She was going to do her spying after the Sunday School children had finished their rehearsal and gone home and what happened then would depend on what she discovered. Mrs. Sweetland had promised to let her in the side door, so that she had access to the gallery. Alison was going to stay in the house and await developments. When I pointed out that Mrs. Sweetland would probably oppose my attachment to the expedition, Esta said she had told her I would be on hand, just in case there was a dramatic scene and a witness was needed. This made me half regret having allowed myself to be drawn into the farce but I promised to meet her in the yard fronting the Sunday School building after dark.

She was there waiting for me at eight and as soon as I arrived she let herself into the parsonage by the back door, telling me to follow the moment the rehearsal was over. I stayed on in deep shadow, out of range of the porch light, until all the little missionaries and all the Zulus the missionaries had converted came tumbling out to disperse on East Stump. Then I followed Esta in, found my way through to the front parlor and tapped on the door. She came out at once and I had a fleeting glimpse of the strained face of Alison Sweetland as she sat hunched over a smokey fire. We didn't exchange a word as Esta piloted me through the mock-Gothic door that led to the southern end of the schoolroom. We stopped to listen on the landing outside the gallery and from the big room below came the tinkle of the piano, playing a Hungarian dance. It could only be Angela Tapper, entertaining Rex, and the music, played on those premises and in those circumstances, struck me as wildly incongruous, like *Chopsticks* emerging from a cathedral organ.

We went cautiously into the gallery and negotiated the rows of forms that were banked there, feeling our way to the rail where we could look right down into the room. They were both there and we could see them clearly in the light of a single electric bulb above the piano. Angela Tapper was playing and he was standing behind, one hand resting on her shoulder. I was acclimatized to his wide, let's-give-God-a-chance grin, but he wasn't wearing it tonight. Instead his smile was what some might have called seraphic but the word fatuous would have described it equally well. For all that, the scene we looked down on was innocent enough, although I could see that Esta was right about Angela's transformation. She didn't look much like a deaconess but more like a woman working hard at seducing and was wearing a red party frock from which too much was expected. Her hair had been bleached the color of straw and this, in those days, was an act of desperation for a woman in her mid-thirties. She was, I suppose, a handsome woman. Her features were heavy but regular and even from up here I could see that she had been reckless with lipstick, which she would never have used in public. She was also showing a certain amount of cleavage and Rex Sweetland was positioned to appreciate it.

Then, quite suddenly, the music ended and the fun began. He put both hands on her shoulders and lowered his head to kiss her neck, and her hands left the keys and pretended to caution his as they roved about a little before finding their anchorage. I began to shake with laughter but Esta gave me a sharp nudge and hissed into my ear. Then, just as though he had been shot in the back, Rex's knees buckled, his head was in Angela's lap and she was stroking his hair. It was a touching scene of love locked out, or love about to be admitted, I couldn't decide which, and I was never given the opportunity to find out.

The first hint I had that Esta's plan was amended came with a metallic chink at my elbow and as I swung round, intending to warn her to keep quiet, I saw what she was doing. She had the gallery fire bucket level with the rail and in the second before she tipped it I saw that it was full to the brim with scummy water. It seemed to go down in a solid sheet and her aim was deadly. It struck Angela on the crown of the head, cascaded over her shoulders and then shot off into her lap and down the length of Rex Sweetland's back. There seemed to be far more than a single bucketful, enough to engulf both of them and overspill halfway across the schoolroom floor. They both let out a shriek, tenor and treble, and then Angela, in leaping up, lost her balance so that they rolled together under the keyboard of the piano. Then Esta was dragging me by the hand up the steep stairs of the gallery and we were through the Gothic door and back inside the parsonage.

I was so astounded by the enormity of the deed that I was speechless and she had pulled me into the presence of Mrs. Sweetland before I realized it. Alison Sweetland looked even more startled than I expected.

"I heard shouting!" she said. "What happened over there?"

"Nothing that can be traced to you," Esta said, and then, frowning with concentration, "I don't know though! Perhaps he *might* think you did it and that's better than ever! He'll have to pretend he thinks it was done by one of his boys, however!"

I began to feel genuinely sorry for the wretched woman. She wasn't far off breaking-point and was making a terrific effort to control herself. Her hands were shaking and she kept blinking and staring round the room, as though she expected Rex to come bounding in with a hatchet. I said, breathlessly, "Tell her, Esta! Tell her what happened! It was a crazy thing to do and I'm getting out before he gets here!"

Esta didn't seem in the least perturbed. She took Mrs. Sweetland by the hand, sat her down and addressing me over her shoulder, said, "He won't come here, you idiot, not until he's changed, not until they've both changed!" Then, readdressing herself to Alison, "I tipped a bucket of water on them! You do it to cats, don't you?"

Alison's jaw dropped and for a moment I thought she was going to faint. She didn't, however, but gave a little shudder, as though some of that scummy water had found its way down her neck. After that, to my profound astonishment, she laughed outright, not in the least hysterically but with genuine mirth.

"You did *that?* You mean, when they were . . . ?"

"They weren't," Esta said briefly, "they were just fooling around at the piano but you can take it from me, Mrs. Sweetland, that if I hadn't cooled them off while I had the chance they would have been lovers next week, or the week after! It looked that way to me."

There was wonder in Alison's gaze as she said, in her low and very attractive voice, "Well, and what do I do now? You started this so tell me how to finish it!"

"It will finish itself, as from now," Esta told her. "The point is, they know someone is wise to what's going on, and they can't be certain who it is. My guess is that he won't say a word to you about it but I'll tell you one thing—that Tapper woman will be out of here inside a week and he'll leave it at that, you see if I'm not right!" She paused for a moment and with a glance at me, went on: "Do you mind Pip Stuart being in on this, Mrs. Sweetland? You can absolutely rely on him, he won't say anything to anyone, will you, Pip?"

All I wanted was to be out of there before Rex came in trailing water, but before I could give her the reassurance she sought I heard the key turn in the front door and steps go pattering across the tiled hall towards the stairs. Esta was right. They needed time and a towelling before they made up their minds what to say and do. I felt even more relieved when I heard footsteps on the floor above.

"I won't say a word to anyone, Mrs. Sweetland," I promised

and was again surprised by her cheerfulness, as though the dousing Esta had given Rex and the deaconess had washed away most of her fears and doubts. She addressed herself to Esta, however, treating me as a spectator.

"You've got something else in mind, haven't you?" she asked, and Esta, taking the chair opposite, said that she had and was going to say it and risk giving offence.

"You've got to *do* something about yourself, Mrs. Sweetland," she said. "You're quite pretty really and could be far more attractive than that Tapper woman if you tried, if you really set out to make an impression on him!"

"What kind of impression, exactly?" asked Mrs. Sweetland.

"A sexy one if you must know! And an up-to-date one too! That's why I asked if you had any money of your own, and advised you to go out and spend it on yourself! I'll tell you what, I get a day off on Wednesday and we'll both go to Paxtonbury. It's no good kitting yourself out here because it will be all over the town in an hour or so. You need a new hair-do and an entire new outfit. After that you need a new approach. Angela will be gone by then and he'll be in the right mood to appreciate you. He'll be feeling as guilty as hell but still mooning after a woman, and you'll be handy, all spruced up and secretly forgiving. Do you see what I'm driving at?"

"I think so," Alison said, with a tight little smile, "and thank you for everything, Esta. I don't know what I should have done if I hadn't told someone about it and I think maybe you're right, he'll lose his nerve and persuade her to go after this. Will you call for me about ten on Wednesday? We can catch the ten-thirty and I'll pay the fare and give you lunch in Peabody's. We could get everything there, couldn't we?"

"Yes," Esta told her, hoisting herself up, "we could and will! Come on Pip, let's have a drink. It's his twentieth birthday, Mrs. Sweetland."

"Really? Congratulations!" said Alison gravely, and we went out, just like that, as if we had been paying a social call and had overstayed our welcome.

It wasn't until we were crossing behind the Stump that the

full impact of her initiative hit and humbled me. I wasn't quite ready to admit it, however, so I said, "You're so damned sure of yourself! How do you know it'll work out like that? Suppose it doesn't. Suppose there's a showdown and he settles for that other woman?"

"You don't really think that's possible," she said, and I didn't. I was as certain as she was that Rex would panic, Angela would leave town and Alison's transformation would head him back to the straight and narrow in a matter of days. Esta stopped within yards of the Lamb and Flag, held me back for a moment and spoke the epitaph on the incident. "Sometimes you just *know* what you have to do, Pip, and this was one of those times! Thanks for coming along, anyway."

"I didn't do anything but watch," I reminded her, but she said, "You were there! That's what mattered to me!"

[2]

As it turned out I had a surprise for her that week. I bought my first car. At least, Birdie Boxall and I bought it between us, and he undertook to pay for the petrol I used on business trips. It wasn't much of a car, a battered 1926 Austin Seven tourer, with a perished hood that was difficult to raise, worn tires and about ten thousand miles on the clock. It cost us twenty pounds but it could travel up to forty-five miles an hour and I was proud of it. I collected it from Bedwell's Garage when Esta was in Paxtonbury, keeping her date with Alison Sweetland, and since I knew that they would be catching the four-thirty home I drove across the moor and parked in the station yard, sounding the hooter when I saw them approaching the booking hall.

Between them, Esta and the firm of Peabody's, the biggest store in Paxtonbury, had done an impressive job on Alison. I could see that at a glance as they turned and came across to me, Esta's eyes widening as she saw the car. Later she described the ecstasy of spending indulged in by the parson's wife. Once she had begun trying on new clothes, neither Esta nor the saleswoman could stop her; she spent over sixty pounds of her Post Office Savings in that shop, and finished up with a face massage and an elaborate hair-do at Pompadour's, just across the Square. Even then she wasn't through. She bought herself new suede shoes and a whacking great handbag, and left all her old things behind for the junkman. Esta said it was like taking Cinderella to the ball. Judging by the parcels Alison was carrying, Cinderella must have won most of the prizes.

It was a little dodgy getting her home and into the parsonage without anyone noticing. I drove into the broad alley at the rear of the Sunday School building and dropped Esta off to scout around and make sure neither Rex Sweetland nor his organist was on the premises. As luck would have it they were not, so Alison slipped in and twinkled up the steps in her new shoes, silk stockings, grey two-piece and saucy little beret. It was only when she turned to wave that I identified her new hairstyle as the low, eye-masking style of Norma Shearer, then one of Hollywood's reigning goddesses.

Esta seemed well satisfied with her day's work but she needed my confirmation.

"Well, what did you think?" she wanted to know, as I made my third attempt to back out of the alley without losing the last three inches of my exhaust pipe.

"Sensational," I said, "but I'm hanged if I know what the Reverend will make of it! He'll probably assume she's found herself a boy friend in Paxtonbury."

"Wait until he sees her in her lemon silk camiknickers and black negligée," Esta said. "If you ask me the Congregationalists are in for a short sermon next Sunday!"

"How about Angela Tapper?" I wanted to know.

"Packing," Esta said, "just like I told you! She's got herself a job in Nottingham," and then, and not before time in my estimation, "I'm so glad you've got a car, Pip! With summer coming on we can have fun in this, especially as I'm back on night duty in April. We can go farther afield in the afternoons!" and she snuggled down in the worn leather seat as if she was riding in a Bentley.

Much later I heard what happened at the parsonage. Angela Tapper left town the following Saturday and the same night poor old Rex made three or four stumbling attempts to confess, but Alison wouldn't let him shed his guilt that easily. He had to peel it off a little at a time. The black negligée, the lemon camiknickers, or the transformation as a whole, must have had an even more salutary effect than we had anticipated. They had been married thirteen years and were still childless, but by late spring Alison was pregnant and so proud of the fact that for a week or so she was the standing joke on our side of town. She always stopped and had a word with me when we met. Clearly she seemed to think that I had had a hand in making Rex sit up and take notice.

I have recounted the Sweetland–Tapper story in detail because on looking back, I see now that its successful conclusion had a curious effect upon Esta's thinking and, to some extent upon our relationship, in the months ahead. I think it was this personal triumph that headed Esta down the path of total reconciliation with Redcliffe Bay, in the sense that a prospector might abandon the idea of setting out for the goldfields after discovering a sizeable nugget in his own backyard. It wasn't very noticeable at first. We still talked about a moonlight flit but it was obvious that she had become reabsorbed to some extent in the day-to-day routine of the town, for in early March she amazed me by entering her name as a contestant for the title of Water-Carnival Queen, an honor very much sought after by every local girl with the necessary qualifications.

In the years before the spread of railways Redcliffe Bay had been no more than a large fishing village. It got its first boost in the decade following the French Revolution when a group of *émigrés* discovered it and built Frog Terrace, the town's first distinguished houses. After the Restoration the *émigrés* went home, but some of the zest they had injected into the town remained and the Water Carnival was an example of this, for it became a strong local tradition, with many features elevating it above most of the annual carnivals in adjoining Westcountry towns. One such tradition was the Burning of Bonaparte and another, the Progress of the Water Queen across the bay between the two headlands. People would come from miles around to see a Redcliffe Bay carnival; and the celebrations, which had developed into a shopping festival and a seasonal opening, lasted a week. It was always a busy time for me and sometimes, if national news was in short supply, I sold carnival pictures to the dailies, even to London dailies. In those days every newspaper had a page or two of pictures and relied, to some extent, upon local photographers.

Esta asked my advice about entering and I told her she had as good a chance as most local girls and a much better chance than some. There were very strict rules about qualifications. A girl had to be over seventeen, under twenty-one, unmarried and resident in the urban area, but what gave Esta a fair prospect of winning was the committee's preference for a girl who, in addition to possessing good looks and a good figure, was able to make a speech and carry herself with dignity. Redcliffe Bay was old-fashioned in most respects, but regarding its carnival, which was its major holiday advertisement, its residents anticipated the techniques of postwar public relations officers.

Well, she put her name down and moved onto the short list, and secretly I was proud of her because, in the preliminary canters, she began to look like having a first-class chance. There was a by-product that probably influenced her entering the competition. The winner was awarded a twenty-guinea prize, most of the regalia outfit and a ball dress. She probably thought these bonuses would be useful additions to her trousseau.

I don't want to give the impression that at this stage we had made up our minds irrevocably to get married, to leave Redcliffe Bay singly or to leave it as a team. We had not, but we still talked of these things and each of us thought about them a great deal and I am sure we were already thinking of the town as a place we would soon be looking back on as one looks back on childhood. It was this that distinguished us from all the other youngsters growing up around us and a factor that contributed as much to our partnership as did our mutual attraction.

I took a good many pictures of Esta round about that time and because they were good pictures, staged and presented with more care than I lavished on other clients, I think I contributed to her ultimate success for the photographs were drooled over in private by all the Committee members, most of them elderly tradesmen. You could see which way the wind was blowing at the two preliminary contests. The girls, originally two dozen in number, had to parade the dais at two local events in the Church Hall—the Licensed Victuallers' Ball and the Civic Ball—both launched in early spring. Here again postwar TV beauty contests were anticipated, for the girls paraded twice, once in their dance frocks and once in bathing costumes, although the latter were nothing like so revealing as the modern bikini. They were usually made of a much heavier material and some kind of skirt, even if it was only a couple of inches long, was obligatory.

Esta bought herself a crimson costume that went very well with her dark curls and pale complexion, and it gave me a comfortable feeling to reflect that she was my girl as she strutted to and fro along the boards under the beady eyes of the Committee men. Judges included Doctor Morney-Sutcliffe, as Vice-Chairman of the Council, and his sole dangerous competitor for civic honors, Fred Hopkins, owner of the local timber yard. There was no love lost between these two and at this time Hopkins was enjoying his year of office as Council Chairman.

The short list for the Water or Carnival Queen had to be ready by the first day of spring and the selection of the final winner was then in abeyance until the last Saturday of May, the week prior to the carnival. All the unsuccessful finalists were automatically enlisted as maids-of-honor and some of them performed their duties with turned-down mouths. It was not unknown for one of them to try and trip the Queen with her train during one or other of the ceremonies.

The night that Esta won through to the final was a memorable one for the Wallaces and for me. Indeed, her success was shared by the whole of East and West Stump, for we had never produced a Queen on our side of the town. Almost always they came from families owning the larger shops and businesses in High Street and Fore Street, or from one of the few Avenue families taking an active interest in town affairs. I saw Mrs. Sweetland there, with her eyes shining and her husband's hand clasping hers, and the Wallace family turned up *en masse*, Scatty Wallace wearing a dickey that showed grease spots put there by his latest invention. It was no surprise to me to discover that Scatty entered his workshop in evening clothes. He sometimes went out there and got on with it in his nightshirt. Birdie Boxall was there, smelling of rough cider (a drink he favored when he anticipated mixed company), and so was Myfanwy Pritchard, who kept the West Stump Gift Shop, and Myfanwy's loved one, Owen Rees, headmaster of the Church School. Esta already had her eye on these two and was giving her mind to a plan to bring them together but in the event her assistance proved unnecessary.

Another star-crossed romance that bothered her at this time was one that I believed existed in her imagination, a possible alliance between Ken Pigeon, manager of Olaf Hansen's music shop, and Olaf's solemn daughter, Greta. As usual, where Redcliffe Bay matters were concerned, I was wrong and she was right, for it was at that dance that she fired her opening shots in the Hansen–Pigeon campaign. They were only range-finders but they hit their mark.

Ken Pigeon was an old friend of both Esta and me. He was a short, dapper, cheerful young man about my age, so sleek and glossy that he always reminded me of a rook. He sauntered over to us and congratulated Esta, freely prophesying her election as Queen and she asked him if he had been able to persuade Olaf the Dane to hoist his business into the twentieth century. Ken said he hadn't and he had given up hope for Hansen wouldn't even stock jazz sheet music or records. "According to Olaf," he said, "*Just a Song at Twilight* is still the rage of Denmark Street!"

Esta said bluntly, "You'll never do a damned thing with that old fuddy-duddy until you pounce on his daughter! She could bring him round in two seconds, take it from me!" and then, when Ken shrugged, "You are keen on her, aren't you? Everyone assumes you are!"

When Esta came out with a loaded question like this I always felt embarrassed for her and I hastened to Ken's defense, saying, "Why the hell can't you leave people to settle their own affairs? Why do you always have to jolly them along? Maybe Ken's got his own ideas, maybe he'll set up on his own somewhere." But Ken shook his dark, brilliantined head and said that Esta was right, that he was keen on Greta, and that a town the size of Redcliffe Bay could never support two music shops. Olaf's place, he said, could make a lot of money if the old man would let him try out some new ideas. As to Greta, she had never given him the slightest encouragement, although she didn't seem interested in anyone else. It had been this way, he added gloomily, ever since he had gone there to work when he was fifteen.

"Well, it's time you tried your luck, Ken," she said. "What have you got to lose? He only pays you fifty shillings a week, doesn't he?"

"That's so," Ken said, his natural ebullience reasserting itself, "but don't forget the commission on harmoniums and music-stands! That works out at all of two pounds a quarter!"

The dancing recommenced at this point and Esta and I went on the floor. They played *Auf Wiedersehen* again and it made me think of the beautiful Lorna for the first time in weeks. She wasn't there; in fact I hadn't set eyes on her since I had parted from her at the foot of her drive after the Hospital Ball. It was odd that I should remember her that night for within a matter of hours I was talking to her.

The gaiety of the occasion, and the pleasant close-up I had had of Esta in her tight-fitting bathing costume, made for an affectionate ride home that night. We didn't go straight home of course but out along the front and up the back road to Coastguard Hill, one of our favorite spots on a fine night. It was particularly clear on this occasion. At three hundred feet we could not only see the town, with just a few lights winking, but the soft glow in the sky over Paxtonbury, fifteen miles inland, and also the regularly spaced flashes of the Sharksnose lightship, ten miles out to sea. We both appreciated Redcliffe Bay at moments like this, sitting in blue-black moon shadow cast by the knob of Mitre Head and sniffing the wet, salty wind that came off the sea. We didn't feel shut out and cut off, but free to go or stay as we pleased and always relaxed, the way Huck Finn used to feel on the raft when he was drifting down the Mississippi by starlight.

Esta was never much of a reader—she found it difficult to sit still for more than an hour—but she was always interested in what I had read or was reading, and liked me to tell her stories, usually potted versions of the classics, and describe scenes that had a local parallel, like this one. She thought of me as a well-read man which I wasn't, but I let her go on thinking so; it flattered me and it did no harm. She was fond of poetry too, so long as she didn't have to learn any, and I used to quote her extracts from anthologies Birdie Boxall kept on his shelves, mostly modern verse by war poets, like Sassoon and Wilfred Owen. She liked Sassoon's irony and Wilfred Owen's compassion, but she also enjoyed the shorter poems of Masefield. I tried to interest her in painting but I didn't get far in that direction. She had too much of her father's respect for things that went bang or bobbed up and down in response to steam pressures and electric currents. She could always get the car started again if it went wrong, as it did not infrequently, whereas I, with no mechanical bent whatsoever, would have walked home on account of a flat tire or a jammed carburetor needle if she hadn't been handy.

We stayed up there a long time on this particular night and if there had been more leg room in the back of the car I daresay we would have watched the dawn. As it was, we cruised back into town about three A.M. and I kissed her goodnight on her doorstep. It was a very satisfying kiss, the last of its kind we were to exchange for some little time.

Birdie gave me a shout while I was shaving and said I was wanted on the phone by a customer. I never let him answer the phone. He not only forgot important messages but coughed and spluttered so much the callers often hung up on him. I went down to the cash desk and picked up the receiver and a voice that I didn't immediately recognize said, "Is that Kent?" and waited.

My given name was used so infrequently in Redcliffe Bay that I had to think who "Kent" was. When I repeated it, with a note of query, the woman on the phone laughed and I recognized the laugh at once as Lorna Morney-Sutcliffe's. Nobody ever laughed quite like Lorna. The note was pitched very low, like her voice, but it had within it the same contempt for her audience. She said, "People don't usually forget their own names, do they? Or did you invent it, just for my benefit?"

I waffled a moment longer, needing time to readjust myself to her. Her voice, after this long interval, had a disturbing effect on me, not exactly stimulating and certainly not alarming, but portentous, as though she was the bringer of very bad news or very good. It did something else to me too, something that Esta's voice or presence never did achieve. It made me think of women not as potential wives, mothers, aunts, friends or helpmeets, but wholly and exclusively as instruments of pleasure. To feel this way about Esta I needed a couple of drinks, or to be kissing her in propitious circumstances, but Lorna could turn on sex appeal like an electric light.

I said, "Where have you been all this time? I heard you were abroad?" and she said she had been abroad, to the Dolomites, but was ringing because she had an idea that might put money in my pocket. This interested me less than the prospect of seeing her, or even talking to her, but I listened carefully when she said she had heard I sometimes illustrated magazine features and wrote the accompanying text, and that if this was true I could call on her that afternoon, make a selection of her father's paintings, and photograph them for an article she was writing for *Apollo*, then running a series on the French Impressionists.

I said it sounded a wonderful idea and thanked her. "You can write the article as well if you like," she said. "I'm no good at it and it's been commissioned. They pay pretty well and, to be honest, you would be doing me a favor. What shall we say?

About three-thirty? We could give you tea up here." I said I would be there on the dot and after I had rung off I wondered whether to pop across Stump and tell Esta before she left for the hospital. I decided not. Somehow I knew she wouldn't be enthusiastic and I didn't want to be talked out of it. I was meeting her that evening anyway. It was a Thursday and the Tivoli changed its program on Thursdays.

I botched what little work I did that morning and was too excited to eat much lunch. About two o'clock I changed into my best suit, shaved very carefully and polished my shoes. Beryl, our cashier-receptionist, looked so surprised when she saw me emerge from the studio that I had to tell her I was covering a big wedding and couldn't show up in the usual slacks and windcheater. That satisfied her and I drove the car up to within a house or two of "Heatherdene" and parked it. I wasn't going to drive up to the home of someone who owned an M.G. sports and a Daimler in my kind of transport. It was far more dignified to arrive on foot.

The house was a good deal larger than I had realized but not impressive architecturally. It was mock-Tudor and tile-hung, with wisteria trained along the south aspect. The flower beds were very tidy and full of daffodils and narcissi, bending in the stiff March wind. An aged gardener, weeding the central bed, glared at me as if I had overlooked the "NO HAWKERS" sign on the gate.

A uniformed housemaid answered my ring and took me through the hall and along a corridor to a room in the west wing. If I hadn't been impressed by the house on the outside I was by the evidence of affluence here. The floors had wall to wall carpeting and there were deep recesses with bowls of flowers and here and there a choice piece of porcelain, Rockingham or Colebrookdale at a guess. The furniture was genuine antique, not French, as I would have expected, but early nineteenth-century English. There were several good pictures on show and a general air of taste and elegance as well as wealth. I had always supposed the Doctor to be wealthy but I was surprised by the opulence of "Heatherdene," viewed from the inside; it was something quite extraordinary in Redcliffe Bay at this time.

She was awaiting me in a small drawing room at the end of the long corridor. There was a bright coal fire burning and tea was already served, so that I suspected she must have seen me trudging up the long drive. She looked a little older and more matronly than she had appeared at the dance; she was also more composed and less inclined to advertise her impatience with her surroundings. She was wearing a close-fitting, short-skirted cocktail dress of dark blue shiny material that brought out the color of her eyes. Seeing her, so decorous and well-groomed, I was glad I had spruced myself up a little. Her manner was polite and friendly without being the slightest bit intimate. Looking down at her as we touched rather than shook hands, it was hard to believe that I had kissed her in a way I had never kissed any woman up to that time.

She invited me to sit opposite her and served me with tea from a silver pot, and then buttered crumpets from a silver muffin dish warmed by a tiny spirit stove. It was all very formal, as though I was paying a duty call on a rich young aunt. She said briefly, "Glad you could come, Kent. After all, if they really want to do a display of my father's work, I don't see why some-one shouldn't benefit from it. There's no one else in this desert who would have the faintest notion how to set about it."

For the next twenty minutes or so she went on to talk of her father, of his work and background, of the small niche he occupied in modern art and also, to some degree, of her own youth in Paris and her private evaluation of the work produced there during the twenties. She illustrated her talk with a fat portfolio of her father's drawings, some of them originals, others reproduced as prints. He was, according to her "a *genre* painter" and such talent as he had, limited in her view and mine, resided in catching a trivial aspect of a street scene involv-ing a hawker, a waiter, a tired old tart or, in some cases, a passerby who had no idea that he was being limned for pos-terity. It was all very interesting and I listened attentively but with no more than the surface of my mind. At a deeper level I was pondering both her and our relationship, and it was not until she began using her legs in a way that I easily recognized that I had a glimmering of why I was here, why indeed she bothered to cultivate me and what, if anything, I was expected to do about it.

As I said, her skirt was an inch or two shorter than the current fashion. It was the length that was fashionable about the time I left school and the use she made of this fact was the one unsophisticated aspect of her ploy. She held her knees closely together but every now and again she shifted her position in the tub armchair she occupied, crossing and recrossing her legs once every three minutes and using the bulky portfolio as an excuse. After pretending not to watch her knees for longer than I could bear I surrendered, letting her talk of Paris and her father flow over me while I waited for the next peep behind the scenes. We had progressed this far when the maid came to remove the tea things. Then, with a final flourish of suspender clips, she stood up, yawned, tapped her mouth and said, "Well, Kent, that's the general idea! Does it interest you? You had better be frank, one way or the other."

I said, a little too fervently, that it did interest me and not solely on account of the fee the magazine might pay but because I was genuinely interested in painting and always had been. She looked at me doubtfully and said, "Really?" and in an attempt to convince her I told her, half jokingly, about my rush home to compare her with Gainsborough's *Mrs. Graham* after our last meeting. This piece of information had an exaggerated effect. She loosened up quite considerably and became far more relaxed and accessible. It also seemed to me that she was flattered for she said, with the nearest she could ever come to genuine enthusiasm, "But I *know* that picture! I always thought it was one of Gainsborough's best. She was rather hoity-toity, don't you think?"

"You're hoity-toity when you stop being yourself," I said and she laughed very pleasantly, tilted her head on one side and said, "You're an odd one, Kent! You don't belong here at all, do you? You're rather sweet, really!"

She didn't fool me for a moment so I wasn't much surprised when she said, with elaborate unconcern, "The rest of the stuff I brought back from Paris is in a folder in the attic. You had better glance through it and see if there is anything you want to take away with you. Leave the portfolio here, I'll have Lucille wrap it before you go," and led the way down the long corridor and up the stairs to the first landing where there was a door flush with the wall that gave access to a story revealed by the dormer windows I had noticed outside. I might have been mistaken but, with her hand on the latch, she seemed to hesitate a moment too long. Then she opened the door and went on up, apologizing for the litter when we arrived in a large attic that was used as a junk store. "Some of this stuff is mine and some belonged to the Doctor's mother," she said. "We've never got round to sorting it out."

"Where is the Doctor?" I asked but she didn't duck the question as I had been certain she would. She just shrugged and said, "He's in London, at one of those local government conferences he attends. Him, the Town Clerk and Mr. Hopkins, the Council Chairman. I'd sooner them than me!"

I remembered then that this was so, that there had been a paragraph about it in the *Messenger* the previous Friday, and although, by this time, I was beginning to think I knew the form, the realization that she had waited until he was out of town before inviting me here was sobering for, by now, I was almost sure that the painting article was a smoke screen. In five minutes I was handed the proof.

She went over to a trunk in the corner and took out a folder made of thick cardboard, carrying it over to an old plush sofa that stood under one of the dormer windows. She put it on her knees, hitched her skirt a point or two and patted the space beside her. "Come and sit here, with the light behind you!" she said, and I went very willingly although I was aware of a qualm in my belly that wasn't put there by her China tea and buttered crumpets.

The drawings in the folder were much the same as those downstairs, at least, that's what I thought when she began to sift through them, but then we came to one that had little in common with the gendarmes and flower-sellers but was the kind of sketch that every stay-at-home in Redcliffe Bay would expect to find in the luggage of a person who had visited Paris. It was a watercolor of a Can-Can girl, all roguishness and naughty-naughtiness, a study of frilly knickers, red garters and plump, pink thighs. It was, in fact, a poor imitation of Toulouse-Lautrec, representing the dancer in the final flourish of the dance when she flaunts her bottom at the stalls and peeps over her shoulder to watch the effect. I had seen a dozen pictures exactly like it in *La Vie Parisienne*, which was as near as we came to bookstall pornography in Redcliffe Bay.

"Very ordinary," she commented, as if she was telling me something new, "and not even father's! René did it. A rather silly attempt to prove that Toulouse was overrated."

"Who was René?" I asked dutifully.

"A writer who thought he was in love with me. He was a good writer but a bad painter and a worse lover. However, to be fair, he admitted using palette and easel as decoys."

"How did he do that?"

"How do you think? They gave him an excuse to undress me. Like this."

She flicked her way past the Can-Can girl and pointed to a study of a nude standing beside a window, her back to the painter and both hands resting on the ledge as she peered into the street.

"Is that you?"

"I'm afraid it is—or was. I was slimmer in those days," and she sighed, as though regretting not only excess weight but a moment of frolic from her past that still had the power to produce a whiff of nostalgia. "That one isn't too bad, as a matter of fact, but René couldn't do faces. That isn't surprising. He wasn't the least interested in faces, certainly not my face."

"You said he was in love with you."

"I said he thought he was in love with me. There's a difference. Or didn't you know?"

I was accustomed to being patronized. Run a business in a

small town and you are patronized by all kinds of people, rich, poor, young and old, but I didn't have to take this kind of thing from her, not after that kiss and those furtive pressures at the dance. I made a move to put the folio aside and stand up but she must have had considerable experience with men and beat me to the exit. With one of those wintry smiles that were common currency between the tradesmen and the Avenue folk she said, quickly, "I'm sorry. I shouldn't have said that. I'd forgotten boys of your age are very sensitive on the subject of romance."

This time I did manage to land a glancing blow. "I'm not exactly a boy, Mrs. Morney-Sutcliffe. I found that out dancing with you last January!"

It wasn't bad for an amateur and at least it forced her to change her tactics.

"That's so," she said, pretending to yawn, "I'd almost forgotten. Then I daresay you're old enough to tackle red meat. This is what I meant about René's approach," and she turned a page and showed me a crayon sketch of herself lying flat on her back, her upraised arms holding a kitten and a long shaft of sunshine highlighting her spreadeagled loins. It was well drawn and readily recognizable but so frankly pornographic that it came close to being comic. Nothing whatever was left to the imagination, and in displaying it she had made an accurate guess at the strain that could be placed upon my self-control. Suddenly, as though someone had turned a valve, the attic became insufferably hot and the temperature absorbed the last doubts I had about her purpose in summoning me here. The devil of it was that I hadn't the least idea what to do about it.

I knew so little about women of her type that I had to rely solely upon instinct. I was like a bumptious youth playing bridge with a first-class player and although it seemed to me that I held a strong hand I was not only at a loss to know what to call but what to lead. This gave her an enormous advantage and she wasn't slow to exploit it, letting me flounder about for a moment trying to come to terms with my own inadequacies. I never did, of course, for the correct play was to pass and let her do the calling, instead of which I pushed the portfolio from her lap, grabbed her round the waist and kissed her mouth, expecting her to melt like a heroine in the final clinch of a Tivoli epic.

She did nothing of the kind. I might have been embracing a wax doll lightly sprinkled with expensive perfume, and when I relaxed my hold she still didn't move but went right on smiling, her eyebrows drawn together in a judicious expression of interest, stiff courtesy and amusement.

Her smile, her pose, her entire, slightly pitying bearing made me so furious that I could have seized her by the hair and flung her onto the floor and I can see now that it might have resolved matters more satisfactorily if I had done just that and walked out. As it was I sat gaping at her with my ears tingling until she said, crisply but kindly, "You do take rather a lot for granted, don't you? When I want to be mauled in my own home, I'll ask. Perhaps you'll remember that another time, Kent!"

I was baffled and horribly embarrassed but not quite so reduced as she imagined and there were reasons for this. Not only was I certain that the gibe was her revenge for my remark concerning the dance, I was quite sure that I had been correct in assuming the sole reason for her enticing me here had to do with her desperate need for a man. Not perhaps a lover, but at all events someone who would prove a captive audience for her charms and make her feel coveted. I was so convinced of this that reflection steadied me a little and gave me the breathing space that I badly needed.

There were two obvious courses I could have taken. I could have sneered back at her and called her bluff, brushing aside her phoney protests and using the then popular caveman approach; or I could have played dumb and bruised and in that way saved a few rags of my dignity. That I did not make a deliberate choice of either role was due to the fact that I was far too flustered to show any kind of reaction for a moment or so and the involuntary respite not only rescued my dignity but turned the tables on her in a way she neither liked nor expected. Having said her piece, as it were, she turned on a mood of sweet reasonability, pushing me down just as I was about to rise and patting my hand in the manner of a reproving but tolerant schoolmarm. She said, with her infuriating smile, "You don't imagine I asked you here with this in mind, I hope? You aren't that young, Kent!" And then, with a coyness that I found quite sickening, "Oh, I admit to teasing you a little when I realized those silly sketches were in the folder, but you can stand a little fun, can't you? Have you forgotten how to laugh at—twenty now, isn't it?"

This pious disclaimer only made me growl so she tried again, even more patiently. "Come now, Kent dear, think back a little! I let you kiss me goodnight in the car that night because you had been sweet enough to waste your evening on a married woman and missed the chance of taking a pretty girl home, but that doesn't imply that I'm available in my own home, does it? Well? Say something! At least I didn't scream, or smack your face. Most women would have done one or the other!"

I found my tongue at last and it gave me savage pleasure to use it. I said, "Most women wouldn't have asked me up here to show me sketches of themselves lying naked on a couch! Most women wouldn't offer a man a second-hand preview of their fanny!" Then I stood up, pushed past her and made for the door.

For the first and, as it proved, the only time in our association, I really scored over her and in a way that made her gasp and flush. She wasn't smiling now. Her face was as flushed as mine and her mouth was half-open. She looked almost ill with amazement. I was two stairs down before she recovered sufficiently to cry out.

"Kent! Come back!"

I stopped and half turned. I had hoped to shock her but not to this degree and I knew, the moment I returned to the attic, that our positions had been sharply reversed and that for the time being at least I was master of the situation. It gave me the greatest satisfaction to watch her stand there fumbling for a formula of surrender that wasn't quite unconditional. In the end she found one, although to announce it required a considerable effort on her part.

"Sit down," she said, almost inaudibly, "sit down and . . . and try and act like a man, instead of a spiteful boy!"

I sat down on the couch. I was feeling so sure of myself that nothing she could say had the power to wound or belittle me. She crossed over to the window, preferring to talk with her back to me.

"You must think of me as a pretty desperate case," she said, and when I made a sound that could be interpreted any way she chose, "Well, I suppose I am! And there *was* some kind of reason behind asking you here. I couldn't say what that reason was in so many words except that it didn't have much to do with an article in a magazine!"

I said I had guessed that when we were downstairs. I was behaving badly I knew but I didn't care, not a damn. You can shrug off humiliation at forty plus but not at twenty. I was after my pound of flesh and to do her justice she was prepared to give it to me or more than half of it. She hesitated a moment before going on and in that pause I began to feel slightly loutish. She said, slowly, "All right, Kent, you don't have to listen. Walk right out and forget the whole thing if you like. I daresay you'll wish you did in the end."

She was right about that but already I was beginning to feel sorry for her. She looked and acted as though she didn't care whether the roof fell on her and I noticed something else, she wasn't pretty any more, just drained and tired, with the color gone from her cheeks and her teeth clamped over her lip. I said, taking the first step or two towards a qualified apology, "Nobody likes to be made feel that much of a fool, Lorna. Damn it, it was pretty obvious what you wanted, wasn't it?"

"I didn't think it was," she said unexpectedly, "but clearly it must have been. All right! I was depressed, and moody, and so damned lonely that I had to talk to someone. Then I remembered how young and unpretentious you were at the dance. That's what I was really looking for, someone who wasn't a bloody humbug! Someone who had a bit of sparkle left in him! You can take that as a compliment, for I don't know a single other person in Redcliffe Bay who qualifies!"

"Thank you," I said, a good deal less gruffly, and then, our eyes meeting for the first time since I had come back into the room, I could have laughed and even that surprised me. "We don't have to have an inquest, Lorna. I like talking to you and I like being with you. If anything else is going I'm not the one to say no to it, not after the way you kissed me when you brought me back here last time. But I didn't come looking for it, not until I realized you were getting a kick out of pushing me."

"I do that sometimes," she admitted, "I've been doing it off and on since I was a kid. I believe men have a word for it, haven't they?"

"Yes, they have, and I don't have to tell you what that word is."

She laughed at that. In her own, miserably distorted way she was as honest as Esta. The trouble was, then and later, we graduates from the Tivoli one-and-sixpennies had never played in her league. Here I was, within minutes of feeling so cocky, ready to eat out of her hand and both of us knew it.

She said, moving away from the window and coiling herself on the sofa, "I've gone through a bad time since we last met, Kent. You probably gathered at the dance I was nearing the end of my tether then but it's been a lot worse since I returned from the Continent."

"You and the Doctor?"

"Yes," she said, with one of her patronizing smiles, "me and the Doctor. Or the Doctor and Redcliffe Bay! They can be lumped together, you know, in one big, soggy ball, equated with boredom, stuffiness and what are known as fantods!"

"If it's that bad why don't you leave him?" I asked.

In those days, I believed that ecstacy was insoluble from marriage and from any kind of association between a man and a woman who shared the same house and bed. She must have realized this but she was wise enough not to challenge it. All she said was, "I would have done that two years ago if I had money of my own. I'm not one of those idiots who have to sleep in a bed just because I've made it, but you would have to know a good deal more about how it began and how it has developed to understand, Kent. Maybe I'll tell you one day but I'm not in the mood at the moment and I don't think you're in the mood to listen. Another time, perhaps."

"You've told me that much you might as well tell me the rest," I urged, as much out of curiosity as sympathy. I began to understand that it wasn't only vanity or even ruttishness that drew me towards Lorna but also a sharp awareness of crossing into a world that was utterly foreign to a small-town boy, growing up in a place like Redcliffe Bay and having, as his fellow-travellers, people like Birdie Boxall and Scatty Wallace, with Scatty Wallace's daughters for light relief. It was a world that had to do with big, shiny cars, shareholdings, trips to and from the Continent, Savile Row suits, expensive perfumes, nightclubs, divorces and Ascot. It was a world that none of us had ever entered or expected to enter and our door-chink glimpses of what went on in there were limited to paragraphs in London gossip columns, or the passage of shadows on the Tivoli screen. The closest I had ever come to crossing the threshold was the few seconds I had held Lorna in my arms, and it says something for the impact she made upon me that I was now ready to sit in her attic all day and all night without a thought to the Doctor's return or the conclusions of the servants downstairs.

"I'll tell you one thing," she said at length. "The Doctor married with the idea of raising a family. It has now been established that he bought a pig in a poke. I can't have children."

"Does that disappoint you as well?"

"What do you think?"

"I think not, I think you'd be as bored with children as you are with everything else in Redcliffe Bay!"

"You're learning, Kent."

She fumbled in her bag and took out a small, ivory cigarette case, lighting two De Reszke cigarettes and pushing one towards me. I noticed that she inhaled in a way that people in the shiny-car world inhaled. They didn't puff, as we did, and they held their cigarettes in a special way, as though the price of the packet wasn't worth bothering about.

"I suppose, at your age, money isn't important," she said suddenly.

"It's damned important and don't run away with that idea about anyone living down there."

"Ah yes," she said, "but you could get by without it, or with a few pounds a week."

"Almost every one of us has to but very few of the girls here ever think of marrying money. I don't say they could if they wanted to but just that it never occurs to them."

This interested her. She thought about it a minute and then smiled. She was looking more herself now, more as she had looked when we chatted over our first drink together.

"Well, I was flat broke when my father died," she said, "and up pranced the Doctor, seeing Paris for the first time, and feeling the way every middle-class Englishman feels when he visits Paris. I think they expect to find all the girls doing the Can-Can in Place de la Concorde, and red-light districts stretching from the Arc de Triomphe to Notre Dame."

"He never struck me as that kind of chap," I said, "but go on."

"I suppose it was his mood that took me in as much as his openhandedness. It's funny, he was quite gay that first month, and he did something I've never seen him do since. He threw his money about."

"Maybe he was in love."

She shook her head slowly. "He isn't built that way," she said and then, quite seriously, "Did you know he kept a purse?"

I did know. I had seen him pay bills over our cash-desk counter and had long since written him down as a purse-owner. Nearly all men keep loose change in their pockets. Purse-owners are rare and almost invariably mean about money. It was one of the first things you learned in a shop.

"Never mind his purse. What happened?"

"I used to hang around his hotel," she said. "I knew people who stayed there for long periods and they would often buy me a drink, or pay me as a guide. One of them introduced me as the daughter of a Left Bank English artist who had died in debt and the Doctor was interested. He's got a romantic streak. Did you know that?"

I didn't and I doubted it. Pawky and sentimental maybe, but

not romantic as I understood the word. She went on: "He took a fancy to me and bought some of my father's pictures at an inflated price. Then I showed him the sights. It was amusing taking him to places like the Casino. He was more interested in the girls' appendix scars than in their dancing. I remember him saying that they must have some very clumsy surgeons in Paris. Finally, during the third week, I landed him."

"How, exactly?"

"How do you think? I got him to bed when he was full of good food and Beaune, and then set to work on his Puritan conscience. I daresay he would have come up to scratch anyway but I wasn't taking any chances. Why the hell am I telling you all this?"

"You said you had to tell it to someone."

"That's right, so I did. Well, that's about all there is to it. He thought he was rescuing me and in a way he was, but I honestly didn't bargain for Redcliffe Bay, or hospital dances, civic ceremonies, Colette's Hairdressing Salon and a Friday night housekeeping accounting! Even if I had I would have bet on being able to change him, or getting him settled in a London practice, but above all learning a little about women!" She looked at me speculatively for a long moment. "Do you know, Kent, even a boy like you could teach him something on that score. If he'd listen that is, which he wouldn't."

"He never listens to anybody," I said. "We've all got used to that."

"No," she said, "he doesn't. You see, he never thinks. He's like that Head Prefect I was reading about in a book called *Some People* the other day . . . although stuffed with opinions he had never had a thought in his life. I remember saying to myself when I read it, That's him! That's our Basil!"

"He knows how you feel?"

"About what?"

"About everything. About hating it down here, about small-town life and feeling shut in. Surely he must have realized it by now. Most people have, you know."

"Most people have warm blood," she said.

I knew that she wasn't telling me the whole truth. A medium-sized slice of it perhaps but not the essentials, things like Basil's performance as a husband, as a man married to a sensual woman vain of her looks and her power to attract men. My intense curiosity about them almost tempted me to risk a direct question but I was learning about her at a prodigious pace and I did not want another setback. I said, "About not having children, is he resentful? Does he refer to it much?"

"He's resentful all right," she said, "but he lives up to his own conception of the chivalrous English stuffed shirt, so he can't refer to it directly, can he? That's part of the trouble."

"How do you mean, Lorna?"

She smiled and leaned back, shooting out her legs and reaching behind her to crush the cigarette stub on the window ledge. "You're just dying to know, aren't you? I believe, under all that earnest innocence, you're the randiest cub in town, Kent!"

"If I said that's the reason why I'm here we should be back in Square One!"

She laughed again, stood up, smoothed down her skirt and put an abrupt end to any hopes I had of that particular session.

"Not here, not now, and never in this house!" she said. "Go home and practice on the locals and maybe I'll look you up sometime. But don't go away thinking I'm ungrateful! I'm not. You've been a tonic in all sorts of ways. Do you want to kiss me?"

"Like hell," I said, "but I'd sooner save it up. I'm the saving sort even if I don't carry a purse."

She looked at me for the first time with a glint of respect in her eyes. "You don't have to bother writing that article," she said, "but you're welcome to the portfolio."

"No thanks," I told her, "I'll wait for that too," and I led the way down the stairs to the landing.

Five minutes later, having been shown to the door with elaborate courtesy, I was walking down the long drive and getting another glare from the gardener. I wished then that I had not been too proud to drive the battered Austin Seven up to the porch. It would have made him blink and probably made Lorna laugh.

The trivial lie I used to cover that afternoon visit to Lorna was the means of causing the first rift in my relationship with Esta Wallace. Within an hour of leaving "Heatherdene" and returning to the studio, I was improving on the story I used to explain my best clothes when I went out. The first thing Esta said to me that evening was, "Why did you have to spin that yarn to Beryl about wearing your new suit? What were you really up to anyway?"

I was a good deal taken aback at first but then I recalled having told our cashier that I was on my way to a wedding and that Esta would know to a decimal point who was getting married, and when, within a five-mile radius of the Stump. So I said, "I didn't want Birdie to know I was freelancing," and the answer satisfied her but left me under an obligation to tell her a little more. "I had to go up to Doctor Morney-Sutcliffe's place," I added. "His wife wanted some blow-ups of her father's paintings. As a matter of fact I had tea there. Do you mind?"

At that age a man believes he can stop a woman prying by taking the offensive. Years pass before he learns that this is the quickest way to arouse her deepest suspicions. Esta said, "Why do you resent my asking?" She said it reasonably. After all, it was a reasonable question but my nerves were ragged and I snapped back at her.

"Do I have to explain all my movements to you and Beryl?"

She looked at me with mild astonishment and I realized I had overdone it, so I said, in a more conciliatory tone, "I'm sorry, Esta, I've had a bad day. She kept me messing about all the afternoon and then decided against publishing. It was for an article in a magazine and I would have made a fiver on it if it had worked out the way I planned."

Esta was mollified, accepting the statement at face value. "What's she like?" she wanted to know, "to talk to I mean. Is she as stuck up as she looks?"

"No," I said, wondering how to dismiss the subject, "she's more approachable than he is but she's like most women and can't make a decision."

Esta didn't pick me up on this the way I hoped she would but stuck to the particular with a doggedness that made me uneasy.

"She's making a monkey out of the Doctor," she said, and when I replied that I was glad somebody was and we ought to be grateful to her, Esta added, with uncharacteristic piety, "No, Pip! I think he's an ass but that isn't the point! She made a bargain and she ought to stick by it, so long as she lives in his house, drives his swanky cars and puts half his income on her back!"

I was curious to discover how much she knew, or thought she knew, about the Morney-Sutcliffe *ménage*.

"You've never even spoken to the woman," I said, "so how do you know so much about what goes on up there?"

"I don't know much, except that she doesn't play the game."

"You mean she goes with other men?"

"No, not necessarily. How would I know a thing like that? What I mean is she makes it damned obvious that she thinks of all of us around here as animals in a tinpot zoo, and that's bad for his practice and his silly ambitions on the Council. She knew what he was and what kind of set-up was in store for her when she married, so why doesn't she either settle for it or go back to wherever she came from?"

I remembered what Lorna had said about not being content to lie on a bed because she had made it and almost gave myself away by rushing to her defense but checked the impulse just in time, reminding Esta that we had promised ourselves a visit to the Tivoli and that I had had more than enough of the Morney-Sutcliffes for one day.

We went in and settled down to watch the new Jack Hulbert–Cecily Courtneidge film but that night our luck was out. The picture, being British, was entirely unconvincing, even as a knockabout comedy. You knew you weren't following a story about imaginary people but watching a couple of light comedy artists earning a living. You could always lose yourself in a second-rate American film because the backgrounds were fresh and the speech idioms incisive but the home products of that period were even cornier than the early silent pictures. Then the lights went up and there he was again, Cecil Trumper, sitting two rows in front and still looking as though he had been marooned on a sandbar with his foot chained to a stake. For some reason the sight of him brought me to the boil.

"Why the hell does he have to follow us around everywhere we go?" I demanded, and Esta, after lifting her hand to Cecil, got up, saying, "Let's go, there's no pleasing you tonight, Pip."

There wasn't either. I followed her out into the dusk of a mild evening and we crossed the Stump to the lane behind the studio where I kept my car, but fresh air didn't improve my temper. At the time I put it down to the frustration I had undergone that afternoon but now I know there was a good deal more to it than that. Two hours in Lorna's company had conditioned me to look at Redcliffe Bay through her eyes and already it was smaller and shabbier than yesterday. I didn't recoil from it, as she regretted every minute of her waking life spent in the place, but I was beginning to tap the springs of her contempt, to look for crinkled bubbles of brown paint on the fascia boards of the shops, to notice the empty Woodbine packets in the beds of narcissi in the enclosure and, above all, to resent the vacuity of Cecil Trumper's moonstruck face. I was even conscious of this and as she took my arm the stain spread a little until it touched the girl beside me and I found myself comparing her off-the-peg jumper suit to Lorna's cocktail dress. Esta could judge my moods better than anyone and when we reached the car, and I got into the driving seat without opening the nearside door for her, she said quietly, "You don't want to drive anywhere with me tonight, Pip. You'd rather go somewhere by yourself and you don't have to apologize for it. There's no point in us going together if we can't respect one another's privacy, so I'll go home and finish the dress I was altering for the final."

She went off before I could say a word and I was so grateful to her I almost ran after her and apologized. I didn't, however, but drove down the Stump, out along the sea front and swung left up Links Road to the Valley. It wasn't until I passed "Heatherdene" and glanced right to see if there were any lights showing, that I realized why I had taken the long way out of town.

CHAPTER FOUR

[1]

If it had not been for the excursions and alarms of the next month I think my association with Esta Wallace would have sputtered out before the final of the Water Queen competition. As it was, in the flurry of all that happened that spring, we soon forgot the tiff and the urgency ebbed from my desire to receive another summons from Lorna. I thought of her, of course, and often looked at the Gainsborough reproduction. Sometimes, when I was alone, I remembered details of the sketches she had shown me and would wonder about her life in Paris before she met the Doctor, and how many men like the painter René had seduced her. It is unreasonable to be jealous of a woman one has kissed on a couple of unlikely occasions and was, moreover, safely married to a middle-aged man, but already I was half-resentful of strangers who might have seen her without her clothes and even jealous of her florid, baby-faced husband, who tripped all over town booming at people as though they were lazy coolies.

I don't think my feelings regarding Lorna were exclusively sexual, however. My two conversations with her had enlarged me in a way that I found hard to rationalize, even to myself. The alchemy of her discontent had touched me emotionally, so that I had turned away from our world without more than a very slender hope of entering hers, and the uncertainty of my future made me restless in a way that I had not been during the winter. Perhaps, also, spring itself had something to do with it, for Redcliffe Bay was an invigorating place in April, when huge banks of daffodils and narcissi covered the lawns and banks of the big houses and the sky over Mitre Head was blue and cream-puff white, the light catching the sandbars in the bay and all the chestnuts in the Stump enclosure bursting into bud. The weather was good, a month of gentle sunshine shot through, every now and again, with silver slivers of rain that dropped almost as soon as they began and were never more than sprinkles. I was busy too, with more than two dozen Easter weddings to cover, so that I had little enough time to brood during the day.

Lorna made no attempt to get in touch with me and as time went on I resigned myself to the certainty that she never would, having probably thought better of the impulse that made her lure me to her attic for no better reason than to prove she could still whet the appetite of someone eight years her junior. Esta played it quietly. Either she was absorbed in the prospect of winning the carnival crown of Redcliffe Bay, or she sensed that I was going through a period of uncertainty and self-searching. We continued to see one another several times a week and once or twice, when I had been thinking of Lorna, she benefited from my impatience to establish myself as a man instead of a front-porch adolescent. I believe she would have broken our pact readily enough but held on to it because by this time she had convinced herself that it was important to me and to our relationship generally, and this sometimes gave my conscience a twinge because she still gave me credit for abounding strength of purpose. Strength of purpose it was, I suppose, but not of the kind she imagined. My instinct told me to hang on to my independence simply because I was going to need it sooner or later. I wanted room to maneuver, or so I told myself at the time. I realize now, of course, that what I was bent on preserving in our relationship was just enough room to back down if I had to.

I suppose it must appear from this account of life as we lived it in that time, and in that backwater, that we were as earnestly preoccupied with sex as press, pulpit and TV pundits are today. Perhaps this was so but at least we weren't morbid about it. Ordinarily, we didn't pursue sex to the point of boredom and I think this was because there was far more fun about in those days and, with so much less money earned and spent, far more improvised leisure. Redcliffe Bay, with a population of about twelve thousand, had a total of sixty-seven clubs, social groups and voluntary organizations where the young of both sexes mingled very freely. Introverts like me were rare and I wouldn't have admitted to being one until Lorna really went to work on me. It was she, not Esta, who planted the seed of active discontent in me, converting the vague possibility of a breakout into an ultimate certainty. After that second *tête-à-tête* I could almost feel it happening to me and once I had adjusted to Lorna's focus I challenged premises that I had previously taken for granted, asking myself what life was all about, and on what targets my sights should be set if I had any serious intention of enlarging my experience. Was it money, or acclaim? Or travel, or professional reputation? Or was it a simple gratification of the senses that could be achieved by the simple process of seducing a woman like Lorna, someone who, unlike Esta Wallace and all the other Estas in town, demanded nothing in return in the way of loyalty? The heat had gone out of the day before I realized that the answer to this question, if there is an answer, depends upon chance and a combination of imponderable factors, like moods, inherited tendencies, and even weather; yes, weather even, like the long hot spell that ushered in the Carnival that year.

I mentioned the spring, and the spate of Easter weddings, and the latter must have helped to incline my thoughts towards marriage. In the month leading up to the West Stump fire, the event that lit the fuse of the most talked-of wedding of the year, I must have pointed my camera at a score of brides and grooms emerging from the west door of All Souls' Church, or from one or other of the free churches in the district. I seemed to photograph nothing but weddings and the marshalling of so many mums and dads, so many mittened bridesmaids and scowling pageboys, became tedious so that Esta, who always took a lively interest in my work, would ask me "How many this week, Pip?" or "Was it true Angela Brompton's mother and the groom's mother chose exactly the same frocks at Marcelle's?"

She read all the wedding reports published in the *Messenger* every Friday and as I often compiled them from the specially-printed forms sent round by Ben Dagmar, editor of the *Messenger,* she would sometimes shriek with laughter at my mistakes, such as the occasion when I wrote "belge" for "beige." These reports were the very devil to concoct, for Ben liked to vary the introductions and this, in a week when there were as many as a dozen in a single issue, was not easy. One soon used up the routine opening paragraphs beginning "*A pretty wedding was solemnized* . . ." or "*All Souls' Church was the scene of* . . ." and Redcliffian mothers-in-law were very particular about the spelling of their names or the omission of an item from the list of wedding gifts, for which they paid Ben Dagmar sixpence a line.

The weddings themselves fell into three categories. An Avenue, or Valley, event, a semidetached occasion, and a modest affair, based on one of the jerry-built terrace houses in the Colony beyond the railway line. One thing they had in common—an album of photographs mounted for posterity—but in most other particulars they differed a good deal. There were one, two, three and even four-tier wedding cakes; there were batches of six, four, two or a single bridesmaid and sometimes no bridesmaid at all but "a small attendant carrying a basket of rose petals." There were expansive fathers, pernickety mothers, shy brides, brassy brides and brides who were four months pregnant; there were glassy-eyed grooms, trapped grooms, happily captive grooms and tipsy grooms, although the latter were rare, for the hangover from stag parties usually kept the menfolk from anything more lethal than sherry on the forenoon of the ceremony. For my part, however, one curious factor began to emerge and harmonize with all my previous experience of small-town weddings which, by this time, was considerable. A study of the proofs established beyond any reasonable doubt that a sense of achievement was confined to the women, whereas the men, even the most gallant of them, could never quite banish the hunted look from their eyes when they took their places in churchyard or garden setting. It was Esta who first pointed this out. One of her favorite pastimes while waiting around for me to finish my work was to sift through the week's weddings and pronounce on the probable failure or success of the match. She had a very arbitrary process of assessment based not only upon the expression of the sitters, but on the degree of possessiveness she pretended to read into the grip of the bride upon the arm of the groom. She would say, tilting back on a stool and staring hard at a print, "Bert Mallow is hooked! Look at Sheila's curling fingers!" or "*That's* better! Madge is nestling already, isn't she?" I have never since been able to look at a wedding group without applying her slide rule and although, even then, it was amusing, her general preoccupation with match-making (which, until then, I had regarded as a failing shared by the entire female sex) alerted me. Somehow I found it difficult to rid myself of suspicion that the prospect of marriage—and by inference *her* marriage to me—took precedence over every other thought that entered her head and this made nonsense of her avowal that she despised girls who baited traps for men. That was why I sometimes looked over my shoulder in an attempt to determine how Esta, her mother, her sisters and our mutual acquaintances like Cecil Trumper viewed our association. What I saw there was enough to make me brace myself against closer involvement. Marriage meant roots and roots meant putting on a paunch in Redcliffe Bay. Lorna's doctrines had made that much impact. I was not going bald or grey as a photographer of small-town wedding groups. The perambulator under the stairs began to look a little like a hearse but I told myself it had no claims on us so long as I kept my head and Esta her virginity.

[2]

Things were jogging along like this when, in common with everyone else on East and West Stump, my own concerns were engulfed in the tremendous excitement that burst over us on the night of the schoolhouse fire.

Redcliffe Bay Council School for Boys occupied the northern, or inland half of West Stump, midway between Myfanwy's Gift Shop and the Rainbow Café that stood at the junction of Stump and High Street. The school itself was set back in about a half-acre of asphalt playground, enclosed by formidable iron railings. The schoolhouse that Owen Rees, the headmaster, shared with his aged mother was nearer the pavement to the south or sea side of the school buildings.

Owen was an exceptionally likeable man and a very popular headmaster, one of the very few in those days who did not keep a bunch of canes in his cupboard. He had lost his left arm on the Western Front and when I first knew him he was an old-looking and rather ravaged thirty-two, with tired eyes, dark, greying hair and a sweet-tempered mouth. The boys loved him and he loved the boys and his music. Myfanwy Pritchard loved him too, having worshipped him through schoolhouse railings (that divided her yard from the playground) for the better part of a decade. He liked her well enough but I don't think he knew that she was longing for his old mother to die and leave her a clear field. He wasn't the kind of man who thought about things in that way.

Myfanwy wasn't the spinster-tradeswoman you might expect to find in any gift shop along the coast. She was a cosy, talkative, red-cheeked little body, with a neat figure and the rare sociability and intelligence of the Welsh. It was no secret to anyone except Owen that she wanted to mother him, but what with his obsession with his raggle-tailed boys, his glee choruses, and his mother, she made no progress at all in the years leading up to the climax. By the spring of 1932 hope deferred was beginning to show in her round, cheerful face. She was several years older than Owen and could hear the clock ticking. Esta was desperately sorry for her. Myfanwy had been in the van of the procession of Esta's lame ducks for years and the fire was not only a Godsend to the spinster. It gave Esta the opening she had been awaiting for some considerable time.

It happened very late on a Saturday night, about halfway through April of that year. Owen Rees's choir had fought their way into the final of the Westcountry School Song Festival, and were due to perform in London and stay overnight. Owen, as their conductor, was desperately keen that they shouldn't miss their chance through his inability to attend, but he was reluctant to leave his mother alone and would have sent one of the masters with the choir had not Myfanwy offered to come in and sleep the night at the schoolhouse. They had to bluff the old woman. She wouldn't have let such an obvious rival set foot in the place but it worked out well enough until Owen and his boys were safely away and Myfanwy took the old lady's supper in on a tray. She wanted to know where Owen was and Myfanwy tried to explain, the old crone's eyes glinting like a snake's when she learned that Owen was to be away all night, and that Myfanwy was to occupy his bedroom. She said she wouldn't have any supper but would boil her bedtime cocoa on an oil-stove that she kept in her bedroom. She often did this when Owen was over at the school rehearsing and Myfanwy had no option but to let the old lady enjoy her sulks.

I heard what happened over there from Myfanwy herself when the dust had settled and town talk had reverted to the carnival.

Just before midnight, when Myfanwy was enjoying the novel experience of snuggling down between Owen's sheets, and almost persuading herself that he was within touching distance, she smelled smoke and ran across the landing and down the stairs to the old lady's ground-floor room, at the rear of the house. She found that part of the building well alight, with a sheet of flame separating her from the old woman crouching in the far corner of the room. It was a situation that would have scared a professional fireman but Myfanwy was equal to it. She ran through the kitchen and out into the yard, seizing a heavy pair of fire tongs en route and smashing her way into the old lady's room via a small window opening on to the playground. She got into the room at the cost of several cuts from the broken glass and managed to check the fire for a few moments by damping it down with bedclothes and rugs. By this time, however, Mrs. Rees was unconscious and Myfanwy, not much more than half her weight, had to drag her to the window and somehow bundle her through into the yard. She never could have managed it if she hadn't kept her head and she told me later that the thought of what Owen would say when he came home to find his mother had been burned alive while in her charge had given her the strength and resolution to try. She nearly succeeded and had the old lady halfway over the slate sill before help arrived in the persons of Bruce Brayley, the cinema owner opposite, and, a moment later, Birdie Boxall and myself, who had been alerted by the uproar. Mr. Brayley dragged the old lady clear and Birdie, who had just gone to bed after a heavy session at the Lamb and Flag, staggered into West Stump bawling for help.

The moment he had gone Brayley grabbed my shoulder and shouted, "Someone's in there! Someone else!" and I naturally assumed it to be Owen for I was unaware that he was out of town and supposed him to have fought his way through from the front. I shouted, above the roar of the flames, "Jump for it, Mr. Rees!" but instead of Owen's face appearing at the opening I saw Myfanwy's and she was looking exasperated rather than terrified, and shouting, in her sing-song Welsh accent, "It's a crazy old woman she iss! Her and that old oil-stove of hers!" It seemed to me a remarkable time to put her protest on record.

Bruce Brayley took hold of her by one arm and I by the other and between us we yanked her through at the cost of inflicting more lacerations on her body and leaving the remnants of her shredded nightdress hooked to the window frame. With a final lurch we all rolled together on the gritty surface of the playground and it wasn't until I scrambled to my feet that I realized Myfanwy was stark naked and bleeding from a dozen wounds. I think her nakedness shocked me more than her injuries, even though it occurred to me, as I threw my dressing gown over her shoulders, that she might be bleeding to death. She obviously wasn't. Without pausing to slip her arms into my gown she scampered across to the spot where Bruce had laid the old lady under the railings and at once began to apply artificial respiration, calling on us to help. At that moment Birdie reappeared, with Abe Gorman, from the Rainbow Café, and Police Sergeant Wright, all three bellowing that they couldn't get in at the front and feared Owen Rees was suffocated. Myfanwy must have heard them for she looked up and said, in the sharpest tone of voice I ever heard her employ, "Don't talk nonsense! Owen's safe in London, isn't he? Fetch an ambulance, you fools, and get his mother to hospital! There's no one in that old place any more!"

In her frenzied efforts to revive Mrs. Owen my dressing-gown had slipped off her shoulders, and in the glare of the flames the playground was as light as day. Birdie and the Sergeant were so astounded to see her throwing herself to and fro like a naked Dervish that they stood there openmouthed for another moment until she stood up, carelessly hitched the belt round her waist and said, "She's breathing! Do something one of you, will you now?" whereupon the Sergeant, still far too astonished to comment, bumbled off along Stump to the kiosk behind the Stump headquarters.

Between us we got old Mrs. Rees down the alleyway to the Stump pavement and by then about a dozen others had gathered, all bawling "Fire!" at the tops of their voices. Soon the engine was clanging down High Street but it was far too late to save the schoolhouse. Before they had run the hoses out the first floor fell in and a shower of sparks shot up and came down on and around the gazing lifeboatman, who continued to stare across the bay as if a wreck was of more concern to him than a gutted school. Then, but only then, Myfanwy fainted, so that she was taken away in the same ambulance as Mrs. Rees. It was typical of her that, a fortnight later, I received my dressing-gown back cleaned, pressed and with a new piece of matching material neatly sewn on to a threadbare patch between the shoulders.

Myfanwy's cuts were superficial and she was out and about and enjoying her ovation within days of Owen's return. The *Messenger* went to town on her rescue and even the London dailies gave us a paragraph or two. But public commendation was not the chief by-product of her courage and clearheadedness. Owen had nowhere to live, so he accepted her offer to board with her while the authorities thought about rebuilding the schoolhouse. He had no spare clothes either, so she superintended a shopping expedition that resulted in him acquiring what turned out to be his trousseau. Her luck was really in that season. Old Mrs. Rees died a fortnight after the fire, not from burns, which might have prejudiced Owen, but from heart-failure, that Doctor Morney-Sutcliffe declared had nothing to do with her recent experience! I don't know how he got away with such a barefaced declaration in a Coroner's Court, unless it had to do with the Coroner being a fellow-Mason, a fellow-Councillor and one of the Doctor's patients. Myfanwy could therefore cosset her lodger with a clear conscience. She brought him up to scratch in a matter of weeks and their engagement appeared in the *Messenger* a few days before the carnival, but in the meantime I learned through Esta that this was not achieved without a push from behind. The propelling power was applied by Esta herself.

She admitted this one glorious afternoon in May, when we stopped on our way back from Shelly Bay, a village several miles east of Redcliffe Bay, where I had gone to take what Birdie always called "environ" pictures, for the *Redcliffe Visitors' Guide,* issued by the Chamber of Commerce.

Esta was back on night duty then, standing in for a probationer who had gone sick, so we saw a good deal of one another in the daytime. On occasions like these, when she had been working nights, she would take a short nap in the morning, have her lunch, and accompany me on my jaunts about the countryside. She was usually rather sleepy and sometimes, if the weather was good, we would stop on the way home and she would take another nap in some nook on the common, while I wasted a reel of film on long shots that took my fancy. Summer was right on the doorstep up here, with the smell of gorse reaching us on the land breeze and the variation of the sea, cloud and rock colors sitting up and begging for color photography, then in its experimental stage.

On this particular afternoon I left her slumped against a bank of purple heath, starred with a few late primroses and seasonable bluebells, her face turned to the sun and her hair still rumpled by the tousing it had received in the open car. I didn't bother much with pictures of the landscape but I took one or two of her without her knowing it. She looked, I thought, as serene as a princess in a fairy-tale book, and again the thought came into my mind that she was about a century behind the times if you could look beyond her little grey skirt and white blouse. She ought, I thought, to have been wearing sprigged muslin and chisel-shaped slippers, with her hair in ringlets, and as I watched her I felt very much at peace with the world and proud that she belonged to me and no one else in town, for I was now convinced that she would sail through the final and become Redcliffe Bay's Water Queen for the year.

I stood there looking down at her a long time, noting the texture of her pale skin, her dark eyelashes and the neatness of her feet in a pair of cheap, strap-over sandals, and I remember comparing the feelings she roused in me with the less complicated ones inspired by Lorna. Although I did still continue to think about Lorna a good deal, day by day association with Esta was strengthening my assessment of her as a companion and friend. She was a confidante as well as a pretty, happy-go-lucky girl, and it was as a confidante I found her rewarding. I never had to pretend to her and when I weighed her trust and affection against the uncomplicated lust I felt for Lorna, it seemed to me I would be making a bad bargain by staking one against the other. I think at that moment I was deeply in love with her, and I put aside the camera and settled myself beside her, rousing her and settling her head on my shoulder and intending perhaps to make some attempt to express my feelings, even if it meant admitting to the truth of the situation between myself and Morney-Sutcliffe's wife. It might have shaken her a little but I don't think it would have damaged our relationship. She might even have laughed a little, once she had got over the shock of someone like me rampaging about Morney-Sutcliffe's attic and French-kissing his wife in her car outside the Doctor's gate. The moment passed, however, as all such moments do if you aren't a natural gambler and I wasn't. She said, drowsily, "Times like these I'd hate to live anywhere else, Pip darling!" and all I said was something about my having two moods on the subject of Redcliffe Bay, a spring–summer mood and an autumn–winter one.

"Oh, it's not just a question of locale!" she said, settling herself but wide awake now. "I think maybe that's where people like us can't see the wood for the trees. It's much more a matter of—

well—*belonging*, it's a kind of tribal feeling, if you follow me. Lately, ever since we've been going together in fact, it's been growing inside me. I feel I belong and I enjoy belonging. I feel I can—well—justify myself, contribute something! It's difficult to explain, even to you, Pip, but what happened yesterday is the kind of thing I mean."

"What did happen yesterday?" Yesterday, as far as I was concerned, had been a day like any other day although, now that I thought about it, I remembered we hadn't seen one another. I had been too busy preparing a mock-up for the Chamber of Commerce handbook and she had gone about her own concerns.

"Well, I finally got it across to Owen Rees!"

"Got what across to Owen Rees?"

"About Myfanwy. After all, somebody had to. Myfanwy was as mixed up in her way as Alison Sweetland and we managed to solve that one. I get a kick every time I look at Alison now. I think I willed that baby on her!"

"You're not trying to tell me you persuaded Owen to put Myfanwy in the family way?"

"Well, no," she said, laughing, "I don't think it will come to that. They're both too long in the tooth but he did propose to her last night!"

"*Owen did!* But for God's sake, how on earth did you come to have a finger in it? It was an ultimate certainty, wasn't it, once his mother kicked the bucket?"

"Don't you believe it!" she said emphatically. "He would never have got around to it if I hadn't jogged his elbow. But he was grateful really. He's very fond of Myfanwy, and always has been, and he needs someone to look after him. He's not a natural bachelor, any more than Myfanwy is a natural spinster. They'll get along marvelously, you see if they don't! The wedding is to be quite soon. In July, I think."

There was such a note of achievement in her voice that I had to laugh and she smiled too, half apologetically I thought, as though she realized very well that she was a busybody but didn't mind me knowing.

"If he only got around to it last night," I said, "how the devil do you know the date so quickly?"

"How? Why, because Myfanwy rang me up at the hospital," she said. "She was crying into the phone and ever so grateful. It was very touching really, but I was glad for her."

I said, "All right, tell me! I can see you're bursting to, and you can't preen yourself in front of anyone else without them thinking you're crazy! What happened, exactly?"

She told me then that, in spite of so much promise, things hadn't worked out as Myfanwy had hoped once Owen had settled into her spare room over the shop. They got along well enough, and Owen was sweet to her in all kinds of ways, but he treated her like a genteel landlady and it eventually occurred to Myfanwy that the longer they stayed on that plane the more formal their relationship would become and might even atrophy. She tried all kinds of dodges to raise the temperature about the place, getting herself a new hair-do, cooking him special dishes, playing classical records he liked on her gramophone, but he went right on opening doors for her, tidying up after her, smiling his dreamy smile and complimenting her on her window displays, without any reference to a change in status now that they were living cheek by jowl and the principal obstacle to a full life had been laid to rest in the overflow acre behind All Souls' churchyard. Finally the state of suspension between heaven and hell began to get on Myfanwy's nerves and she broke down in front of him after smashing some plates she was unloading from a crate in the store behind the shop. Even then he attributed her tears to a loss of profits and after sweeping up the pieces patted her shoulder and told her that she was suffering from delayed shock and should take a holiday. As it was term-time there was no question of her interpreting this as an invitation. Esta, who seemed to have an instinct for happening upon women in confiding moments, came into the shop that evening to look over some artificial jewelry for the Water Queen final and Myfanwy told her everything she didn't already know about the situation. Esta didn't hesitate. She made up her mind on the spot to go into action, insisting that Myfanwy might as well know where she stood for anything was better than indefinite suspense.

She buttonholed Owen the following Saturday evening, when he was busy marking a pile of exercise books in the front room

Myfanwy let him use as a study. Owen and Esta were old friends. He remembered her as a toddler, when he first took the headship of the school after his discharge from the army, and when she said she wanted to discuss something serious with him he pushed his exercise books aside and said he was at her disposal. There was nothing odd about this. Owen Rees was always at everyone's disposal. There was something about him that invited confession and promised absolution. Esta didn't say so but I gathered that he obviously took it for granted that she had come to him with some problem of her own and he must have been horribly embarrassed when Esta said, without so much as a token preamble, "I daresay you'll think it very rude of me, Mr. Rees, but I simply have to tell you something important about yourself!"

"What the hell did he say to that?" I demanded, knowing I would never extract the whole truth but settling for half of it.

"Well, he did look a bit confused," she admitted, "almost as though I was going to tell him his fly was open but I didn't give him much chance to bluster, even if he can bluster, which I doubt."

"Get to the point!"

"I'm trying to if you'll let me! I said, 'It's about poor Myfanwy. She's breaking her heart over you, and has been for nearly ten years! I'm very fond of you both and I know that neither of you would like the gossip to go on and on, without anyone having the nerve to come out with it, as I'm doing.' "

"What gossip?" I asked, but Esta waved her hand impatiently. "I had to pretend there was gossip—I mean about him living there with her, and it wasn't really bluff because you can be absolutely certain that the old women of both sexes are sniggering over it! Anyway, I let him assume that they were and he must have because he went bright pink, scratched his ear, and finally said, 'You mean people are talking about *us?* In *that* kind of way?' and I said, 'If they aren't they soon will be, so if you intend getting married why don't you do it or move over to the Railway Hotel until they build you a new school house?' I was a bit frightened right then," Esta admitted, "because his face and neck turned a kind of puce and he sat up so straight that all his exercise books spilled on to the floor. He didn't bother to pick them up either but just sat there looking at me but at last his mouth twitched and I saw that he was trying not to laugh, and then I knew everything was going to be all right and that it had been worth taking a chance on him telling me to mind my own damned business!"

She paused for a moment. Even a recital of the incident had left her a little breathless. I didn't say anything, I was too absorbed wondering how the plain, practical Mrs. Wallace and old Scatty, whose thoughts had never strayed outside workshop and kitchen in twenty years, had produced this intense little creature who felt compelled to double for fairy-godmother everywhere she went. She seemed, at that particular moment, both very young and very old, a kind of sprite or white witch, who had wandered out of the early morning of the world and was still going about her business with charms, magic talismans and love-potions in a world of carbolic soap, motor cars and rubber goods. Finally I said, "I think you're dotty but I have to admit you're also unique. Go on, tell me the rest."

She looked up at me under her long lashes as though relieved that I hadn't shown more impatience with her meddling in other people's affairs. "He said, very quietly and civilly, 'Tell me, does Myfanwy know you're holding a pistol to my head like this?' and naturally I denied any idea of collusion. Well, I had to, didn't I? And I convinced him too, I'm quite sure of that, because he said, 'It was a very kind gesture on your part, Esta, and I'm glad you brought it up. As a matter of fact, for your ear alone, I would have come to an understanding with Miss Pritchard years ago if it hadn't been for this!' and he lifted his left shoulder to display his pinned-over sleeve. 'After all, who but someone like her would be interested in half a man? I've got other disabilities, besides being short of an arm.' "

I was interested in this and asked her if he meant the kind of injuries that would result in further frustration for Myfanwy but Esta said no, it wasn't that at all, although the same thought had occurred to her. He told her then that he had a damaged lung and several bits of shrapnel travelling about inside him, but now that he was convinced Myfanwy would settle for what was left he was prepared to let them take their time about sending him back to hospital for further treatment. He went on to say that he had always considered Myfanwy an exceptionally kind, intelligent woman, and a pretty one as well, and that if Esta would excuse him he would propose that same night and the exercise books on the floor could go unmarked for all he cared. He then paid her the compliment of asking her to stand in as Myfanwy's bridesmaid "so that Redcliffe Bay would have the privilege of seeing the Stump's two most personable females play major roles in a single ceremony!" "He's got a terrific line in woo when somebody encourages him," Esta declared, "and looking back on it all I can't help feeling that Myfanwy must have gone the wrong way about it. What I mean is, she relied on the 'Command me, oh master!' technique, whereas he's pre-Victorian, one might almost say medieval, in his conception of women. He's the kind who would fix her glove in his helmet and joust in her honor. If she had realized this I wouldn't have had to go to work on him the way I did!"

"You would have found some excuse to get in on the act," I said and she looked a little shamefaced and said, "You think I'm an absolute idiot, don't you, Pip? Go on, say so!"

I wondered if I did. On the face of it she was, of course, and some people might have doubted an innocence that I knew to be genuine and possibly labeled her intrusion into the affairs of people like the Sweetlands, Ken Pigeon and Myfanwy Pritchard as a kind of prurience, masquerading as do-goodery but this wasn't so. She was curious all right, but the goodwill was there and I related it in my mind to what she had said earlier on about her urge to justify herself to neighbors whom she saw as members of her tribe. In that moment I envied her, envied her sense of kinship with these nonentities, and her simple directness and sense of purpose that relied, almost exclusively, upon instinct. I said, meaning every word, "I wouldn't have you any different. I daresay most people would because you could land a man into a peck of trouble the way you think and act, but I don't want you to change. I'm sold on you as you are!" and I rolled her over on the grass and kissed her a dozen times.

[3]

If I had what all of us sometimes long for, a brief, limited period of our youth to relive with the benefit of hindsight, I think I would settle on the month of May 1932, a time of sun-drenched, relatively uneventful suspension between the period of seeking, that had begun in the New Year, and the months of folly and stress that followed Carnival Week in June.

It was then, I think, that Esta and I came closest to attaining the kind of harmony one searches for all one's life. It seems to me, on looking back on this interval, that Lorna, until then, had played little more than a fantasy role in my daily being. She was still there in the background, a kind of waiting experience, but I had no real expectation of improving my acquaintance with her and certainly no suspicion that she would associate herself in any way with prospects I had for changing the direction of my life. On the contrary I believe that I had half-settled for the near-certainty of fifty years as a small-town photographer, which meant, almost inevitably, marriage to Esta, the acquisition of Scatty Wallace as a father-in-law, and perhaps, if I was lucky, the sufficiency of a man with a modest but slowly expanding future. In other words, the perambulator under the stairs now began to look less like a hearse and more like a piece of equipment most men have to acquire sooner or later.

This apparent change of heart was due to the continuing silence of Lorna and a growing affection for Esta, hastened perhaps by her involvement with a variety of parish pump events, like the carnival, the sorting out and shaking down of the Sweetlands and the Owen Rees–Myfanwy Pritchard romance. Until I had time to reflect on these things I had always seen myself as the dominant character of the partnership, the man who would make the decisions of when and how we would sally out, but now I wasn't sure. She was so unlike her sisters, and all the other girls I had seen emerge from gymslip to adolescence and finally to the pram-pushing stage, that I found myself turning to her for the answers to questions I would never have put to a girl the year before. As she began to flower under the impetus of local triumph, and as more and more people whom I already regarded as halfway through their lives behaved towards her as though she was a contemporary, I would have expected her to put on the side, and perhaps moderate her devotion to me, but the exact opposite was true. Whenever we were alone, and removed from townsfolk and town affairs, she deferred in every way and I began to realize that her dependence upon me was due, in part at least, to extreme nervousness and a sense of insecurity.

It may seem absurd that we were inclined, even at that age, to take an event like her possible election as Water Queen as seriously as we did, but you have to remember the unsophistication of the time and the place in which we lived. As I say, in those days (it seems almost unbelievable today) not one in five Redcliffians had ever spent a night in London, and not one in fifty (veterans excepted) had ever crossed the Channel. I don't suppose there were more than a hundred privately-owned cars in the urban district and our metropolis was Paxtonbury, a small cathedral city reached by a very slow, inadequate train and bus service. Very few of us owned our own houses and, at a guess, not more than ten per cent of us earned more than three hundred a year. We were a self-sufficient community, partly from choice and partly from geographical reasons, and the majority of us liked it that way. We thought of ourselves as the equal of most city-dwellers inasmuch as they flocked to us between June and September but we seldom or never returned the compliment. Setting seasonal profits on one side there was very little money to be made in Redcliffe Bay but most of us had led enclosed lives for so long that money seemed far less essential than it does today. Not one of us, not even the most forward-looking progressive on the Council, envisaged the evolution of Redcliffe Bay into the kind of town it became thirty years later. If one of our elders had prophesied that, within thirty-three years, the population would have swollen from twelve to thirty thousand, and that housing estates would lap over the edge of the moor and scale both crags enclosing the bay, his fellow-councillors would have tapped their foreheads.

I suppose it was this sense of remoteness and timelessness that kept everyone except a few youngsters like me more or less content with their prospects. Health and family loyalties mattered, and so did the holding of a steady job bringing in anything up to five or six pounds a week; after that the rest of the world could go hang.

Apart from these reasons for general complacency the year itself was a national watershed and even now it continues to look like one. The worst of the Slump was behind us, and the fashion of obsession with world politics had not yet caught on in Redcliffe Bay. The latter began, I fancy, about a year later, with the Reichstag fire and the emergence of Hitler, but at the time of which I wrote none of us had ever heard of Hitler, whereas Mussolini was regarded as a posturing clown. It was only later, as the possibility and then the probability of a second world war edged closer, that people in places like Redcliffe Bay felt themselves involved in international events. It was not until Munich, six years later, that people started to discuss continental events in places like the public bar of the Lamb and Flag.

On the last Saturday in May, nine days before the carnival was scheduled to begin, the Water Queen final was held in the Church Hall and it was soon clear that Esta stood a very fair chance of winning, for three of the five finalists came from outlying villages and were thus unlikely to earn much support from the ten judges, exclusively local tradesmen serving on the Council Foreshore and Entertainments Committee, with one or two diehards from the Valley who would be guided by men like Doctor Morney-Sutcliffe and Fred Hopkins, the local timber merchant.

Esta's principal rival was Hazel White, a High Street dairyman's daughter. When they stood side by side people said they looked like the Erasmus Twins, a blonde and a brunette then seen on all the hoardings advertising "Erasmus Soap." Hazel was a handsome girl with a good figure but she knew it and local boys made very little progress with her. She could be numbered among the ambitious in Redcliffe Bay and it was even rumored that her father had paid for elocution lessons in order to dispose of her Westcountry accent. Only the malicious believed that folly and extravagance could go as far as this but it was known that Hazel hoped to become a model at Peabody's, Paxtonbury's most fashionable shop. She had corn-colored hair cut in a long bob and her eyes were as hard and blue as Lorna's. I had never been attracted to her. She looked frigid and her mouth indicated that if things didn't go her way she would soon develop into a nag. She was a year or two older than Esta and the odds on her victory were about five to four.

I knew all the other finalists. There was Mabel Boxall, a niece of Birdie's, a tall girl called Sally Havill, who was a fisherman's daughter from the village east of the town, and Mavis Purcell, a frightened little redhead with green eyes, who came from one of the outlying farms and was said to be free with her favors among the agricultural community.

They all five clacked around the specially-erected dais for the better part of the afternoon and the Foreshore and Entertainments Committee took their time making up their minds. Nobody blamed them for that. They had the best view and were entitled to make use of it.

After the parades each competitor was gently quizzed by the comedian of the resident concert party, a group having their headquarters in a large marquee at the bottom of Frog Terrace, and called, God forgive them, the Tiddly-Pom-Poms. The comedian asked each girl a number of questions and after that they had to make a little speech, extolling the merits of Redcliffe Bay as a holiday resort.

Hazel White's elocution lessons—if she ever had any—did her no good. She stumbled over the word "amenities" and dried on the phrase "a mile of golden sand for the kiddies," whereas little Mavis Purcell, who had never made a speech in her life, burst into tears and threw in the sponge. Esta got through her speech very well. Standing beside the wise-cracking funny man she was able to call on fresh reserves of dignity, so that, one way and another, nobody was much surprised when Mr. Hopkins, Chairman of the Council, led her forward by the tips of her fingers and pronounced her Water Queen of Redcliffe Bay for the next twelve months.

The choice seemed very popular, except with Hazel White, who looked as if she was going to have a seizure. There was sustained applause and Esta's pale face stayed rose-pink for ten minutes. I took a dozen pictures of the crowning ceremony (performed by last year's Queen, who had broken the rules by getting married before her term of office was up), and then I left Esta to spend the next two or three hours getting fitted for her ceremonial robes, a job fussily supervised by Councillor Mrs. Rowbotham, who traded in Fore Street under the name of Madame Marcelle and, on occasions like this, gave the Council a seven and a half per cent discount on materials purchased.

About nine o'clock that evening, just as it was getting dusk, I locked the studio and went across to the Church Hall dressing rooms to see if Esta was through. As I approached the stage door I heard an imperious toot on a car-horn and turning saw Lorna sitting in her red M.G., a cluster of golf clubs protruding from the passenger seat. She looked very sporty and a good deal more vivacious than usual, as though she was finding life supportable now that summer had come and she could get out and about but for this reason she didn't make the same impact upon my senses. In well-cut tweeds and squarish brogues she looked like something out of *Tatler* and that much further removed from my world. She greeted me with sardonic gaiety, an approach that was new in our relationship.

"Well, Kent, getting all steamed up for the revels? There'll be plenty of hey-nonny-nonny in the old town this time next week, eh?"

I was surprised to find that her studied contempt irritated me, particularly when she went on to say, "Who is the Queen of the May? Do you know her?"

"Esta Wallace," I told her civilly, but making sure I didn't share her derision for small-town high jinks and she was quick to note as much, looking up at me with a half smile and saying, "Pretty? Girl friend of yours?" so that suddenly I wished she had let me go by without tooting. It seemed almost an act of disloyalty to talk to her.

"Esta Wallace is a nice kid," I said, "and they couldn't have chosen anyone who will do the honors with more dignity!" and I felt better for having said it.

Lorna said, lazily, "I stopped by to pick the Doctor up. I daresay he'll tell me about it when we get home. What have you got there? Photographs?"

I showed her a sheaf of proofs of the crowning ceremony and she examined each of them carefully. "Yes, she *is* pretty," she said finally, "and not really a local type, is she? What does she do for a living?"

"She's a nurse up at the Cottage Hospital," I said, and at that Lorna chuckled and said it all made sense, for the Doctor had a bevy of vestal virgins dancing attendance on him up there and Esta's profession had almost surely influenced his decision.

It seemed to me a bitchy thing to say and I challenged it. "There were ten on the Selection Committee," I told her, "and the Doctor only had one vote!"

She looked straight at me, still smiling her patronizing smile. "I say! You are prickly tonight, Kent! Have I been probing the sensitive spot again?"

I didn't know what to reply to that. I wasn't going to admit to the fact that Esta was my girl, so I took the obvious course of pretending they were awaiting my photographs inside and said I would have to go. She looked quite surprised at my virtual dismissal of her and her change of expression did something to restore my morale. I lifted my hand and went in at the stage-door, feeling I had scored over her at last. She called after me, in a sharpish voice. "Tell the Doctor I'm waiting!" It was a pleasure to note the irritation in her voice.

I told the Doctor and he went out at once. I heard the car start up and roar away and then I went along to the main dressing-room and knocked on the door. Esta's voice answered and when I said it was me and I was alone, she said, "Come in, Pip, I'm nearly ready!"

I went in expecting to find her still cluttered with Councillor Mrs. Rowbotham and hedged around with pins and lengths of silk and ermine, but she was alone and standing in front of the full-length mirror in her panties and nothing else. Coming on top of my unexpected meeting with Lorna it was a shock and besides, I had never seen her that way before, all our petting having been conducted in the dark. She seemed to me to be extraordinarily casual about the encounter, as though we were already married and I had just walked into her bedroom. I had enough self-possession left to lock the door before I kissed her and held her close for a moment, transferring a large smudge of powder to my jacket in the process. Then, but without any hurry, she pulled on the rest of her clothes and looked through the pictures.

"They're a bit starey," she said. "I suppose it's the flash-bulbs. They make everyone look as if they've been caught with their hand in the till."

"I'll take some better ones of you later on," I promised. "By the time you abdicate we shall have a stack six feet high in the files. I'm sending one of today's up to the *County Herald* and when the water procession takes place I'm going to try for one or two of the glossies."

She looked pleased, sitting with her chair tilted in the way she used to sit in the studio. I could see she was relishing her triumph but trying hard to sound modest about it.

"Were you surprised?" she asked and I said I wasn't and neither was anyone else in and around Stump. She said that after I'd gone half the town had been milling round the stagedoor and that she felt like an actress on a first night. Cecil Trumper had bumbled in and left a large bouquet of red roses, with a card reading "For the Gloriana of Redcliffe Bay." I was amazed at this, never having suspected that Cecil had that much nerve or originality. "I gave him a kiss," Esta said, "just a peck or two on the cheek. Sometimes I do feel so desperately sorry for him. Couldn't we find him a nice, fluffy little thing, who could use all his St. Bernard devotion?"

"You can't pair people off like that," I argued. "I know you think you can but you can't! He's never looked at anyone else since we were all in 2a together and it's my guess he never will. He'll hang on hoping and hoping until he's about fifty and then he'll go into a monastery."

That made her laugh and she bounced up and hugged me. "Oh Pip!" she said, "I'm so happy! I don't think I've ever been so happy in my life but it's not just winning and having people make so much fuss of me, I can tell you that!"

"Then what is it? The clothes and the twenty guineas in the offing?"

"No," she said, "not that either! I'll be an idiot again and tell you. It's having something for you. That's all that really counts!"

I was touched and who wouldn't have been? She looked so young and innocent and eager, and there was a sparkle about her that hadn't been there before, not even when I gave her the locket. "Oh, I know it's nothing much really," she went on, as though half-regretting her admission, "and I daresay I'm getting it out of proportion, but when I entered in the first place it seemed to me a way of putting a feather in your cap rather than mine. However," and her brown eyes flashed mischief, "now that I have won I've made up my mind to put the pressure on and play hard to get for the next twelve months!"

"You do that," I said, "and I'll try my luck elsewhere. Hazel White looked as if she could do with a consolation prize."

"That doesn't scare me. She's not your type, neither one thing nor the other. You like doormats, like me, or the sexy and safely married ones, like Mrs. Morney-Sutcliffe!"

She said this quite innocently but it gave me a bad moment. I was glad she had her back to me when she said it and could thus pass it off easily enough.

"Mrs. Morney-Sutcliffe wouldn't hold hands with a local for first prize in the Irish Sweep," I said. "It's my belief that even the Doctor has to sit up and beg for it!"

"Well," said Esta, cramming on her little grey beret that looked incongruous after seeing her under a crown, "she has a lot more sense than me. I've resigned myself to being taken for granted. The girl next door whose panties you've always seen hanging on the line."

"There's a lot to be said for that," I said, thinking of Lorna's ability to play a man like a fish. As she turned to me, ready to go, I kissed her and we stood together for a moment in the last patch of evening sunshine. It was a moment that was to return to me often during the next thirty years.

CHAPTER FIVE

[1]

It always interested me to watch Redcliffe Bay shaking out its skirts for the summer and its biggest annual event, the Water Carnival, which usually coincided with our first spell of really warm weather.

It was a slow process, beginning at the tail-end of April, when the daffodils were beginning to wilt in the gardens above Frog Terrace and in the enclosure triangle between East and West Stump. Very few visitors showed themselves in May so the month was devoted to a spring-cleaning marathon on the part of the town's five hundred landladies. You would see them, turbanned and unsmiling, thrashing the life from their rugs at first-story windows, while their husbands retraced the names of their establishments on signs and billboards in front gardens, St. Helens, Resthaven, Kia-Ora, Shangri-La, Trafalgar Lodge, Bayview or simply Apartments; Enquire Within.

Then, about mid-May, the famous trident standards would rise along the sea-front, symbolic of Neptune but with an interlaced "R.B.U.D.C." on every shield boss. We were on very familiar terms with Neptune, for he emerged from beneath the jetty each year to kiss the Water Queen and garland her with bright green seaweed, still damp but partially dried on a breakwater. Unsuccessful candidates for the crown enjoyed brief office as Neptune's mermaids, appearing in scaly silver tails, stored all the year round in the Town Clerk's office so that fresh regalia was no charge upon the rates.

Then, in the third week of May, the seasonal brass band would arrive and install itself in the wrought-iron pagoda opposite the lifeboat house, and soon, weather permitting, the strains of *Iolanthe* or *The Gondoliers* could be heard as far west as the Dock if the wind was right, and towards evening, when middle-aged Gilbert and Sullivan fans had been driven indoors by the sea breeze, the green-jacketed bandsmen would play shorter-lived melodies, like that year's popular *Auf Wiedersehen*, or the previous year's hit *Red Sails in the Sunset.*

Once the promenade fairy lights were switched on there would be dancing on the sanded surface of the band enclosure but this was hard on the feet and even harder on shoe leather, so that the dancing never attracted more than a score of teen-agers; the others waited for the waxed boards to go down after the carnival.

In the final week of May the Tiddly-Pom-Poms would arrive, a party of six usually, led by Jimmy Lemont, whose rubbery face was as familiar in Redcliffe Bay as Doctor Morney-Sutcliffe's because Jimmy had been telling jokes about his wedding night from that same trestle stage since he emerged from the famous "Splinters" Concert Party, in 1919. Two of his company were almost as well known, Charles Tregaskis, Cornish baritone, and Charles's sedate wife, a contralto billed as Gilda Gay. The remaining trio, light comedian, pianiste and soubrette, changed each year. The light comedian was usually a good-looking Irishman and the soubrette was invariably pretty, with twinkling legs that ensured her popularity among the male regulars at the marquee.

By this time the town was practically *en fête*, with the Queen's gondola decked out and her escort of gilded dinghies moored in the boat-shelter near the jetty. Private prayers would be offered up for a fine opening day and usually they were answered, for although we were resigned to gusty Julys and dripping Augusts, we could bet on unclouded skies in June and September.

This particular year there was added excitement, for word came that a film was being made on the dunes, between Coastguard Point and the village of Shelly Bay, four miles to the east.

Two of the leading roles were to be played by then famous names (it says little for the radiance of starlight that I have forgotten who they were!) and the celebrities were said to have booked rooms at The Marino, our leading hotel. Shooting was to begin out on the dunes in mid-June and the film, a smuggling epic, was provisionally entitled *Brandy for the Parson.* I never saw it and never even heard if it was finished, but the rumor put a fine edge on our Water Carnival program.

On the night before the carnival was due to open I accompanied Esta in a practice trip in the gondola. She looked very regal in her gilded chair, clamped to the raised sternsheets of Marty Hocking's camouflaged yawl. She was clothed in a full-skirted gown of white satin (the program called it "samite"), with a crimson sash, a lace ruff, and elbow-length gloves of white kid. Her shoes were gold, with three-inch heels, and her crown a great improvement on the counterfeit crowns of most carnival queens, being made of beaten silver, encrusted with a colorful assortment of imitation rubies, sapphires and emeralds. She had an orb and a sceptre and her three finalist attendants wore green organdie. The fourth, the infuriated Hazel White, had gone absent without leave at the last moment. A message came from her saying that she was attending a relative's funeral in Nottingham. It was far enough away to discourage attempts to corroborate.

Esta didn't seem nervous, just grave and dignified, but she kept me close to her throughout the rehearsal and afterwards made me wait for her while the royal party unrobed at the Church Hall. I was hoping she might invite me into the star's dressing-room and receive me in her panties again, but my luck was out, there were too many people milling about behind the stage. When she had changed and everybody had dispersed she asked me to run her out to one of our favorite spots, the highest point of land between Coastguard Hill and the downsweep of the cliffs to Shelly Bay, close to the place where she had told me about her part in getting Owen Rees and Myfanwy Pritchard married and I, for my part, was very willing to oblige. I had been congratulating myself all the evening on the way she looked perched on the stern of that gondola. She seemed to me to have matured overnight, so that she was no longer a pert eighteen-year-old, with pleasing rather than pretty features, but a girl any young man would have been proud to display at a Paxtonbury Pump Room dance, or in a smart city restaurant, a girl with a freshness and charm people of Birdie's generation would have called a chocolate-box beauty.

As soon as we were alone I praised her for her lack of temperament, reminding her that all the queens I remembered had had tantrums at least once during rehearsal. I also told her that, with a little luck, we might use the pictures to get her entered in a county or a national beauty contest. She showed a flutter of excitement at this but then she laughed at the idea and said, "I don't think that's in the cards, Pip! This is just a local affair and I'm getting a lot of pleasure out of it but it's all make-believe. I'm not the kind who wins real beauty competitions, I haven't the features, the figure or the ambition for that matter. As long as I can encourage you to convince yourself that I'm pretty I'm satisfied because that's all I entered for really. I thought the clothes, and the treatment generally, might do something to you and apparently it has, so let's leave it at that. To be honest I shall be glad when the week is over."

I said I would be glad too, for as long as the carnival lasted every minute of her time was at the disposal of Redcliffe Bay, and who wanted to share a Water Queen with twelve thousand subjects?

"Well," she said, smiling, "as long as I'm on show you'll have to keep dodging around the outskirts, like poor old Cecil Trumper! We shan't see much of each other until it's over and that's why I wanted to make the most of tonight!"

I was glad she had admitted that. I felt the same as she did about the carnival, that it was no more than a narrow spotlight in which she could stand for a few days, but already I was beginning to resent the demands it made on her time and energy. She had been given the week off from the hospital and it occurred to me that we could have used her holiday to better advantage, perhaps on a jaunt to the Cotswolds in the Austin

Seven. Thinking this was no more than a step from a moment of self-revelation that brought me up with a jolt. I was able, from that instant, to gauge her essentiality, and remember how profitless was my daily round when it did not end with an hour or two of her company in the evenings, or maybe a shared trip in the afternoons. I had a hundred acquaintances in town but no real friend, certainly no one in whose company I was wholly at ease, or able to discuss the kind of things that kids our age liked to wonder at and talk about.

Suddenly I heard myself talking with an earnestness unique in our association and I do really mean "heard myself," because the words tumbled out involuntarily and even as I said them I recognized them as a means of release from the accumulated loneliness of all the years I had spent in that place, first as a stray dependent upon the kindness of relatives, later as keeper and breadwinner for a seedy old drunk like Birdie Boxall. I knew then that I wanted most desperately to put a term to this isolation. Like Esta I wanted to belong, to be needed by someone, and in that moment of clarity the fabled lure of the big world outside Redcliffe Bay seemed not only fictitious but fatuous.

I put my arm round her and pulled her round facing me. "Listen Esta, it's finally got through to me—I mean, what you said the last time we were up here about not wanting to live anywhere else! We belong here, and we belong to each other, and I ought to make a go of what I've already got before I start chasing rainbows! I could be happy enough here if I had you and that studio to myself. I'm sick to death of Birdie's frowzy old rooms and his daily help's God-awful meals! I'm sick of working ten hours a day to keep him in booze, and if I tell him so he'll have to listen, and draw up a proper agreement at the solicitors. He can take his six pounds a week out of the business on condition he moves into digs, or finds a home with his sister. As soon as he goes I'll spend the hundred and fifty I've saved on doing the place over and buying some modern equipment. Once that's done you could move in and take over as cashier and receptionist. That way how can we lose? In five years' time, if we still want to go places, then at least we'll have something to sell. If we don't then we'll get along somehow and have a place of our own. What do you say? Would you take a chance on things working out for the two of us?"

She hadn't taken her eyes off mine all the time I had been speaking and there was enough light from the dashboard, and the half-moon suspended over the bay, to see her expression of wonder, as though I had proposed setting her up in the Grand-Cham's palace instead of a rundown old flat over a poky little studio, with its smell of dust and dry rot, and the paint peeling from its frontage. There was wonder in her eyes but uncertainty also, as I realized as soon as she spoke, slowly and carefully, like a witness with a desperate regard for truth.

"'Move in and take over?'—'Take a chance on the two of us . . . !'—I'm sorry to sound stupid, Pip, but it isn't clear, or not clear enough! You've always been so careful to avoid committing yourself. . . I've been happy as things were, ever since that day you gave me that locket, but the two of us, working there . . . you getting rid of Birdie, you paying Birdie off . . ." and suddenly she became angry with us both on account of her inability to say what needed to be said, to find words that would avoid making a fool of herself and of me. "If you mean what I hope you mean, then *say it!* You can't expect *me* to, can you?"

Her despairing protest did more than anything I could have done to rescue our sense of humor. I can see now what confounded her. I had overweighted the proposal with the business and her absorption into it, so that it was really more of a commercial proposition than an offer of marriage. I floundered for a moment and then opened the car door and by common consent we both stepped out. You can propose to a girl in the front seat of an Austin Seven but you can't follow it up, or not in comfort. I felt that I couldn't do either of us justice in that cramped position. She got out the other side and we stood by the warm bonnet where I embraced her so enthusiastically that she was swept off her feet. It seemed to me a natural thing to lift her clear off the ground, so that for a moment we must have looked like the figures on the dust-jacket of a romantic novel in Applegarth's threepenny lending library. Perhaps it was a realization of this that we found amusing, for suddenly she laughed and said, "Go on, *say* it! Don't put me down until you *say* it! You and your offers of housekeeper-cashier-receptionist!"

I carried her the few yards to the stile that gave access to the cliff path and from here you could see the great sweep of the bay, east of Coastguard Hill. The surface was ruffled and the soft rasp of the waves breaking on the shingle reached us clearly, like the hiss of a saw pushed by a lazy woodsman. I propped my elbow on the stile and said, "I've rehearsed proposals and I've read them in books and magazines but they either sound daft or like something out of a solicitor's preamble to a contract! Can't we just leave it at that?"

"No!" she said, emphatically, "we can't, Pip, because I can't honestly be sure that it was a proposal!"

"Well, it was but the fact is I couldn't do much about it until I get that place to myself. Can't you understand that?"

"Of course I can understand it—that part of it—but, oh gosh, how can I make you understand without sounding like someone writing to the Lonely Hearts column? You've never once told me you love me!"

She said this earnestly but not resentfully. Women never seem to understand that men, as a sex, don't put a great deal of reliance on the word "love." I know I didn't, maybe because it smacked too much of the Tivoli and popular sheet-music. It means less now than it did then but even in 1932 it was a verb that had become debased.

"Look, Esta," I said, rather desperately, "I've enjoyed every minute we've spent together since New Year and I can't imagine life without you. I enjoy being with you and talking to you and I enjoy having you at the back of me, as someone I never have to pretend to. You're different from all the other girls round here because—well, because you don't make a lot of silly demands on a chap but let him go on being himself if you see what I mean. If that's what people call love, then I love you and I should have thought it would have been obvious by now!"

"Not all that obvious," she said obstinately. "Is that all there is to it?"

"Good God, of course it isn't! I realized what was special about you that day I came up to your bedroom on your birthday but I don't see why we have to hold an inquest on how I feel about you. It isn't complicated to me. I never touch you without wanting to hold you all night and when I saw you looking as you did at that rehearsal I wanted to get into that old boat of Hocking's, throw everyone else overboard and sail off somewhere where there was just the two of us. It wasn't the way you looked in those fancy clothes, either! I'd have had those off you the minute we were out of sight of land! Does that do anything towards convincing you?"

"A lot more than all that talk about me taking over Beryl's job as receptionist at the Grosvenor Studios!" she said, calmly. "Now move back from this stile. That post is hurting my back!"

I put her down and she threw her arms around my neck, kissing me with the kind of enthusiasm she had shown the night we opened a bottle of Birdie's vintage champagne. We clung to one another up there for a few minutes without saying anything more and I passed my hands over her taut little body, so that presently she said, in the same quiet tone, "I'm sorry if I sounded ungracious, darling. It was just that I had to be sure. I mean, quite sure that I wasn't jumping to conclusions!"

I apologized then for my hamfisted way of putting things but she interrupted me, saying, "Never mind that now. You've said everything that matters. You could have had me any time. Any time at all, Pip, but you already know that, don't you, and have known it from away back!" She paused for a moment, then she added, "Do you want me now? Before we get separated when all that carnival nonsense begins?"

"I want you every time I touch you," I said, "but only subject to conditions and if that sounds pompous I can't help it!"

She nodded. "I know, not in places like this, or the car, or at home with other people around?"

"Not stealthily!" I said, and that was what I meant. "You just aren't someone like your sisters, to be taken and chalked up on the spur of the moment, and that's something I've known from the time we were kids at school!"

It was about half a minute before she spoke. Then she said,

very quietly, "Thank you, Pip. That's about the nicest thing you've ever said to me, not excluding everything else you've said tonight! Let's go back now. I want to think about it all and I daresay you do, although we won't be thinking the same things I imagine. Of course you've got to consider the practical aspects but I don't feel in the least practical. I've never been so happy in my life and I'll make you happy, I swear I will!"

We went over the smooth turf towards the car and neither of us spoke again as we drove down the long slope to the bend where we could see the broad triangle of lights, now bounded by the winking beads of the carnival illuminations looped on strings between the festal tridents of the promenade. She said, as I changed down for the last quarter-mile, "It looks prettier than ever tonight, Pip!" and I said it certainly did. We were back to banalities again but although I realized this I didn't care a jot.

When we reached her shop door she got out. She said, kissing my cheek, "Don't come in tonight, Pip! I know it seems silly but I'd rather you didn't." I was a little put out at this and almost wished I had taken her up on her invitation on the cliff, but then I reflected that once we settled in her front room we would be there until the small hours and she had a very heavy day ahead of her, beginning with a special hair-dressing appointment at eight A.M. I said, "Okay, Esta, but tonight is rather special. It calls for something more than a railway-carriage-window goodbye!"

"Yes, it does," she said seriously, "so get out of the car. We're through with doorstep goodnights and I don't care who knows it!"

We embraced under the lamp, in full view of anyone on Stump who was looking down on the enclosure. I think she rather hoped somebody was, for she clung to me, showering kisses before she turned and went in. I drove round behind the sea-gazing lifeboatman, parked the car in the alley behind the studio and let myself in. The next moment I was flat on my face on the kitchen floor, having fallen headlong over something soft and bulky lying between sink and stove.

I picked myself up feeling slightly dazed and groped for the light switch. Birdie was lying on his back, with his arms spread-eagled in a way that made my stomach turn over. I saw at a glance that he was dead or dying.

[2]

When I had recovered from the first shock I got down on my knees, opened his jacket and felt his heart. It seemed to be beating very feebly but I couldn't be sure, so I held his shaving mirror over his mouth and cried out with relief when I saw that it misted slightly. I left him then and ran through to the studio to the telephone, whirling the handle of the little box to summon the operator. Modern telephones were installed in most of the shops in town but not in Birdie's. He didn't own the place and refused to spend a penny on improving it.

After what seemed to me a long interval the night operator answered and I asked him to call Doctor Morney-Sutcliffe. There was another long pause during which I could hear my heart thumping. I felt terribly guilty standing there waiting, as though, by finally resolving to have things out with him, I had somehow willed his death. At last Lorna's voice answered and for once it produced no other effect but to startle me. I said, "I'm ringing from Grosvenor Studios on West Stump. Mr. Boxall's had an attack of some kind and is unconscious. I think he's terribly ill. Is the Doctor there?"

She said, with what I thought maddening deliberation, "Is that you, Kent?"

"It's Pip Stuart!" I said, savagely, "and I want the Doctor at once! Mr. Boxall's very ill! I think he may be dying!"

"I'll put you on," she said quietly, and I heard the bed creak and her footsteps cross the room. It wasn't until I heard her voice call "Basil" that it struck me they must occupy different rooms and then I found myself wondering why she had answered a night telephone call. In a few seconds she came back. "He'll be with you in less than ten minutes, Kent. If the ambulance arrives first, wait on the doorstep and tell the Doctor. He'll go straight on to the hospital. I'll phone the ambulance for you. Go back to Mr. Boxall right away!"

Suddenly I felt immensely grateful to her. She sounded cool and organized but at the same time deeply sympathetic. I stammered my thanks and ran off, opening the front door of the shop and looking both ways in the hope of seeing the night-duty constable, who usually made the rounds of the Stump about one in the morning. I was lucky. He was standing in the shadow of the lifeboatman's plinth, thinking that he couldn't be seen while he smoked half a Woodbine. I called, "Frank, I want help!" and the portly figure of Constable Frank Oldham moved out of the shadow, disposing of his dogend as though by magic. He was an old friend of mine, a mild, unambitious officer serving his final year with the Constabulary. He had been trying doors around town since I was a child and convictions resulting from his arrests and reports averaged no more than three a year. I took him through the shop to where Birdie lay, telling him I had phoned the Doctor and that the ambulance was on its way. He lifted the old scarecrow as if he had been a small package, laid him gently on the couch and sucked his gingery moustache in a way that could only mean one thing.

"He's on his way, kid," he said. "Looks like a heart attack. Did he suffer with his heart?"

"No," I said, "it was always bronchitis." I didn't add that he was a heavy drinker because everybody in Redcliffe Bay knew that. Frank Oldham loosened Birdie's tie and unbuttoned his high Victorian collar. The old man stirred faintly and then slumped; by the time we heard cars arriving outside he was dead, at least, I think he was, for his features became rigid and Frank said, gently, "I'll stay with him, kid. Go out and bring the Doctor through the front."

Doctor and the ambulance arrived simultaneously and Morney-Sutcliffe came bounding in at his customary pace. He didn't address a word to me but went straight over to the couch. The ambulance driver stayed in the studio, plying me with questions that I couldn't answer. I was glad when Morney-

Sutcliffe barked at him and told him to bring the stretcher and a few moments later Birdie crossed the studio for the last time, disappearing into the vehicle. The Doctor came bustling out again and then, as though responding to an afterthought, checked his stride. "Are you a relative?" he demanded, and when I told him I was not, and that Birdie had a sister living in New Church Road, he told me I had better telephone her and tell her to go to the hospital. "He's dead," he added, brutally, "and I can't say I'm all that surprised! I've warned him times enough over the last ten years!"

That was all. He didn't give me a chance to tell him Birdie's sister didn't own a telephone and he didn't invite me to come along to the hospital, or offer a word of sympathy. I might have been someone returning home late, who had found a dead tramp in the gutter.

I needed company badly and was going to suggest I make some tea and share it with Frank Oldham, the Constable, but then I realized he had gone with the ambulance and that I was alone again. I dithered a moment, still reeling with shock, and thought fleetingly of going across to rouse the Wallaces. At that moment the telephone rang and I answered it mechanically. It was Lorna and the sound of her voice was very welcome, even though I assumed she was only ringing to contact the Doctor.

"He's gone," I said, "and they've taken Mr. Boxall away in the ambulance. He died a minute before the Doctor got here."

"He was the old man you worked for, wasn't he?" and when I confirmed this she asked the same question as the Doctor. "Are you related?"

"About as close as I came to having a relation," I told her and she must have detected bitterness in my voice. I was still smarting under the Doctor's abrupt departure and when she asked me if he was still there I said he wasn't. He had popped in and popped out in thirty seconds flat.

"You mean you're all alone?" She sounded mildly astonished.

"Yes," I said, "nobody lived here but Birdie and me. I came in very late and he was lying on the kitchen floor. The Doctor said it was a heart attack and implied that drink had killed the old boy!"

"He said *that?* To you? Just now?"

"Yes. Everybody knew Birdie knocked it back but well—somehow it didn't seem right to say it, not with him lying there."

"What are you going to do now, Kent?" She sounded, I thought, genuinely concerned and the gentleness in her voice touched me.

"You mean, right now? Or in the way of a job?"

"Both," she said.

I told her I would probably take over the studio when things were sorted out but I didn't know upon what kind of terms. Maybe his sister would want me to pay her for a goodwill, or maybe Mr. Trumper, the landlord, wouldn't grant a lease to a person my age. As to tonight, I supposed I would make some tea and wait for sunrise. There wasn't much prospect of sleep and anyway, someone might ring.

There was a pause during which I could hear the studio clock ticking. Finally she said, "Would you like to drive up here? You've got a little car, haven't you?"

I was surprised on two counts, that she should propose I make my way up to the Doctor's, and also by her knowledge that I owned "a little car." Apart from that one brief encounter outside the Church Hall I hadn't seen her since the day I had driven up to "Heatherdene" and parked the Austin Seven three gates short of her drive but I gathered she must have seen me and the knowledge awakened in me the kind of interest she had always aroused. I would certainly have accepted her invitation had I not been reluctant to run into Morney-Sutcliffe again that night. As it was I said, "That's very kind of you, Lorna, but I'd sooner stay here in the circumstances."

"It's not kind, just civilized," she said, "and I'm sorry Basil was brusque. I suppose he's a good deal more familiar with sudden death than you are, and anyway, he isn't famous for his bedside manner. If you won't come, will you promise me something? Will you ring me in a day or so and tell me what your plans are, and what's going to happen to the business?"

"Yes, I'd like to do that," I said, "and thanks for talking to me like this. I feel a lot better for it, Lorna."

"I'm glad," she said, and then, "Goodnight, Kent dear," and the phone clicked.

I sat in the little cash-desk staring at the telephone and wondering why the shop was so drafty. Then I noticed that they had left the street door open and went across to close it, returning to contemplate the telephone as if it represented Lorna, and feeling comforted by it on that account. I sat there for a long time, not thinking of Birdie, or Esta, or my future, but simply about her in the various moods I had encountered her at the hospital dance, in her drawing-room, in her attic and on her way home from the links. She had just entered a new dimension. I had thought of her as a pretty woman, a desirable woman, an almost detestable woman, but never as a human being to whom one might be glad to turn in time of trouble. I wondered how many of the cosseted wives living in the Valley would bother themselves about a badly-shocked lad in my social niche and concern themselves to the point of inviting a tradesman into their home in the middle of the night. I wondered too, if a single one of them, on the strength of so short an acquaintance, would have shown the slightest interest in my future. The answers to both questions were not flattering to Redcliffe Bay's upper crust.

Presently I got up, went into the storeroom and took down Volume Three of *Masterpieces of the World's Galleries*, opening it first time at Gainsborough's *Mrs. Graham* because I had turned down the corner of the page. Mrs. Graham looked cool and arch and beautiful, but not in the least sympathetic. If you wanted a bosom to cry on you wouldn't waste much time there but would hunt up something cosier or more expansive. To-night there didn't seem much in common between the two women, except the slightly prominent lower lip and the smooth curve of the cheeks.

Suddenly I felt terribly tired and used up, so that I could only think of lying down. I went upstairs, half undressed and flopped on the bed, telling myself I would take a short nap before driving round to Birdie's sister and reporting what had happened. In the few seconds before I slept I thought of Lorna's voice, controlled and very gentle, coming out of the phone as she concluded our conversation with the unlikely words "Kent dear." I was probably the only man of my generation who, on the night he had proposed marriage to one woman, devoted his final waking thoughts to another.

[3]

The crunch of traffic in the street outside awakened me and I was alarmed to see that it was eight-thirty and that I had been asleep for more than six hours. I jumped up and was halfway to the wash bowl before I remembered, with a sense of tremendous shock, why I was still wearing shirt and trousers. It seemed a month ago since I had sat beside Esta in the car making my qualified proposal. As for the Water Carnival rehearsal, that seemed to belong to another life.

The house was very still and again I wondered why until I remembered that this was the opening day of the carnival, and that custom decreed all Redcliffe Bay tradesmen gave their employees a day's holiday with pay. Mrs. Crispin, the daily woman, would not be coming in and neither would Beryl, the receptionist-cashier.

I went down to the kitchen and drew the curtains aside. It gave me an unpleasant feeling to look at the spot between sink and stove where Birdie had lain, and the frayed plush couch on which Frank Oldham had placed him to die. I found it about as much as I could do to make myself a cup of tea. The toast I tried my hand at was burned black and I threw it away before fetching my jacket and running a comb through my hair, with some idea of going round to Birdie's sister in New Church Road, in case no one had told her of her brother's death. Then I thought I should ring the hospital first and while I was hesitating the phone rang. It was Esta, calling from the hairdressers, and sounding very agitated.

"Pip? Thank goodness! I heard on the way over and I knocked and knocked but couldn't get an answer! I wondered where you were. I'm terribly sorry, and I know you will be. It's just awful happening as it did, after last night, and you finding him like that! I'm so sorry I can't come over now but you could come here. I'm all in curlers but Madame Colette says she doesn't mind as there's no one else being done except me."

There didn't seem much point in me sitting beside Esta in a hairdressing salon and recounting the grisly details, so I said I had to call on Birdie's sister, then go up to the hospital to get particulars for the death certificate.

"Oh Lord!" she said, "does that mean you'll miss the procession?"

"I suppose it does," I said, without regret, "there's a hell of a lot to do and nobody but me to do it."

"When will I see you, then?"

"As soon as I've done what I've got to do. I'll have to call Dudley Snell, the solicitor, and I can't very well attend the dance tonight. Maybe I'll pick you up afterwards. Don't worry about me, I'll cope."

I rang off, rather abruptly. It might seem odd but I didn't want to discuss it with her, perhaps because Birdie's death, preceding anything but a verbal agreement concerning my succession, involved her too closely after what we had agreed last night. Then it had seemed so straightforward. All I had to do was to get Birdie to Dudley Snell's office and make him sign some kind of agreement that would include the transfer of lease and a splitting of profits over an agreed period, but now it was by no means as simple. Birdie's sister, a cross-grained old widow called Annie Vetch, was a noted miser and I had a strong suspicion that she would make all kinds of difficulties. I was right about that. As soon as I called on her she stormed at me for not coming round the moment it happened, declaring in her strong brogue, that she would have "liked to zee un go!" In vain I argued that he was dead when he left the studio, and that no purpose would have been served by dragging her out in the middle of the night. She still said I had failed in my duty to her and to Birdie. I had certainly got off on the wrong foot with her, so I went on up to the hospital and saw the Sister, who wasn't any more co-operative because we had fallen foul of one another on a number of occasions over Esta reporting late for night duty. She said Birdie was in the mortuary and the Doctor had all the particulars. If I got the certificate from the registrar I could leave it for him to sign and fill in the cause of death. She did ask me if I wanted to see Birdie but I said I didn't. The sight of the old chap lying under a sheet on a marble slab wouldn't have done a thing for me that morning.

I went down to the registrar and hung about in his poky little office for half an hour or so. He was a member of the Carnival Committee and not disposed to waste more time on me than he could help. I gave him the particulars and he handed me the certificate. Then I went back to Annie Vetch's to talk about the funeral. On the way I passed any number of decorated floats and tableaux moving towards the assembly point for the street procession. They made me feel like the Ancient Mariner bent on putting a brake on the jollifications. Everybody but me was in high carnival mood and although Birdie's death must have got around by then nobody stopped me and referred to it, which seemed to me very insensitive on their part, for Birdie Boxall had served Redcliffe Bay all his life. I stress this mood of self-pity for it had a direct bearing on what happened that day. I am certain that if someone had forgotten the carnival for a few moments, and paid me a little attention, the entire course of my life would have been altered.

By midday, the time the gondola procession was due to begin, I began to feel hungry. I should have been down on the jetty, of course, taking pictures of Neptune's meeting with the Water Queen, but I knew the *County Herald* photographer would be there and that Ben Dagmar, editor of the *Messenger*, would realize why I had let him down. He already had plenty of pictures of Esta and her retinue and in any case the carnival was due to last for the rest of the week.

I bought some Cornish pasties and went back to the empty studio, pulling down the blinds less out of respect for Birdie than to keep out the blinding sun and the noise of the crowds surging up and down Stump. It was a blisteringly hot day and the air in the studio was stale, with any number of trapped flies buzzing in the windows and last Easter's wedding pictures curling at the edges. I found a bottle of warm beer in Birdie's meat cage (it was before the age of refrigerators in establishments like ours) and sat in the coolest corner of the room to eat my lunch. The beer was burpy but the pasties were satisfying and cheered me up a little, so that I got up halfway through the last one and raked out Volume Three of the *World Masterpieces* again, opening it at Mrs. Graham and propping it up in front of me as I ate.

I didn't hear her come in. I suppose I was too deep in my sulk and beginning to enjoy my misery. The back door had been left open and she must have found her way down the alley and up the short garden path to the kitchen. The first advertisement of her presence was her perfume, which banished the frowstiness of the studio in a second and made me look up from the book, so that I saw her standing beside the potted palm Birdie had used for sittings back in Edward the Seventh's reign, and would never throw in the dustbin. She looked as cool and fresh as a white rose, in a well-cut linen suit and white suede shoes with very high heels. She had a large white handbag in one hand and a bottle of French brandy in the other, one of those shapely bottles with a fancy label. I couldn't have been more surprised if the Hon. Mrs. Graham herself had rustled into the studio.

"Still all alone, Kent?" she said, and there was the same note of concern in her voice. It was genuine concern, at odds with Esta's rather gossipy expressions of sympathy earlier in the day.

I was so astonished by her appearance that I was unable to make an immediate reply but simply stood up, gaping at her. She crossed over, her heels striking hard on the parquet floor, and looked curiously at the reproduction, then at me. A smile lurked in the corners of her mouth but it wasn't her usual, patronizing smile. She said, "Is that the portrait you were telling me about? The Hon. Mrs. Graham? The woman who reminds you of me?"

"Yes," I said, finding my voice at last, and alarmed by its

hoarseness. "I took it out again last night after you had phoned."

She studied it very carefully. I could see that she was flattered, as much by the fact that she had caught me gazing at it as by the comparison.

"She is rather beautiful and I like her pearls and hairstyle but there isn't much promise about her is there? To a man, I mean. She looks is if she might dole out her favors like mortgage payments!"

It was an aspect of Mrs. Graham I had not considered. "Her husband was crazy about her," I said. "After she died he hid that picture and it wasn't rediscovered until half a century later."

"Is that so?" she exclaimed with interest. "What kind of man was he?"

I told her he was one of Wellington's generals and had an impressive military record and she asked how old Mrs. Graham was when she died.

"She was married at eighteen and she died when she was thirty-five. She was about nineteen when that was painted."

"She looks older," Lorna said, "but I suppose it's the clothes." Then, in a more businesslike tone, "What's happened since last night? How is it you're moping here eating pasties. Shouldn't you be taking part in all the fun and games outside?"

I told her briefly how I had spent the morning and she seemed indignant that no one had bothered to come round and give me a hand to straighten things out. "Haven't you got any friends in this terrible place?" she demanded. "How about that girl you were so prickly about last time we met? The one I just saw curtseying on the jetty, with lots of seaweed round her neck?"

"Everyone is out enjoying themselves," I said guardedly. "Esta Wallace is Water Queen and has her hands full for the rest of the week. I've got friends. Everyone around here is friendly enough, but this is Redcliffe Bay's big day and they've all made their plans."

"Then you had better take a drink," she said. "You look as if you need one. Do you use glasses round here?"

"I'll get some," I said, and went into the kitchen, returning with two tumblers that I had washed and carefully dried before setting on a tin tray. I remembered to bring a jug of water, knowing that I couldn't drink neat brandy even if she could. She poured me a very generous measure and it was the best brandy I had ever tasted. I was glad I had watered it down, however; it had a snap like the jaws of a crocodile.

The drink made me feel very mellow so that I forgot all about Birdie, his sister, the registrar, the hospital Sister and the carnival, and was able to concentrate wholly upon her.

"What made you come?" I asked. "Did you tell the Doctor I was in a fix?"

"No," she said, "I haven't seen him since last night. I answered the phone when you rang because he was downstairs but he was gone when I came down to breakfast. He's caught up in all that mummery out there, isn't he?"

I said that he was, very much so, and would be for the rest of the week if he could spare time from his patients. She said she had suspected as much and that was why she had made the effort to get the boat ready. I remembered then that she and the Doctor owned a small cabin cruiser, moored in a tiny inlet about three miles along the coast, just below the spot where Esta and I had left the car last night. The Doctor didn't use it much because he was a bad sailor but she spent a great deal of her time there in summer. She now told me she painted from it, seascapes mostly but very bad ones. She only did it to pass the time; she was always looking for some way of passing the time. That brought her to the point. If I didn't intend to work that afternoon why didn't I come out and take a swim with her? "There's peace and quiet in the cove," she said. "Everyone for miles around will have trudged into town to watch the processions."

"I always got the impression you hated peace and quiet," I said.

"Mostly I do," she said, "but on a day like this it's preferable to all that yammering!" Then she asked me if I was a swimmer. She liked bathing, she said, when the water was warm enough, but she could only do the breaststroke and fool around on her back.

The prospect appealed to me and not only because it would change the direction of what promised to be a very depressing day. I was a good swimmer and it occurred to me that here was a chance to show off a little. Apart from that, the prospect of seeing her in a bathing suit was worth any number of torchlight processions. I said I would be very happy to come and asked if she had got the car outside.

"Well, I didn't walk here," she said, "but you had better follow on in your own boneshaker. Give me about half an hour's start and drive to the goyle. You can get partway down to the beach and park in a clearing. I'll leave the brandy. You'll probably need some when you come back from the funeral."

The entire aspect of life changed for me as soon as I heard her start her engine and honk her way up the Stump. Suddenly life seemed gay and adventurous again, and I ran up the stairs three at a time to rummage for my bathing costume and towel. I didn't give Esta or the carnival another thought, and the half-hour delay she had advised seemed to stretch itself into hours. I changed into silver-grey flannels, put on a sports shirt and went over my face twice with a safety razor. Then, right on the dot, I locked up and backed the car onto the Stump, turning inland to avoid the crowds now surging towards the sea-front.

The gully, or "goyle" as we call gullies in the West, ran down from Phillips's farm through a wilderness of gorse, dwarf oaks and other half-grown trees, and at this time of year the banks were gay with foxgloves, honeysuckle, periwinkles, wood anemones and campion. The bay was a polished blue plate and the sandstone crags enclosing the inlet looked red-hot in the sun. I found the clearing and drove the car behind a clump of young beeches, where it couldn't be seen from the farm track. I wouldn't have thought to do that had she not dropped the hint about us making our way out there in separate cars. Then I went on down the winding footpath to the tiny beach that had a makeshift jetty and a boathouse looking like a backwoods cabin. The cabin was a solid little structure built under the lee of the most westerly crag that overhung it by a hundred feet. I had been there before, in the days when I was still at school and much addicted to beachcombing, but the cabin was new to me.

It looked as if the Morney-Sutcliffes had staked a permanent claim on the cove.

The cabin cruiser, a smart little craft, all shining paint and polished brasswork, was moored about a hundred yards from the tideline in what I knew to be about fifteen feet of water. There was no means of getting out to her so I put my hands to my mouth and shouted "Ahoy, there!" in the best nautical fashion. Before the echo had died she bobbed up from the foredeck and waved and a moment later she had dropped into the dinghy and was pulling ashore.

She handled the rowboat very expertly and brought it shooting alongside the jetty as neatly as a Redcliffe Bay longshoreman. She was wearing a striped singlet of vaguely piratical design, a pair of blue slacks then known as beach pajamas and open-toed sandals. Hers were the first painted toenails I had ever seen. They matched the sunbaked sandstone of the cliffs.

"Jump in, we'll do our swimming from the boat," she said, and then, scrambling onto the jetty, "Wait a minute, I've got some records to collect."

She disappeared into the boathouse and reappeared a moment or so later with a case containing about a dozen records. "Old favorites of mine," she said. "I only play them when I'm here alone. You'll be too young to remember them!"

I said I doubted this and she scrambled in and fell to with the oars so that the boat fairly flew across the water and I found myself wondering at her explosive energy. Back in town she had always given me the impression that she found it an effort to go anywhere without a car. I had never seen her do anything in a hurry. She took about twenty seconds to lift a tea cup or light a cigarette, but here she was behaving like a tomboy trying to outdo an elder brother. All her carefully cultivated languor had gone, and she spoke and moved as if she was enjoying life, even life in Redcliffe Bay.

The boat was called "Linda" and its name was picked out in gold lettering above the rudder. She told me, as we climbed aboard, that it had been her mother-in-law's name. "She was killed in a riding accident," she said gaily, as though this was a very good reason for naming a boat after her.

"Would you like some tea now or later?" she said and I told her I preferred to take a swim and cool off. It had been hot work driving and walking down that suntrap of a goyle and the water looked placid and inviting. It was so clear out here you could see the head of the stern anchor half-buried in the sandy bottom. She pointed to the cabin and I went in to change while she slipped out of her singlet and slacks on the deck. Underneath she was wearing a blue and silver bathing costume of a kind you didn't often see around Redcliffe Bay. It was an ancestor of the bikini and not a very distant one. It fitted her like a skin and was open to the waist at the back. It didn't have a skirt, like the Water Queen finalists' costumes, but was cut in a way that emphasized her thighs and buttocks, like those of a Principal Boy at a pantomime. Striding about the deck in that costume she reminded me a little of a Principal Boy, the one in *Robinson Crusoe*. She seemed to take on a kind of pseudo-nauticality that was entirely uncharacteristic of the Lorna I knew, or thought I knew. I said, emerging from the cabin, "You're so different out here, Lorna. You just aren't the same woman!"

"Improved or otherwise?" she said, smiling and showing her exceptionally white teeth, a feature I had noticed the first time I met her but had since forgotten.

"Well, I'm not sure," I said truthfully. "A man would require notice of that question. It's just that you seem so much livelier and happier."

"Then why is there any question of it being an improvement? 'Lively' and 'happy' are complimentary adjectives, aren't they?"

"I'm sold on both land and sea personalities," I said, "but there's no link with the Hon. Mrs. Graham in that costume! She wouldn't have worn it and you wouldn't if we were swimming off the town jetty. It would stop the Water Carnival in its tracks!"

She could take any amount of that kind of talk and pirouetted just for the pleasure it gave her to watch my expression. Then, with a flash of her attic technique, she said briskly, "Come on, you need cooling off already!" and jumped overboard with a splash, bobbing up just in time to watch my first show-off swallow dive. I went threshing round the boat at top speed and then dived under it, bobbing up beside her like a terrier who has performed his tricks and now looks for his titbit. I got it too because she was looking at me admiringly and saying, "You're terrific, Kent! I've always wanted to swim like that. Do you think you could teach me?"

"I should enjoy trying," I said and I did, for the better part of twenty minutes, swimming round her and under her and getting an occasional mouthful of water as I explained the kick and the trick of breathing after every fifth stroke. She made some progress but not much and at length lay flat on her back ten yards on the seaward side of the boat, and I lay beside her enjoying all aspects of the scenery. Presently I thought up another approach and asked her if she knew anything about lifesaving. It was naïve on my part to try this hoary old excuse to get a little closer but she humored me and I demonstrated both popular methods, pulling her along with my hands cupped over her face, and propelling her backwards with her hands resting on my shoulders. One way and another it was the most enjoyable swim I had had in a long time but it didn't do much to lower my body temperature.

When we had had enough we climbed the little rope ladder to the foredeck and I suggested we sunbathe. She said she never made a practice of lying in the sun because she was one of those unlucky people who didn't go brown but merely blistered and peeled. With her fair complexion I could believe it, so I stretched myself out and she went into the little galley leading off the cabin to make tea on a primus stove. Presently the gramophone began to wail, a number called *Valencia*, that had been enormously popular when I was about thirteen. I did a little arithmetic and deduced that this was a tune likely to promote nostalgia in a woman aged about twenty-eight. She had probably danced to it in Paris, perhaps with that writer René, who had painted her so often. I was nearly asleep when she called "Tea up!" and I went through the sliding door into the cabin.

It was a large and very comfortable cabin considering the size of the boat. There were two bunks that were really well-padded locker covers. There were even flowered curtains over the portholes and the place was scrupulously clean.

I was more than satisfied with what I was getting and wasn't looking for a bonus but one awaited me. She said, "I'm dripping all over the floor and I only set to and scrubbed out yesterday. Here, dry me!" and she handed me a soft white towel the size of a blanket, turning her back and slipping the straps from her shoulders but leaving the costume clinging to the lower part of her body.

It looked very much like a variation of the ploy she had used in her attic and I took it as such, remaining very much on guard and casually dabbing her back and shoulders which were dry anyhow. Up to that moment I was behaving, I thought, with heroic restraint, but when she leaned her weight against me I lost my patience, deciding that this was too much after all that dolphin play in the water. I dropped the towel, spun her round and kissed her, first on the mouth and then on her breast, and then she was down on the nearest locker cover. The joke was the portable gramophone was still grinding out *Valencia* and it was this that finally demonstrated how mistaken I had been regarding her intentions. She threw out her arm and pointed and I interpreted the gesture as a protest. With a tremendous effort I stood up, pride winning a very narrow victory over lust, and shouted down at her, "You've been making a bloody fool of me ever since we met! Why do you do it? Why don't you leave me alone?"

She looked quite amazed for a moment and very undignified too, sprawled half on and half off the locker cushions, with her skimpy little costume peeled down to her navel and the straps brushing the floor. Then she sighed and swung her feet down to the deck saying, in a restrained and patient voice, "Nobody's making a fool of you, Kent. Not this time. Turn that thing off and don't be in such a tearing hurry!"

I was far too gratified to apologize for my idiotic misjudgment and she didn't seem to expect an explanation. There was a kind of fatalism in the way she stood up and pulled off her costume, tossing it into the waist of the boat and slamming the sliding door after it. Then she turned back and kissed me very lightly on the cheek and because I had done nothing about the gramophone reached behind me, lifting the needle from the worn old record. She looked and behaved as though she was resigned to comforting a child rather than displaying her beautiful body to a gawky boy with whom she had made up her mind to commit adultery, and yet, behind all her manifest gentleness, there was a flicker of her familiar coquetry, of a woman wanting and waiting to be praised and admired and at least this hint wasn't quite lost on me.

"You're lovely! Quite lovely, Lorna!" I said, and without pretention I knelt and clasped her round the body, letting my hands slide over her hips in a lover's gesture that had no link with the purely physical yearning I had felt for her from the moment of kissing her outside her gate on the night of the hospital dance. She seemed to find this homage moderately pleasing, for she stroked my face and pressed it gently to her belly. There was no salacity about the movement. It was executed gently and with infinite grace, a woman receiving a tribute from a man as a right yet with an element of humility and thankfulness.

We must have remained like that for several minutes and neither of us spoke a word. What was there to say, anyway? I was enslaved by her and she had evidently come to some kind of decision about me. That it proved not to be the decision I imagined, indeed, took for granted at the time, was of no importance at all. We had reached this stage by a long and roundabout route and there was nothing to be gained by talking about it, the way we had tried to when she flirted with me at her home. In what followed I must have demonstrated my clumsiness and gross inexperience but she seemed to take this for granted. The initiative was all hers and she didn't match my excitement or enthusiasm, but what young man cares a jot about that in these circumstances? It was only later, as we lay together in the dry heat of the cabin that I noted, or thought I noted, a touch of sadness about her. She said, presently, "I don't expect you to believe me, Kent, but that's the first time I've behaved that way for a very long time. As a matter of fact since coming to this place!"

This surprised me very much. Until then I had convinced myself that the indecisive results of our previous encounters had been attributable to my youth and callowness, that she thought of me as a mooning boy, immensely flattered by her graciously bestowed attentions such as they were. Now, it appeared, I was mistaken and also, in spite of the real contempt in her voice whenever she spoke of her husband, there was a small part of her that still wanted to play fair with him and this inclined me to think that her lazy pursuit of me over the past six months had been conditioned by her moods. In other words, she had no special preference for me as Pip Stuart, small-time photographer and potential cuckolder, but was driven, every now and again, to find relief from intolerable loneliness. The fact that I had overcome her scruples today was due less to her own desire than to a sudden awareness of my own isolation.

"I'm glad," I said, "and grateful! I'll always think of you as the most wonderful thing that ever happened to me."

She sat up, resting her weight on her hands and smiling down at me. "Oh no you won't!" she said. "Lots of exciting things will happen to you if you'll let them and you'll enjoy most of them a lot more than that bit of nonsense!" Then, with a note of query, "Did you ever think of me as anything more than a person to go to bed with? You don't have to be gallant, just tell me the truth."

I would have told her the truth anyway. "Not until last night, when you rang a second time. And maybe not even then, not until you came into the studio with the brandy. Then I did; then there was no one else I cared a damn about."

"It's strange," she said, in a voice she might have used if she had been talking to herself, "strange the way they prick the few bubbles of illusion left to you in a place like this. I mean loyalty, comradeship, ordinary human compassion. I wouldn't expect any, and I've no right to expect any, because I'm new to the backwoods but you aren't, you've grown up in the place, gone to school here, worked here day after day. Now why *is* that? Can you explain it? Can you offer any excuses for all those chawbacons wandering about and gawping at dressed-up brewery wagons when one of their own kind is facing the first real trouble of his life?"

If I had been honest I should have told her about Esta, about the peculiar complexities of the situation and of all that being Water Queen meant to a Redcliffe Bay girl. I should have told her that Esta Wallace hammered at my door the moment she heard about Birdie's death and had then telephoned from the hairdresser's chair. I didn't, however, being reluctant to invest my relationship with Esta as anything more than a light flirtation. I knew that if I explained the truth she would ply me with questions that would expose the fact that we were engaged and it did not require much imagination to picture what would follow. Lorna would make it her business to get to know Esta Wallace and weigh the prospects of marriage, just as Esta herself did with everyone who looked as if they needed help and advice. It would complicate and perhaps end the hard-won intimacy between Lorna and myself. There would be no more occasions like this but instead a helpful-aunt approach on her part, with any number of arguments for or against committal, dependent upon the impression she got of the girl and our prospects here or elsewhere. I hadn't the slightest wish to deny myself access to a woman who promised so much ecstasy, and so much boost to my morale. I found it very difficult now to contemplate Esta as a rival attraction and, although I already felt slightly guilty at disloyalty on this scale, I was ready to accept the guilt as a generous exchange for the pride and pleasure I had achieved in the last hour. It was because of this that I hedged an inch or two. "You've never begun to understand small-town life," I said, "and to do it you would have to stop thinking of Redcliffe Bay as a backwater. It's a backwater to you but it isn't to them! It's their whole world!"

"Doesn't that go some way towards proving my point?"

"No, it doesn't go any way at all. Not much happens here but when it does, something like the Water Carnival, it generates the kind of excitement the country as a whole would feel for a coronation or a declaration of war. For the time being the affairs of individuals don't count for a thing. Today was Carnival Day, and this week is Carnival Week. When it's all over, or maybe before it's over, they'll get around to realizing that poor old Birdie Boxall has snuffed it, and that I'm still there wondering what's going to happen to me, and then they will all chip in one way or another. Ben Dagmar, the editor of the *Messenger*, will give me advice, and all the townspeople living round Stump, people like Scatty Wallace and Myfanwy Pritchard, will put pressure on Birdie's sister to let me carry on and not make things too tough for me. Maybe old Rufus Trumper, our landlord, will give me a lease and a year's credit, but you can't expect this kind of thing to take precedence over the one week of the year Redcliffe Bay is in the news. I don't expect it anyway."

She listened carefully but all she said in reply was, "You're a rum boy, Kent, and I'm hanged if I know what to make of you! Sometimes I think you'll amount to something and then again, not. I suppose, in the end, it depends on how singleminded you are, or how ruthless, if you put it that way."

I would have liked her to elucidate. There was nothing better I liked than hearing her talk about me and, fantastic as it might appear, I honestly believed at that moment that our futures were linked. She put an end to speculation, however, by getting up and crossing to the galley, saying, "To think I made you tea! It's stone cold now; shall I make fresh, or shall we take another swim?"

I said I would prefer to swim so she opened the sliding door on to the waist of the boat where her costume lay crumpled in a ball. She picked it up, studied it and tossed it down again. "We'll keep the boat between us and the shore," she said. "I always did think it stupid to dress yourself for a dip!" and she slipped into the water, rolling over and letting her beautiful hair trail, a perfect parody of a mermaid on an ancient navigational chart.

It was evening now and the fierce heat had gone from the day but the water was tepid, the warmest I ever remembered this early in the season. We fooled around in it like a couple of kids and it struck me how rapidly and effortlessly our relationship had enlarged itself. It was as though a single act of intimacy had not merely leveled the age gap between us but also whetted our appetites for fun and mischief to a degree that made the episode a kind of practical joke played upon the entire population of Redcliffe Bay. I could imagine what was happening back there at this moment. The tableaux and floats would be assembling in Broadheath Lane as far as the first inland farm, with old Luke Applegarth, the bookseller, mounted on his grey cob as marshal of the torchlight procession. Behind him, first in line, would be Trumper's dray, dressed up to represent the Water Queen's palace and bearing Esta's throne and the crêpe-covered footstools of her attendants. Behind Esta would be Ned Bradford as Neptune, breathing beer fumes over his nymphs. Then would come a dozen or so tableaux, the Scouts' entry, a snow scene composed of cotton-wool blobs spun on innumerable threads through which, as Captain Oates, the Scoutmaster would be staggering into the blizzard, the very gallant gentleman of Scott's expedition. Then would come the Women's Institute entry, *The Last Moments at Fotheringay*, a mournful group of matrons snuffling into handkerchiefs, as they watched Mrs. Butcher, their President, lay her head on the block. There would be any number of "comic" entries, old favorites like *A Visit to the Dentist*, *Uncle Tom Cobleigh* and *The Better 'Ole*, and these would trail back a hundred yards or so to the decorated cars, flower-decked perambulators and finally the carthorse parade. From out here, floating on the water beside a nude and accommodating woman, it all seemed desperately provincial and something told me that never again could I take pleasure in it. It was an odd feeling, and a rather chastening one, like discovering the truth about Father Christmas. Lorna said, "You look very worried! Having second thoughts already?" so I dived under her, pinched her bottom *en route* and ducked her as I came up on the other side. She bobbed up spluttering and protesting and made for the ladder, calling. "Just stay where you are for five minutes or we'll never get any tea!" and I suddenly realized how hungry I was for apart from the pasties I had eaten nothing for twenty-four hours. When I told her this she said I could start on cucumber sandwiches while she rummaged for something more substantial. She came up with scrambled eggs and several slices of bacon, watching with a smile while I wolfed them down. That afternoon and evening we were more like honeymooners than a boy and a married woman making fools of ourselves and each other. It was never quite like that again. In all our subsequent encounters there was an element of tension and unease.

We stayed out there until it was dusk and the sun was dipping into the bay beyond Coastguard Hill, flooding the water with pinkish light that reduced the orange glow over the town to a blur. We could have heard the faint and intermittent sounds of revelry if we had listened for them but we didn't, preferring to sit in the cabin with the door open and work through her repertoire of records on the portable. She loved that portable and those nineteen-twentyish records. Playing them was almost a ritual and she played at least one of them every time we met, so that I can never hear a vodeo-do number without thinking of her, her legs coiled under her, her shoulders swaying to the beat of *Yes, Sir, That's My Baby*, *Aint She Sweet?*, or *Crazy Words, Crazy Tune*. She was probably the first person in the world to make a cult of the twenties.

When the last record was spinning, and I was getting tired of rewinding the handle, I drew her attention to this, saying that it seemed to me eccentric on her part to go into mourning for a vanished youth before she was thirty.

"It's not the number of years," she said, "but what you've done with the time! You wait, Kent, I daresay you'll feel the same when you're my age."

"But it's crazy," I persisted. "There's only eight years between us and people don't think of themselves as middle aged at twenty-eight! You're prettier and have a better figure than any young girl for miles around, and you're a lot more fun to be with! Why pretend otherwise, even to yourself?"

She looked at me speculatively through half-closed eyes, as though weighing the sincerity of this compliment. God knows, it was offered sincerely enough, but Lorna never took anything on trust.

"Okay!" she said, abruptly, lifting the gramophone arm and

slamming it back into its socket. "Make me feel young again and then go off home to bed, you young devil!"

I was by no means sure, when she said this, whether she was inviting me to engage in a more or less innocent romp or repeat the afternoon's performance.

I was not left in doubt for long. The moment I kissed her, intending to observe her earlier advice to manifest some kind of patience, perhaps even gentleness, she launched herself on me with such unsmiling violence that it was as though she meant to resolve any doubts or regrets she might have had, employing my body as a target for her accumulated discontent. It was an astonishing enactment on her part. Whereas, earlier in the day, she was the giver and I the receiver, now our roles were exactly reversed and I was left breathless, bewildered and vaguely resentful, for it seemed to me she had used me far more selfishly and painfully than I had used her. That moment of climax was the first blink of a warning light but it only winked for a few seconds before being doused by a flood of conceit. In that moment, however, I was sufficiently alerted to wonder if the fire I appeared to have lighted wouldn't explode a powder barrel that would blast me all the way to hell and back. Then everything changed again, so suddenly that I was neither frightened nor exalted but infinitely perplexed, for the fury of her lechery was spent and in its place was a curious blend of sulkiness, expressed by her abrupt withdrawal to a corner of the cabin where she began to tug at her hair with a comb. Standing with her back to me she looked like a greedy child deprived of a toy and banished to her room to work off her temper.

I watched her for a moment, far too bemused to speak and thinking she might offer some kind of explanation but when she did not, but went on tugging at her hair as though she would strip the teeth from the comb, I said, in a voice that proclaimed awe as well as astonishment, "*Why?* Lorna? Why like that?"

"Why not?" she flung at me, over her shoulder.

It was, I thought, not so much a challenge to me but to every man who had ever laid hands on her. It was as though, in those two savagely emphasized words, she was expressing contempt for every male animal in the world, those who had looked at her tenderly and those who had looked at her ruttishly. I understood this very well and somehow it went some way to explaining her abandonment so that for a brief space I could wonder about her objectively. I could see her as something beautiful and desirable but also freakish.

This moment, had I known it, could have rescued me from her because it opened the door again on a safe, sane world, where affection did not necessarily have to translate itself into frenzy. I realized this at the same time as I recognized her as a wholly destructive force but I was far too naïve to conceal it and she must have realized from my expression how close she had come to scaring me off. When she turned and smiled the warning light went out again and stayed out. She laid down her comb and sauntered back to me, letting her gaze travel from the floor to the level of my eyes. She said, calmly, "I'm sorry, Kent, I shouldn't have done that to you. It was only because I thought you might be getting into something you'd regret and I wouldn't want that, believe me!"

"You were trying to scare the hell out of me?"

"Something like that."

"But why? This afternoon . . ."

"This afternoon I was just mothering you!"

"You mean you were sorry for me?"

"Yes. And right now I'm sorry for myself."

"Sorry it happened at all?"

"No. Sorry I need a man that much!"

The fearful complexities of women and of this woman in particular! I didn't understand her then and, in spite of everything that lay ahead, I was never to understand her, or not entirely. I said, abjectly, "Does this mean we won't see one another again?"

She lifted my hand and studied it as though she were palmreading. Her voice was that of the woman who had comforted me over the telephone in the small hours.

"I don't know, Kent. I honestly don't know! It depends on the answers to so many questions, some important to you and all vital to me." She threw up her head. "I'm doing my damnedest to persuade Basil to sell up here and buy a London practice!" Then, improbably, she laughed, picked up her handbag, took out a little tortoiseshell case and lit a cigarette. "I really have been a bitch to you, haven't I? You know what the old wives in Redcliffe Bay would call it—'Leading him on,' they'd say. Poor Kent! Led on, and at such a furious pace!"

"But everything's different now, Lorna!"

"Is it? Because you've tumbled me twice in a few hours? Because you've seen me with my clothes off! Nonsense! That isn't nearly so important as you think it is, at least, not to you, though I can understand you thinking so. I didn't invite you here because I was sorry for you, and saw you getting a raw deal back there. I imagined I did but it was only the excuse I was offering to myself up to a few minutes ago. It put me in a better light and enabled me to half-fool myself, until I got my second wind. I asked you here because I wanted to prove something to myself and I've done it. The first time didn't count because it was passive but the encore set my mind at rest. Do you follow me, or do I have to spell it out for you?"

"You have to spell it out."

"Very well," she said, equably, "I'll do that. I don't have to tell you my marriage was on the rocks but what you don't know is that you might have saved it! Even if you haven't you've done me a good turn. You've convinced me that I haven't petrified and I was beginning to think I had. Basil and I haven't slept together in a long time and I was losing my nerve, particularly after the showdown a few days ago."

"You asked him to divorce you?"

"It wasn't that kind of showdown!" She smiled and anyone more experienced than I might have seen malice in the smile. "We both put our cards on the table—or on the bed. He's got no more sensitivity than a hulking peasant but he's a good doctor. He realized that we couldn't go on pretending indefinitely."

Suddenly I didn't want to hear any more. The prospect of learning precisely what had passed between them at a crisis in their married life seemed repugnant. "You don't have to tell me the details," I said, but she made an impatient gesture with her hand. "You'd better hear them for your own peace of mind, and for mine too, now that we've gone this far! You know Basil as a small-town bully and a hustler, but some of his other characteristics aren't so obvious. He's a pedant, precisionist, in everything he does, from a diagnosis down to the act of making love! Friday is his weekly day off, the day the junior partners take over. He plays a round of golf every Friday afternoon and he dresses for dinner and drinks claret. Friday night is his connubial night, to round off the day I imagine, and it's been that way ever since he brought me here. Maybe there's a memo in his daybook—'Friday, ten-thirty P.M. Make love to Lorna. Leave Lorna twelve-five A.M. latest; heavy day tomorrow.' Something like that. I told him so when he finally realized I couldn't function, not even as an instrument. You thought it silly of me to will myself into middle age but it isn't all that silly. Up to a few hours ago I was beginning to think of myself as a woman who had been deprived of every vestige of sexual feeling, as someone who could never give or receive affection again. Now do you understand?"

I believe I felt a deeper compassion for her than I had ever felt for any human being, but how do you express sympathy for someone in that kind of predicament? I hadn't the words then and I still don't have them. All I said was, "When he realized . . . what did he say?"

"Oh, he had a word for it. 'Vagisimus' it was, something attributable to a pelvic spasm. Apparently it's not all that uncommon. I looked it up in one of his books and found it under 'Frigidity.' There it was in black and white but still about as communicative as the slogan on a pill wrapper! It didn't say much about the emotional causes. It never does in his kind of books. Maybe that's why he's like he is!"

"But good God, Lorna," I protested, "how can you even think of going on with it? How will persuading him to swap this practice for a town practice make any difference if you're still married to him?"

"It would make a lot of difference to me," she said blandly, "apart from change of environment. And particularly now, when I'm over the worst of my fears."

"But it's ridiculous! How could anyone call you frigid, or think of you as frigid? That time in your attic—even then the thought never crossed my mind! To tell you the truth I've always thought the exact opposite! And this afternoon, well, you were gentle and patient. I've never really had a woman before."

"You don't have to tell me that, dear," she said but not unkindly, "and I'm glad for you. If you had begun on one of those dimwitted little geese in the town it might have disappointed you, and somehow I don't think I have. You can forget what happened just now. It's like I said, I was simply proving something to myself."

"I still don't see why you don't leave him. It can't be money. Money can't be that important to anyone."

She gave me a very soft glance. It sounds trite to call it a caressing glance but that's precisely what it was. "If I did leave him it would be on impulse," she said. "After all, I've got this boat, the world is wide, and I might even need a crew. Who knows?"

There it was, a hint that might have been worth a sixpenny bet on a two hundred to one outsider, or a sop to my pride, or no more than a few flippant words, forgotten as soon as uttered. I didn't know and there seemed no prospect then of my getting to know, for once again she had withdrawn into herself, almost as though we were talking over our first drink at the dance back in January. Before I could attempt to grapple with the maddening complexities she posed she was brisk, businesslike and friendly again. "You'll have to go now, Kent. They'll be coming back to the farm and they know I sometimes spend the night here. Make as much noise as you like driving that boneshaker of yours up the goyle. I don't want furtiveness on your part to start a lot of silly gossip; it would only complicate things."

I made a technical stand. I knew that it wouldn't do much good but I made it nevertheless. "When do I see you again?"

"When and if I ring," she said, "those are the terms, Kent. Take them or leave them."

"I'll take them," I said, and my humility must have reassured her for she gave me a sisterly kiss and said, "Thank you, Kent. You're a nice boy. For Redcliffe Bay uniquely nice."

She rowed me ashore and set me down on the shingle with the impersonality of a ferryboat operator. Before I had started for the foot of the goyle she had pushed herself clear of the jetty and was sculling back to the "Linda." I watched the dinghy merge into the gathering dusk and trudged up the slope to where I had left the car. I was incapable of selecting and following through any single line of thought. I felt as if I had just stepped off a roller-coaster after two hundred whirls in a row.

CHAPTER SIX

[1]

I didn't look in on the dance as I had promised and it wasn't because I didn't care to face Esta after what had occurred. I felt completely removed from the life of Redcliffe Bay, and from everyone beating it up in the Church Hall that night. I was an experienced traveller who had seen pretty well everything and was returning to his native village to wait around between voyages for the next week or two. Apart from that I wanted to think, to enjoy in retrospect the hours I had spent in the cove, to ponder Lorna's situation and what prospects there were of seeing her again under similar circumstances. So I went back to the studio, took a sip or two of her brandy and went to bed. I didn't have much chance to revel in my experiences. I was asleep in three minutes.

I had left the bedroom and studio inner doors open in case the phone rang and it was the shop bell that awakened me about eight o'clock the next morning. I came pounding downstairs trying to convince myself that it was Lorna, but it wasn't. It was that old trout Annie Vetch, Birdie's sister, here to tell me that I had better go round and see Dudley Snell, the managing clerk of the firm of solicitors Birdie had used all his life. There was a sour note in her voice that didn't augur well for my prospects of getting the business for nothing.

I was shaving when Esta rang from her home across the Stump. She wanted to know what had happened to me yesterday. She had looked out for me at the dance and refused a lift home in the Council Chairman's Humber, in case I showed up at the last minute. Then, just after one A.M. she had telephoned without success. I was thankful I hadn't heard her ring.

"It's dreadful!" she said. "Here we are, more or less engaged, and I haven't set eyes on you for ages! Come over and see me right away, you brute! I'm slutting round in my dressing gown. I feel absolutely all in after yesterday. Didn't you see anything at all of the carnival, you poor dear?"

"No," I said, "I didn't because I wasn't in a carnival mood!" Her chirpiness irritated me and her enthusiasm for me aroused uncomfortable feelings of guilt. I went on to say that, after running around doing all the things that had to be done, I had driven over the moor to Shelly Bay to get away from people. She was immediately contrite for sounding cheerful and said, "Oh, you poor darling! It's awful me not being able to be with you at a time like this, but I've no engagement until the children's fancy dress competition this afternoon. Don't let's waste time talking, come on over!"

I said I couldn't because I had to see the undertaker and then talk to Dudley Snell about the business. She sounded very disappointed but didn't comment on this, except to ask when and where Birdie would be buried. I said I imagined he would be buried in the family grave up on Cemetery Hill, but I didn't know when, that was something I had to arrange.

"Well, when *am* I going to see you?" She sounded as if we were already married and I had been out on the tiles all night.

I said I would come to the Church Hall for the children's afternoon ball and watch her select the prize-winner from the baby show that was due to precede the fancy-dress parade. She brightened up at once and said, "I've never asked you, Pip! Do you like babies?"

The question made me jump but I went right on bluffing. "I'd like yours, Esta!" I fancied I heard her purr into the receiver.

As I put the phone down I saw my reflection in the little mirror our receptionist used to powder her nose, and I was surprised to see that my ears were pink. I learned the technique of this word-juggling later on but that opening bout was unnerving. I finished shaving and made tea and toast. It still seemed odd eating breakfast alone. I couldn't get used to Birdie's absence, to not hearing his cough and his stumbling tread in the room above. Mrs. Crispin, our daily woman, looked in to talk interminably about "the tragedy," and "how much she would miss the dear old chap." It made me wince to listen to her. She never had a good word to say for him when he was alive because she was a Baptist and he was a town drunk but that was only Redcliffe Bay running to form.

I telephoned Mr. Pyne, the undertaker, and we fixed the funeral for the following day, subject to Annie Vetch's confirmation. He had already seen her about it and told me, in a pained voice, that she had ordered a plain coffin, without mountings. I said this wouldn't do at all. Birdie was to have oak, with brass fittings, and if there was any dispute about it I would pay the extra. He said this was not only generous of me but wise, because people would talk if a Redcliffian of Mr. Boxall's standing was buried on the cheap, and then he expressed his sympathy and said I could safely leave all arrangements to him. He was a good undertaker and took himself and his profession seriously, not like his rival, old Thorley Harrison, who was known to refer to the people he measured as "fat parties" or "rashers of wind" as soon as the relatives were out of earshot.

Dudley Snell ran the firm of Voss, Voss and Pickering, without any help from the surviving partner Henry Voss, or his son Arthur. Dudley wasn't articled but he knew his law and he knew Redcliffe Bay, treating his employers with the cheerful contempt they deserved for they were both useless. Old man Voss was a garrulous ass and his son Arthur, the made-to-measure product of a small public school, was the self-appointed leader of Redcliffe Bay's Smart Set, spending most of his time at the Sailing Club or on the golf links. I climbed the stairs to their offices over the Midland Bank in Fore Street and Dudley treated me like an important client which I wasn't, for Birdie had never troubled them much in all the years he had been in business.

"The old chap didn't leave much," he said, "but I believe there's a couple of hundred for you. The rest goes to his sister and nieces. I suppose you'll want to carry on, won't you?"

I said I would and I didn't like the narrow look he gave me. He was a plump, fresh-faced man about forty, with an incisive manner. He rang for coffee in order to give him a few moments to think. Then he said, with a ring of sympathy in his voice, "She's a hard woman, that sister of his! She buttonholed me down by the jetty yesterday and more or less stated what she expects you to do. I was pretty short with her, pouncing on me like that while I was watching the water procession, but she'll be here again and she won't waste much time about it! She expects you to buy the goodwill. If you don't she's going to put the place up for sale as a going concern. She says Trumper will give her a new fourteen-year lease on the premises."

I wasn't all that surprised but I was when he mentioned the figure. She wanted a thousand pounds, paid over a period of two years. It was more than twice as much as I had anticipated.

"It's a damned silly price," I protested. "Any goodwill there is down there is really mine already. Anyone will tell you that, Mr. Snell."

"I'll do what I can to get her down," he said, "but I doubt if I can budge her below eight hundred. She says there are all kinds of fittings and equipment."

I told him that the equipment came out of the Ark, that Birdie would never spend a penny on modern gear or on dressing the place up, and that the value of the business, if there was any, rested on the fact that we had a local monopoly that was unlikely to last much longer.

"How much have you got, not counting Boxall's legacy?" he wanted to know, and I told him about two hundred, and would need every penny of it for redecorating and buying decent cameras and studio furniture. The only way I could pay her anything for the goodwill would be so much a week, over a period.

"Well, I could bluff her," he said. "It would depend on how much you wanted it. You're well known around here and your work is good. She couldn't get much for that place as it stands and I believe she knows it but she's a tight-fisted old harridan and will hang out as long as she can. Do you want me to try?"

Did I? I didn't know. It depended on all kinds of imponderables; how deeply I was committed to Esta, how interested I was in attempting to build the studio into something worthwhile, but above all, how much I meant, if anything, to Lorna. I said, "Try her anyway, Mr. Snell. Say I'll pay her five pounds a week out of income but not a penny more. I had it in mind to try my luck in London, or some other city. What I should really like would be press photography on a big paper, but jobs like that must be hard to come by, wouldn't you say?"

"Any job nowadays is hard to come by," he said gravely, "and I should know. I've been stuck here for twenty years and still haven't got a partnership. There are certain advantages living in a place like this, I suppose, but affluence isn't one of them. However, leave this to me and I'll do the very best I can for you, Pip!"

I thanked him and went out into the bright sunlight of the street, wishing like hell that I could discuss the situation with Lorna but unwilling to risk her displeasure by ringing her home and leaving a message. The only other alternative was to drive over to the cove and hail her aboard the boat but that had its disadvantages too, for I was reluctant to give her the impression that I couldn't stay away from her. In the end I went to see Ben Dagmar, the editor of the *Messenger*. He seemed to me the best source of advice about the prospects of a job in Fleet Street, or on a big provincial paper.

Ben was an interesting character. At this time he was over sixty and a confirmed old bachelor, living in a large flat over his newspaper premises on East Stump. He was a first-class local journalist but a bit of a misanthropist and we all knew how this had come about. His father, Simon Dagmar, who founded the paper in the eighteen-seventies, had been one of those savage old Puritans who could be found anywhere among Britain's small-town tradesmen up to and even after the First World War. Ben's childhood and youth had been purgatory. Older residents told me that he had been kept hard at work from the age of about eleven, learning his trade in the printing office, and later doing the books. He was thrashed for the slightest fault and he spent all day Sunday and most week nights at the

Wesleyan Chapel. In spite of this he somehow found time to meet, woo and ultimately seduce Hetty Harding, the former pilot's daughter. The scandal resulting from this had rocked the town.

Harding, himself a prominent member of the Wesleyan Community, took it out on Hetty in the way Victorian fathers usually did when their womenfolk went off the rails. He skinned her hide and then marched round to see Simon Dagmar, having got more than a hint of who was responsible for his daughter's pregnancy. Ben Dagmar admitted paternity and there was a frightful scene in the printing office, where Ben stood up to his father for the first time in his life and told both him and Harding that he would not only marry Hetty at once but take her away from Redcliffe Bay, even if they had to beg their way to a town where there were people who could show a little more charity. Then, learning of Hetty's thrashing, he punched his prospective father-in-law on the nose and hurried down to the Quay Cottages where Hetty lived. He was about half an hour too late. Hetty had drowned herself in the dock, after tying a half-hundredweight anchor to her neck.

Ben never really recovered from the shock of seeing her body fished out. He never spoke to his father after that, and at the inquest he indicted old Harding as a murderer. Old Simon must have relented somewhat for when he died, soon afterwards, he left his son the business, one of the best in town, and Ben had been editor of the paper ever since. His troubles had done something to develop a natural originality and all of us around Stump liked and respected him. He was fairly well off for a Redcliffian tradesman and, unlike most of them, extremely generous. He lived frugally and gave most of his money away. He wasn't once fooled by a plausible hard-luck story but selected his beneficiaries with care. He had given me good advice in the past and I went to him now, telling him how things stood with me.

He surprised me by his first comment. "I should hang on if you can, Pip," he advised, "because this place won't stay like it is. It's going to grow and an established business here is going to make money in the forties and fifties. It's hard to believe right now but it is so. People are going to have more money to spend on non-essentials and holidays are top of the list! Holiday-makers spend money on photography and my advice to you is to scrape together all you can, do the place up and worry Trumper into selling it! I could lend you a deposit and I dare-say the bank would give you a mortgage. After all, you're young and keen and this town needs young blood. Let me talk to the bank manager and Rufus Trumper and see if I can persuade them to meet you."

I thanked him for his interest and his generosity. His proposal put a different complexion on things and as I went back along Stump I thought ruefully of Lorna's snide comments on the impregnable selfishness of small townsfolk, for here were two of them already offering me practical help.

I kept my promise to attend the children's fancy-dress competition and baby show that afternoon. The Church Hall was a pandemonium of Little Bo-Peeps, Robin Hoods, Dick Turpins, gnomes, elves, fairies and ballerinas, with rank after rank of mothers trying to hypnotize the judges into pinning a first on their offspring. The din was frightful. Some children were screaming with disappointment, others with triumph and all were sliding up and down the polished floor and cannoning into one another, the impacts provoking renewed uproar.

Esta, who was not acting as a judge, sat on the platform with her attendants, beaming down on this revel. She saw me at once and gestured with her sceptre. I waved and smiled and then took a batch of pictures. During the tea interval I had a few words with her when she came down into the hall to judge the baby show, which had been postponed because there were far more entries in the older groups than had been anticipated. I approached her cautiously, as though I sensed she could read of my recent experiences on my forehead, and she must have noticed something odd about my manner for she said, "You look peaky, Pip! I had no idea you were so attached to poor old Birdie. You never gave me the impression that you liked him that much."

"He was a habit," I said, feeling grateful to him for handing me a red herring. "It was a shock to find the old chap lying there dying when I came in that night."

At that moment who should bustle up but Doctor Morney-Sutcliffe, barking, "Now, now, come, come, Your Gracious Majesty! Get these infant subjects of yours sorted out before they begin caterwauling!" and I looked at him with morbid interest and no guilt whatsoever. It seemed to me, in fact, that I was looking at him for the first time. He was no longer the Emperor of Redcliffe Bay but a puppet ruler, sustained by his own bluff and everyone else's ignorance. It was not difficult, studying him objectively, to see a baffled husband making a cheerless Friday-night visit to his wife's bedroom and finding himself faced with a situation that he could not begin to understand and was therefore forced to treat with his own prescription of medical bluff. Somehow, bouncing up and down on his small feet, and chivvying officials this way and that, he seemed almost pathetic.

Then I was able to dismiss him and concentrate on Esta, as she moved smilingly along the line of cribs and perambulators, trying to equate pinkness and plumpness with physical excellence. She looked, I thought, not only regal but much prettier than I remembered, with her dark, freshly-waved hair compressed by the crown and her trim little figure flattered by the panels of her close-fitting bodice. Her cheeks had their bright spots of color and her make-up had been professionally applied. She was clearly enjoying herself and had more or less dismissed me, despite the urgency of her voice on the phone earlier in the day. I thought, a little sourly, she just wants me dancing attendance on her like everyone else. My presence here was only needed as the last piece in the jigsaw, and I probably did her a gross injustice when her sister Jonquil sidled up, saying, with a fatuity that I found disagreeable, "What's all this I hear about having you wished on me for a brother-in-law? Is it true, or is Esta pulling our legs?"

I don't know why this should have annoyed me. I had said nothing to Esta about keeping it a secret and she had every right, I suppose, to tell her family that we intended getting married sooner or later. I said, brutally, "A good deal has happened since then and things aren't the same as they were! As long as this bloody nonsense accounts for every minute of her day we can't even discuss it!"

It was an unnecessarily blunt disclaimer and I knew it, even at the time, and before Jonquil's face went blank with surprise. The fact was I didn't want to talk about it; all I wanted to do was to reopen my line of retreat in some way, and for the life of me I couldn't find a way of doing it in a way that wouldn't devastate her. It wasn't that I wanted to drop Esta altogether, or that in my heart I regretted having discussed marriage with her. It was just that at the moment we were occupying completely separate worlds and that I thought of hers in the same terms as Lorna thought of it. This wouldn't have mattered much had it not been for the fact that she had been elevated to a very prominent position in that world and could no longer sit on the fence, as we had both done since January. She had now jumped down into the safe side, whereas I had crossed over into the unexplored. I began to think of her then not as a partner but as a child to whom it was impossible to communicate the advantages and disadvantages of becoming an adult. Jonquil said nothing in reply to my churlish remark but just gaped, obviously out of her depth, and then one baby's roar touched off another and then another until the hall rocked with discordant uproar. It was all I needed. The chorus of wails was an alarm bell counselling flight. I went out of the hall, down Fore Street and back across Stump to the studio. I had to have time to think and plan.

I locked the door and pulled down the yellow blinds, sitting in the darkened room as though I was afraid of sunlight. I tried to evaluate Ben Dagmar's offer but the pounds, shillings and pence of the situation had no power to engage my concentration. All I could think of was the threat behind them which, reduced to its simplest terms, meant lifelong detention in Redcliffe Bay and the perambulator under the stairs. I was prey to the kind of panic bridegrooms experience a day or two before the wedding, and I fought it with a generous shot of Lorna's brandy, taken neat. I wasn't used to brandy and it made me splutter but once it had gone down it not only steadied me but made me feel reckless. I got up and took down the painting book, but in opening the pages to have another look at the Hon. Mrs. Graham, I came across Titian's *Venus of Urbino*, described there as the most perfect of all nude portraits. Discounting the slightly simpering face the body reminded me sharply of Lorna's as she lay on her back in the water, and the combination of painting and brandy made me feel so amorous that I began to shake. I have a conviction that this particular moment was a new watershed as far as my feelings concerned Lorna. In the beginning I had been immensely flattered by her interest but after our meeting at her home the certainty that she was using me as an emotional safety valve, and would never risk engaging in more than a patronizing flirtation, checked any sympathy I might have felt for her as the frustrated wife of the local bigwig. Then, when she rang back the night Birdie died, I saw her less as a sophisticated woman, who might or might not use me as a means of hitting back at the Doctor, but as a friend who understood my situation far more intelligently than anyone, not excluding Esta. All my mixed feelings about her were resolved, however, by the afternoon and evening on the boat, and that not so much by the pleasure of possessing her as a woman but because I could not help but sympathize with her, seeing her as a local Andromeda awaiting a champion. This idealization survived our parting and was reinforced by my observation of the Doctor at the fancy-dress parade but now, as I turned the pages of the painting encyclopedia, I began to identify her with every sensual beauty whose charms had been transferred to canvas over the centuries and there was nothing particularly idealistic about the way I thought of her. She represented fulfillment, but fulfillment on a physical level. She was my private Venus of Urbino and my personal Venus of Giorgione, Corregio, Titian, Veronese and Rubens. She was endowed with all the revealed delights of a mythological goddess, as seen by all the painters of the great romantic period. She was Leda,

Danae and Eve, especially Baldung's Eve, the superb nude he painted in 1525, in which his model is seen flirting with fig leaves yet preserving the elusive modesty that expresses the contrast between the sexuality of male and female. The more I looked at these pictures and compared them with the memories I had of Lorna's pink and white flesh, the more certain I was that I was not only in love with her but had been, as it were, converted by her. She was a symbol of freedom from the moral shackles of all places like Redcliffe Bay. She not only offered physical gratification but also—and I think at that time this was the more important—freedom from all the restrictions and frustrations of my life up to that time. Separation from her became refined torture and prevented me from concentrating on anything else.

Not even Birdie's funeral, conducted in blazing sunshine and in the presence of a knot of familiars taking time off from the carnival, succeeded in banishing thoughts of her for an hour. As for the trivialities of the carnival itself, and my work in recording them for the local newspapers, I hardly bothered to focus my lens, resenting the distraction they represented. I slept badly and when I was asleep I dreamed of her and awoke yearning for her. Mr. Snell came through with what he thought a far more reasonable offer from Annie Vetch—I could buy the goodwill for eight hundred pounds, to be paid in quarterly payments over a period of two years—but I didn't clinch, telling him I would think it over. Ben Dagmar was better than his word. He bullied Rufus Trumper into renewing the studio lease for five years on existing terms, and also persuaded the bank manager to advance me four hundred for redecorations and equipment, on his guarantee of that sum. One way and another things were falling out for me far better than I had any right to expect but I couldn't put Lorna out of my mind for long enough to congratulate myself. What was going on around me might have been the distant blare of the municipal band on the sea front, or the passage of a covey of gulls across the patch of open sky between East and West Stump. All I thought of was Lorna's mouth, Lorna's breasts, Lorna's thighs and, in my less urgent moments, Lorna's voice and Lorna's hair spread like a mantilla as she floated in the bay. I was like a man on a hunger strike tormenting himself with mirages of exotic banquets and I watched the telephone as a castaway scans the horizon for a sail.

I have no clear recollection of the remainder of that week. I saw Esta now and again but never alone and had she not been so absorbed in her obligations as Water Queen she must have noticed my total abstraction. As it was I don't think she did, beyond presupposing that I had taken a surprisingly hard knock over Birdie's death. She probably put off thinking about me until the carnival ended with what was called "Cavalcade Day," a Saturday evening procession of Queen, Neptune and prize-winning tableaux to all the villages north and west of the town. The following day, Sunday, would be her first real break and she would almost surely cross the Stump and tackle me about the future. In the event this is what she did but by then she was too late by twelve hours.

I should have accompanied the carnival's progress to the villages, of course, but I didn't. I was sick of the sight of flower-decked drays and the pom-tiddly-pom strains of the local British Legion's martial music. On Saturday I came in off the street about six o'clock with the serious intention of composing a long letter to Lorna, confessing that I found life insupportable without her. I put off thinking how I would convey such a letter to her without dispatching it through the post and thereby risking enquiries by the Doctor, but I had to find some emotional outlet for the terrible yearning I felt for her and it seemed to me, in my muddled state of mind, that a declaration might prompt her to communicate with me.

I locked the studio door, shut out the light as usual, and had carried notepaper into the cashier's cubicle when the telephone rang for the first time that day. I jumped as though someone had taken a shot at me through the fanlight. Even before I lifted the receiver I knew it was her.

Her voice sounded warm and friendly but by no means

urgent as she greeted me with "Hullo there! How's tricks? Is it still on with the motley, you poor devil?"

I must have gobbled into the phone because she asked me to repeat what I had said and the pause gave me a chance to control the tremor in my voice. I admitted that I had given the carnival a miss that night, and then went on to tell her something of what had occurred in the way of securing the business.

"You sound undecided," she said, when I stopped talking. "Are you, or is it my fancy?"

"Look, Lorna," I said, clutching at this straw, "I've got to talk to you about everything! I am undecided, but I have to make up my mind about the lease and about Mrs. Vetch's proposition within a day or two. When can I see you?"

"Why not tonight?" she said lazily, and my heart seemed to leap onto the table and bounce across the floor to Birdie's potted palm.

"Oh God, I should love to!" I blurted. "Where are you phoning from?"

I heard her chuckle but the sound did nothing to shame me. I didn't give a damn what she thought of me or what mood she was in. All I knew was that I was to see her within hours.

"From Phillips's Farm, on top of the goyle," she said, "where I park the car when I'm over here."

"You mean you'll meet me there?"

"No, of course I won't, idiot, but I'm here for the weekend. I shan't go aboard tonight because it's clouding over. I shall sleep in the boathouse. Don't come via the goyle. Go along the cliffs as far as the iron ladder, above Shelly Beach, then back along the shingle bank. You'll be able to get round the point, the tide will be at full ebb by the time you get here."

"You mean I'm to wait until dark?"

"Well, let's say dusk!" and I heard her chuckle again.

I remembered then that you could get down to the beach a mile or so east of her cove and pass the enclosing headland when the tide was out. I said joyfully that I would be along about ten o'clock but that it would help if she kept a light burning to guide me across the shingle.

"Naturally," she said gaily, "in the best romantic tradition!" and then the phone went dead, causing me to wonder if one of the Phillips family had clumped into the hall of the farm-house.

I had about three hours to fill somehow before I set out and I knew I couldn't work. I let myself out on Stump and looked up at the sky. She was right about the weather. It was clouding in the west and I saw that the long, fine spell would soon be over and that rain would fall before dawn. I went across the enclosure and down to the sea front as far as the Municipal Gardens, where the carnival sideshows were competing for the last pennies of the week. The patrons were few but there was a small group at the miniature rifle range where a tall, broad-shouldered young man was winning too many prizes. As I moved closer I recognized him as Mike Shapley, manager of the recently-opened Duckworth's on the premises of the old Penny Bazaar. It was the first time I had got a good look at him, although I had heard Jonquil Wallace and other girls around town describe him as the Sheik. By 1932 Sheiks were going out of fashion but they were still to be found in places like Redcliffe Bay, where the Valentino legend lingered. Personally, I wouldn't have given Mike Shapley that label. The Buccaneer, maybe, or the Wide Boy, but not the Sheik, in spite of his sideburns and suntan. He was more masculine and much beefier than the silent screen heroes. You couldn't imagine him stealing into Vilma Banky's tent and running a scale of kisses up and down her arm. He would have been more at home in a flashy West End bar, exchanging jokes with the boys and wearing a public-school tie that he was not qualified to wear, but perhaps this does him an injustice. He would have worn the tie but he would almost certainly have boasted of his disqualification. He was that kind of man, cheerfully aggressive and very sure of himself as a lady-killer and a good mixer. They were already saying he was making a go of the store and also that he had a sharp eye for a buxom assistant and was a paid-up member of the Wandering Hand Society. He drove a green, three-wheeled Morgan and sometimes breezed into the bar of the Lamb and Flag, wearing a scarf as long as a winding sheet with its ends trailing. He played a bit of golf and seemed to have money to burn. I had taken a vague dislike to him on sight and this was reinforced by the negligent way he handled the rifle and enjoyed impressing us with his marksmanship. I saw two or three of the local girls eyeing him appreciatively and when he distributed his trumpery prizes with an air of a baron's son showering largesse on the peasants, I wondered how long he would last in a conservative little town like ours, and how spectacular would be his exit. He had that air about him; everything that happened to him would fizz and crackle but somehow, in the end, he would never amount to much.

When he turned away and lounged over to his car I noticed that, discounting his flashiness, he was what most people would regard as handsome, at least by the standards of that day. He had dark, crisp hair, with a natural wave in it, and regular features, with a thinnish nose and a slightly jutting chin. His eyes were brown and impudent and he walked like a man who believes he has only to drop an eyelid in any woman's direction to make her want to go to bed with him. He was, I suppose, about Lorna's age, maybe a year or so older. I don't know why I took such careful note of him that particular night but I did, watching him pile a couple of girls into his passenger seat, give a devil-may-care flick to his trailing scarf and accelerate with unnecessary emphasis in the direction of the Esplanade. Then I forgot him and tried my own hand at several sideshows, willing the minutes to pass before I could set out without the certainty of arriving at the iron ladder in daylight.

It seemed an outrageously long evening and was still light when I passed the head of the goyle and drove down the rutted lane that ran parallel to the cliffs. High above Shelly Bay I found a spot to park and sat smoking a cigarette until a few heavy spots of rain arrived with the fall of dusk. Then I wrestled with the perished hood of the car and set out for the iron ladder, dropping down onto the beach about three quarters of a mile east of the cove.

It was difficult walking here in loose shingle. Several times I tripped and almost fell over drift logs and other flotsam marking the tideline, but once I had worked my way down to the narrow strip of sand I struck out and rounded the point, still lapped by about six inches of water. Her light was burning, a tiny orange glow at the foot of the goyle, and I made straight towards it, like a fogbound wayfarer careless of his shinbones. I walked noisily, rattling the pebbles, so that she heard my approach and opened the boathouse door, standing silhouetted with the lamplight directly behind her. I called, eagerly, "It's me, Lorna!" and she called back, "I wasn't expecting anyone else!" Then she was in my arms and the thrust of her tongue told me she was as impatient as I was. The thought gave me a sense of triumph that no personal relationship since has yielded.

She said, as soon as the door was closed and locked, "Did you really come here for sisterly advice, Kent?" and I said no. She said, laughing, that she was relieved to hear it, for she wasn't in the mood to give it. When I kissed her again she inclined her body towards mine so sharply that my back struck the protruding key and I gave an involuntary yelp and her laughter gave me a brief opportunity to study the interior of the place over her shoulder.

It was not really a boathouse but more of a chalet, with oak benches, cupboards, a big cushioned divan and large rugs covering the space where the boat was housed during the winter. There were chintz curtains drawn over the little window facing the sea and an oil lamp on the mock refectory table at the back. There was even a brick fireplace surrounded with large pebbles set edgewise, the empty grate screened by a three-panel oval on which an amateur artist had drawn pictures of clippers and paddle-steamers riding a rough sea. It was cozy but the taste wasn't Lorna's. I could see that at a glance and assumed she had rented it from the Phillips family at the head of the goyle, who probably built it years ago to store the seaweed they collected for manure.

I sat on the divan and pulled her down on my knee, feeling far more at ease with her than at any time since we had been paired off by the Doctor at the dance.

"You're getting to be quite a habit, Kent!" she said, and as a remark it was a rangefinder. We were given to that kind of thing in the early stages of our association. The moment we met we began probing one another's moods, both trying it on a little and sometimes, as now, achieving a compromise between jocularity and lust. I told her that I hadn't had a thought in my head that didn't concern her since we had last met and she said she was glad to hear it because she had "warmed to me in retrospect." She qualified this by saying, "I daresay it derives from having a lover fresh from school! That would help any woman to slough off the years!"

"For God's sake don't start on about your age," I told her, gruffly. "I daresay it gives you a sense of superiority but it makes me feel about fourteen, with a pash on the Latin mistress!"

"Did you have mistresses like that up at that dreary Secondary School?"

"We had one, but she only lasted a term."

"Tell me about her!"

"Are you serious?"

"Certainly I am; I hardly know a thing about you, except that you were a poor orphan boy, sold into slavery with that awful photographer, Boxwell."

"Boxall," I said, "and go easy on him, I've just come from his funeral."

"Oh, never mind him. Tell me about the Latin mistress."

I told her of the old scandal—it seemed old to me—of Miss Gould, who had set the town by the ears during my last year at school. No one ever understood how she came to be appointed unless it was a grim joke on the part of a retiring headmaster. She was in her late twenties, possessed a figure she liked to emphasize with tight jumpers and was reputed to have her hair peroxided once a month. She had pretty legs too and there was great competition among the senior boys to sit directly under the teacher's dais, where they could study them at leisure while memorizing declensions. We boys clubbed together and bet Bob Thatcher, the most enterprising of our monitors, that he wouldn't take her to the pictures in Paxtonbury. He accepted the bet and against all probability Miss Gould agreed to go and they held hands but that was all. On the way home they were spotted sitting close together in a first-class railway carriage and any plans they might have had for improving the occasion were scotched by Prebble, the Maths master, who saw them when the train stopped at Moorend Halt. He went into their compartment and refused to be shaken off until he had seen Miss Gould enter her lodgings alone, and he must have reported the matter for Miss Gould disappeared at the end of the term and Bob Thatcher had to be satisfied with his winnings, the pooled pocket-money of 5A, 5B and the Sixth.

"How absolutely typical of Redcliffe Bay!" Lorna said, laughing. "What happened to her afterwards?"

"Nobody knows," I said, "but there were plenty of rumors. One had it that she ran off with a Persian carpet-seller who sold rugs from door to door, and another that she married a Bristol undertaker. It was probably the undertaker."

"Did you enjoy your schooldays?"

I said more than most people, largely because the Secondary School was co-ed, and she said that this made sense because I was obviously a precocious boy as far as girls were concerned. She didn't believe this, of course, but said it as a half-hearted attempt to shift some of the responsibility onto my shoulders.

We sat on the divan a long time, talking of this and that, and listening to the steady drumming of the rain on the roof. I thought briefly of the effect the storm must be having upon the royal progress round the villages. By now the decorated drays and floats would present a bedraggled and woebegone spectacle, colors running from the folds of crêpe paper, and the Queen and her attendants huddled under umbrellas and mackintoshes if they had any. I was glad I hadn't gone along. It was warm and cozy here with Lorna and I began to feel smug about my progress with her. Her gaiety, enjoyed in such delightful isolation, appeased the demands that had brought me here in such a tearing hurry. It was quite dark outside now and the rain was still lashing the western wall of the cabin and skittering along the shingle roof so that for once the clandestine element was absent from the occasion. We fooled around a little between spells of talk, but lightly and inconsequentially, more like a couple of kids sheltering from a storm on the way home from a ramble than a married woman entertaining a randy young cub in a boathouse. I remember being surprised at the tenor of the evening and I had reason to be surprised. All that week, and especially since I had heard her voice on the telephone, I had yearned for her like a bridegroom deprived of his bride in the middle of a honeymoon, but now that we were together, with no one closer than the Phillips family at the head of the goyle, I found that I could enjoy her company in a way that would have been unimaginable earlier in the day. She sprawled on the divan, half her weight resting on my shoulder, as though we sat like this every night of the week and it was because of this that I was startled when she said, in an incidental tone, "I suppose you realize you're here for the night, Kent? You can't go round that point again until the tide ebbs. Did you think to check the time before you left?"

I said I hadn't given the tide a thought and that I could easily find my way up the goyle and back to the car in the dark. "I used to go beachcombing when I was a kid," I told her, "and know the country between here and Shelly Bay like the back of my hand!"

"I'm sure you do," she said, "but you don't know Mrs. Phillips. If you passed that farm in the dark the dogs would start barking and Mrs. Phillips would listen to hear me drive off in my car. When she didn't hear my engine start she would know damned well I had company down here. Why else do you suppose I told you to come along the beach?"

It crossed my mind for the first time that perhaps she had been lying when she told me she had never taken a lover since marrying the Doctor. The sudden spurt of jealousy, prompted by the thought that other young hopefuls had visited here when her husband was otherwise engaged, was like a sharp twinge of rheumatism and I at once gave expression to it, saying, "Since when have you been concerned about Redcliffe Bay gossip?"

I regretted the remark the moment it was out because she swung her legs to the floor and hoisted herself up, but she didn't have to reprove me. I had apologized before she had straightened her skirt.

"I'll go back the way I came," I said abjectly, "but won't there be just as much chance of someone seeing me from the cliffs?"

"No, there won't," she said, sharply, "because you'll leave before it's light and wade around if necessary!"

"I'm sorry, Lorna," I said, certain now that I had offended her but she wasn't offended, or no more so than a mother might have been when a child questioned the wisdom of a road safety precaution. She smiled down at my chapfallen expression and said, quietly and reasonably, "You've nothing to be sorry about, Kent, or not so long as it's understood I do the thinking for both of us! I told you on Saturday that I'm not ready to make the break yet, and I don't want to be hustled into having to make it by the kind of confrontation thrust upon your Miss Gould!" Then she dismissed the subject and suddenly became very businesslike, saying, "I've got a lobster and I can make coffee on the Primus. Or if you're not hungry I've got drinks. There's gin, whisky and wine. Beaune, I think. Do you like Burgundy?"

I said I had never had an opportunity to find out and she laughed and kissed me, saying, "That's what's refreshing about you, Kent! You don't pretend, do you? Almost everybody back there does in one way or another. We'll eat later but in the meantime treat your palate to a little Beaune. You haven't lived until you've acquired a taste for French wines. You can't even buy a good Burgundy in Redcliffe Bay, did you know that?"

I said that I didn't know it and watched her open a bottle of Beaunc as casually as I would have opened a tin of pineapple chunks. The wine was every bit as pleasant as she promised and after two brimming glasses I began to feel almost as amorous as when she had asked me to dry her back.

She wasn't in any hurry, however, or perhaps she was bent on teasing again, for when I tried to lay hands on her and pull her down on the divan she sidestepped me and held up her glass of wine, daring me to rush her and spill it. She really was in a playful mood that night, just how playful I didn't fully appreciate until she put down the glass and began to undress, saying, "No rough stuff tonight, Kent! That's my prerogative, remember."

She took off her clothes in what I later came to recognize as a ritual, rather like an extremely conscientious whore who insists on giving value for money. At that time striptease had not been elevated to an art but her leisurely shedding of garments anticipated the cult. She didn't indulge in any fancy gestures, but all the time, and in every movement she made, she studied the effect upon her audience. First she eased the sweater over her head without disturbing her hair and then she stepped out of her sandals, very delicately and deliberately, like a cat walking over wet ground. She slipped off her skirt and petticoat and stood smiling at me for a moment in a brassiere and a pair of wide-legged panties. Both garments were novelties to me because we were still within hailing distance of the flat-chested twenties when girls tried to pretend that bosoms didn't exist, whereas the kind of knickers she was wearing would have drawn a small crowd if they had been displayed in the window of Madame Marcelle's, Redcliffe Bay's leading dress shop. She was having fun and, in a different way, so was I. But by the time she had disposed of these two items and was standing there to be admired, I wasn't looking for laughs but was finding a new kind of meaning for the line from the Ancient and Modern hymn they taught us at Sunday School—the one describing pilgrims as being lost in wonder, love and praise. In a way, I suppose, I was a kind of pilgrim, worshiping at a shrine a good deal older than any set up by Christianity. Years later, when I came across the old Greek story of the Cnidian Venus who, knowing herself to be overlooked by male worshipers, laid aside all pretense of Olympian majesty and accepted the desire she roused as normal, healthy tribute to her perfect proportions, I thought of Lorna Morney-Sutcliffe as she appeared to me at that moment, cool, detached and accessible, her lips parted in a smile, one hand poised on the back of the divan, the other pretending to shield the reddish-gold tuft between her thighs. To me she was quite perfect; to me she was the Venus of Urbino, Giorgione's Venus, and the model of every artist of the great romantic period of painting. On another level she was Madame Du Barry, Madame Pompadour and every Restoration beauty painted by Lely and bedded by Charles II. Naked, she had a kind of innocence that made me half-ashamed of the frankly carnal thoughts I had entertained of her up to that time.

"You're beautiful, Lorna!" I said fervently. "Nobody could be more perfect!" and although this was no more than an echo of what I had said to her on the boat, this time she did not dismiss it as the cry of a lovesick boy after his first clumsy attempt to possess a woman. Neither was there any hint of the maternal attitude she had demonstrated on that occasion, but instead a restrained thankfulness that she was able to bring someone so much delight with so little effort, and this thankfulness was latent in her submission. This time there was no haste or impatience on my part and certainly none on hers. There was no sense of guilt either, for afterwards, when I held her and listened to the thrumming of the rain on the roof and the spaced gusts of the gale, it seemed to me that nobody but myself had any right to her, that Morney-Sutcliffe had somehow blundered into her life and would soon blunder out again, surrendering his rights, if he ever had any, to me. I wasn't worried about the complications and I gave no thought at all to the future or to where this involvement would lead us. Time, and the tide outside, had ceased to exist for me. There was only Lorna's body, Lorna's red-gold hair and the ecstacy of knowing that I was her lover.

I remember that she confirmed this sense of triumph when she broke the silence between us and said, running her hand over my hair, "I'll tell you something, Kent. Don't go on underestimating yourself. You do, you know, and you shouldn't. You might have something special for women—or a certain type of woman, and it's not common. You learn quickly about them and most men never do, but there's more to it than that."

It was exciting to know that I could bring her as much fulfilment as she brought me and I pressed her to explain. I had no impatience to dominate her. I was more than content to remain a student in her academy. She said, beginning to dress, "This would have gone to most boys' heads. They would have strutted around telling themselves that they were personally indispensable to a married woman, and a woman a lot older than themselves!"

"It's gone to my head," I admitted.

"Not in the way I mean. You're content to be led and you don't crow about it the minute it's over."

"Do most men?"

"Most men under forty. They're timid enough to begin with but on the third or fourth occasion they behave as if they were the only male animals in the zoo who could perform!" She thought a minute. "It has to do with your approach to a woman's body," she said, at length. "It's a romantic and semi-reverent approach, and I've decided that it isn't solely because you happen to be young and totally inexperienced. I think it's part of your make-up, so don't squander it. It's pleasing and flattering and rather rare!"

I supposed then that I owed this gracious compliment to Morney-Sutcliffe's abysmal ignorance of her susceptibilities, and perhaps her Paris lovers had fallen into the error of approaching her with the same brusqueness, so that she was vulnerable to my humility and perhaps genuinely moved when it was not at once translated to dominance. If this was so then she had as much to learn about me as I had about her. The truth was, of course, that I never did overcome the handicap imposed on me by our age, experience and above all, the difference in our social status in Redcliffe Bay. Physical possession of her was such an achievement that it suspended the power to make any accurate assessment of her as a person. She was always someone who had descended the long flight of steps to meet me and I never ceased to regard her bestowal as a kind of miracle performed by a local goddess in a moment of earthiness.

I don't think she ever really came to terms with this so that she thought of my humility, and the gratitude I displayed towards her, as a deliberate surrender of male triumph, as though

I acted from motives of chivalry and perhaps modesty, whereas it wasn't like that at all. As she said, she knew little or nothing about me, or the forces that conditioned my approach to her. She did not understand, for instance, that I was hamstrung by a sense of loneliness and isolation that was uncommon even among people who lived out their lives in places like Redcliffe Bay. Almost everyone back there was a member of a family unit, and most of them had ancestors in the local churchyard. I had no family and was aware of no ancestors, so that I had to hunt for the component parts of a makeshift background. In the light of what I learned of her much later, maybe I am wrong about her appraisal. Perhaps she sensed that we were far more alike in this respect than either of us knew at that time, and perhaps it was this intuitive feeling that led her to cultivate me in preference to all the young lovers she might have attracted among people of her own class, young officers home on leave in the big Avenue houses, or even the sons of well-heeled professional men in Paxtonbury. I like to think this was true. It softens the outlines of our association.

We had our supper, lobster, homebaked bread from the farm and strong, bitter coffee. We smoked some of her Turkish cigarettes and listened to her obligatory gramophone recital. She had picked up one or two more up-to-date numbers, our old friend *Auf Wiedersehen*, and the dirge *Muddy Water*. She also had an excerpt recording of Noel Coward's *Private Lives*, telling me she had seen the comedy during one of her frequent trips to town. The rain had stopped now and when I looked at my watch I saw that it was past four o'clock, and realized that it would be dawn by the time I regained the point and climbed the shingle banks to the iron ladder. She hadn't mentioned anything about Morney-Sutcliffe's decision, if there was one, regarding the possibility of him taking a London practice, and when I asked her if there had been any developments at home she said that the Doctor had been so absorbed in town affairs during the past week that she had had no opportunity to speak to him. She made it clear that she had no wish to reopen the subject of their relationship, so I thought it best not to persist but to let things take their course, especially as some kind of master plan was even then forming in my mind. The prospect of devoting serious thought to this plan moderated my regret at parting from her without a firm arrangement about another meeting. All she said when I hinted at this was, "I'll get in touch; you're still on the telephone, aren't you?" It began to dawn on me that she enjoyed this arrangement of having me poised and ready to run to her side, like a dog to a whistle; but I didn't resent it, not at that time. I was satisfied with the near-certainty that I was necessary to her and that the last traces of patronage were disappearing from her overall attitude towards me. She kissed me goodbye like a young wife dispatching her suburban husband to catch the eight-forty-five and this in itself represented a substantial advance on our last parting.

Faint streaks of light were showing beyond Shelly Bay as I picked my way along the tideline to the point. The tide still had two hours to ebb, and the water round the sandstone knob reached to my thighs but I hardly noticed it. The air was sweet and fresh after the storm, and the sea was empty of everything but gulls riding the swell. I climbed the ladder, found the path and reached the car just as the sun peeped over the edge of the bay. The birds in the thicket were singing in chorus and raindrops gleamed on every twig. There was a pool of rainwater on my driving seat but I didn't mind that either. I was riding life like a clipper under full sail and wherever I went Lorna went with me, the scent of her hair mingling with the smell of wild flowers coming out of the woods. Down I went, through steep-banked lanes, until I struck the head of the gradient leading to the Valley, and there, as I swung hard left at Posthorse Cross, was Redcliffe Bay, looking as if it had been poured into the triangular cleft between the high masses of sandstone spreading inland from Coastguard Hill to Mitre Head.

I stopped the car, as I often did when I was returning home this way, and sat looking down on the sprawl of houses contained by the wide curve of the Esplanade. A few wisps of smoke rising from terrace-house chimneys beyond the railway picked out the early risers, but the narrow streets converging on Stump were so still and empty that the town looked as if it was awaiting the first French *émigrés* in the eighteenth century. Not a gull crossed my line of vision; the only signs of animation down there, on my side of the goods yard, were the spirals of smoke and the twinkle of sunlight on the glistening, trident lamp standards and their festoons of fairy-lights. It was at that moment that the idea formulating in the back of my mind fizzed and exploded. Suddenly I knew precisely what I had to do and how to go about it. As I released the handbrake and coasted down the Valley road to Stump the church clock struck six.

I parked the car in the alley and went in through the back door, pausing only to put the kettle on the gas stove. Then I went on through to the studio, raising the blinds, opening the shop door and stepping out onto the gleaming pavement to take a good look at the premises, wedged between Myfanwy Pritchard's Gift Shop, and Applegarth's book store to the south. They were not impressive now but there was nothing a jobbing builder and a couple of coats of paint couldn't put right. I went back inside, closed the door and foraged among a pile of trade journals until I found last week's issue. My memory had not deceived me. The small-ad page displayed a half-column of wants on the part of photographers from all over the British Isles, and among them were at least three whose requirements fitted my plan. Every week, I recalled, advertisements like these were inserted by professionals seeking to invest in modest businesses in a holiday town—aging men tired of city life, who fancied semiretirement beside the sea; junior partners hoping to break away from prosperous studios in London, Leeds and Manchester; young hopefuls like myself, with a small amount of capital to invest in a shop. The solution was so simple that I was surprised I had not thought of it long ago. All I had to do was to get a long lease from Trumper, accept Annie Vetch's offer about the goodwill, and use the overdraft Ben Dagmar had arranged for me, to modernize and redecorate the place so that it looked more prosperous than it was and offered someone the chance of making a modest living. It would cost, I calculated, around four hundred pounds, but it would be money well spent. Once it was done I could advertise it at something around two thousand pounds, including goodwill and apparatus and this, after Annie Vetch had been paid off, would leave me around one thousand two hundred. I had enough savings to pay for more than half the renovations, so that when all was settled I would be left with about a thousand plus to start a new life with Lorna. It seemed to me a very substantial sum indeed, the basis of a fortune, and if this sounds impossibly naïve it should be remembered that a thousand pounds then would be worth at least four times as much today. With a thousand pounds in my pocket I could afford to pick and choose a city job, perhaps even buy my way into a fashionable studio in London or abroad. I didn't pause to reflect upon how Lorna would view this amount in terms of a float. I had confidence in my earning ability and my professional skill and it seemed to me more than enough to give me the necessary breathing space I needed to prove this to her after she had turned her back on Morney-Sutcliffe. I sat down in the reception cubicle and did a series of little sums, and then I made a tour of the premises, listing what had to be done and estimating what it would cost. I was so happy at my work that I forgot I had put the kettle on and when I reached the kitchen it was full of steam. I finished my calculations, made some tea and found myself yawning over it so I stretched out on the couch intending to take a cat nap. I was there when roused by an imperious rapping on the shop door and rubbed the sleep from my eyes as I went through, certain in my own mind that it would be Esta, asking why I hadn't shown up for the royal progress the night before. I was actually rehearsing excuses as I fumbled with the bolt but I need not have bothered, or not with the kind of excuses she would accept. When I opened the door, there, on the slate step, stood the Doctor and behind him, parked against the curb, was his big, shiny Daimler.

[2]

I don't think I have ever been so astounded in my life. I stood there, one hand on the door handle, the other knuckling my eyes, blinking in the strong morning sunlight and telling myself I was still asleep and having an exceptionally harrowing nightmare. He looked as impatient as usual but not enraged, and not even testy. He was wearing his usual summer clothes, a well-cut gabardine suit in dove grey, a striped shirt and a blue silk tie, with shoes that twinkled and trousers that had knife-edge creases in them. He carried under his arm a folder, and for a moment the insane notion struck me that it was the folder Lorna had shown me in her attic, back in the spring. I then noticed, however, that its buff covers were stamped with the letters "R.B.U.D.C." which meant that it was directly connected with the local Council and this piece of deduction was the first check on the tide of panic that rose in my throat and almost emerged as a cry of despair. I only stopped it by clamping my jaws together and taking a long, deep breath that whistled, and then I noticed a puzzled expression in his pale blue eyes that remained there until replaced by the familiar, purposeful gleam.

"Well, young feller-me-lad!" he barked, "are you going to keep me on the step all morning? Young chap of your age should have been up and about long before this! I've got a job for you! Might amount to something if you stir your stumps and get busy!"

"It's Sunday," I faltered, and this was about all I could manage, for the relief engendered by his cheery greeting came close to choking me. It gushed over me like a torrent and its effect was as potent as half a bottle of Lorna's cognac taken neat. His presence here was obviously nothing to do with his wife, or my association with her. He was after my camera not my blood, and his business concerned the Redcliffe Bay Foreshore Committee and not the law courts. I have had a number of narrow escapes from death since then, but not even the closest of them afforded anything like as much easement as his words and those tell-tale letters on the file he carried. The experience was unique. It was like hearing and seeing the hangman turn aside and announce the reprieve when his hand was already on the drop-lever.

We went into the studio and I offered him tea and when he

refused this, a glass of beer. I only just stopped offering him some of his own brandy, which was standing on the studio table waiting to be labelled Exhibit Number One in an investigation. Brushing aside my offers of hospitality he said, "No time for that! Not a social call! You and I are going to take a little walk and collect evidence for those fools back there! Fetch your camera, the one you use for outdoor pictures. Ideal morning! Couldn't be better!"

He always employed this clipped form of address when confronting a patient or ratepayer. It had about it a feudal ring, as though he was a bluff Norman baron going his rounds among Saxon tenantry and addressing each of them from the saddle of a mettlesome horse. I was accustomed to it of course but I was particularly aware of it on this occasion. I had to keep reminding myself that, only a few hours before he knocked on my door, I had held his wife in my arms and it was this that made his presence so hard to accept. His request for the camera I used when taking long-range land- and seascapes gave me the respite I needed so badly. I mumbled something about going upstairs to fetch it and then scuttled to the bathroom, locking the door, resting my weight on the washbasin and looking at myself in the spotted mirror.

I was not very flattered by what I saw: a tousled and badly rattled young man, hair distorted, stubble on the chin and naked fear in his eyes. It required a very great effort to pull myself together, wash myself and slip into a sports jacket before going downstairs and asking if he would mind waiting while I shaved.

"Yes, I would mind, young feller-me-lad!" he said, but genially. "I can only spare an hour or so and I want coverage of more than a mile of the dunes from the south, north and east. You can take the eastern shots on the way down, from the elevation of Frog Terrace. Took some myself a week ago but I'm no damned good with a camera. Too impatient maybe!"

It was the first time I had ever heard him admit to a shortcoming and it humanized him to a degree that I found disconcerting. I said, "What are they for, Doctor?" and he told me he was making a private survey of the part of the foreshore that related to his plan for the development east of the bandstand. I knew all about this plan. You couldn't live in Redcliffe Bay and not know about it, for Ben Dagmar, who was the Doctor's eager ally in this respect, regularly paraded it before his readers in every issue of the *Messenger*.

As Chairman of the Foreshore Committee Morney-Sutcliffe was then in a minority of two. Ben Dagmar's championship was useful to him but Ben wasn't a Councillor, and what was then recognized as the Progressive Party consisted of the Doctor himself and Garfield Pyne, the West Stump undertaker. They had plenty of active allies in the town as a whole, tradesmen and professional men, who wanted Redcliffe Bay to expand, but so far none of these had been elected and the diehard faction, led by the Doctor's chief rival, Fred Hopkins, the timber merchant, had packed the Foreshore Committee and succeeded in outvoting a progressive policy by six to two. We all knew that this state of affairs couldn't last, and that sooner or later the Doctor's ascendancy would result in him browbeating the opposition and getting younger and more vigorous men elected. But this was how matters stood in the summer of 1932 and the Doctor wasn't the kind of man to wait upon time. He regarded the shelving of his foreshore development plan as a personal insult, aimed at him by Hopkins and Rufus Trumper, and he was very annoyed about its recent deferment by the Committee.

What I didn't know about the plan itself I soon found out, as we drove up to Frog Terrace and positioned ourselves to get some seaward shots of the dunes, taking in the entire area embraced by the scheme. It was a much more ambitious plan than I had supposed and consisted of a parking ground, a pagoda to be leased as a refreshment room, a paddling pool, swimming pool, yachting pool, four hard tennis courts and some beach chalets. It would cost, the doctor said, about thirty thousand pounds but would be partially financed by the Government under one of their crash unemployment schemes set up during the slump the year before. Locally, it would not mean more than a penny rate and the Doctor said it would establish Redcliffe Bay as the most popular holiday resort in the West.

The way he talked one might have supposed him to have

designs on the holiday trade of places like Cannes and Deauville but this was not so; all he really wanted was to assert himself and make the front conform to an orderly pattern. He hated disorder of any sort and he saw the clumps of marram grass on the dunes as evidence of a policy of drift. He liked concrete paths and well-weeded flower beds. He liked pretty little iron railings and Chinese-style shelters, and if it had been left to him, a new public garden east of the bandstand would have fulfilled his requirements. But it wasn't left to him. Ben Dagmar and Garfield Pyne, the undertaker, were deeply committed progressives, who saw big money in town development, and they were using him as their spearhead to initiate a policy that was bitterly opposed by stick-in-the-mud tradesmen and also by the retired army and navy families living in the Valley.

I don't think Morney-Sutcliffe ever realized this. He was so accustomed to deference that the charge of betrayal, levelled at him more than once by neighbors numbered among the town élite, had no power to dismay him, or make him wonder if he was being used by essentially local men, like Dagmar and Pyne, both far better versed in the subtleties of local government than he would ever be. Service on the Council was a hobby to the Doctor; it was a matter of simple economics to the editor of the local paper and the town's most prosperous funeral furnisher.

We went on down to the sea front and took pictures of the dunes as far as Links Road. He made me concentrate on all the untidy patches and things like an overturned litter bin, or a broken bit of fencing, and I became so interested in his approach that, for a spell at least, I was able to relegate Lorna to the back of my mind. He was much more affable than he had ever been and there was something almost likeable about his enthusiasm and the way he took me into his confidence.

"I don't know why I should concern myself to this extent," he said, when he had shown me where the swimming pool would go, and calculated the rent we could get by putting the refreshment pagoda out to tender. "None of it will benefit me a threepenny piece but you ought to support it, a young chap with his way to make in the world! We could make this town into a resort that would be known all over the world!"

"You mean like Blackpool?" I asked him and he winced.

"No!" he snorted, "*not* like Blackpool! Blackpool is a sham, dreamed up by people with a fairground mentality! The only thing good about Blackpool is its sea air, which is very stimulating I'm told, but this place has great natural beauty and all it wants is a little money spent on it, and a little discipline. Now that the slump is receding people are going to have money to spend. In ten years' time every family in the land will have at least a fortnight in which to do nothing. The Trade Unions will see to that, mark my words! Well, why not encourage them to come here, where they can do themselves some good and put money in the pockets of young shavers like you?"

It was the line of propaganda taken by the *Messenger* and that was where he learned it, although he certainly thought of it as original. As a prophecy it was accurate in all but the time factor. In ten years' time the sea front was to bristle with beach obstructions, and the sandbars and groynes were to be sewn in with barbed wire, but you couldn't expect him to guess that. At the time his confidence in the future of Redcliffe Bay impressed me, so that I thought I might raise my asking price for the studio to two thousand five hundred, but this made me remember why I was contemplating a sale and again I felt desperately embarrassed at my presence here on a bright Sunday morning, chit-chatting with a man whose wife I was currently seducing.

The strain increased when he asked me to join him in a pint of beer at the Conservative Club adjoining the grass courts under Frog Terrace. Until then I don't think I had felt any shame over what was happening. I had always thought of him as a pompous ass and since Lorna's recital of his inadequacies as a husband I had begun to look upon him with the arrogance that is the prerogative of the young when they encounter something they can't understand. Now, however, as he handed me a tankard of the best draft you could buy in Redcliffe Bay, I began to have my first doubts. What kind of man was he underneath that familiar façade of bouncing, bustling bossiness? He was a good doctor. I knew that, and wondered how it was possible that a man as stupid as he sometimes seemed could be a competent healer. I also wondered about the impulse that sent him trotting into Lorna's bedroom every Friday night and whether, indeed, her account of this was strictly true. It seemed to me that a man who could pass exams in Edinburgh, build a prosperous practice and also plan a new layout for the foreshore, must possess some glimmer of common sense and dignity. He didn't seem such a bad chap after all when you got to know him, overbearing maybe, and far too satisfied with himself, but weren't we all the moment the people around us gave us our heads? The more I thought about it the less I liked remaining in his company and drinking his beer. I gulped down the pint and said I would go back to the studio and get the pictures developed, and then he made things a great deal worse by insisting on paying in advance for the photographs and announcing that he wanted a full-dress studio portrait of his wife and would make an appointment for the sitting later in the week. Only lack of perception on his part enabled me to extricate myself without giving him the impression that he had made an outrageous proposal. A more astute man, or one who knew me rather better, must have noticed and remarked upon my reaction to this suggestion. As it was I managed to mumble something unintelligible and withdrew to the forecourt of the Club. Once there I took a deep breath and scuttled back to the studio like a fox making for the nearest den.

A day that had begun so promisingly was now threatening to become one that I would be thankful to put behind me. There was no immediate respite. When I let myself into the studio I heard someone rattling pans in the kitchen and then Esta called from the bowels of the house, "Is that you, Pip? Come on in, I've cooked lunch for you!" This time I crossed into the passage like a man expecting the roof to fall on his head.

At first she didn't seem to notice anything odd about me. She was wearing our daily woman's apron and there were two or three pans simmering on the gas stove. She said gaily, "Where have you been? Did a job turn up?" and I was glad to prattle about Morney-Sutcliffe and his plan for confronting the Foreshore Committee with photographic evidence of a near-derelict sea front. She said, "Well, the old pig! On a Sunday! Just who does he think he is?" and I disposed of a little of my guilt by hurrying to his defense, saying that he had not only stood me a beer but paid for the pictures in advance. She gave me another helping hand by saying that she wasn't much surprised at my failure to turn up for the tour of the villages the previous night, as I could not have taken a single picture under those conditions. "It was a shambles!" she said, "and we all got soaked! The rain brought the canopy down and we gave up after we got to Stourford Magna. I rang when I had had a hot bath but I couldn't get you. Were you over at the pub?" I accepted the excuse she offered and said I was. I realized that, sooner or later, I would have to do something about Esta but I wanted time and nobody seemed disposed to grant me any.

She served the lunch and kept up a ceaseless rattle of conversation and it wasn't until we were facing one another over the kitchen table that I realized she was making a heroic effort to steer clear of the subject that was really bothering her, namely me and my desperate avoidance of her during the past seven days. I could see now that this was how she was beginning to look at it, but she had obviously made up her mind to give me the benefit of the doubt, not out of consideration for someone who had been through a trying week but because she was afraid to face any other conclusion. We knew each other far too well, however, to maintain this farce for more than half an hour, and once she had dumped all the plates in the sink, and waited in vain for me to praise her cooking, she suddenly faced round and said, with a note of desperation in her voice, "What's *happened*, Pip? What is it that's bothering you? Is it what I think? Have you gone back on what you said up on the cliffs? I mean, about me coming here as receptionist, about . . . well—us getting married?"

I said, feeling about as wretched as I had ever felt in her presence, that the situation had changed for the worse since Birdie had died and that her part in the carnival had denied me the opportunity of talking it over with her. She grabbed at this straw, saying, "Jonquil told me you were angry about me being chosen as Water Queen but I didn't believe her! She said you snarled at her like a bear when she spoke to you at the fancy-dress parade. I said you were upset over Birdie dying and that it was idiotic to say you didn't want me to take on the job because it was you who had pushed me forward and were more excited than I was when I was chosen! That's true, isn't it?"

"Yes, that's true," I said, conceding a grain of honesty but wondering how I could get rid of her without hurting her too much. It would have been easier, and much kinder, to have made the break there and then, but how was it possible to do this without involving Lorna, without actually mentioning her name and telling some of the truth. I didn't see any way of doing this then and I still don't, after more than thirty years to think about it, so I fell back on my old line of defense, arguing that Birdie's death and Annie Vetch's demand of a thousand pounds for goodwill had thrown our original plan out of the window.

This didn't fool her for a moment, not any more. She said, "Look, one night last week we got engaged. At least, that's what I thought at the time. Since then we've hardly exchanged a word, and when you came in just now you didn't even kiss me! I might have been the daily woman, rustling up some dinner for you. Since then you haven't even let your face slip, not once! You're not telling me the truth and that's crazy! Of course I realize things have changed, but I can't see why Birdie's death, and the future of this dump, should change how you feel about me, or how I feel about you! I was in love with you last Sunday and I'm in love with you this Sunday. All that prancing about as Water Queen doesn't mean a thing to me one way or the other, and neither does what happens to this studio and where we go if you ever decide to leave here. What's obviously happened is that you've had second thoughts about us but haven't got the guts to admit it!"

She had given me a clear opening and I should have used it. I still don't know why I didn't, simply telling her that I wanted to see the world a bit before marrying and settling down. She would have believed that, even though it would have made her miserable after all our talk of making the break together. She would have understood it too, for she knew how I felt about being rooted here for life, without so much as a peep at the world outside. I could have tried another and riskier tack. I could have invented a job I had written after and landed against all expectations, a job for a single man with a small starting salary but good prospects. She might have swallowed that if I had made it sound plausible, but the encounter with Morney-Sutcliffe had slowed my thinking processes and left me nervous and edgy. I felt that I was being crowded and driven into a corner and I let fly instinctively, without any attempt to justify myself in a way she would be likely to accept. I said, "You damned girls are all the same! You always have to rush things, to panic everybody! A fellow only has to make a few passes and what happens? You smell the orange blossom and dive headfirst into your bottom drawer!"

I can see her face now, after getting on for a third of a century, and the expression on it still makes me ashamed. She stood quite still, with her back to the sink and her hands mottled with soap suds. She didn't look regal any more and not even pretty in the elfin way I had grown to like so much over the last few months. She looked like a child forced to watch while someone made a big bonfire of her dolls.

It would have helped, I think, if she had reacted like any other Redcliffe Bay girl under identical circumstances—that is, burst into tears and rushed home to mother with her tale of woe, and if she had done this maybe it would have helped both of us, even if it didn't succeed in setting things right. It was our loss that she had more guts and more dignity than any two people in that town. She untied the apron, wiped her hands on it and folded it into its original creases. Neither of us spoke another word until it was back inside the dresser drawer. Then she said, very quietly, "That's a lie, Pip, and you know it's a lie as far as I'm concerned! I never tried to corner you although, as I said, there never was anyone else for me. I'll tell you something else you've conveniently forgotten in eight days! You were quite free to come or go until you got carried away after the dress rehearsal last week, and even then, if you had been straight with me, I wouldn't have held you to it! I'd have shed tears maybe but I wouldn't have held on to you. Do you believe that? If you had wanted to break out on your own I would have agreed and just hoped. But you haven't played straight with me, have you? And not for some time now! There's somebody else, isn't there, somebody I don't even know about, that none of us know about! That's a fact, isn't it?"

I was more scared then than I had been when I found Doctor Morney-Sutcliffe on my doorstep. You could fool a man like the Doctor maybe but you couldn't fool Esta, or not for very long, and the knowledge of this sparked off a barrage of indignant denials. They made as much impression as slingshot fire at a rhinoceros. All she said when I stopped for want of breath was, "Don't worry, Pip. I won't pry. Good luck to you both; it looks as if she's going to need it, whoever she is!"

She would have left then but I stood in front of the door. My scattered wits were reporting back on duty, not *en masse* but in sufficient strength to make me understand that it would be folly to let her go in this frame of mind. She said she wouldn't pry but that didn't mean she wouldn't keep her eyes open, or discuss the company I was keeping with her sisters and other people on Stump. Soon enough everyone would join in the guessing game and there were far better private detectives in Redcliffe Bay than we saw in the gangster films at the Tivoli. I said, "Wait, Esta! Who did you tell about us, besides Jonquil?"

She looked surprised. "I didn't tell Jonquil; as a matter of fact I didn't tell anyone! But I shall have to have some kind of story pat, won't I? I daresay someone has noticed we've been going together since January. What would you like me to tell them? That I wouldn't come across, or that you decided you were still in love with Shirley Temple?"

This kind of talk was new from Esta. Until then I hadn't known she had a gift for irony. "But Jonquil made a crack about having me as a brother-in-law," I protested, for all the world as though I was the injured party.

"She was just fishing. That's our Jonquil!"

I still wasn't satisfied. "If you didn't tell her about us getting engaged why should she say a thing like that?"

She looked at me patiently, as though I was being tiresome rather than brutal. "When we heard about Birdie dying mother make a joke at breakfast. We make jokes sometimes, even about dead people. Mother said, 'Now's your chance, Esta! I daresay Birdie has left Pip a fortune!' "

"But you still didn't say anything?"

"I still didn't say anything."

"Then how will you explain it if people do ask about us?"

She came back into the room and her eyes never left my face. There was a good deal more in her expression than bewildered misery, something midway between serious concern and furious exasperation. She said, patiently, "Are you sure you aren't sick, Pip? I don't mean lovesick, just sick! Something bad has happened to you! I don't know what, but something! You just aren't the same person any more!"

I told her gruffly that I had never felt better in my life but she went on, as though I hadn't spoken. "Come to think of it, why should you be so interested in how I explain the fact that you've thrown me over for Miss X? What is it to you, anyway? It's none of your business if I told the exact truth—that I was engaged to be married last week and quietly ditched exactly eight days later! You've got an awful nerve trying to extract conditions from me! All I want from you is a promise to keep up appearances until next Wednesday!"

"What's special about Wednesday?"

"My God, you must be in love! On Wednesday I'm bridesmaid at Myfanwy's wedding, and you've promised to be Owen's best man! I don't want you letting them down as well."

"I had forgotten," I mumbled, "so much has happened since then," and she said grimly, "Yes, it has, but don't let it worry you. Father isn't likely to shotgun you into making it a double wedding! We never got around to giving him cause, did we?"

She walked round me then, as if I had been a puddle on the floor, and I watched her go down the garden path and out through the backyard door. She didn't even slam it.

I mooched back into the studio, trying to convince myself that what had just happened was irrelevant, that nothing mattered now except selling out and whisking Lorna away on the proceeds, but no amount of reassurance could stop me feeling cheap, boorish and cruel. I couldn't forget the expression on her face, when she finally realized everything was over, or the curious fact that she had seemed to lose her prettiness, as though it had been withered by a blight. I honestly thought of myself as head over heels in love with Lorna, but I realized even then that Lorna's contempt would not have had so much power to wound and diminish. I did what I had formed a habit of doing lately. I took a quick nip from Lorna's dwindling bottle of cognac.

[3]

The Stump turned out in force for Myfanwy's wedding at All Souls' the following Wednesday.

Esta and I didn't meet during the interval and Lorna didn't ring either, but I discussed arrangements with Owen Rees on the phone and turned up at ten-thirty to get him to the church. He wasn't anything like as nervous as I had expected but prowled about the hotel room he had hired in a radiant daze. All I had to do was find his collar studs and pocket the ring.

It was interesting watching him dress with his single arm. In the years since he had lost it at Passchendaele he had become very dexterous and could knot a tie using his teeth and one hand as quickly as most of us can with fingers and thumbs. He seemed to regard Esta's part in precipitating the marriage as a joke and took it for granted, just as Alison Sweetland had done, that I had had a helping hand in the plot. "I really don't know why I didn't get around to proposing myself!" he said, when we were ready and waiting, and sipping a couple of beers brought in by a beaming landlady. "I suppose I was just as hagridden by Mother as my father was! You can make altogether too much of this filial duty business, Pip. When you make up your mind to do anything go ahead and do it, don't keep asking yourself if other people might get bruised in the process!"

I wondered if he would have stood by this advice if he had

known my situation at that particular moment and I doubted it. He was very fond of Esta and an exceptionally gentle soul.

Myfanwy looked and behaved as if Esta had given her too much to drink. She was just that much too self-assured but she looked smart in her neat little two-piece and a hat that was a serious challenge to Alison Sweetland's hat on the occasion Esta equipped her to banish the deaconess. Afterwards, at the church porch, there was a flurry of confetti and rose petals, and I took a number of wedding pictures near the west door. Esta, unsmiling but looking moderately pretty again in apple-green organdie and a hat that might have been made of green cobwebs stretched on wire, didn't look in my direction once, or address a single word to me at the reception. We might have been two complete strangers, drawn together for an hour or so by the marriage of mutual friends.

One other person paid her a great deal of attention and he was Cecil Trumper, son of Redcliffe Bay's wealthiest tradesman. He must have heard that we had quarrelled, for he positively danced attendance on the bridesmaid and even managed to shed half his stutter. I saw Esta smile at him once or twice but in a tired sort of way, as if he was a trifling addition to the load she was carrying. Then, when we were all gathered on the pavement outside, and the bridal pair were on the point of driving off on their honeymoon tour of the Lakes, Cecil called, "Throw your bbbbouquet, Myfanwy!" and Myfanwy, obviously forewarned, reached behind her and threw it so that it struck Esta's shoulder and was caught, not by Esta but by Cecil, who bowed and presented it to her. I don't know why this little send-off scene irritated me, but it did. It smacked so much of Redcliffe Bay in its conventional holiday mood and made me think of Lorna's oh-what-a-dump philosophy.

I was still thinking of Lorna when the guests dispersed and I went home to change. I was very busy just then. Hundreds of rolls of film had been expended by Redcliffians on the carnival and most of them still had to be developed and printed. I was hot and sticky, however, and almost decided to take a swim first but changed my mind, settling for a shower, which was one of the few modern amenities available on Birdie's premises. I was standing in the bath under irregular gushes of cold water when I heard the shop doorbell ring and cursed it. It was Beryl's afternoon off and there was no one to answer it, so I threw a bathing wrap over my shoulders and went downstairs calling "Who is it?" through the door. Lorna answered, "It's me, Kent! Dressed to kill and ready to pose in front of the potted palms and the pedestal!"

I tore open the door in a frenzy of excitement and she came in, her eyes opening wide when she saw me in my bathrobe with water streaming from my hair.

"You must have second sight!" she said. "Basil didn't make an appointment, did he? I told him not to bother. You made quite a hit with him on Sunday. He thinks like me, that you're too good for Redcliffe Bay. Shall I wait, while you make yourself presentable, or do you photograph all the girls in the altogether?"

I was so surprised and pleased to see her that I began to stutter almost as badly as Cecil Trumper. Then I stopped trying to talk, pulled her into the annex where we couldn't be seen through the shop windows and kissed her the way she liked to be kissed. She said, laughing, "Well, I had a notion I would be welcome, and maybe qualify for trade discount, but I didn't expect to be ravished on sight! How is it you take showers in the middle of a day's work? And where is that awful pimply girl who usually sits in the cash-desk, looking like a madam in a small-town brothel?"

I explained about the wedding and told her that Wednesday was half-day and that I had made up my mind to tackle the backlog of work in the order book.

"Well, don't I qualify as work?" she said. "Basil was quite insistent about a studio portrait and I really don't know what gave him the idea, unless it was his way of thanking you for devoting Sunday morning to him and his crazy foreshore scheme. Where would you like me to pose? Here, or out of range of Stump? Suppose you lock the shop door and put 'Engaged' up? I parked the car in the courtyard of the Marino, so if it turns out to be a lengthy sitting no one is likely to comment. You do *want* to photograph me, don't you?"

"I can't think of anyone I'd sooner photograph," I said, "and that includes Greta Garbo in the nude!"

"You'd probably find her disappointing. She's all soul and that doesn't show above the neck!"

She looked round the dusty studio with a distaste she never attempted to hide whenever she came here. "This place is grisly," she said. "I can't understand how anyone your age could spend a day in it."

"I don't intend spending many more," I said, breaking my resolution to say nothing about the sale until contracts were signed. "I've made up my mind to do it up and sell it as a going concern. You might be surprised to learn that a certain type of pro is always looking for a little business by the seaside and if you want proof run your eye down that 'Wanted' column while I get some clothes on," and I gave her that week's issue of the trade paper.

She sat down and addressed herself to the magazine. I might have been wrong but it seemed to me that I had at last succeeded in convincing her that I had a brain as well as a body. I left her there, returned to the bathroom and ran the safety razor over my chin. I was still in my bathing wrap when I heard her heels clack on the stairs and glanced across the landing to see her on a tour of inspection. It made me smile to watch how carefully she carried herself, as though contact with the walls and banisters and doorknobs would mean sending all her clothes to the cleaners as soon as she returned home. When I went into my bedroom, which the daily woman had cleaned out only that morning, she was sitting in the wicker chair by the window glancing through an album that contained a selection of my best pictures.

"Basil's right," she said, "you *have* got a special kind of talent. I couldn't put a name to it, exactly, but it has to do with lighting and choice of subject. Some of these are very good indeed! I think you're doing the right thing to sell up and try your luck in town. Why didn't you do it a couple of years ago? This picture of the old gaffer at Mill House is dated 1929. You must have taken it when you were seventeen."

"I hadn't met you when I was seventeen," I said, "and if you hadn't nagged me I would have settled for being my own boss at twenty. That might not seem much to you but it's very unusual in Redcliffe Bay."

"Ah, big fish, small pond?"

"That's it; just like Basil!"

"Basil met me six years ago. It didn't make him want to up stumps and away."

"He isn't in love with you."

She considered this seriously, laying the book aside and leaning back on her hands. A shaft of afternoon sunlight lost itself in a stray curl over her right ear. I could hear my heart hammering and there were about a thousand things I wanted to say but I kept silent, telling myself that this was it and that I had a right to something more than a half-joking promise to sail as her crew, in her time and under her conditions.

She said, after what seemed a long time, "What do you really want to do with your life, Kent? Apart from me, I mean. Do you want to make money, travel, be famous and sought after? Do things like fast cars and the Riviera trappings interest you? Or are you more or less dedicated to your own form of creativity?"

"Whatever I want to do has to be done with you, Lorna. I've made up my mind to that. There isn't anything I wouldn't do with you and for you and if that sounds corny I can't help it. It's how I feel and how I have felt for a long time now."

"How long, exactly?"

"Without knowing it? Since I first set eyes on you at the Hospital Ball. Knowing it, since you asked me out to the boat."

"How much do you think you'll get for this place when you've finished doing it up and cooking the cash ledger?"

"I might get as much as two thousand five hundred. More than half of that will be clear money."

"Say twelve hundred. And then?"

"I've never known a good press photographer or a good studio photographer out of work. It depends what you can do and where you're prepared to go, of course, but I'll always make a good living."

She took her time thinking about this. Today, it appeared, she was in a contemplative mood. "When will all this happen?"

"By about October. It will take that time to do the place up and find a buyer and besides, I shall want to show a good season's takings in the books."

"October," she said, thoughtfully. "It's a good time to go south. It might even be my time."

"Then you *would* leave him? If I had just that much capital?"

"I'm not that bothered about capital," she said. "I've got a certain amount of my own but I'm damned if I'd buy any man alive! I've also got the boat. That's in my name."

"You mean you were serious about sailing that boat to the Continent?"

"Not just to the Continent. That boat was built for blue water and why should we stop at a weekend in Cherbourg? What's wrong with the Gironde, Lisbon, Las Palmas, Naples and the Aegean? The sun shines a long time down there, Kent, and you can live cheaply if you don't need to find your fun among the fashionable set. I don't say it would last, of course, but what does? It might be fun trying. If you ever had the nerve, of course."

"I've got the nerve!"

I walked over to her, hauled her out of the chair and away from the window. "I'd match my nerve against yours any day, Lorna!"

"Yes," she said, smiling, "I believe you would, Kent, but you'd better prove it again. Right here. In your own dinky little masculine bedroom!"

We stayed there the better part of an hour and afterwards I took a dozen photographs, most of them formal studies, but one or two in the kind of light and pose I had long decided would be likely to bring out the best in her. It was a gay and silly session and both of us had some difficulty in addressing ourselves to the work. Perhaps it struck us as a curious way to finish the afternoon, her turning this way and that in response to my suggestions, me fiddling with the lights and backgrounds, just as if she were another young wife from the Avenue having herself photographed for Auntie Edna, in Kenya. Then, with a pretense of panic, she was gone, and I pulled the blind and watched her cross the enclosure and turn up Fore Street to the hotel, where her car was parked. I didn't feel bad about Esta any more and I didn't feel guilty about the Doctor. I felt as if I, personally, had drunk all the champagne served at Myfanwy's wedding.

Looking back on that single year, on the twelve months covering my entire association with Lorna, I see now that it falls into a number of phases. It does this so clearly that I can pinpoint the month, almost the specific day, when one phase ended and another began.

There was the fantasy period between the night of the Hospital Ball and the night Birdie Boxall died. Then the feverish week or so following my first visit to the boat that led on to the night we spent in the cabin and ended with Esta's confrontation. After that came a period that I can only describe as the trance phase. Finally there was the phase of suspense that ended in dissolution.

It is of the third, or trance phase, that I now write, for it began the day of Myfanwy's wedding when Lorna called at the studio and perhaps this interval, which lasted for about twelve weeks, is the most difficult to rationalize. It seems as though our brief tumble in my narrow little bedroom visited each of us with a special kind of madness and recklessness and this new twist encouraged us to throw aside discretion and transfer our intrigue from the comparative security of the cove to our own doorsteps. Perhaps the spell really was broken by a change of background, or perhaps it would have lost its magic in any case. I only know that from that moment we began to leech upon one another with a selfishness that had been absent from all our previous meetings, except for that single predatory sally of hers on the boat. From then on there was certainly nothing playful or casual about our association. Where there had been gaiety there was a kind of desperate harrying of one another, so that we ceased to be friends or mutual comforters in anything but physical terms, and behaved more like a couple of animals than people prepared to disguise our appetite for one another in the words and trappings of love, or even comradeship. She behaved like a bitch in season and I exploited her salacity in a way that even now has the power to disgust.

I suppose it could be argued in my favor that she, as a mature woman, was the more to blame for coarsening our relationship, and that I was too young to distinguish between love and lust, but even this is debatable. As I came to understand, she too had her tensions and they were far more complex than mine, demanding a release that would have taxed the self-control of a far less sensual woman than Lorna was. However, there it was. One way or another we very quickly destroyed any chance there might have been of establishing a worthwhile relationship and we set about sowing the seeds of disillusion with equal energy. I daresay that no two people in a similar situation have ever entered upon the business with less dignity or more relish.

With our dignity went any mutual tenderness that strengthens a relationship between a man and a woman, so that neither of us acknowledged any kind of responsibility towards the other. My instinct was not at fault. I knew well enough that we were set upon a course that must end in disenchantment, and possibly disaster, but in the absence of any kind of signal from her I cheerfully ignored the warning, for I had now arrived at the stage where I found no abiding interest in anything except her body. As long as it was available, and as long as she fed me evidence that I was equally essential to her peace of mind, then I was happy to put past and future aside and enjoy the present. Neither of us referred to the half-formed escape plan we had discussed in my bedroom, she, no doubt, because alternative plans were already forming in her mind, me because I sensed her reluctance to reopen the subject and hesitated to say anything that threatened to change the crazy rhythm of our lives.

It was the maddest kind of frolic. At first we continued to act with reasonable caution but soon we were ready to take all kinds of risks in order to spend a few hours together. We continued to meet by stealth, of course, but she had a party telephone line installed in the cabin and at any time the Phillips family, who shared it, could have listened in to our conversations. It wouldn't have taken a very discerning eavesdropper to break our schoolboy code. Over the telephone she called me "Basil" and I called her "Darling" or "Dearest." If anyone at the farm did hear us they must have had some revolutionary thoughts about the Doctor.

Sometimes, if we had been separated for more than a few days, I wrote to her, adding a touch of absurdity to the situation by leaving letters in a niche of the drystone wall that separated the rear shrubbery of "Heatherdene" from the golf course. She encouraged me to do this and often left a brief note in return. Naturally, I didn't destroy her messages and I later discovered that she didn't burn mine, in spite of assuring me that she had. We didn't often meet in the cove or on the boat, although I invented the convenient fiction of a photographic survey of the coastline and used it as a cover story to account for my frequent appearances down there. Occasionally she came to the studio and several times she drove me out to an isolated little cider house in the woods, where the owner, a bucolic old crone in her dotage, was seemingly hypnotized by Lorna and gave us the free run of the place, busying herself in her vegetable patch while we remained inside, keeping a casual eye on her through an inglenook window in the great stone fireplace.

At other times she would pick me up at a point five or six miles from town and we would drive inland in her car. On these occasions we made love in the open. I preferred this kind of setting if we were unable to use the cabin or the boat, thinking it not only less sordid but safer, but she had very little feeling for the works of nature other than those she saw in her mirror and would complain petulantly of briars, wasps and damage to her clothes. She always preferred a more conventional setting, surrounded by four walls that offered her the privacy to indulge her individual impulses. Three decades later, when there was all that fuss about *Lady Chatterley's Lover* and *Fanny Hill,* I found myself remembering things about Lorna that I had forgotten. She had none of Lady Chatterley's whimsical approach to sex, but she did have something in common with Fanny in her more boisterous moods. Once we had established the rhythm of that summer she was always completely uninhibited, but the whole structure of our association remained based upon my appraisal of her physical perfection and on what she continued to regard as my subjection. This was the only thing I had to offer that was of the least value to her, and if it occurred to her that it might be insufficient to sustain me indefinitely then she almost certainly didn't give a damn. She remained the senior partner, I the willing accomplice. It was always Lorna who decided when and where we should meet, how long we should remain together, and even how and in what precise manner we should use one another.

When young, one imagines that physical gratification, particularly that arising from a partnership as frenzied and single-minded as ours, is enough to build a permanent and mutually satisfactory relationship between two people. She must have known otherwise, of course, but then, she wasn't interested in building one. As far as she was concerned I was an instrument, and if I hadn't been so besotted by her I should have recognized this and either settled for it or proposed some kind of conditions. As it was, I did nothing of the kind. I was far too eager to hold on to the single advantage I thought I had, that I was a physical necessity to her. And if I did look for anything else it was based on a hope that, as time went on, and I became a kind of habit, she would demonstrate the less selfish side of her character that I had glimpsed when she came to my rescue the night Birdie Boxall died. The hope was never realized. I have met, and tangled with, all kinds of women since then, but I have never encountered one more slavishly devoted to the senses, or less dependent upon the more homespun threads that all of us throw out in the direction of others in order to survive as individuals. Neither have I met any woman who had such a compelling need to be worshipped in the purely physical sense while totally rejecting any other kind of devotion. I did not, of course, understand this at the time and not solely because I was raw and inexperienced in the business of assessing people's worth. I was far too absorbed in her physically to quarrel with what I thought of as an astonishing piece of luck on my part and also, I suppose, with my own vanity gorged by her acceptance of me as a lover.

In the meantime, however, I clung to the bare bones of my plan and without once seeking her advice or confirmation. Away in the back of my mind I saw it as the one means of making sense out of our involvement and providing some kind of lifeline we could use to haul ourselves back to a starting point that promised a settled pattern and an end to all these furtive comings and goings and subterfuges.

Cecil Trumper's father gave me an estimate for renovating and redecorating the studio and the living premises above it, and when he said it could be done for just over five hundred I told him to go ahead. The builder's men moved in towards the end of June and I shifted my headquarters to the Nissen hut in the garden. The weather was fine and I was kept busy with holiday snapshots and the usual spate of weddings and baby pictures. I didn't do any real freelance work; there was no time to think of it, but I earned my weekly running expenses with press pictures for the *Messenger* and *County Herald*. My financial situation caused me no worries at all. The bank loan covered the building estimate and I was grossing round about fifty pounds a week, of which one third was profit.

I composed a cunningly-worded advertisement that brought replies from four prospective purchasers and of these I chose a pleasant couple called Palfrey, man and wife, who were entering their sixties, had saved a little money, and were willing to pay two thousand five hundred pounds for lease, goodwill and fittings as soon as they had disposed of their own business in South London. This part of the original plan seemed to be working without a hitch, but I put off thinking about it in direct relation to Lorna and her boat, telling myself that as soon as I could go to her and say that I had a substantial amount in my account she would make her own plans. I even flattered myself into believing that a little coolness on my part would ensure her ardent participation. At twenty most men have that kind of confidence in their loins and sometimes it lingers there for another ten years or so. Mine didn't; too much was demanded of it in too brief a period. The first check came the night after Basil Morney-Sutcliffe put on the mantle of hero, to add to all the other fine clothes he used to dazzle Redcliffe Bay.

It happened about midday one sunny morning in August, at

the peak of the holiday season. I had just heard that the Palfreys had sold their studio in London and were ready to sign a contract giving them possession on the last day of September. The news put me in a good humor, especially as I had a tentative arrangement with Lorna that evening, she having proposed that I come for a swim after tea, make a show of taking pictures, leave openly by the goyle, and double back again via the iron ladder after dark. Basil, she told me, had plans to attend a dinner in Paxtonbury and there was no chance of him coming down to the cove when he returned after midnight. He very rarely did visit the anchorage, taking no interest in the cabin cruiser, except to use it for inshore fishing about three or four times a year.

I finalized things with Dudley Snell, who was acting for me, and whose opinion of me had soared several points since our first business discussion the morning Birdie died. I was leaving Dudley's office when the ambulance rushed by, scattering holiday makers and making for the junction of High Street and Fore Street, about a hundred yards north of Stump. I went after it. I had my camera with me and there was always a chance of an exclusive picture.

A few yards up High Street, where the road widened, the ambulance stopped and the crowd moved in from all sides. Two workmen were being helped away from an excavation outside Gorman's, our biggest grocery store, and word reached me that a third man was still trapped down a fifteen-foot hole. I opened up the crowd with the magic word "Press" and looked into the pit where I could see a man's head and shoulders showing above a heavy slide of earth and a tangle of splintered timber. I recognized him at once as Ben Boyland, an old drinking companion of Birdie's, and from where I stood I didn't see much chance of him coming out alive. There was a smell of gas from fractured mains and water was already seeping into the hole. Workmates scrambled down and managed to keep his head clear of cascading earth and gas company men managed to seal the pipe, but every attempt at digging on the part of his rescuers started another landslide and it looked to me as if Ben was trapped by a bulk of revetting timber that had fallen across his thighs. Inspector Crisp and the police sergeant shepherded the gaping onlookers back to the pavements, but they didn't order me away and Crisp said I should take a couple of quick shots because this shambles was likely to end in a lawsuit and photographic evidence might be important.

The firemen arrived and kept the water-flow in check, and then Ben began to harrow us all with his cries. He was obviously in great pain and it was terrible just standing there, listening to him and not being able to help. Suddenly there was a stir on the pavement outside Gorman's and up bustled Doctor Morney-Sutcliffe with his little black bag. The Inspector shouted, "Watch your step, Doctor!" but he brushed him off in the way he disposed of a fussy mother when he was treating a family for measles. In five seconds he had stripped off his coat and was down the hole, using the tackle rope they had rigged up beside the pump.

I never saw a man his size move with such speed or precision. He gave Ben an injection and then began to scratch away with his hands, ignoring a warning outcry from above. He might have been down there alone, miles from the nearest succor, and I took another picture of him at work, with his back bent over Ben in a protective arc and his big hands scooping out half a spadeful of earth at every thrust. He looked a little like a St. Bernard after a rabbit and when Ben's workmates saw that he wasn't going to be stopped by the threat of subsidence they rallied round and began using the planking to contain the shower of earth he threw over his shoulder. It was more exciting to watch than anything I had ever seen at the Tivoli. In a matter of minutes he had exposed the cross beam that was pinning Ben by the legs and with a little help from one of the workmen he raised it high enough to enable Ben to be drawn from under it. Then he barked for a stretcher and one came down on four lengths of rope. In another five minutes Ben was on his way to hospital, a cigarette protruding from his mouth like a miniature periscope.

They gave the Doctor three cheers when he came up and stood dusting his hands and putting on his jacket, but he didn't acknowledge the applause by so much as a lift of his eyebrows. All he said was "Both legs broken! There'll be trouble for someone over this! Where's the foreman in charge of that damned hole?"

The foreman couldn't be found. Luckily for him he had been one of the two injured men taken away as I arrived, so Morney-Sutcliffe told Inspector Crisp to follow him to the hospital and the Inspector did, even saluting on receipt of the order. The cars roared off with the Doctor in the van. It was like witnessing the departure of a general whose emergency measures had converted disaster into victory.

I went back to the studio with my tail well down. All the misgivings I had experienced on the day the Doctor took me on the foreshore expedition returned tenfold, for it was obvious that not only I, but the entire town, had badly misjudged Morney-Sutcliffe. He wasn't just a blowhard. He had more guts and initiative than any of us, and the thought that I had been playing games with his wife for weeks, and had been encouraged by her to regard him as a pompous, ineffectual ass, made me feel so contemptible that I sat in front of the telephone for a long time, trying to make up my mind to call Lorna and tell her I wasn't free to come along to the cove that night. I didn't, however. Somehow it wasn't the kind of scruple you could explain over the telephone.

About seven o'clock, shortly after I had heard that poor old Ben Boyland had had his right leg amputated, I drove over to the parking spot that I used below Phillips's farm and went down the goyle to the cove. I walked slowly. For the first time in weeks I was in no hurry at all to see Lorna with her clothes off.

It was my bad luck that she was in a hilarious mood, and I noticed this by the way she hailed me from the boat as soon as I set foot on the shingle. I asked her if she had heard about what happened in town that morning and she said she hadn't because she had slept aboard and had not been ashore during the day. I gave her a detailed account of what had taken place in High Street and it didn't surprise me to note that she was less impressed than the most casual bystander who had witnessed the rescue.

"Well now, what a turn-up for the Doctor's daybook!" was all she said. "Things couldn't have worked out better for him if he had staged the drama and written his own part!"

It wasn't in my power to accept this without a protest.

"That's damned unfair," I said, "and if you think about it you'll admit it was! Basil saved old Ben Boyland's life and he took a terrific chance down there. Ask anyone in town and they'll tell you the same. It was the bravest thing I've ever seen done, apart from being the quickest and most sensible way of tackling the job! The police, firemen and ambulance people were all there, and not one of them had the guts or the brains to go about it the way he did!"

She looked at me with the familiar patronizing smile on her lips, the one she had often used in the earliest days of our association.

"Well, well, *well!*" she said, "just listen to the little hero-worshipper! This is something new, isn't it?"

I could have hit her across the face. "I can't help how I feel," I told her. "Watching him gave me a kind of shrinking sensation, as though I was a football someone had punctured and thrown aside ready for the dustcart. Why didn't *I* throw the damned camera aside and go down and help him?"

"Well, and why didn't you?" she asked, still smiling in that irritating way.

I wondered why and decided that, in the first place I hadn't thought of it, in the second place I valued my hide and in the third place it would have seemed a monstrous presumption on my part to join forces with a man whose wife I took to bed twice a week. When I told her this she laughed outright. One might almost say she guffawed.

"It looks as if I've been fooling myself all this time," she said. "You brag a lot but I wonder if you're any different from him, or anyone else back there? In some ways you're even more of a hypocrite, because you want large helpings of cake without sacrificing the smugness that comes from eating bread and dripping!"

I flared up at this and told her that I couldn't see why acknowledgment of Basil's nerve and initiative should be regarded as evidence of sloppy-mindedness on anyone's part.

"It is on yours," she said cheerfully, "because you come running here with your tongue hanging out whenever you feel like it but still observe the self-denying ordinances they practice in that stuffy little town yonder! You can't have it both ways, Kent, and why the hell should you? Why should anyone, come to that? Either you're my kind and don't give a damn for their rules, or you accept their values and their limitations!"

She was right of course and privately I had to admit it, but I didn't care to climb down without another attempt at self-justification.

"I'm in love with you, Lorna," I said piously, "and that means I'll go to any lengths to be with you. It wouldn't matter who you were married to but it does make some kind of difference to discover that he isn't the person we thought he was."

"You really believe it makes a difference?"

It made more difference than I was prepared to admit, enough to make me wonder whether I would ever enjoy her in quite the same way again. As long as I could think of Basil Morney-Sutcliffe as the man who made those egregiously punctual visits to her bedroom, as a bustling, small-town bully radiating pomposity and arrogance, it was a simple matter to put him out of mind the moment I had her in my arms. That wasn't the same thing at all as making a fool of a man who would walk up to a German machine gun with a bomb in one hand and a bayonet in the other and this was how I was beginning to think of him now. I realized, however, that no amount of discussion would make this clear to Lorna, who had been patronized by him at unpleasantly close range for years, and thinking this, I took a plunge that I had not contemplated taking when I made my way over there that day. I said, "I've signed the contract, Lorna. The new people are moving in at the end of the month."

"What contract and what new people?"

She wasn't trying to be funny. She had really forgotten every word of the conversation we had had in my bedroom back in June, and the full understanding of this came as only slightly less of a shock than discovering the real Morney-Sutcliffe.

I swallowed my resentment and disappointment, telling her precisely what I had done about the business and how I had accumulated, or soon would accumulate, some fifteen hundred pounds. She seemed no more than mildly interested. It was like going over a lesson with a jolly but rather inattentive child, and when she made no final comment, but just sat there with her teeth clamped over her lip, I knew that we had arrived at another crisis and that it would be madness to drift on and on evading the real issues.

I said, "I did this—sold up I mean—so that we could go away together. Not at once, perhaps, but certainly as soon as I land a decent job with better prospects. I never really believed in that crazy idea of yours about sailing off to the Mediterranean but I did believe you had made up your mind to let him divorce you. If I was wrong about that you had better say so now. I can't go on like this indefinitely."

She looked not so much astonished as pained. "All this? Because dear Basil jumped into a sewer and fished somebody out?"

"No, not just because of that! I want to marry you and I want to get out of this place as much as you do! You've told me often enough that you intend walking out on him sooner or later. All I want to know is when."

"When I intend leaving him?"

"That, and when you're going to start thinking of me as something more than a means of spending the occasional afternoon or evening!"

"You think of *me* as more than that? Honestly now, Kent! Yes or no!"

It was a genuine offer of retreat with the honors of war. I didn't see it as that at the time but I do now. The physical pull she exerted over me, however, was far too strong to enable me to face facts as nonchalantly as she faced them. Her candor not only knocked me from my high horse but reduced me once again to the role of the infatuated supplicant.

"I've never thought of you as anyone but the woman I wanted to share my life with," I said, "and I don't much care where, so long as it's about a thousand miles from here! What I don't want is to go on behaving like someone in a French farce."

"Well, that's an honest enough answer," she said gaily, "and I suppose I must give you credit for honestly believing that's how it really is."

"Meaning you don't?"

"Meaning I don't! I'd like to, and I would have a few years ago, and been flattered to hear it from a boy as beefy as you. Come to that I'm flattered now, but flattery, plus the odd roll on the bed, is a thin diet for a lifetime."

"Just what does that mean? That you want to finish here and now?"

"Not unless you do. What it means is, if I left Basil I wouldn't necessarily ask him to divorce me. He probably would, in due course, but I wouldn't badger him. Why should I? I haven't the slightest intention of marrying again!"

"Then all that about us going away together was some kind of joke?"

"No, it wasn't a joke, but a woman isn't obliged to marry a man because she leaves home with him. Lots don't. You'd be surprised."

In a way it was a kind of relief. I had spent a great deal of time picturing Lorna as a permanent instead of a transient bedfellow, a sharer of all kinds of extravagant adventures in the far corners of the world, but no time at all as the dutiful little wife bustling about the kitchen preparing my breakfast, and welcoming me with a wifely kiss when I came home after a day's work. I had thought of Esta in these terms, because Esta was inseparable from the prospect of connubial comforts and the inevitable perambulator under the stairs, but in Lorna's cards there was nothing to suggest she might win a perambulator. Neither were there any baking ovens, three-piece suites, frilly aprons or even contraceptives in the dressing-table drawer. It was almost laughable to think of these things as ever having a part in Lorna's future.

"All right!" I said, "let's take that as read, but it doesn't mean we can't make some kind of plan now that I've gone this far. We can't just sit around and wait for something to happen."

"Why can't we? I've never cared for plan-making. The only time I set about organizing my life I ended up right here and is that much of a recommendation for drawing up a schedule?"

I stuck doggedly to my point but there was no convincing her, not only because she was deliberately evasive but also because I had not even convinced myself, as she was quick to point out in her next brutally accurate assessment of our relationship.

"Before you stampede into something you might find yourself regretting as much as I regret marrying Basil," she said calmly, "you ought to take time off and think hard! I mean, really think, without wandering off into pleasant little backwaters where, as like as not, you'll see me not as I am but as the girl in that picture *September Morn* that Basil's mother kept in her bathroom, I can't think why! Just what have we got, you and me? What does our association amount to, once you remove the Christmas wrappings? A woman getting on for thirty who has to be constantly reassured that she's coveted by at least one normal, healthy male, and a young man looking for something more rewarding than the occasional fumble on the back porch! I know, I know, it all sounds horribly unromantic and sordid but life isn't a bloody magazine serial and no amount of self-delusion can make it one. I daresay I've been selfish encouraging you the way I have, but I'm not apologizing for it and never will, and do you know why? Because I see now that it was the one way to help you to grow up and begin thinking of yourself as someone a bit more adventurous than all those other drips, the men who spend the last thirty years of their lives wondering where and why they took a turning that led them slap into a cul-de-sac! Some older women might have done that much for you with their heads, or even their hearts, but I'm not the maternal type, so all I did was to roll over on my back and do it with what interests you the most. I'm not pretending I had your interests in mind, but that's how it worked out as far as you are concerned. Here you are, ready and willing to burn your boats, and that, in Redcliffe Bay, is really something! I'll lay you a hundred to one it doesn't happen down there once in a generation!"

Her candor was as stimulating as her lust and it had approximately the same effect upon me. I needed as much of it as it was in her power to give, but it was hard to throw all my illusions away in a single parcel.

"Don't you believe it is possible for two people to find permanent happiness in one another's company?" I asked.

"It might be, in a small minority of cases, but even then they would have to be free to come and go as they pleased and they never are. People talk a hell of a lot of nonsense about love and marriage and romance. Particularly married people. Once they're fenced in themselves they seem compelled to pontificate about it, and make it sound as though, without marriage as an institution, we couldn't survive as a civilized community. Some even believe that, I suppose, but I never did. I always recognized marriage for what it was as far as a woman is concerned!"

"What, exactly?"

She looked at me as if my romantic expectations were tiring her out. "A meal ticket, the rent and rates paid in advance, and somewhere to go when it's snowing!"

"And for a man?"

"Two things. The most important one, no matter how many fancy ribbons you tie around it, a private pussy at his disposal without the bother and expense of going in search of one. The other is more complicated. It's a cast-iron excuse for not doing all the things he dreamed of doing when he was your age!"

"And where does that leave us?"

"Where we came in when you arrived here spellbound by Basil's latest bit of see-what-I-can-do! Get your money and get your job, Kent. I'll still be here and I daresay just as needy, but for God's sake don't ask me to plan. I don't know who it was who came up with that advice about treating each day as a separate existence but he was on to something! It's not a bad philosophy for want of something better, and who ever does know what's coming out of the bag?"

That was all that came of this particular crisis, one that I had more or less forced on her, and I suppose there was more satisfaction to be distilled from it than from any of our previous or subsequent discussions. The occasion ended the way it always ended, with a roll on the bunk, a swim to cool off, a few drinks, a jazz session with me winding the handle of the portable and, finally, a few breathless moments before I set off along the shingle to the iron ladder. I thought of all manner of things on the way home but the Doctor's heroics were not among them. She had succeeded in blinkering me again as far as he was concerned.

CHAPTER SEVEN

[1]

It was strange how subtly but completely my involvement with Lorna isolated me from the community in which I had lived, more or less contentedly, since childhood.

I don't think I was aware of this until about the time we had our inconclusive showdown on the boat, the day that the Doctor found his way, via my photographs, into the national press. Right up until the day Birdie died, on the opening day of the carnival, I was Pip Stuart, Birdie's dogsbody, one of the bright young sparks about town whose professional duties put him on easy terms with most of Redcliffe Bay's worthies, people like Ben Dagmar, the editor, Bruce Brayley, proprietor of the cinema, and councillors like Hopkins, the timber merchant, and Garfield Pyne, the undertaker. I was friendly with the police and many of the local tradesmen and artisans, most of whom were affiliated, in one way or another, to one or more of the dozens of amateur societies whose activities I followed with my camera. I was on nickname terms with people like Scatty Wallace, Esta's inventor father, and my obligatory attendance at local weddings kept me in touch with all the anonymous Redcliffians, who lived in the terrace houses west of the goods yard. Most people called me "Pip," a few "Mr. Stuart," and whenever I went along Stump I was sure to run across a friend or acquaintance, somebody like Myfanwy Pritchard, Alison Sweetland, Ken Pigeon, or Esta's long-range suitor, Cecil Trumper. Once I had become Lorna's lover, however, all this changed, and the initial withdrawal must have been mine, for I was absolutely certain no one in Redcliffe Bay had an inkling of what was going on. I could tell that by the general approach to me; in Redcliffe Bay you couldn't contain a secret of that kind for twelve hours once it had leaked.

Throughout the months of June, July and August a great deal of the friendliness ebbed from my life and by the end of the season I was more like a day tripper than someone who had gone to school and grown up in the town. Nobody except Esta and her sisters showed me any hostility, or even chilliness, but there was a restraint in the way people greeted me, so that I began to wonder whether the news that I was selling up (which had almost certainly been broadcast by Annie Vetch, Birdie's sister) had been received with a certain amount of resentment by local tradesmen. Redcliffians automatically opposed any change, however slight, in the traditional pattern of the town.

It might have been that, or it might have been a desultory whispering campaign started by Esta's gossipy sisters, but I am more inclined to believe that, basically, it was no more than a reflection of my own attitude. Maybe some of Lorna's contempt for our way of life had rubbed off on me and this was sensed by those with whom I came in contact.

I saw nothing of Esta except at a distance, where she was performing one or other of the Water Queen's chores, and I had to attend as a photographer. She never looked in my direction and we had exchanged no single word since she had walked round me in the kitchen and down the garden path to the back gate. I never ran into her on Stump, as I was accustomed to do three or four times a week even before we began going about together, and this in itself seemed strange, for I could look right across the enclosure at the kettles and oil stoves hanging in her father's shop doorway. It made me wonder if she had sharper eyes than me and turned aside when she saw me approaching.

From time to time I got news of her, once or twice through Cecil Trumper who, despite his heroic efforts at Myfanwy's wedding, had not yet succeeded in replacing me, and then again from Ken Pigeon, the manager of Hansen's music shop on East Stump. It was from Ken that I learned she still practiced her private hobby of matchmaking and matchmending, for she finally talked him into making a grab at the statuesque Greta, the Dane's only daughter, and having made sure of her, he then tackled the glum old man about a partnership.

The results of this interview startled East Stump. Almost overnight the music shop became a satellite of Tin Pan Alley. Gone were the copies of *The Indian Love Lyrics* and *In a Monastery Garden*, and in their place came the kind of numbers Lorna played on her gramophone. The gilt music stands disappeared too, and where they stood in the window were rows of gleaming saxophones and piano accordions that we called "squeeze-boxes."

I don't know what Mr. Hansen thought about it all, but business began looking up at once, and by the end of August Greta Hansen was wearing an engagement ring, bought at Frobisher's Jewel Box in High Street. We even knew how much Ken had paid for it and the figure, a few shillings under twenty pounds, confirmed the suspicion that Ken had had a substantial rise. It would have taken him a long time to save twenty pounds out of his original salary of fifty shillings a week, less his share of a national insurance stamp.

Ken made a half-hearted attempt to patch things up between Esta and me, inviting us both to his engagement party, but he lacked Esta's flair for marriage-broking. When she heard that I was going to be there she excused herself and went off to Paxtonbury for a late-night dance at the Cricket Club. I heard that Cecil Trumper escorted her there but I couldn't be certain.

Morney-Sutcliffe did me a good turn by jumping down that hole and Police Inspector Crisp did me another by allowing me to take a batch of photographs. I earned five guineas for my action shots, and the insurance company paid me another five in anticipation of a claim from Ben Boyland, the injured man. I put the money away in my private account, now hovering around the four hundred mark.

Apart from my regular hole-in-corner excursions with Lorna I didn't have any social life. I worked round the clock to save the expenses of an assistant, and in any case the holiday season was in full swing and Redcliffe Bay's internal sociability, like that of any small town dependent upon a ten-week season, was confined to the period between October and Easter. From then on, until the tail end of September, everything was geared to the holiday-maker. We all had to make enough money in this period to keep us through the autumn, winter and early spring.

The visitors never descended upon us in a flood. The invasion began as a trickle, with the arrival of elderly couples in May, and to this was added a modest number of professional people, of an age when their children had grown up. These kept us going until mid-July. Then, with school holidays, the real rush began, and the town went into top gear. By August Bank Holiday we were bursting at the seams and most of us worked a daily fourteen-hour stint. By the second week of September, however, the place was half empty again, and by the last day of that month we were more or less back to normal, except for a rearguard of elderly couples who took a second holiday in early autumn.

I didn't anticipate seeing much of Lorna during the peak of the season and neither did I, seldom meeting her more than once a week. Apart from the rush of work I had a good deal of clearing up and sorting out to attend to, and what remained of Birdie's household goods to pack up and get across to Trumper's auction mart. By this time the studio had been renovated and it gave me a pang to contemplate leaving it when, for the first time in my memory, it looked worth having.

The front of the shop had been painted a pale primrose and the studio was done in ivory and gold. A new stairway had been built and the flat over the shop partially refloored and painted olive green. Taken all round, and having regard to my turnover that summer, it was well worth the money the Palfreys were paying for it. Mr. Snell, the solicitor's clerk, who inspected it the day the builders moved out, said I had shown too much impatience and that we could have got a better price by waiting. Ben Dagmar, who had always opposed my selling out, told me frankly that I was an idiot to exchange an established business in a growing community for the uncertainties of the labor market in the city. As I couldn't tell either of them my real reason for going I had to agree with them.

Lorna came in on the last day of August and made a cool

assessment of the place but showed no sign of improving on her original advice. "So it's tidied up a bit," she said, "but it's still small town. Nothing short of a gold strike on the prom could alter that! There's no future for places like Redcliffe Bay, despite that old editor's pipe-dreams. In twenty years communities like this will be faced with a straight choice. Either they'll wither away, like the ghost towns in some parts of the States, or they'll become dormitories for the nearest city. By that time the bucket-and-spade holiday trade will have given way to continental flips. I think you're doing the right thing, Kent, so don't let anybody talk you out of it!"

In view of what she knew of my reasons for making the change, and having, no doubt, more than an inkling of her own future, this was the closest she came to acting a blatant falsehood in our association.

It was during that busy month of August that I became more aware of Mike Shapley, the buccaneer-style manager of the new Duckworth's, the man I had seen showing off at the shooting range in Carnival Week. I remembered taking a dislike to him then but it was an impersonal and instinctive dislike. He was nothing to me nor I to him. We were no more than nodding acquaintances and my antipathy towards him, if it merited the word, was the kind I had for the snobbish half-grown sons of retired service people in the Valley who buzzed about town in sports cars, wore university scarves ten feet long, and called a tankard of beer "the odd jar" when they were honking opinions in the saloon bar of the Lamb and Flag.

It was when Shapley came in to have a roll of film developed that I first became conscious of him as a kind of jeering observer of my status, someone who apparently thought of me as a glorified errand boy, and who was just that much too big for his boots. He had an unpleasant habit of looking you straight in the eye and staring you down, and while he was thus engaged his mouth twitched in a way that implied mockery and cynical interest, as though you were a child pretending to be a man and he was a much-travelled uncle unable to make up his mind whether to clout you across the head or tip you half-a-crown.

Nobody had ever looked at me quite like that and nobody has since. The approach was peculiar to Mike Shapley.

To me his snapshots were further proof of his conceit. They were all lively holiday-type pictures of himself and girls, mostly girls I did not know and assumed to be visitors. In every one he had struck a proprietary pose, with his arm round a waist or over a breast and the girl inclined towards him in an attitude that suggested voluntary enslavement. Some of the girls were in their bathing costumes and others were showing a great deal of leg, so that I could imagine him gloating over his array of scalps in the privacy of his lodgings and sticking the pictures into an album over carefully-printed headings, like "*Joanna and me, Redcliffe Bay, 1932*" or "*Freda and me in the old jalopy, summer, 1932.*" He was the kind of man who would keep a snapshot album of that kind. There was impudence and sexual aggression in everything he did, said and thought, but sometimes his aggressiveness was disguised by a cheerful nosiness, as when he commented on the studio's renovations.

"Gone to town here, I see! Was it worth it? Not much money in your racket, is there? Wouldn't have thought so, or not here, any road! Going to flog it, I hear! Good idea, son, good idea!" and he went out before I could think of a smart rejoinder.

That was another thing about Mike Shapley. He always left you wishing, with all your heart, that you were endowed with a gift for witty repartee of the kind that could cut people down to size. He irritated me so much that I made enquiries about him from people on Stump whom I supposed knew him rather better than I did, but that didn't result in much. He was from somewhere up north, they said, and had been specially picked to break new ground in this area. Beyond that nobody seemed to know anything about him.

It was a week or two after this encounter with Shapley that I took the initiative for the first time and rang Lorna, suggesting I come over to the cove. I did it because, in the first place I was lonely, and in the second place Dagmar told me the Doctor and some of his allies were attending a dreary conference in Paxtonbury that had to do with our application for a grant in respect of the Foreshore Development Scheme. He had won the last round against his stick-in-the-mud opponents and it now looked as if he was going to be the man charged with the dubious privilege of converting Redcliffe Bay into a shrine for city sun-worshippers. Dagmar was very excited about the prospects and said the Doctor was proving a great asset to the town. I thought so too but not in the way Ben Dagmar meant; it was eight days since I had seen Lorna and I was getting desperate.

She piqued me a little by sounding hesitant, but I persisted and she said she supposed it would be all right, so long as I waited until dusk and came in via the iron ladder route. "The tide will be half in," she said, "so you'll probably have to swim for it!" I said I would swim the width of the bay to spend an evening with her and she laughed and reminded me of what happened to Leander under parallel circumstances.

I got down to the beach about nine-thirty, when visibility was reduced to about ten yards owing to the sea mist. The sea was fairly calm but we often got a summer sea fog if the day had been windless and it didn't bother me at all, even when I found that there was eight feet of water washing round the point.

I was wearing only a sweater, slacks and canvas shoes, so I stripped, rolled my clothes in a ball and weighted them with a large pebble and tried to throw them as far as the tide-line on Lorna's side of the point. The throw fell short and the clothes landed in the shallows, but I knew I could dry them in front of Lorna's oil stove and swam round to the cove, arriving on her doorstep stark naked, clutching my sodden clothes. I thought she would be amused but she wasn't. She said I must be crazy to come along the shingle bank like that, even though the beach was invisible from the cliffs.

She wasn't in a very forthcoming mood and seemed nervously expectant. I lit the oil stove and that made the cabin stink like the engine room of an elderly paddle-steamer, but I was able to dry my clothes. In the meantime I walked round in my spare bathing costume that we kept in a space under the plank floor. It was when I was putting the costume back into this compartment that I saw the tin box and asked her what she kept in it.

The box was about ten inches square and looked like a cash-container.

"Souvenirs," she said, "heave it out and open it up!"

I did so and was astonished to find that it contained not only some of the saucy paintings she had shown me in her attic but several bundles of letters tied with string. Mine were among them and others had French stamps and postmarks. There were also two large envelopes stuffed with snapshots, and sifting through these I came across several pictures of myself that she had taken on the boat.

"Flattered?" she asked, watching me closely and unsmilingly and I said I wasn't, not because I shared the keepsake box with others but because it seemed to me an unnecessary risk to keep them there as indisputable evidence of our association.

"Oh rubbish!" she snapped. "Who the hell is going to pull the shanty to pieces looking for proof of your visits? René's snaps are there. Take a look at them, I know you've always been curious about him."

She was right about that and I sorted through the snaps until I found several of a slim young man wearing the traditional French beret. He didn't impress me much. He looked a little like an onion-seller and I said so. She snatched the photographs out of my hand and slammed them back in the box, together with the letters.

"You promised to burn any letters I wrote to you," I protested.

"Well, I thought better of it!" she replied, closing the box and replacing it under the floor.

"What's the matter with you tonight, Lorna? You seem in a tetchy mood. Do you want me to go?"

She considered a moment and then said no, she didn't, but she had been irritable all day, partly as a result of a row she had had with the Doctor over their gardener. When I questioned her further into the cause of the dispute she seemed reluctant to elaborate but finally she did; the gardener, the one who had glowered at me on the occasion I first called on her, had been very insolent and she had sacked him, but Basil reinstated him over her head.

"What was he insolent about?" I wanted to know, and she looked almost shifty as she said, "He dropped a hint that he knew what was going on. It happened when I ticked him off for digging up some of my plants. He said he took his orders from the Doctor and that was that!"

"I don't see how you could read anything more than surliness into that," I said. "All these old countrymen hate taking their orders from a woman."

"There was more to it than resentment," she said. "As I was walking away he called something after me!"

"Well?"

" 'It's the Doctor us respects yerabouts!' "

I thought about this and reflection made me uneasy. Lorna wasn't popular in the town and the Doctor was, particularly since his spectacular rescue of Ben Boyland in the High Street, but a statement like that, made to her face, probably did imply that word was getting around of her flightiness. Thinking it over it occurred to me that it was miraculous we had kept our secret so long. I said, "What do you think we ought to do about it?"

"Nothing!" she said. "I should want a good deal more evidence than that to stampede me into doing something silly!"

"Like running away as soon as I've moved out of the studio?"

"Yes, something as silly as that! If I do 'run away,' as you put it, it's going to be done with dignity. With packed cases, a taxi to the station, and somewhere to run to, if you follow me."

I followed her. Already, in the back of my mind, the original plan of whisking her from under the Doctor's nose had undergone extensive modification. I had now more or less settled for moving to London, getting a job and sending for her when I was ready and she had had plenty of time to miss me. I told her this but it didn't improve her temper. It wasn't until we had had a few drinks and played that damned gramophone of hers, that she mellowed enough to let me kiss her, but even then she was unusually passive.

I suppose I should have taken the hint and gone. In the light of what followed it would have been the sensible thing to do but common sense had no place at all in our partnership. Instead I made a valiant attempt to rouse her and to an extent I succeeded. I kissed her and recited the usual litany in praise of her charms, and when she seemed to warm a little I carried her over to the settee and laid her down on it as though she was made of brittle glass. This was at odds with our usual program. In spite of what she had said in praise of my humble approach to her she much preferred a rough-and-tumble the moment she had made up her mind to it. Tonight, however, she reacted to reverence and even smiled up at me, saying, "Any woman you fancy after me will be a cakewalk, Kent!" and I said that there wouldn't be another woman, adding, with my obligatory earnestness, that I was more in love with her than ever.

"That's nonsense," she said lazily. "After this kind of apprenticeship you'll make a real killing with some poor kid." Then she hoisted herself up, sighed and added, with an unflattering note of resignation, "Come along then, you won't be happy until you get it!" and began to pull off her sweater.

Her mood was so uncharacteristic of all our recent meetings that I found I could look at her for the first time with a certain amount of detachment. The grudging quality of her voice and gestures piqued me for they implied I was back in her attic during my probationary period and she was teasing me with those idiotic drawings done by René. It might have been the memory of this that nerved me to say, "If it's that much trouble on your part, Lorna, no thank you! We'll skip it and just talk!"

The face that emerged from the neck of the sweater wore such a wildly indignant expression that in happier circumstances I could have laughed, but I soon saw that this was no laughing matter and that she considered herself insulted. Her voice had a cutting edge that she had never used on me in the past.

"What the hell do you mean—'*skip it*'? What kind of talk is that to a woman taking the kind of risks I take to please a kid of your age? I told you long ago that I'm available only if and when I choose, so for God's sake do what you came here to do and get to hell out of here!"

The effect of this outburst, and the sense of personal outrage it conveyed to me, was such that, notwithstanding desire to make amends, I was physically incapable of achieving what I had hurried here to achieve and when this became obvious she hovered for a moment between extreme indignation, incredulity and sardonic amusement, somehow subsiding into a compound of all three that passed for resignation. Oddly enough it was not wholly an unsympathetic mood. She said, at length, "Well, that's something else you've learned. There's no joy in taking a woman to bed if you happen to catch her in the wrong mood. Go along home and think on that. Maybe it would be better if you didn't see me for a month or so."

I was so utterly humiliated by what had occurred that I missed the substance of this remark and after a moment or two she shrugged herself off the settee and stood with her hands on her hips, looking down at me with an expression of exasperated dismay. "My God!" she said, "things have come to a pass, haven't they? What's happened to you? Is it that damned silly conscience of yours again?"

I said, making a supreme effort to pull myself together, that it wasn't. "I haven't got a conscience about you, Lorna," I mumbled, "it's just that I know I'm in love with you and having you this way isn't enough any more. Can't you begin to understand that?"

She poured herself a stiff drink and one for me. I didn't touch mine but she finished hers in a couple of gulps and went back to the table for another. Finally she said, "Of course I can understand. I've been twenty myself and I've thought of myself as being in love, but take it from me, nothing comes of it except waking up one morning and finding that all the fun has gone off to find somebody else to play with. All you're left with is a padlock and a short length of chain. Maybe that's what I've been trying to prove to you all this time but I don't seem to have got very far, do I? About as far as you got a moment ago!"

The drink had mellowed her. She sat down beside me and lifted her hand to turn my face towards her. "Listen, kid," she said, "we've had a lot of fun and I daresay we'll have more when you've grown up a little and can see our kind of frolic for what it is. I'm fond of you, of course I am, and I'm grateful to you for making life liveable over the last few months, but you're going the way everybody goes back there unless you get one thing straight! Love—the kind of love you and I have enjoyed—is one thing, natural, worth having for its own sake, and something most of us are equipped for the way we're equipped to enjoy a square meal when we're hungry. But this other thing that is beginning to bother you is phonier than those speeches Basil makes at the Council meetings, or all that cant that goes on round the town war memorial on Armistice Day! What I mean is it's invented, cooked up, part of the trappings people drape around themselves because they haven't got the guts to see sex as a bodily function, like any other bodily function! God knows when people began looking at it that way. Not so long ago, I imagine, but the fact is it has such a hold in places like Redcliffe Bay that when somebody does call its bluff it gets its own back doing what it just did to you. Just ask yourself, how long are we here and how long are we young? How much time do we have to enjoy each other the way you and I have done when you don't come here cluttered up with a lot of half-baked hopes of eternal fidelity and death-till-us-part drivel? I'm not saying I was entirely free of them at your age, but I soon ditched them, and if I hadn't you wouldn't be here at this moment. In fact, I'll tell you where you would be—scuffling round some little huntress trying to get as much as you could without getting lugged into church. And because of the set-up you wouldn't stand an earthly. All the little fillies back there have got 'love' in reserve and that means the parson, the twopenny magazines and public opinion. Before you knew what had hit you some little hussy like that Carnival Queen would have you home, dry, mortgaged and bed-rationed! 'No, Pip dear, not tonight, Pip dear! We've got to be up early to start the spring cleaning and besides, you've been drinking! And even if I forgave you, suppose we had another baby when little Pip is still in the nappy stage and the radio isn't paid for?' It's the truth and you know it! And while I'm at it I'll tell you something else even more basic . . ."

I never did discover what that something more basic was for at that moment, silencing her with the immediacy of a factory siren, the telephone rang. She stopped in the middle of an emphatic gesture, and I jumped from the settee as if it had burst into flames.

It had never once rung while I was there and for a second or two she seemed almost as startled as me, but then she frowned, crossed the room and lifted the receiver as though its summons had been no more than a tiresome interruption. She said, standing with her back to me, "Yes?" and I heard the indistinct crackle of a male voice and kept very still. Lorna said "Ah-hah!" once or twice but nothing more until the very end of the conversation when she said, "Very well, just as you like. I'll be here," and rang off.

"Was it Basil?" I asked breathlessly.

"Who else would it be?"

"He's coming *here?*"

"In about half an hour!"

"Good God! I'd better go straight up the goyle now!"

"You better hadn't! It's only ten-thirty and Mr. Phillips won't be in bed. One of the family might even be in the yard and what would they think if they saw you go by and the Doctor arrive ten minutes later? You'll have to swim for it again. Take your costume and wrap your clothes in this old mackintosh."

There was no time to argue and anyway she was right about the risk of passing the farm before midnight. I slipped off my clothes, put on the costume, rolled my sweater, slacks and shoes in an oilskin she handed me and slipped out. She came as far as the first shingle bank and as I slipped away into the mist she called, "French farce again, Kent! Better luck next time!" It was a curious valediction from a woman who had meant far more to me than any person I had ever known in Redcliffe Bay.

When I reached the point the tide was not far short of high-water mark. The wind had freshened, disposing of the sea fog but raising a modest swell. It wasn't anything to worry about, and I would have made nothing of swimming the eighty yards into the next bay, but I didn't put much reliance on the oilskin and neither did I care for the prospect of driving back to town in wet clothes. It was partly this, and partly the dissatisfaction I felt at such a shattering evening, that made me take the idiotic course of scaling the cliff.

The bluff wasn't very high just there, no more than about eighty to a hundred feet and seamed with crevasses worn into the sandstone by streams. There were also plenty of ledges and a good deal of scrub growing on them. In daylight I would have been at the top in five minutes but it was a foolish risk to take in starlight. I dressed, discarded the oilskin, found an easy place to reach the first ledge and started the climb.

[2]

It must have happened less than halfway up, otherwise I would have broken my neck and perhaps every bone in my body. Two factors saved me, the series of ledges sown with gorse that helped to break my fall, and the remains of an insignificant landslip at the base of the cliff where the hard core of rock was cushioned with loose soil.

I can remember very little of the actual circumstances beyond a sharp rattle of stones, a swirl of panic and a deadening but not painful blow on my shoulder. Then nothing. No falling sensation and no impact.

From then on, however, after the first dance of lights and far-off murmur of conversation that marked, I imagine, a transient moment of returning consciousness, my memory is sharp and clear, even at this distance. There is no time factor in the recollection but there is a definite pattern that recurred with the monotony of wavebeats on a rocky shore, when the whole weight of the Channel is driven by a south-westerly gale. Over and over again the kaleidoscopic sequence washed through my brain and it never varied, not in the smallest particular, so that it seemed to me like the slow flicker of one of those *What the*

Butler Saw epics that could be enjoyed for a penny in the machines on our jetty until they were carted away at the instance of the Rev. Donald Avery, Chairman of Redcliffe Bay's Free Church Union.

In my case, however, the photographs had been shuffled, so that they were out of order. There had been a beginning, a middle and an uproarious finish to *The Naughty Wife* and *Husband's Night Out*, whereas the sequence of my delirium had the perversity of most dreams. In themselves the facets were convincing but in relation to one another they were gibberish.

First there was the all-pervading smell, a hospital smell that I associated with Esta. Redcliffe Bay Cottage Hospital had a particularly potent hospital smell, so that whenever I walked Esta back there for night duty, the marriage of floor polish, ether and disinfectant conjured up scenes of disaster, the rush of an ambulance, and a knot of stooping figures beside a stretcher. My own physical presence as the central figure in such a scene may have impressed itself upon my memory from the moment of arrival, later merging into a general background of which Esta herself was the dominant character.

It was not an unpleasant sequence. I would see her in her prim probationer's uniform and dazzling white coif, passing to and fro among the beds and along the corridors. I could even hear her smart heel-taps on the parquet floor but although, in my fantasy, I was under strong compulsion to stop her and talk to her, I never succeeded. Always she smiled and brushed by, hurrying importantly upon some medical errand.

Then came the Morney-Sutcliffe sequence, dominated by his big baby face, that seemed to fill the room until it looked like a vast pink balloon decorated with two pale blue eyes and a small, clipped, ginger moustache. The Doctor was not hurrying about any particular task. Mostly he just loomed over me, talking and talking in a low earnest voice, but I never made sense of a single syllable he uttered. Luckily, his appearance in the pattern was hardly more than a walk-on part. He never stayed long, and because the monstrous size of his face frightened me, I was glad of this, even in the dream.

The third sequence was tumultuous and incoherent. It was

acted out within the frame of Stump by a small army of characters, drawn from the people closely involved in my life down there. Scatty Wallace was almost a fixture, working away at one of his absurd patents in the workshop behind his premises, and so absorbed in what he was doing that he never looked up but remained crouched over his home-made forge that glowed red in the strong draft from the door. The dream had that much validity. There was always a fierce draft from the door of Scatty's workshop. Back on Stump, I identified Myfanwy Pritchard in her wedding costume and could even distinguish her corsage spray, a brace of white carnations and a wisp of maidenhair fern. Owen Rees was there and so was a crocodile of his boys, on their way somewhere but never arriving. Garfield Pyne, the East Stump undertaker, crossed the enclosure in his tall hat and rusty frock coat. I knew that he was on his way to bury Birdie Boxall, which was odd, for Birdie was dressing the studio window and clearly in liquor for everything he touched crumbled or subsided. Ben Dagmar drifted in and out of focus, and so did Alison Sweetland, who enlivened the scene by directing a fire extinguisher, not upon the deposed deaconess, which would have made some kind of sense, but upon her husband's congregation. The scene was very animated and interesting to watch, but the effort of trying to make sense of so much confusion was exhausting and, from time to time, I turned away and deliberately lost myself in the deep goyle that ran down to the cove where the cabin cruiser was moored.

It was here, without being observed, that I saw Lorna, and the contrast between her solitude and the crazy complexity of Stump was balm. I never went all the way down to her but stood off about halfway up the cleft, watching her poke about the rocks with a shrimping net, or stoop to pick up and discard a shell, or piece of driftwood. Then she would go into the cabin, emerging again almost immediately without clothes or costume, so that she seemed to be mocking my identification of her with a classical Venus.

Then I would try and join her on the shingle but this proved impossible, for the long grass and trailing briars tangled with my feet and in one foot there was a sharp, localized pain, as if the instep had been punctured by a shoe nail. I would struggle to free myself but always, before I had won clear, the hospital smell would return and there would be Esta again, rustling up and down the corridors on her endless errands.

Then, in the early morning light, the edges of the epic fantasy became blurred and I saw an aperture of light that was recognizable as a window, a real window and not a fragment of the Stump backdrop in Reel Three of the dream. I stared at it a long time, lovingly and with relish, for I recognized it as a symbol of relief from the terrible fatigue of fever. I have never been so grateful for light.

There was a swift rustle of starch beside the bed and I tried to turn towards it but could not because I was trussed as thoroughly as was Gulliver when he woke on the shore of Lilliput. Every part of me except my face seemed to be swathed or clamped, and it was not until Esta leaned directly over the bed that I recognized her as flesh and blood and not the teetering Esta of the dream.

I said, startled by the rattle of my own voice, "What time is it?" and she said, "About six-thirty, Pip!" There was a suppressed jubilance in her voice, as though she was speaking the first line of a joyous proclamation, and when I let my glance travel up to her eyes I saw that they glistened with tears. It seemed too ridiculous to assume that she was distressed over me so I asked, enunciating each word, why she was crying. Her hand came up at once and she drew back out of my limited range of vision, saying, "Because I'm pleased. You haven't said anything that made sense since they brought you here."

I digested this. Slowly, like an amateur juggler assembling a formidable assortment of balls, cubes and loops, I began the process of explaining to myself where I was and what had occurred. By no means all of it came back but enough to re-establish the cliff climb and the exit from the cabin that had preceded it. Then, like a wink of a light, caution caught up with me and whatever I had been going to say I was content to leave unsaid as she walked round the bed, put a cup to my lips and slipped her arm under my head.

It was pleasant to feel her hand brush my cheek and hear the sound of her finger rasp lightly across the stubble. I thought, I can cope! Esta's around! I can cope, and apparently I'm not more than half dead. The drink inside the cup tasted like Arcadian nectar. It was probably barley water.

The room sorted itself out into a normal shape and so, to some extent, did I, gingerly canvassing my system as Tom Sawyer might have put it, for ailing portions. As far as I could determine, nothing was missing. I was trussed but whole. My left shoulder felt like the face of the cliff down which I had fallen, my right arm was in plaster and my head seemed as vast as Morney-Sutcliffe's face in my dreams.

"What day is it?"

"Don't bother about days."

"I want to know. How long have I been here like this?"

"Getting on for a fortnight; eleven days actually."

"I've been flat out all that time?"

"More or less. You came round now and again but you were still heavily concussed."

This roused a more urgent interest in my injuries. She told me, in defiance of hospital protocol, that I had been admitted with a badly fractured arm, a broken collarbone, a damaged kneecap, several large bruises, innumerable cuts and scratches and severe concussion.

"No ribs broken?"

"No, and no serious damage to your head. I told them it was the least vulnerable part of your make-up."

She was slightly perky now and I asked her to tell me what had happened after I had fallen to the beach but she said, "Go to sleep now."

I wanted to sleep but I remembered, just in time, that she would go off duty at eight and that it was essential I should know something of the circumstances in which I had been found and brought here. It would surely be by the Doctor himself, who, according to my very hazy recollection, would have been about half a mile west of the spot where I landed if in fact he had made his way down to the cabin soon after I parted from Lorna.

"I'd like to know, Esta. It's important that I know."

She gave me a cool glance and there was no perkiness about it now. She was judging the distance between us and deciding that it was still considerable.

"Tom Havill found you," she said. "He was fishing offshore and heard you yell. He thought it was someone cut off by the tide and came ashore to get them. He and his boy took you along to Shelly Bay where the policeman phoned for the ambulance. You were damned lucky, a lot luckier than you deserve. Now go to sleep. I'm taking your temperature."

She stuck a thermometer in my mouth and I drifted off to sleep before she withdrew it. I slept most of the day and the day after that and in the brief intervals I was awake I didn't feel like talking to anyone, least of all to Morney-Sutcliffe, who looked in every afternoon. The only sound I recall him making was "Ur-huh!" which I accepted as doctor-jargon for "making steady progress."

Esta came in again about nine on the second evening, when I felt a great deal less hazy, although localized parts of my body hurt like the devil, notably a half-healed area of grazing on my knee.

I was able to study her as she moved about the private ward I occupied. It seemed about a thousand years ago that I had promised to marry her and take her on as a partner in the studio. She hadn't got her prettiness back. There was a taut look about her face, and her eyes seemed to dwarf the rest of her features. The only thing about her that hadn't changed were the small areas of dark hair not confined by the starched coif. It had a familiar lustre and glowed in the light of the bedside lamp when she bent to tinkle the thermometer in a beaker.

"Did I have any visitors?" I asked, vaguely embarrassed by our prolonged silence and she said no, I wasn't allowed any, but a lot of nosey-parkers had enquired by phone and on Stump.

"Who?"

She gave me another of her long, cool looks, compressing her lips in a way that suggested primness.

"Not her!" she said. "She's keeping well clear of it!"

It was obvious then that she knew and I made a guess at how she had acquired the information. The guess scared me, for it surely meant that everybody knew about it, including the Doctor. I tried to make a joke of it and a very feeble joke it was. "They always come clean under an anaesthetic! That's why policemen sit by bedsides, with pencils poised over notebooks."

"You didn't come clean," she said, and was obviously reluctant to pursue the subject, for she gathered up a tray and made for the door.

"Esta!"

It was a direct appeal and it stopped her, one elbow wedged in the swing door, the tin tray braced against her small breasts.

"Well?"

"I'm in a jam and I need help. How much does everybody know?"

She came back into the room and set down the tray, looking down at me with an expression of profound exasperation, the kind of look a mother might give a tiresome child who is demanding his fifth drink of water after being tucked up for the night.

"Nobody knows, I'm certain of that! They probably had the same hints that I had but they weren't in a position to make use of them, or maybe they just weren't interested! After all, Lorna is a common enough name around here. I know three Lornas, not counting her, but they aren't married and they don't play around with little boys! In any case, I had my suspicions some time ago, although I paid you the compliment of thinking them ridiculous!"

"I suppose you think I should have made a clean breast of it when we had that row?"

She considered this; she might have been pondering an academic question.

"No," she said, "I could hardly expect that. A person prepared to involve himself in that kind of mess and in a place as small as Redcliffe Bay would naturally keep his mouth shut about it. In a way it expained a lot of things about you, and about us. In a way it was a kind of relief to find it was as stupid and as incredible as it was!"

"How can you be sure that you are the only one around who has put two and two together?"

"I should have heard, shouldn't I? Do you think Redcliffe Bay wouldn't seethe with that much heat under it?"

It was true of course. If my involvement with Morney-Sutcliffe's wife had been general knowledge I should have been able to tell from the way the other nurses looked at me, and almost certainly from the Doctor's bedside manner.

"You say I've been here a fortnight. Do you know where she is?"

"Is that still important?"

"It's important."

"She went off on one of her trips in the sports car and she's due back in a week or so. I heard the Doctor telling Matron."

Somehow, in conveying this information, she managed to impress on me that she thought of Lorna Morney-Sutcliffe as trash, but at a deeper level there was a flicker of curiosity.

"What's so special about her?" she asked.

How did you answer a question like that without sounding as fatuous as a lovesick schoolboy mooning after somebody like Jean Harlow or Norma Shearer? I wasn't even sure myself what I found special about her, even when I was able to dismiss her as a person and think of her as a symbol. I worshipped her body, but I knew by now that she was morally worthless and that even her sophistication would pass almost unnoticed in any city with a population of over fifty thousand. She might have impressed Paxtonbury but she would have found plenty of strong competition in a Bournemouth or a Torquay, and far too much in Deauville or Le Touquet. I knew this but it didn't make any difference. I would have still preferred her to the Queen of Sheba, Helen of Troy or even the Venus of Urbino. She had become a habit during the trance period, and even in my present state of health, I realized that the habit would be very difficult to break. I don't know whether Esta surmised this simply by looking at me, but what she did deduce was enough to cause her to make a snap decision on the spot. She glanced through the glass panel of the door in order to make certain the corridor was empty then sat in the visitor's chair between me and the window.

"You can't expect me to go on discussing it without giving me the broad outlines," she said. "I don't want to know all the dirty details and I'm not asking out of motives of good, old-fashioned jealousy, but you said you were in a jam and you are in one, or will be sooner or later. How on earth did it *start?* Why did she pick on you, of all people?"

Her voice was so strident, and her approach so unflattering, that I must have smiled. She said, grimly, "It isn't funny, Pip! You'll laugh the other side of your face when you're out of here, but before I start preaching I want to know the background. I thought I knew most things about you but it seems I knew very little. You only showed a bit of yourself to me all the time we were together. If you want any help, or advice—and I'm not in the least sure that you do—you've got to show rather more. Otherwise we'll pass! God knows, I don't want you to confide in me. Right now I'm sorry for you but that's about all! Can you get that into your thick skull?"

I told her the broad outlines of my association with Lorna but very little more. I wasn't contrite and I wasn't apologizing to her and I'm sure she was aware of this, but nothing I said generated self-pity on her part. She heard me out without a blink and when I had finished all she said was, "I only made one mistake but it was a big one. Up to now I assumed that she made all the running!"

"She did make it!"

It was an ill-advised thing to say and I soon discovered as much. I had never seen Esta lose her temper but she lost it now. My attempt to saddle Lorna with the major share of the blame produced a curious effect upon her. She seemed to quiver with rage as she bounced to her feet and glared down at me.

"You men are insufferable!" she shouted and then, lowering her voice somewhat as a door banged down the corridor, "You never show the least guts, discrimination or even fairness! Nearly all of you are guided by penis rather than brains but you don't even have the honesty to admit that! I must have been crazy to imagine I could waste my life on a rabbit like you! I suppose there must be quite a few men around who want more from women than a few seconds' sweaty excitement on a bed, but you don't qualify! I was wrong about everything I thought about you, up to the moment you backed down on me and started lying and lying about everything that mattered, but even then it wouldn't have been so bad if you had told me what you really wanted and not let me go on believing you were a special kind of person. You pretended about everything from the very beginning. You don't want affection, loyalty or even friendship from a girl. To hold your interest for more than five minutes a woman has to be flat on her back when she isn't preparing something to put in your belly. I'm not saying any man is much different, but I thought you were and you encouraged me to go on believing you were. As to that Morney-Sutcliffe woman, you took everything she offered the minute she offered it without a thought of how much misery you might cause, or what would become of either of you when it was over! But all the time you were telling yourself it was you who was being seduced and that made it fine with what was left of your conscience!"

It was a blistering assessment but not, strictly speaking, a very fair one. Even now it seems that way to me and I know I thought of it as such at the time.

"I daresay you're right about most things," I growled, "but don't run away with the idea I didn't have any reservations. I did, on the day the Doctor saved Ben Boyland's life in that pit in the High Street, and I would have broken it off then if she had given me the chance!"

"You'll break it off now," she said, "and I'm hanged if I don't tell you why and leave you to think about it! If it hadn't been for Morney-Sutcliffe I doubt if you would have pulled through —and even if you had you would have lived out the rest of your life with one arm and a four-inch stump! You were pretty much of a mess when they brought you here, and the surgeon they fetched from Paxtonbury was all for amputating. But Morney-Sutcliffe dug in his heels and Morney-Sutcliffe was right! I always thought of him as a man who knew his business but I never realized how good he was, or how much moral courage he had, until he stood up to that Paxtonbury quack and accepted full responsibility! Quite apart from that he watched over you like ten fathers during the crisis. He was here three times one night, and the night before last was the first unbroken sleep he's had in ten days and all on your account! How does it feel to owe that much to a man whose wife you've been seducing twice a week and three times on Sundays?"

With that she was gone, whisking up the tray as if she would have been delighted to bang me over the head with it, and she didn't look in again for twenty-four hours. I was glad she didn't; I had plenty to think about one way and another.

[3]

I don't think I was fully aware of the impact of this denunciation until I was through the worst of it and beginning to mend. It was early October then and with the season ending I began to get visitors from the town. Their solicitude put a sharper edge on the guilt I felt in respect of the Doctor, who spent about fifteen minutes in my ward every day. I believe I could have set my face against him, anaesthetizing what Esta had called "the remains of my conscience" with all the odds and ends Lorna had fed me when discussing him as a husband. I could never see him cross the room, with that slightly tilted, cat-on-a-roof walk of his, without imagining his Friday night visits to Lorna's bedroom and his alleged affronts to her dignity. I never doubted her story, perhaps because it exactly fitted my conception of Basil as a lover. It was so much in character with his bossy impatience, with the impression he always gave of being so much wiser and better informed than anyone else in Redcliffe Bay. I didn't even doubt it when I began to realize how essentially kind he was, once you had discounted the shattering arrogance of the man. No one could have devoted more skillful attention to a patient and no one could have shown more thoughtfulness and consideration in a variety of ways. He let me stay on in the private ward usually reserved for critical cases, and my presence here would have cost me five guineas a week if he hadn't written me down as a Hospital League patient, who belonged in a general ward and paid according to his circumstances. He also rooted out an insurance policy Birdie Boxall had taken out on my behalf, and arranged it so that I could claim the entire cost of his and the other surgeon's fees. He told Matron (whose dislike of me dated from my occasional late delivery of Esta) to get me a radio that worked properly, and after a time he began to treat me, if not as an equal, then at least at one with his cronies on the Council. All this, of course, made me very uneasy in his presence, but he wasn't solely responsible for lifting the curtain on a new aspect of Redcliffe Bay. His unwitting allies in this respect were numerous, and included several of the people whose daily life I had shared on Stump since I became Birdie Boxall's apprentice five years before.

Alison Sweetland looked in at least once a week, bringing grapes, cigarettes, and magazines. She was almost seven months pregnant now and looked like a little blonde penguin, but she was so obviously pleased with herself that she wanted to share her *joie de vivre* with everybody she met. She had grown prettier I thought, as though to offset Esta's loss of sparkle. There wasn't a trace of the mousey, desperately-frightened little woman who had talked with us in the living room of the Manse on the night Esta emptied the fire bucket over Rex and the deaconess. Perhaps Rex himself was working overtime on Alison to salve his own conscience, or perhaps it was the new personality Esta gave her when she persuaded her to spend her Post Office savings on clothes and a new hairstyle. She seemed very concerned over my injuries and more so over the fact that Esta and I had decided to go our different ways. Esta hadn't told her this, she got it out of me one afternoon when I was tired and offguard, and at once set herself to heal the breach in a kind but clumsy way. She might have fooled herself into thinking she had made some progress with me, but she gave up after broaching the matter to Esta, who was sharp with her. After that she didn't say very much when she waddled into the ward but just smiled, laid her grapes or oranges on the locker and made conventional remarks about my progress.

Rex Sweetland breezed in one Sunday after conducting a service in the men's ward. He too, it seemed, was in high good humor, now that a son (he was convinced that it was a son) was on his way, and even went so far as to tell me that lack of children had been a source of permanent disappointment to him. I wondered if the broad, professional smile on his face would freeze if I told him I had been there when he was taking his first stumbling steps towards getting his lady organist in the family way. It was an uncharitable thought, but having seen him kneeling on the Sunday School floor with his head on Angela's plump knees, I found it difficult to take him seriously.

Myfanwy and Owen Rees were regular visitors and usually came on Saturdays when school was closed. Myfanwy wasn't pregnant and unlikely to be, but she had Alison's bouncing faith in everyone's goodness and the same disposition to see Esta and me tidily married and repopulating Stump.

She knew all about the break and tried more than once to set about mending it with rather more tact than Mrs. Sweetland had shown, but Owen checked her with a schoolmastery frown. "Mind your own business, Myfanwy," he said, "and let them mind theirs! Esta Wallace is only eighteen and Pip is only twenty. If they take as much time as we did to make up their minds, he's got another twelve years, and I daren't say how long Esta has got!" That put a stop to any attempt on Myfanwy's part to reverse the roles as matchmaker. She was very sensitive about her age, although everyone on Stump knew she could give Owen four or five years.

Visitors such as these kept me in touch with what was going on about Stump. Scatty Wallace had invented a collapsible coffee table and was trying to get it patented. Mrs. Wallace was thinking of selling the shop and taking a boardinghouse on Frog Terrace. Arthur Willoughby, the golf-mad partner of the practice run by Dudley Snell, was in financial straits and had had to sell Dudley a partnership for a thousand pounds. Linford Scott-Shawe, the tyrannical boss of the Redcliffe Bay Operatic

Society, was currently producing the *Mikado* and had cast Dora Gorman, of the Rainbow Café, as Yum-Yum, to the unspeakable chagrin of Lily Pyne, the undertaker's niece, who had played it twice, the last time when she was thirty-eight.

I would have made very little of all this a year ago and would have joined Lorna in sneering at it in the summer but now, isolated from Stump and entering my fifth week on my back, I could listen to the town gossip with interest and even attempt to engage Esta in discussing it when something really sensational came up, such as the ultimatum Bill Belcher, the East Stump butcher, had recently received from "Her," the mistress he had openly maintained in the flat over his shop for more than a decade. I thought a joke or two about this might mellow Esta's attitude towards me but it didn't, not even when I suggested that "Her's" determination to become the legal Mrs. Belcher after all these years had been prompted by Myfanwy's capture of Owen Rees, which was Esta's doing. All she said was, "It's about time! She was a fool not to insist on it long ago!" indicating that Bill's treatment of his mistress was additional proof of the moral bankruptcy of men.

This militantly feminist attitude of Esta's was not only new but thoroughly uncharacteristic of her. She had always seemed to me a very tolerant person and it was difficult to believe that my affair with Lorna Morney-Sutcliffe had been responsible for souring her entire outlook, as would seem to be the case. I tried to tackle her on this once or twice but she only shrugged herself out of the ward in answer to a bell that hadn't rung. It was not until the beginning of the sixth week that I was able to reopen the subject, but that was a day or two after the curious conversation I had with Ben Dagmar, editor of the *Messenger*, who took time off to spend a whole visiting hour with me.

Ben came shuffling in unexpectedly one afternoon and at first I thought his visit was prompted by a hope of checking on the story I had put about to explain my presence halfway up the cliff after dark. He did mention this, hoping to extract something more plausible than the story I had put about that I was trying out a new camera and taking twilight shots of the bay. When I stuck to this yarn he didn't question it but said, laying aside his green trilby and fiddling with his watch chain, "Seems a crazy thing to do. Would have thought a chap like you would have had more sense! All the cliffs here are treacherous and to go fooling around on them in the half-light is lunacy. Didn't have suicide in mind, I suppose?"

He knew something, I decided, but not much, and I wasn't going to give him any more help than I had to.

"No, Ben," I told him, smiling, "I'm not that disenchanted with Redcliffe Bay. I can't get out of this place fast enough and I'm not referring to hospital!"

"Don't believe a word of it!" he said gruffly. He knew me that well and could see that I was even more confused and undecided than when I had come to him for advice at the time of Birdie Boxall's death.

"Matter of fact," he went on, "I came here with a proposition."

"The place is sold," I said. "Dudley Snell was here yesterday and the new people take over on Monday. I daresay you can come to some arrangement with them about pictures for the paper."

He sat down and used his battered trilby like a rosary, passing its soft brim through fingers seamed with half a century's overspill of printer's ink. I didn't recall ever seeing him so ill at ease.

"Fact is," he said, suddenly, "you could help solve my problems. I'm attached to that paper of mine and when I die I don't want to see it swallowed by one of these damned combines! Those people can't handle local news. You have to grow up in a place before you can write about it. Why don't you sign on with me as a photographer-reporter? I couldn't pay you much but there would be prospects. I don't know how much longer I can trundle round the district on a bicycle. If we got along I'd make you a partner in a year or so."

It was an interesting offer and it tempted me. I had worked with Ben on all kinds of local stories in the past and I hadn't much doubt that I could satisfy him. He wasn't one of those old-fashioned editors who insist on long, chunky reports, good syntax and everybody's name in the column. He believed in modern presentation, with plenty of pungent paragraphs, some of them not much more than amplified captions of the kind I supplied with pictures. I said:

"What's behind this, Ben? Everybody is making a fuss of me now that I've decided to move on. You could easily find yourself a junior reporter and train him."

"Don't you believe it," he said earnestly. "I need someone who has an affection for the place, someone who believes in it!"

"Then why pick on me?"

"Oh, you're just impatient to stretch your legs," he said, "and I can't say I blame you, but you won't find anything out there that compensates you for leaving this place behind."

"Now what gives you the right to say that?" I argued. "I never heard of you going farther than London on a ten-and-sixpenny football excursion!"

"That's so," he said, "but there was a reason for it in my case. You know about me and Hetty Harding I suppose? The girl who drowned herself on my account?"

"Everybody in Redcliffe Bay knows about you and Hetty Harding. It's part of the local folklore."

"They don't know that I still put flowers on her grave every time her birthday comes round. It's her birthday today, I've just come from the churchyard. Ah, I see I've at last succeeded in surprising you!"

He certainly had. Hetty had jumped in our dock with an anchor round her neck and Ben's child in her womb more than forty years ago, but here was Ben, wrinkled, grey and paunched, still hankering after her in the way I hankered after Lorna. It gave me a strong feeling of kinship with him, so strong that I was tempted to tell him the truth there and then if only to see what he would make of it. I might have done so had I not been so sure that he would come down heavily on the side of law and order and I wasn't ready for that. In between Morney-Sutcliffe's visits I still had plenty of Lorna in my system and this, I suppose, was the real reason why I didn't accept his offer. I was pretty certain that Redcliffe Bay wouldn't hold Lorna much longer, and if I signed on with Ben that would mean the end of all prospects of meeting her again. My conscience troubled me but not all that much, certainly not as much as Esta imagined. I knew that, sooner or later, I would have to see her again and the only mental reservation I had as regards continuing the association was one insisting on a clean break with the Doctor. I was by no means clear how this could be achieved but I meant to try again the moment I escaped from hospital. I still wanted her like hell but not at the price of continuing this hole-in-the-corner courtship, and not at the risk of exposing him to ridicule. I was leaving town anyway, and something told me that once I went she wouldn't be long following my example. Somehow there didn't seem anything wrong in our continuing to associate in a place hundreds of miles away and as things were he would be well rid of her. I wish I could have explained all this to Ben but of course that wasn't possible, so I fell back on the argument I had used when I had been challenged by Esta.

"A chap my age oughtn't to bury himself in a place like this, Ben. Surely you, of all people, can understand that. I don't say I'd leave it for good, but I ought to have a look around somewhere else. I ought to travel a bit, and see how I measure up to a wider sphere. Didn't you want to do that when you were my age?"

He was some time answering and I let him ponder. I wanted reassurance from at least one Redcliffian and in the end he provided some.

"Yes," he said slowly, "I daresay both Hetty and I would have gone if things had turned out differently, but in the circumstances it seemed wrong somehow. Hetty going that way, and on my account, rooted me here, like an unquiet ghost you might say. That's why I stayed on but now I can't say I regret it, not when you look at the state of the world today."

"You could have married someone else when the dust settled."

"No, I couldn't," he said, indignantly, "that would have been even more of a let-down! Hetty and me, we were made for one another and I would have thought of her every time I laid hands on another woman. It wouldn't have been fair on whoever that woman was and it would have been rubbing salt in a cut that took a hell of a time healing. Does that make sense to you?"

"More than you know, Ben," I said fervently, "a whole lot more than you know!"

"I thought it would somehow," he said, smiling, and then, after subjecting me to a long, doubtful stare, "You and that chit of Scatty Wallace's—the one who is this year's Water Queen? When you do leave will you go with any kind of understanding?"

"No," I told him bluntly. "There doesn't seem much point in exchanging one set of shackles for another."

His green trilby turned a full circle. More than ever it reminded me of a rosary.

"I see. Ever read Stendhal?"

"No," I said, "but I've heard of him."

"You ought to try him sometime. Taught me a lot. I took him up after reading a single line he wrote somewhere. '*You can make anything in solitude except character!*' Something to bite on there. It's a damned lonely business getting through life solo!"

He stood up, crammed on his hat and shuffled towards the door where he stopped.

"When do you reckon to get out of hospital?"

"Doctor Morney-Sutcliffe says in about a fortnight but I'll have to take it quietly for a month or so. I'm not in that much of a hurry."

"Where are you going to stay now the studio is gone?"

"I'll get digs."

"Don't do that. Digs are depressing here out of season and too damned expensive in season. Why don't you move in with me? I've plenty of room in that barn of a place over the printing office."

I said I would be very happy to do this and he left with a more cheerful expression, obviously half-persuaded that I was won over to his proposal. I suppose I was, and might even have settled for it if there hadn't been several new twists in the road I was travelling.

CHAPTER EIGHT

[1]

That was how things rested when a long, fine October ended in the first gales of autumn, and the south-facing window of the ward was slashed with rain and rattled by a wind that came whooping over Mitre Head, as though to blow the last of Redcliffe Bay's visitors back to their Birmingham suburbs and Clapham terraces.

The room had now become a kind of staging-post between past and future, and because the past held so many regrets, and the future was so full of uncertainties, I came to appreciate the neutrality it offered.

Visitors brought me town gossip three times a week and Esta, although not by any means cordial, maintained a professional approach that I found preferable to the prickliness of my first period of convalescence. She was obviously keeping my secret for none of my visitors came fishing for information, dropping Lorna's name into their conversation as if they were playing charades. This was the accepted way of digging for facts in Redcliffe Bay. As the days passed, however, and no whisper of Lorna reached me, I passed through successive stages of curiosity, anxiety and resentment concerning her and half made up my mind that she had left town for good the moment she heard of my accident. If it had been anyone but her the news of a flight on the part of a married woman would have been flashed across Redcliffe Bay in a matter of hours but people had grown accustomed to her sudden exits and unexplained returns, especially after it was known that the Doctor had found her in

Paris. Erratic comings and goings could be expected of a woman who had lived among Can-Can girls, postcard vendors and Bohemians, which was how Redcliffe Bay thought of Parisians. It was after the Doctor had issued a brief communique to the effect that his wife still had relatives in France (according to Lorna this was untrue) that we stay-at-homes took her disappearances and reappearances for granted. We were also reinforced in our belief that the Doctor must be a very rich man and a very tolerant one to grant a pretty young wife so much license to spend and to gallivant. It may have been Redcliffe Bay's acceptance of this state of affairs that had helped to keep our association such a close secret.

All the same I began to fidget, to wonder where she was, what she was up to and why she had made no attempt to get in touch with me. I also wondered why the Doctor himself never mentioned her in my presence, but the fact that he did not caused me no uneasiness. There was no reason on earth why he should discuss his domestic arrangements with me, or, for that matter, with anyone else in the town. Up here, of course, he was shown an even greater deference than he received in the town and had I been able to look at him impersonally, as I did before I became involved with his wife, I would have derived plenty of amusement from his daily appearance in the ward.

He never arrived alone. There was always a little retinue of Matron, staff-nurse and probationer at his heels. It was like watching a barrack-room inspection conducted by a formidable camp commandant, with a starchy Matron acting as subaltern, the staff-nurse as company sergeant-major and the probationer as an orderly poised to leap in any direction on receipt of a command from one of her superiors. In our more companionable days Esta had described this daily ritual to me but I think she did Morney-Sutcliffe an injustice when she said that he thrived on veneration. I don't think he even noticed it, he was far too absorbed in his work. It was only when one of them got under his feet that he was apt to bark like a mastiff.

Sometimes the realization of all that had happened since that first afternoon on Lorna's boat would return to me in the form of a cold, creeping sweat. Watching him sweep through the door in the van of his pattering little procession, I was half-persuaded that I was still a prisoner of the sequence-pattern of the dream, that Lorna and I had never been acquainted outside that dream and that I would awake at any moment to learn that this man's wife was just another Valley matron who had never given me a second glance. It might have been this doubt on my part that made it possible for me to lie still while he examined me and answer up briskly when he asked me a question. The juxtaposition of Morney-Sutcliffe, myself and Lorna continued to foster this air of unreality until our final encounter.

When he was gone, however, and I was alone watching the wind driving the cloud formations along the crest of the links, I could, as it were, repossess myself of Lorna, and sometimes enjoy in retrospect the furtive hours we had spent together. It was then that I could come to terms with it and Esta's vitriolic denunciation would seem stuffy and provincial, and she herself would appear as naïve as Rex Sweetland before we discovered that he too could be counted among Esta's majority of men who used their genitals as a compass. Somehow, towards the end of my long sojourn up there, all the urgency was ironed out of the situation but in the place of misgiving I was filled by a longing to know where Lorna was, what she was planning to do and, above all, precisely how I stood with her.

There was, after all, a practical reason for wanting to know. I had stalled Ben Dagmar's offer of a job but I hadn't, as yet, rejected it out of hand. Flight from Redcliffe Bay and Lorna were now fused, the one having no purpose without the other. I was not the victim of my own propaganda and was able to keep at least two salient factors of my future in view, no matter how unpredictable that future appeared as a whole. I had received no answers to any of the jobs I had applied for before the accident and, although I reckoned that the money I had in the bank would keep me for a year or so, it was by no means a fortune, and was insufficient to buy anything but a foundering city studio. I had no real faith in my ability to make money and have not since acquired any, despite a succession of well-paid posts over a period of thirty years. I was not the money-making type and Lorna, I knew, needed money in large, juicy dollops. I sometimes wondered if a deserted Basil Morney-Sutcliffe would be sufficiently kindhearted to settle something on her, even if she was the guilty party in a divorce suit, and it occurred to me that perhaps this was the solution towards which she had been working for some time and might even have achieved for all I knew. If she was indeed gone then her long silence surely implied that she had discarded me, in which case I might as well accept Ben's job and make some shift towards feathering my own nest. On the other hand, if she was still in the offing and had resolved to go on seeing me behind Basil's back, it was essential I should explain that I could not accept this alternative.

God knows I wanted her but not at the cost of living my life as a fugitive from justice. Either way it was imperative that I should see her, or hear from her, and it was only after considering and rejecting a variety of half-baked initiatives that I hit on one with a sporting chance of success.

The Doctor usually made his rounds about midday and it seemed to me that I could only rely on complete security if I rang Lorna at "Heatherdene" when he was actually on the premises and more or less in view. It was unlikely that Lorna, if she was in the district, would be weathering out the gales in the cove and even if she was I did not care to risk talking to her on the party line shared by the family at the farm. I could not write to her but if I weighed my chances carefully I could slip out of the ward and telephone the house. If I was in luck I might be able to speak to her directly. If not, as seemed more likely, the maid or cook might tell me where she was and when she was likely to be back.

The hospital telephone was not enclosed in a booth. It was bracketed to the wall about halfway down the long corridor immediately opposite the women's general ward and I could probably make the call before anyone passed within earshot. I decided to make the attempt as soon as I was certain Morney-Sutcliffe was on his rounds.

Luck seemed to run my way. The next morning I learned that he was due to perform a mastoid operation in the theatre, which opened off the corridor a few yards beyond the telephone, and after his brief visit to me I slipped out of bed and put on my dressing-gown as if I was making a visit to the toilet. I was fairly mobile now, although I could only use one arm and my knee was still very stiff. I kept the corridor in view and waited until the patient, her escort and the sister had passed into the theatre. Morney-Sutcliffe came out of the washroom a moment later, an imposing figure in his ankle-length operating kit. The moment he was inside the theatre I darted along the empty corridor, grabbed the receiver and asked the operator for Lorna's home number.

A probationer passed but made no comment and after a dozen or so rings, during which I began to sweat with impatience, the maid's voice answered. I gave my name and she said Mrs. Morney-Sutcliffe was in the flower room and she would inform her who was calling. I was congratulating myself on the success of the ruse, and wondering why I hadn't tried it before, when the door of the women's general ward opened and Esta emerged, standing within a couple of feet of me and fixing me with a cold, speculative stare. I was so exasperated that I could have pushed her back through the swing doors. As it was I just glared back, hoping to outface her.

I had no success. She said, in a strained voice, "Who are you ringing, Pip?" and I said, unconvincingly, that it was Ben Dagmar. This didn't work and I had no faith that it would. She swallowed once or twice, as though nerving herself to take decisive action, and at that moment I heard Lorna's voice say "Kent" with a strong inflection of curiosity in her voice.

Then Esta acted, taking me completely by surprise. She moved forward in two quick steps, snatched the receiver out of my hand and slammed it back on the hook.

"Get back to bed, you fool!" she snapped. "Go on! Get back in the ward, before I make a scene right here in public!"

I was so outraged that I made no protest. My mouth opened and closed and I raised my sound hand, as if to ward off a blow across my face. For a moment we stood facing one another while, at both ends of the long corridor, nurses moved in and out of doors on their way to or from the men's ward and the kitchen. Then she said, in the same husky voice, "Go on back! There's something you've got to know! Don't keep standing there like someone caught with their trousers down! *Go back into the ward!*"

I surrendered and went back, deflated and defeated, and she followed me but remained just inside with her back to the door.

"*Kent!*" she mocked. "I heard her! She called you 'Kent'! She would, of course! 'Pip' would be too cozy for her!" Then with a grimace, "God help me, how stupid can you get?"

"It's none of your damned business!" I growled. "And if I want to phone her, I'll phone her!" It was meant to sound belligerent but it didn't. It was more like the bleat of a small boy refused permission to go out and play.

"Not if I can help it and certainly not while you're a patient in here! I'm going to show you just how big a fool she's made of you and is still making of you! Call it malice, or jealousy, or what the hell you like, but I'm going to bring you up-to-date! Hold on to yourself, you've really got it coming to you!"

I abandoned all attempts to rescue my dignity. Her voice and her cocksureness told me that she wasn't bluffing, that she had a very good reason for slamming that telephone receiver back on its hook and another for backing me in here like an unwary pedestrian being jostled out of the path of a truck.

"Get back to bed!" she said. "Go on, get back into bed!" and the habit of obedience after such a long spell in hospital worked. I got back to bed, trying to make it look as if it was my idea.

"To begin with," she said, "somebody's been keeping your place warm. At least, that's how it looked to me some time ago. By now I'd say you were ditched!"

She didn't say this with relish or vindictiveness but as a statement of fact, and I didn't reply because what she said more or less confirmed the worst of my nagging suspicions regarding Lorna's silence. She went on, in a moderate tone, "It wasn't difficult to check, not once I'd made up my mind to it. She's getting careless, or perhaps she doesn't give a damn any more. Or maybe she thinks this one is old enough to watch out for himself!"

"Who is it and how do I know this isn't a bluff?"

"No bluff, Pip. Does the name 'Shapley' mean anything to you?"

"Mike Shapley? The manager of Duckworth's?"

"That's him. God's gift to Redcliffe Bay's flappers. The Sixpenny Sheik. That's what they call him down there, according to Jonquil."

"So this is something Jonquil has told you?"

"No, it's something I checked for myself, Pip."

There was no urgency in her voice now that we were off the corridor. She had something to say and it was going to be said, whether I wanted to hear it or not. I wanted to hear it.

She glanced through the glass panel to make sure no one was heading this way and then came over and stood by the window. She looked, I thought, like a nervous amateur about to recite, determined, but not sure of her audience.

"You can have the gist first," she said, "and then we'll go back and take it from the beginning. I was down at that blue lagoon of hers last Saturday night and they were both there. In case you feel like telling yourself this means no more than a mutual interest in boating, I had better say now they were ashore. With all their clothes off. And they weren't swimming!" She paused. "Well? Do you want to hear the rest, or will you take it on trust? I may be a Peeping Tom but I'm not a liar!"

I didn't have to take it on trust. Things were beginning to fall into place, all the missing pieces that made a comprehensive picture of what, until then, had been a guessing game. Shapley's name was the most important of these pieces, or rather the recollection of Shapley's voice. With a certainty that made me goggle I remembered the low-pitched mumble I had heard issuing from the telephone that final evening I spent at the cabin. It wasn't the Doctor's voice but Shapley's and that was why I had been hustled away. Morney-Sutcliffe hadn't been anywhere near the cove that night. The man announcing his arrival was Mike Shapley.

Other things clicked into place. The look, manner and personal approach of Shapley when he had called in at the studio for his snapshots and passed some sneering remark about the renovations. I began to gibber. "How long has he been seeing her? How long have you known about it? What put you on to them in the first place?"

"I got a hunch about a week after you came in here, six or seven weeks ago. We were on our way to a Junior Imperial League dance at Paxtonbury and her car overtook us about a mile out of town. I watched it turn down that side road leading to Pendleton Mill. The bus stopped at the junction to pick up a party from Moorend but they were ten minutes coming and our bus had to wait. Just as we were moving off Shapley's car cut in behind us and turned down the same side road. It might have been a coincidence but I didn't think so."

I didn't think so either because I knew exactly where that side road led. Beyond Pendleton Mill there was a lane that wound over the shoulder of the moor to the broken-down cider house that Lorna and I had visited several times during the summer, the place where the old crone was bribed to go out and hoe her vegetable patch, while those inside made use of her deep, cushioned settle. The certainty of what had headed Lorna and Shapley in that direction made me grind my teeth. I said, "What happened after that?"

"Only a surmise," she said, "something I couldn't check on. I heard she had gone off on one of her trips, so I thought I would see if Shapley was missing. Sure enough he was, on a week's holiday, in North Wales. Did she ever take you to North Wales? Has she got another private blue lagoon up there?"

"Tell me what happened at the cove."

For the second time since she had snatched the telephone from my hand she looked doubtful. She hadn't much time for me now but there wasn't a spark of malice in Esta Wallace. She didn't enjoy hurting and humiliating anyone. Not even me.

"They were making love," she said, "some kind of love."

"You actually saw them?"

"Yes, I saw them."

She stopped, now looking almost embarrassed, and her brows drew together in a way I remembered but had forgotten as I had forgotten most of her mannerisms.

"Look, Pip," she said, "I've been straight with you, a lot straighter than you deserve! If I tell you all I saw will you tell me something in return?"

"There isn't anything you don't already know."

"But there is. This affair of yours, was it a straightforward and comparatively healthy roll-me-over-and-be-done-with-it, or was it—well—grotesque?"

"Why do you ask that?"

"What I saw was grotesque, that's why. What I mean is, if you were drawn to her in that way then I don't know a damned thing about anybody any more. I've always thought of you as more or less normal, and of her as a silly, flighty, oversexed woman but not a professional whore, catering for eccentric tastes. What I really want to know, I imagine, is were you in love with her? Did you think of yourself as being in love with her?"

"Does that matter now?"

"It matters to me."

"All right. I loved every moment I spent with her."

"From the start of it all?"

"No, not from the start. At the beginning it was a kind of exciting game, but it soon stopped being and I couldn't get through an hour without wanting her."

"How about now?"

"I don't know about now."

"But you must. You must know how much she means to you and whether it was just a strong physical attraction!"

It seemed a question requiring a simple answer but it wasn't. She had never had, was never likely to have, my kind of experience, and although I had made up my mind to be completely honest with her I didn't know how to put into words the fearful complexities of my feelings about Lorna, particularly after our final conversation in the beach shanty. I told her the only thing I was sure of myself. "I still want her," I said, "but only if she leaves here and makes a clean break with the Doctor. I can't stand any more of this crazy hide and seek, and I won't go on seeing her behind his back!"

"Is that what you were going to tell her?"

"Something like that."

"Well, it's progress of a sort," she said, reluctantly, and then took a deep breath. "I followed Shapley there on my bike. I must be dotty. Four miles uphill and down to prove you had competition with a trollop! His car was parked at the top of the goyle, hers must have been in one of the farm sheds. It was dusk when I went down but there was a light in the cabin window."

"That window is curtained. You couldn't have seen inside."

"Oh, yes, I could, after I'd gone along the lowest ledge and squatted in a muddy stream."

"Go on."

"There's a ventilator slit high up at the back and when the lamp is burning you can see quite clearly. I could anyway."

I remembered that ventilator but it had never occurred to me that the ledge could be used to overlook the cabin. I'm certain that it hadn't occurred to Lorna either or she would have done something about it.

"So you could see in. What then?"

"There was a gramophone playing. *Bye-Bye Blackbird* of all tunes! It was just daft, the whole business. I suddenly remembered that story you told me about Rasputin's murder when the gramophone kept churning out *Yankee Doodle!*"

"For God's sake, get to the point!"

"That's the funny thing, there isn't one, or not one that makes sense to me. I suppose that's what comes of living out your life in Redcliffe Bay. The nearest you ever get to this kind of thing is a glimpse of one of those postcards you told me merchant seamen flashed around the pub when the landlady was out of the way. They were dancing to the record, shuffling round without a stitch on and it looked so silly that I could have laughed if I hadn't felt so sick at myself for watching.

That's odd too when you think of it. After all, I had gone there to watch. It was something I just had to know, do you understand?"

I said I understood and I believe I did. She thought of my entire association with Lorna as something that was stupid and lecherous, but until that moment she had not thought of it as vicious.

"You went back up the goyle then?"

"I was going but I had to move slowly and before I reached hard ground the record wound down and they stopped dancing. He just stood there. He seemed to be laughing and she went down on her knees in front of him. I couldn't see what they were doing, she had her back to me . . ."

"All right," I said, savagely. "I don't want to hear any more!"

She said quietly, "There isn't any more to hear and I wouldn't have told you a damned thing about it if you hadn't tried to phone her just now. I'll have to go, I'm supposed to be serving lunches in the women's ward."

She crossed the threshold and waited a moment to see if I would make any comment. When I didn't she went out and I heard her steps clatter along the corridor.

When the sound died away the place seemed unnaturally quiet, as if it had been switched off like a dynamo. I lay and watched the tatters of cloud cross the brow of the links and the patterns made by the slanting rain streaking the window. In the far distance a hardy golfer humped his bag across my vision on his way to the tee of the sixteenth green. I thought of the cavalcade of Lornas who had passed in front of me just like that golfer since the night of the hospital dance, more than nine months ago. There had been the perfumed and cautiously randy woman I had identified with the Hon. Mrs. Graham; then the ten-a-penny cockteaser, who had gone to work on me in the attic of "Heatherdene" and after that the cool, calm, kindly woman who had steadied me the night I stumbled over the dying Birdie Boxall. Then there was the gay, playful woman who had frolicked beside me in the tepid water that following afternoon; the humiliated wife, with her tale of being visited punctually every Friday by a robot; the woman who had to find solace with a lovesick boy in out-of-the-way corners like the cider house and the cove. There was also the water-gypsy who talked of sailing her boat and her lover to the Hesperides, and finally the jaded, bitterly cynical woman who had called "Better luck next time!" when we parted on the shingle bank the night I came near to breaking my neck. There were so many Lornas that I knew, or thought I knew, but where did Esta's Lorna slot into place? Had that parting remark of hers expressed boredom with the kind of love I brought her? Had she been making a fool of me as well as her husband all this time? It was probable, I thought, but how, and to what extent? At what point had Michael Shapley entered the story? A long time ago, or the moment I went out of circulation? Did Shapley have anything to do with her prolonged hesitation to commit herself? Did Shapley have access to the money she declared she must have before she walked out on a husband? Or was she looking for something other than money that I could not provide, but Shapley, and possibly French lovers like René, could?

I realized I would never know the answer to any of these questions. I could only lie here guessing and humiliating myself and for the remainder of that day, and for many subsequent days, I did just that, looking for a crutch to help me regain some self-respect. I didn't find one and I didn't get very far with my deductions. There were clues strewn along the entire route of our association, and I weighed them as a tradesman uses a pair of scales to separate whole merchandise from spoiled. There were the assets—her beauty, her gaiety, her cheerful sensuality, her tolerance and all the odd flashes of kindness she had revealed. But there were also plenty of pointers to make Esta's Peeping Tom story credible although none of these, flattering or unflattering, explained preoccupation with a tinhorn Romeo like Michael Shapley, the Sixpenny Sheik, who sidled along behind the counters and pinched the bottoms of his salesgirls.

From all this tiresome self-analysis only one thing emerged and that was a resolve to see her once more and force the issue into the open. It seemed to me that she owed me this if nothing else. After that, I told myself, she could go her own way and I could start all over again. It was a truce of sorts and it got me through my final spell in hospital.

[2]

It was early December when I left hospital and took up temporary residence with Ben Dagmar in his rambling premises over the printing-office on East Stump. I was still an out-patient and obliged to take things easy. Ben's place was an ideal roost for a man sick and tired of his own company. He didn't attach any strings to my going there. Maybe he thought pottering about the place would give me an appetite for printer's ink but it didn't work out that way and the reason that it didn't was the location of my room, with its window looking over a part of Stump screened from the other side of the enclosure. From here I could see Scatty Wallace's ironmongery display on my right, and the old Penny Bazaar, now the premises of Duckworth's, on my left. Several times a day I saw Shapley lounge in and out of the big yard at the back, a cigarette drooping from his lips and a kind of insolent jauntiness showing in his amble to and from the stock sheds.

I didn't want to keep him under such close observation but I had to. He hypnotized me into waiting for his irregular appearances and trying to guess what was going on in his mind. The sight of him made me tremble with rage and once, when we passed one another on East Stump and he gave me a casual greeting, I was almost sick with humiliation. I wanted to turn, jump on his back and batter his cocky head to a pulp. My feelings about him made me aware of the terrible provocation under which some murders are committed. But then it went a stage further, and a trivial observation from my window laid the foundations for the final scene in what even I was beginning to regard as a black farce.

One night after his main premises were closed and in darkness I saw him emerge from the back door carrying two leather grips that looked like personal luggage. He did not go to the store, as I had expected, but down to the gate opening on to the alley, or "drangway" as we called it in these parts, a thoroughfare giving access to the rear of all the East Stump premises. There was no street lighting here. The only illumination came from the last lamp post on East Stump stationed a few yards beyond the Duckworth's frontage. It was just sufficient to light up the outlet where the backway joined the incline leading to Frog Terrace. For a moment or two I was able to study him impersonally and wonder where he was going and why he stood so indecisively at the back gate looking up and down the drangway, the inevitable cigarette a tiny red glow in a pool of sea mist that blurred the outlines of the entrance. Then I saw him look at his watch and the glance alerted me. He was waiting for someone and it could only be Lorna.

I turned out my light and sat in the dark, with the curtains drawn aside. I could hear all the late evening noises of Stump, the rattle of window blinds, the song of the wind in the naked branches of the enclosure chestnuts, the clack-clack of footsteps on the glistening pavements beyond Wallace's shop, the rhythmic thud of Ben Dagmar's ancient flatbed, churning out the supplements for next Friday's *Messenger*. No one but Shapley seemed to be about and he stood there a long time, his shoulders propped against the posts of the back gate, lighting another cigarette from the stump of the old one and throwing the dog-end aside so that it spattered a chain of sparks along the slabs. Then a yellow glow of lights showed from the northern end of the drangway and a car approached very slowly from the direction of Stump. Not many cars drove down there at night. It was only just wide enough for a van and this wasn't a van; it was Lorna's sports car and it stopped opposite Shapley.

I had made up my mind that he was going to get in but he didn't. The offside door swung open and the headlights were extinguished but the sidelights, and the faint glow of the street lamp, enabled me to keep both car and Shapley under observation. I couldn't see Lorna, except as a blob of shadow behind the steering wheel, but I watched him throw both bags into the car, slam the door and lift his hand as it moved off at the same crawling pace. Shapley didn't follow but went back into his yard, closed the gate and went inside. As far as I could determine not a word had passed between them.

The more I thought about the incident the more convinced I was that it had something to do with flight. Not just a trip somewhere, there had been too much luggage for that, but something final, of the kind Lorna and I had discussed so often and so profitlessly. It wasn't just the bags, and Lorna driving off with them like that. It was the furtiveness of her approach and her use of the back way at about ten miles per hour. I had never known Lorna drive up to any stop at less than double that speed. The car had acted as if it didn't care to attract attention. Then there was the evidence of obvious prearrangement about the visit, for Shapley had been waiting ten minutes before her arrival and had, in fact, checked the time during the interval. I kept an eye on the light of his flat over the shop and sure enough, near nine o'clock it went out and he appeared in the yard again. This time he was carrying what looked like a bundle of papers. Quite openly, obviously not caring whether anyone saw what he was doing, he put them in the yard brazier and set a match to them. The little bonfire burned for about a quarter of an hour.

I kept my watch and when the lights in the flat didn't go on again I sauntered down to the front of the building and was just in time to see him cross the enclosure. He had no hat or raincoat and obviously wasn't going far so I followed him and saw him cross to West Stump and enter the spit-and-sawdust of the Lamb and Flag. I felt like a drink myself so I went in the saloon bar, where I could watch him through the alcove window behind a row of bottles.

Dick Bannister served me, and Mabel, his wife, was attending to the public bar. Over my own half-pint I saw her draw Shapley a pint and then she came into our bar and rooted about under the counter, popping up again with two bottles of Scotch and one bottle of brandy. She said, "Is there another Martel handy, Dick?" and he gave her one, asking who was having a party.

"Mr. Shapley," she said, "they're all for him," and went out again.

I had been drinking in the Lamb and Flag since I was under age but I had never seen anyone buy two bottles of whisky and two bottles of brandy at one go. Dick must have thought it unusual too for he said, chuckling, "Some party! I always heard the company shops didn't pay their staff much!" I could have told him that Mike Shapley hadn't paid for the liquor but had been commissioned by Lorna to buy it, probably when she called and collected his bags.

One or another of the Stump regulars dropped in and several of them tried to engage me in a conversation about my health. Owen Rees offered to stand me a drink, and so did Garfield Pyne, the undertaker. Dudley Snell came in and told me that the Palfreys, who had bought my place, were a pleasant couple and were settling in. I would be welcome there any time, he said, and went on to ask if I had any plans. I told him I hadn't and I didn't accept anyone's drinks. I was too busy keeping Shapley in view.

After he had finished his pint he played a game of darts. I could hear him shouting, "Double top wanted," and things like that, and ordered another half-pint to see me through waiting time. Then Esta's old admirer, Cecil Trumper, came in and sat down next to me. He asked after my injuries and I thought I could detect a certain amount of satisfaction in his enquiries. I knew that he hated me on account of Esta, but I couldn't do anything about that. He had a clear field now and if he was unable to use it that was his grief.

I got to wondering about him and Esta, however, and whether, since our row back in June, he had improved his position with her. I said, by way of airing the subject, that she had been a trump to me during my long spell in hospital and this wiped the vacuous look from his heavy features. He said, without more than a hint of a stutter, "You and Esta, you're through, aren't you? Really through I mean!" I was surprised at the directness of the question and the undisguised resentment in his eyes. Usually he looked hunted or baffled but right now he looked as if he could spit at me. An odd thought crossed my mind. If they ever did get together and had kids, I told myself, everyone in the family would have big brown eyes, for his were even more like a spaniel's than Esta's. I said briefly that we hadn't been going around together for months now and that he must have known as much. He said he did know it, and I was sure he had done his best to make capital out of it, but he just wasn't her cup of tea and that was that. I felt sorry for him in spite of his hostility, so I said frankly "You're crazy about her, Cecil! Why the hell don't you do something about it? She isn't engaged to anyone. She's still in the market, isn't she?"

His stutter came back as it always did when he faced any kind of challenge. "It's nnno bbbbloody good so long as you're around!" he said, and before I could reply he emptied his tankard and stalked out, slamming the door so hard that Dick Bannister shouted, "Watch it, you clumsy sod!"

I had missed Shapley's exit during my conversation with Cecil but I didn't think he would be going anywhere tonight and neither was he. When I got back to Ben's place his flat light was on again and it stayed on until after midnight.

Ben came in for a chat just before I went to bed, and after a preamble he got around to asking me if I had thought any more about taking the job he had offered. He had a qualifying proposal now. I could take it for six months, with an option on both sides, and I let him go away thinking I agreed to this. It wouldn't please Cecil Trumper but I didn't give a damn about Trumper. I had too many troubles of my own. Privately, I wasn't absolutely sure I would stay and when I turned off the light, and thought about it in the dark, I understood why. It depended on what Lorna did, and also on what Michael Shapley did. In some way—I couldn't have said how—all three of us, plus the Doctor, were linked in an ill-assorted quartet. Whatever either one of us did would set course for the others, and with what had occurred earlier that evening I had a premonition that things were working towards a crisis for all of us. I was right about that. It was about the only thing I did get right that year.

[3]

When I looked out of the window and across to Mitre Head the next morning I could see that heavy weather was brewing, probably a second helping of the gales that had rattled the hospital windows throughout most of November. The sky in the west was battleship grey and the air was very still, as it always was when we were in for a blusterer.

My first thought was to keep Shapley's stairs and yard under observation. He didn't come out but now that it was daylight I could see part of his landing through a half-papered window and while I was shaving I saw his head and shoulders bob past on his way downstairs. That satisfied me that he hadn't left during the night but it was pure chance that I was able to keep track of him later in the day.

It was a Wednesday, half-day for all the shops on Stump, and it was only when I saw Vera Marker, one of his salesgirls, back Shapley's three-wheeler out of the garage that I realized I was out of step. Shapley was very jealous of that car and never let anyone else drive it. I remembered, too, that Vera had a reputation for clumsiness and her presence in the driver's seat could only mean that Mike Shapley was not on the premises. I went down to the drangway and into the yard just in time to see Vera reverse into a dustbin and then shoot forward, stalling the engine.

"Shapley will sack you on the spot if he catches you messing about with that car!" I told her, and she looked surprised and indignant, saying, "You don't think I'm doing it from choice, do you? I'm the only one in there who can drive and he left word for me to take it round to Bedwell's garage as soon as we closed."

"Where has he gone?" I demanded, thinking what an idiot I had been to let him out of my sight for two hours, and Vera said, "How should I know? He doesn't confide in me, not since I slapped his face and threatened to report him. He won't sack me either, I've got too much on him."

"Like what?"

"Like trying to corner every girl we get here in the stockrooms," Vera said. "He might be the Sheik to some of them but I've got a boy friend and to me he's a pain in the neck! Harry would have bashed him if I hadn't stopped him. He put his hand down my neck three days after I started here!"

I wasn't interested in Shapley's stockroom fumbles or in Vera Marker's virtue, but I was very anxious indeed to know where he had gone and by what means.

"Did a car call for him?" I asked and Vera said no, it wasn't a car, it was the station taxi. Apparently he was going off somewhere and seemed in a great hurry. He had cashed up and left about eleven o'clock that morning. While Vera made another attempt to negotiate the narrow gateway I had an idea. I said, "I'll drive it round for you, Vera. You go on home to lunch!" and she said, "Will you? Well, thanks, ever so!" and maneuvered herself out of the seat.

"I can't stand men like that," she said, by way of a cheerio, "can you?"

"No," I said fervently, "I hate his guts!"

The announcement seemed to cheer her up and she went off with a light, half-day-off step.

I drove the Morgan round Stump and up Fore Street to Bedwell's garage, where I called in the little glass office and told Job Bedwell that Shapley had asked me to deliver it. Bedwell said, vaguely, "Ah yes, he's flogging it. He wanted the money in advance and we had a real tussle over the price. Trouble is he's given it a real beating. I've had my eye on it; I've got my eye on every car in town, yours included!"

"Did you clinch the deal?" I asked, trying not to show too much interest, and Bedwell nodded.

"He wanted fifty and I stuck out for forty. In the end we split the difference."

I was piling up a lot of evidence. Shapley had cashed in two hours before closing time. Shapley had been called for in the station taxi. Shapley had sold his car, a factor that surely indicated that he was leaving town for good unless he anticipated buying one further afield and driving it back. He couldn't be going on holiday either, not in early December, and certainly not in the middle of the week. If he had been leaving to take up another post Vera Marker would certainly have mentioned it, if only to express pleasure at his departure. It now seemed almost certain that he and Lorna were decamping together and I thought of a way to check on this at once. I went across to the station yard and dug out old George Talbot, the nearest thing Redcliffe Bay had to a taxi rank. He operated an elderly Humber, round about 1920 vintage, and a local humorist said that before he bought the Humber he drove a coach-and-four. He might well have done, he was at least seventy years old and wore a fringe of grey hair on the collar of his overcoat like a dirty ruff. When he was not on hire he could always be found in the station yard reading a child's comic, usually *Rainbow* or *Puck*.

"Ah, 'ow be 'ee, midear?" he said, as I approached. He had cultivated a broad Westcountry accent for the benefit of the visitors. Actually he came from Bedfordshire.

I told him I had just taken Mike Shapley's three-wheeler into Bedwell's, Shapley having traded it in for forty-five pounds. If you were seeking information from George you had to give him something in exchange.

"Took 'un up the Valley hour or zo back!" he said, and this time it was difficult to conceal my surprise. The weather was far too thick for the cove but I hadn't imagined they would be so brazen as to rendezvous at "Heatherdene" in daylight. I had been convinced George had dropped Shapley at a point several miles inland, where Lorna would pick him up as she had me on several occasions.

"I've got to contact him," I said, "he's forgotten the registration book. Was he going on anywhere?"

"Ah," George said, "zeems he were. That flighty wife o' the Doctor was giving him a lift some place I reckon. Zeed his bags in that bliddy car of hers!" George hated any vehicle designed to travel more than forty miles an hour and spoke slightingly of all sports cars.

"I'll nip up and see if I can catch him," I said, and George returned to the saga of Tiger Tim in his *Rainbow*.

If I had had an ounce of common sense I would have left it there and maybe counted myself fortunate to be out of it so cheaply. It was no longer any business of mine what happened to either of them, what they did, where they went, or how much they meant to each other. The incense I had burned for Lorna since early that year was now used up. The fire was almost out, extinguished by the recurring shame I felt every time I visualized her paying homage to Shapley's insolent phallus in the cabin and now, no doubt, improving on the act in some hotel room. Emotionally I was through with her, or so I kept telling myself, but I still couldn't let her go. Not like that; not with Shapley's luggage in the boot of her car. Pride demanded that I should confront them and humiliate them somehow, that I should do my damnedest to complicate things for them and make them anxious and uneasy about their future. I didn't see how this could be achieved but I meant to attempt it if I could and was prepared, at that moment, to devote all my time and money to the purpose. Only then, I told myself, could I relax and begin to live again.

I went back to Ben Dagmar's yard, jumped in my rackety little car and headed straight for the Valley. In less than half an hour after leaving George I was breasting the incline that led to the big house at the head of the Valley.

It had come on to blow and the storm that had threatened over Mitre Head earlier in the day would burst in an hour or so. The wind was wet but it wasn't cold. The sea was ruffled and empty, with that rejected look it always had at this time of year. I stopped well short of the gate and walked up the first stretch of the drive. I didn't expect to find them there, but I was not going to leave without getting some inkling of the direction they had taken. I had forgotten all about the Doctor. Lorna might have been my wife not his; that was why I recoiled when I saw, on rounding the curve of the drive, his big black Daimler parked in the forecourt.

It was this reminder of his existence that prompted my first doubts about the logic of the enterprise, the first at all events since Esta had hauled me away from the telephone. I could not imagine what he could be doing here at this hour when he should have been on his rounds, or up at the hospital. Apart from his duties there was no reason why he shouldn't be in his own home at two in the afternoon yet the presence of his car, big, black, solid and eminently respectable, seemed thoroughly out of place in the frame of an elopement, so much so that it even crossed my mind that he and Shapley might be friendly, at least friendly enough for him to swallow a cock-and-bull story of Lorna giving Shapley a lift up to town.

Then the improbability of this caught up with me. There was too much evidence of concealment and premeditation. There was Lorna's stealthy drive down the drangway to pick up Shapley's luggage, Shapley's purchase of two bottles of whisky and two bottles of brandy and Shapley's sale of his car and demand for cash in advance. Whatever Lorna and Shapley were up to, the Doctor must be unaware of the truth.

At the same time the certainty that he was inside the house forced me to review my own position and this, in itself, gave me a chance to assess its absurdity. If the Doctor was ignorant of her association with Shapley then he wasn't likely to remain so for long. Sooner or later it would get around that they had left together, for my brief conversation with George, the taxi-driver, proved that they had made very little effort to cover their tracks. If this was so then what was I doing stalking them? The confrontation, when it came, would be far more resounding if it was made by the Doctor. The prospect of Basil Morney-Sutcliffe horsewhipping Michael Shapley all the way to the divorce courts was a very pleasing one.

I was still standing doubtfully on the outside verge of the drive when the cream front door was flung open and the Doctor appeared, moving faster than I had ever seen him move and he was never a dawdler. He hurled himself into his car and I just had time to glimpse the nature of what he was carrying. At this distance it looked like a long metal stick. Then, with a rush, the car shot forward, screeched over the loose gravel, reversed and came speeding towards me. In the fifty yards or so separating us it built up to over forty miles an hour and passed me as a heavy black mass. Even so I was positioned to see that it wasn't a stick he was carrying but a blue-barreled shotgun that had been flung against the nearside window by the lurch of the car on the bend of the drive. Then he was gone, in a spatter of gravel and a cloud of exhaust.

I stood there on the verge like a man who has just evaded the charge of a mastodon. He hadn't seen me, I was sure of that, but I had seen him in spite of the speed of his onrush and it was a Basil Morney-Sutcliffe I had never seen before. The expression on his big face was as tense as that of a dirt-track rider negotiating a sharp bend in the final lap of a race. He was sitting well forward, holding his body in the posture in which he usually walked. He was hatless and coatless and the fury of his exit, plus the gun, paralyzed my wits.

I must have remained staring towards the gate for two or three minutes before I was able to make a guess at the reason for his hurry. It couldn't be a telephone message concerning a patient or an accident for a shotgun is not part of a Doctor's equipment. Neither was he a sporting man. As far as I knew he never played games but, judging from his expression when he rushed by, he meant to use that shotgun the moment the target came in view. The target could only be me, his wife or Michael Shapley. It steadied me somewhat to reflect that, of the three, Shapley was the most likely.

And then I had another thought, one of the very few unselfish thoughts I had had in months. He was clearly in such a temper that anything might happen when he caught up with them, and I felt responsible for whatever happened to them when he did. What was even more terrifying was the thought of what might happen to him afterwards.

I suppose that moment was the first in months when I really saw daylight, the only time in all those weeks that I had been whoring after Lorna that I saw her, without prejudice, as Basil Morney-Sutcliffe's wife. In the period between her original talk of the failure of their marriage and my total enslavement, I had thought of her as a woman doing a kind of penance by having to live with him, and after that I saw her as belonging wholly to me. But now, at last, I was jolted into an awareness of their true relationship, a woman who had consistently betrayed him and a man who had it in mind to resolve matters with a double-barreled shotgun.

The horror of what was likely to happen in the next hour struck me like the blast from a furnace door. I felt so helpless and distraught that my knees buckled and I threw out my sound arm to steady myself on the gate-pillar. My involvement in what was happening made me feel physically sick and for a few moments I leaned there like a drunken man at a crossroads. In a way it was a crossroads. On the one hand was an acute awareness of my personal contribution to the situation and on the other, urging me to take a step in the opposite direction, was the memory of all the skill and kindness he had lavished on me during my weeks in hospital. I don't think I felt alarmed on Lorna's account and I am sure I hardly gave Shapley a thought. What horrified me was the prospect of seeing Morney-Sutcliffe do something in a moment of blind rage that would lay his life in ruins and might conceivably point him into a dock on a murder charge. Someone had to tell him that neither his wife nor Shapley was worth a charge of common assault, much less his neck, and that someone could only be me, the one person alive to the circumstances. I understood this the moment I got a grip on myself and, having done so, realized that there wasn't a minute to be lost.

His car had swung right after clearing the gateway and this meant that he was heading east along the coast, and not inland towards the main road in which case he would have turned left to follow the course of Links Road behind the town. His direction therefore indicated that he was heading for the cove, but it seemed to me unlikely that Lorna could be contemplating putting into practice her crazy notion of crossing to the Continent under her own steam. It was very late in the year for a cabin cruiser like the "Linda" to make such a journey and until then I had assumed the boat was laid up for the winter. I remembered, however, that it had still been at anchorage when Esta had spied on them, and now that I thought about it, it seemed likely that Morney-Sutcliffe had information regarding their plans that I didn't have. Something else occurred to me as I leaned against that gate-pillar, trying to make up my mind what to do. There was, or seemed to be, a thread of panic running through the general pattern of the exodus, as though Lorna, and possibly Shapley too, were acting under pressure. Each possessed a cool head. Lorna had never let me hurry her into anything except coition, whereas Shapley had played it very coolly all the time I had him under observation the previous evening. Sometime during the day the necessity for a speedy decision, perhaps even an abrupt change of plan, had arisen and this probably accounted for Shapley's departure two hours before closing time, without even delivering his car to Bedwell's as arranged.

Then, as clearly as though the answer to most of these guesses had been broadcast over a loudspeaker, I thought I knew more or less what had happened. They had certainly planned to leave, but separately, she by car, carrying his luggage, he by the one-fifteen train to Paxtonbury, which made a connection with the Cornish express at the junction. They would then meet about six P.M. in London and after that where they went was anybody's guess; but something had occurred during the morning to bring Shapley up here for a fresh consultation. It seemed very probable that somewhere along the line the Doctor had intervened, causing them to bolt like rabbits. Whether or not they were on the boat depended, I imagined, on their knowledge of how close he was on their tail. I didn't bother to seek information at the house but staked everything on my guess. I ran back to my car and pushed her over the crest at her maximum speed, about half that of Morney-Sutcliffe's cruising pace.

Either I was on the right track or both the Doctor and I were much in error. As soon as I reached the outskirts of Phillips's farm I saw his Daimler parked at the spot where the cart-track joined the footpath. It was empty and the only person in sight was Farmer Phillips's pigman, an elderly laborer called Coates who, on seeing me, put down his feeding pails and scratched his head, as though searching for an explanation of two townees descending the goyle in a hurry within moments of one another. He had a reason to be puzzled. The weather had worsened a good deal in the last hour and there was not much more than an hour's light in the day. Masses of grey cloud were scurrying north-east and the wind had whipped up, bringing intermittent showers of sleet. Once inside the gully, however, it was relatively quiet and I scrambled down the steep, winding path at a pace that made me agonizingly aware of my partially-mended knee. Stunted trees and a wilderness of bramble made observation of the cove impossible until one was three-fourths of the way down, but the moment I reached the first open patch I stopped, hoping to take stock of the situation before showing myself on the beach.

The boat hadn't been laid up. It was moored about a hundred yards east of its usual anchorage, rolling heavily in the swell and held, it appeared, by a single stern anchor. The tide was almost full and there wasn't much beach uncovered. Between the little jetty and the cruiser, but slightly nearer the land, was the dinghy with one person in it. He was pulling towards the cruiser as hard as he could scull and having all his work cut out to make headway, for the sea was getting wilder all the time. It looked more like Mike Shapley than the Doctor, but at this distance, and in this kind of weather, I couldn't be sure and I didn't wait to find out. I hurled myself down the last stretch of the path to the point where a flight of seven steps, cut in the rock, gave access to the beach. I jumped these and landed on the shingle with a crash, giving both knee and shoulder twinges that made me yell. At that moment the Doctor, gun slung across his forearm in the manner of a duck shooter emerged from the cabin and advanced with leisurely strides to the little jetty.

If I had been in less of a hurry, or had been less terrified by the certainty of what he was going to do, I might have noticed that his walk was unhurried, and reasoned that his chances of hitting the rower with scatter-shot at this range were negligible. I didn't stop to think, however, but did the first thing that came into my head. Scrambling to my feet I charged down the beach and flung myself on his back so that we both rolled the last few yards into the wash. The gun went off, both barrels discharging simultaneously and the explosion sounded like a landmine. Pebbles rattled in all directions and where the double charge was directed there was a hole in the shingle about a foot deep. If he had been carrying the gun any other way, or my leap had depressed the barrels another inch, the pair of us might have been perforated with ricochets. As it was the shingle absorbed the shock and the pellets went off at a tangent, all the gulls in the cove soaring from the rocks. Then we were both sitting among the bladder wrack looking at one another and the first thing I noticed was that he was grinning like a schoolboy. It was the first time I had ever seen him smile with his eyes.

He seemed in no particular hurry, not even when a wave crashed within a yard of us and covered us with spray. Slowly and carefully he rose to his feet, ejected the spent cartridges and looked down at me with what I can only describe as a quizzical, mildly aggravated expression.

"Young Stuart," he said, "you're a glutton for punishment! What, in God's name, are you playing at now?"

Then, as though satisfied that there was no point in reasoning with an idiot, he moved across the shingle to the end of the jetty, where he stood looking across the grey waste of water at the cruiser and dinghy, now within yards of one another. I had an unpleasant feeling that he was going to reload and try his luck, even at this impossible distance, but he didn't; he just stood there, the gun in his left hand, the other hand raised to keep the sleet from his eyes.

"I think he's going to make it!" he said at last, and I stopped trying to relate his imperturbability with the facts and joined him on the jetty, his bulk interposing between me and the tug of the gale. Through the sleet I saw the cruiser and dinghy merge and then Shapley (I could still only assume it was Shapley) make a leap for the stern, where the rope-ladder hung. He grasped it but lost the dinghy in the process. It swirled round the stern and went bobbing away on the cross tide and was soon lost in the curtain of rain. Then I caught a glimpse of Lorna at the rail, helping Shapley to scramble on deck and a moment later they both disappeared.

"Well," Morney-Sutcliffe said, "that seems to be that! If

they've got any sense they'll stay there until the weather moderates and I hope for his sake he's a better sailor than I am. Now for God's sake let's get out of this. You know more about her love nest than I do. Can you light a fire in that shanty?"

I said, without letting my mind dwell on the crazy implications of his enquiry, that there was an oil stove in the cabin and we turned our backs to the sea and climbed the beach side by side. I was glad he had mentioned the heating facilities. It gave me something to think about while he sat, with one leg crossed over the other, in the basket chair under the window. All the time the gale kept on increasing in force and every now and again the old timbers shuddered. When I had finished lighting the stove I noticed he was filling his pipe. His expression now was relaxed to the point of dreaminess.

"Funny thing," he said, stubbing away with his huge thumb as he crammed tobacco into the bowl, "funny thing your appearing from nowhere like that just when I'd written you out of the drama!"

It occurred to me that he was employing these tactics as a means of goading or interrogating me, but when I looked at him, stolidly puffing away at his pipe, I knew that this was not so. He was genuinely relaxed and not just pretending to be. He seemed almost pleased with himself, as though he had stagemanaged the entire show and found it moderately entertaining. I said, at length, "You know about me and Mrs. Morney-Sutcliffe?" and he said, with the briefest of nods, "Naturally. Why else should I be here, wet to the skin?" and went right on filling the cabin with a tobacco reek that rivalled the stink of the oilstove.

"How long have you known?"

"Does that matter?"

"Yes, it does."

He seemed to reckon me up. "Since about a fortnight after you broke your bones on that cliff yonder."

I wanted to ask him how he had found out but didn't; it would have seemed the grossest impertinence, so I said, "About Michael Shapley, too?"

"No," he said, "I can't honestly say that I knew more than the fact that Shapley was hanging out flags. As a matter of fact, I was surprised to see him when I got here. It was you I expected to find!" A wry grin puckered his pursey little mouth again. "That's why I brought the gun! It was to help you to do a right-about-turn whether you liked it or not. It seemed possible that you might strike a chivalrous attitude and argue the toss, don't you know?"

I said nothing. I felt like a boy about nine, standing in his father's study awaiting the verdict on a disgraceful school report. "For your information, however," he went on, "I hadn't the remotest intention of shooting anybody with it! Maybe over the heads of the crowd, like a riot policeman, but only if you proved obstinate. I imagine you thought otherwise, hence the pounce! You spend far too much time at the cinema, young Stuart!"

"What are you going to do about it—about Lorna?" I asked. Even my voice seemed to have reverted to a treble.

"Nothing," he said blandly, "I've done all I intend to do, and even that wasn't necessary as things turned out. I became resigned to her antics long ago—but cradle-snatching a patient of mine—that's something else! I couldn't let that go unchallenged!"

He looked at me shrewdly. It was an expression I recognized from hospital days, when he was making a professional decision and balancing factors in his mind. "Are you beginning to get things sorted out, or do I have to make you feel a bigger fool than you must be feeling already?"

It was an unnecessary dig. I already had things sorted out. He had come rushing over here with the intention of preventing a kidnapping, not an abduction. He knew all he needed to know about his wife, not only about my association with her but the kind of woman she was and perhaps couldn't help being. I must have been blind not to have realized this much long ago, as soon as I came under his hand at the hospital and got to know him as a man instead of a local figurehead. On his own admission he had brought the gun along in case I proved obstinate and although, right now, I felt abject, I was still able to wince at the nearness I came to being marched up that goyle and past Phillips's farm in front of his shotgun, a grotesque reversal of the Triumphant

Lover in one of those steel engravings in the series *Runaway Marriage* that Myfanwy Pritchard sold in her Gift Shop. In a way, I thought, I had rescued my own dignity, or what little was left of it. I said, "I was chasing Shapley myself. When I saw you drive off from your house with a gun in your car I was absolutely certain you were going to kill him and her!"

He considered this. Finally, speaking from behind a cloud of blue smoke, "It's logical. At your age!" and then, "Just who were you so anxious to protect? Her, him, or law and order?"

I was glad to be able to add a little to the credit side. "You," I said, "it seemed crazy to risk your neck over a man like Mike Shapley."

"Ah," he said, "that's what I thought, but taking it all round you don't give me credit for much intelligence, do you?"

"I do now," I said.

"Well, that's something I suppose!"

He went on smoking, and between his smoke and the oilstove the atmosphere in the cabin grew as thick as the weather outside. It didn't seem to bother him. He was clearly enjoying his hour of relaxation and I noticed that not once did he glance out of the window into the cove. He seemed to have lost interest in the cruiser riding out the gale with his wife and her lover aboard.

"Know anything about that small-town Romeo?" he said, casually.

"Not much," I said, "except that he's called the Sixpenny Sheik and has a reputation for bottom-pinching. Some of the local girls go for him but the bright ones don't."

"That's what I thought," he said, "or something like it. He isn't Lorna's type I would have said. That's why, when I got wind of her intention to go, I assumed she would get far more satisfaction putting someone like you through the wringer and watching you come out the other end. She has a penchant for young romantics as a rule. I suppose you know all about that poor devil of a writer, in Paris?"

"René?"

"That's him. He tried to hang himself and nearly succeeded.

It sobered her for a week or two but she soon got over it. Then there was a younger schoolmaster called Donkin. 'Donkey' it should have been. He was rescued by his mother who fetched him home with a flea in his ear, but Donkin wasn't a stayer. You weathered it better than most."

He spoke of us all as if we were patients and his wife a virus. There was no resentment in his voice and no pomposity either. By this time I had adjusted to his cynical amiability, but I wondered where the pomposity had gone and how I and everybody else could have been so utterly wrong about him.

"She talked about me?" he enquired suddenly.

"She said she wasn't happy but it was mostly the place, not you!"

Thumbscrews wouldn't have got me to repeat her stories of his Friday night visits and, anyway, I no longer believed a word of them. They were just part of her fantasy world and I was beginning to understand how completely she could deceive herself as well as others. I even wondered if she was a little mad and as if he could read my thoughts, which he probably could, he touched on this subject.

"She's sick," he said, "but I suppose you realize that now?"

I told him I hadn't known it and that she seemed a very healthy woman to me and when he did not elaborate I asked him outright if it was some secret tragedy that made her act the way she did. He smiled and didn't answer for a moment, then he said, "I told you you spent too much time watching that Hollywood trash! Tragedy sobers people, most people." He stood up, knocked out his pipe and lifted the corner of the curtain. Then he sat down again and refilled his pipe, moving his hands with great deliberation, as though he was operating. Confidence, and a kind of limitless patience seemed to issue from the tips of his fingers. You felt safe watching them. Safe and sane.

"Put it this way," he said, "she's sick enough to need special treatment but where would she get it in this wilderness? I'm not referring to Redcliffe Bay but to Britain as a whole. We prescribed firing-parties for shell-shock cases during the war, didn't we? And we went right on doing it, until there were so many cases that they had to be classified as something other than cowardice in the face of the enemy. Since then we've made little or no progress on her type of trouble. The Continentals have. She ought to have gone into Doctor Hirshmann's sanitorium when she had the chance. He's about the only man I know who could do something for her."

"What kind of cases does Doctor Hirshmann treat?" I asked cautiously.

"Her kind—frightened people who confuse fantasy with reality because they've been compulsive liars since their childhood. She had a very tough childhood. Did she tell you about that?"

"No," I said, "only the fun she had as a Bohemian on the Left Bank. *Was* she a Bohemian?"

"She slept with two or three I believe, but as they too were compulsive liars I daresay they helped convince one another."

There was so much I wanted to ask him. How real was her father artist? How on earth did he happen to meet her? Why did he take the frightful risk of marrying her and why, having married her, did he bring her to a place like Redcliffe Bay? I wanted to find out whether she was classifiably neurasthenic or a borderline case, if her obssesion with sex was a physical impulse or the safety valve for complicated mental stresses. I wanted to know whether the fashionable blanketword "nymyhomania" applied to her, or whether she was driven to lie and fornicate for some other and more precise reason. But suddenly he didn't want to talk about her but the effect she had had upon me.

"You don't strike me as a liar, young Stuart," he said, with a whiff of the directness that had betrayed Redcliffe Bay into regarding him as a bully. "Maybe you had better tell me how it began, and what it amounted to. As far as you're concerned I mean. You don't have to if it embarrasses you but technically you're still my patient."

I told him with far less embarrassment than I would have imagined possible. He asked me a question or two but mostly he listened, puffing away at his pipe and with his head slightly on one side, like Birdie Boxall exchanging Redcliffe Bay reminiscences with a pub crony. I told him about the night of the dance, the rebuff in the attic, the telephone call that had led to her appearance at the studio and my first visit to the cove. I told him I had sold up my business on her account and that I had intended going away with her if I could. I told him about the last time I had visited her in this cabin, and how she had disposed of me by a trick. All he said when I ran dry was, "I suppose you considered yourself madly in love with her?"

"Yes," I said, "I was in love with her all right!" and then, because now there could hardly be anything less than complete honesty between us, "I think I always will be in a way. Nothing like her ever happened to me before."

"She has that effect on youngsters," he said brutally, "that's why I came chasing out here. I wouldn't have wasted petrol on that Shapley fellow. He's old enough to take his chances like the rest of us. Have you imagined yourself in love before?"

"Yes," I said, "but not any longer!"

"Anyone I know?"

"I was engaged to one of the nurses at the hospital. Esther Wallace, Scatty Wallace's youngest daughter."

He must have remembered Esta but his interest was limited to a lift of his eyebrows.

"All off now?"

"All off."

"On Lorna's account?"

It was not an easy question to answer. On the face of things Lorna was certainly answerable to the shipwreck of our relationship but I knew, and with certainty, that it was a rupture that could be healed if we were both willing to retrace our steps. I had thought about this a good deal since leaving hospital and had arrived at the sombre conclusion that, while it might be possible for her, it was impossible for me. It would simply mean staking her future on my good intentions and that wasn't good enough. I had a tremendous affection for Esta but that was all. I had changed a great deal over the last eleven months, whereas she was still the girl with the lame-dog complex, who had emptied a fire bucket over Rex Sweetland's head and bullied

Owen Rees into marrying Myfanwy Pritchard. This much was obvious; if she had been as scarred by Lorna Morney-Sutcliffe as me, nothing could have induced her to follow Michael Shapley to the cove simply to prove that I didn't exercise exclusive rights.

I would liked to have explained all this to the Doctor, but I couldn't put it in so many words. God knows, it is difficult to put it into words now, with the benefit of thirty years' hindsight. So I told the truth as I saw it and said, "No, not really on her account. Esther Wallace is Redcliffe Bay and I don't think I could settle for that now. I might for a time, but if I thought I was taking root I should do what Lorna's been talking of doing ever since you brought her here and what would a girl get out of that but misery? That isn't Lorna's doing. I was damned restless when you introduced me to her on the night of the ball."

He said an unexpected thing, something I would have attributed more to Ben Dagmar than to a man of his experience and ability.

"Everywhere's much the same, young Stuart," he said, "but it's no good telling you that at your age. Never is; wouldn't have believed it myself; but it is so. I'll tell you something else too and maybe you'll remember it twenty–thirty years ahead. People appear to want different things, and go about getting 'em in a thousand ways, but that's just another illusion. All but the freaks, people like my wife that is, want the same things."

"What are they?"

"To be needed in one way or another by a small group of people. Badly needed by one or two, moderately so by a dozen others. That's the most important human requirement and that's what most of us spend our lives trying to achieve in one way or another. Everything else is a substitute!"

Then, in one of his characteristic swoops from the general to the particular, "Esther Wallace? I remember her now and she'll never make the grade nursing. Not a question of brains. Too compassionate!" and he got up and took a casual peep through the window.

I saw him brace himself but he did not exclaim or invite me

to look. He just stood there with squared shoulders, blocking what little light there was in the cabin. Finally he said, "I suppose that Shapley fellow really did think I was shooting at him. They've sailed!"

He stood aside and it seemed to me he looked more concerned than at any moment during our conversation. I peered out into the murk. The sea was running moderately high, although it looked as if the wind had eased off and taken most of the sleet with it. A long way out to sea, standing off somewhere southeast of Shelly Bay, there was a single winking light.

"This man Shapley," he said, "does he know how to handle boats as well as shopgirls?"

"He probably thinks he does," I said, privately deciding that they would stand in for Shelly Bay as soon as they rounded the next point.

"Well, jolly good luck to him," Morney-Sutcliffe said, "and I don't know about you, young Stuart, but I could do with a drink."

He walked out into the dusk and I followed him. Suddenly and unreasonably, he seemed cold-blooded again.

CHAPTER NINE

[1]

I was awakened by the resonant crack of the first maroon and sat up in bed counting the seconds before its successor rattled the window.

I knew that there would be two and that it was therefore a wreck and not a fire. I knew also that the ship in distress was Lorna's cabin cruiser and that this surely meant that every stitch of our dirty linen—mine, hers, the Doctor's and even Shapley's, would soon be flapping from Mitre Head to Coastguard Hill. The gloomy certainty of this must have seeped through to me during the unquiet sleep. That was why the lifeboat summons surprised me less than anyone in town that morning.

In those days we had a fire alarm about once a week but the majority of them were caused by burning chimneys. A lifeboat launching was a looked-for rarity. Any break in town routine was a bonus in Redcliffe Bay, but a wreck was the threepenny piece in every pound or two of Christmas pudding that appeared on local tables.

In less than a minute the Stump was echoing with scurrying footsteps and the whirr of bicycle wheels. A car rushed by and I knew, without getting out of bed, who was driving it. It would be Commander Fergus Wheeler, R.N. (RETD.), who took his duties as Lifeboat Secretary very seriously and would have crawled from a sickbed to organize the launching under the tolerant eye of Coxswain Holbrook. Holbrook was a genuine bluewater man who knew his business, but he never begrudged the Commander the pleasure of convincing himself that his presence was indispensable. After all, Commander Wheeler not only organized the flag days; he also purchased, over the course of a year, the Niagara of draught bitter that found its way down the coxswain's throat.

I looked at my watch and saw that it was about seven-thirty. The full force had gone from the gale but it was still hovering about and liable to snake back on us at any moment. It had been that way all last evening, something and nothing, until it returned in full force in the small hours, when I was lying awake trying to equate Morney-Sutcliffe's indulgence with the enormity of sitting down to chat with a man whose wife I had repeatedly seduced. I knew that he didn't look at it like that, and also that he had had plenty of time to get adjusted to sharing his life with a woman who never denied herself the pleasure of netting any man likely to grab the kites she flew here, there and everywhere. He had admitted this over a glass of whisky when we returned together to "Heatherdene" that evening, telling me a little of her more spectacular antics in the same laconic, impersonal tone that he had used in the cabin.

I didn't ask him why he hadn't divorced her, or thrown her out long ago, because there was no need to ask. To him Lorna was two-fifths a patient, two-fifths a willful, impossibly wayward child and only a wife in the sense that he had made a bad bargain and wasn't the kind of man to welsh on it.

After the Donkin incident, which had cost him hush money, they struck a bargain of sorts. She could have her romps in the hay and still remain his pensioner so long as she kept up appearances. At any time she felt unable to do this she could leave, bag and baggage. In her own way, as I had discovered, she honored this curious arrangement. It seems almost ludicrous that he should have come close to apologizing to me for throwing her my way at the hospital dance, but he gave me this impression, admitting that my youth had disarmed him, and that he never gave me a serious thought until he came across some discarded proofs of the pictures I had taken of her in June. He skated over the positive identification of me as a victim. I think he was protecting someone who dropped him a hint soon after my admission to hospital. That someone might or might not have been Esta, although I didn't think so. It was more likely someone who had seen us swimming together, or travelling inland in her car. He didn't need a handful of clues. He had more perspicacity in one of his huge, back-curving thumbs than most doctors have in their heads.

What he did describe, however, was the curious pattern her fancy was likely to weave once it was started by a chance encounter, such as that cosy limelight dance in the Church Hall, and I saw that this pattern conformed almost exactly with mine. There was the first brush, full of lingering promise, the sudden tug on the rein to keep something in reserve, the bland approach as friend or adviser, the pseudo-reluctant surrender, the climax of possessive triumph and finally a swift tailing-off, like the unspectacular descent of a burned-out rocket.

He did not know what impulse, or combination of impulses, had led up to her final decision to head for the horizon that afternoon. Her thirty-fourth birthday, he thought, might have had something to do with it, and here he read in my reaction the fact that she had lied about her age, as about most things that had cropped up during our association. Or it might, he thought, have some bearing on Shapley, who was probably as unstable as she was and possibly as persuasive a liar.

"I daresay he convinced her he's got expectations," he said, "and I find myself wishing it was true. It wouldn't last, of course, not with Lorna, but it might help to cushion her descent to the pavement. After all, she's been accustomed to creature comforts for seven years and has probably forgotten the tricks of survival."

We left it at that and I went home as sober and chastened as the Reverend Sweetland emerging from under his bucket of scummy water. I can't honestly say that I was depressed by the madly improbable end of the affair. On the contrary I was relieved, and the astonishing tolerance and compassion of Morney-Sutcliffe prodded the cold embers of my sense of humor, absent without leave from the moment Lorna invited me to towel her dry back. I found it difficult to believe, however, that it was all over, that it really had moved to a muddled, farcical conclusion. Perhaps the physical memory of her was too sharp, or perhaps I sensed that such an improbable story demanded a paradoxical climax. I wouldn't know. All I can say is that the bang of the second maroon, heard at seven-thirty on that drab, overcast morning, was just like witnessing a distress rocket soar from the helpless derelict in the bay.

I dressed like a man about to be shot but skipped the traditional hearty breakfast. I wasn't all that concerned for myself, or even for Lorna, but I was deeply depressed by what this would almost certainly mean to the Doctor. Because so few of us had had the opportuntiy to know what manner of man he was, local popularity had always evaded him. The prospect of his wife and the manager of the local chain store being hauled ashore like a pair of half-drowned alley cats, was one that promised to shake even his imperturbability. I could see nothing ahead for him but years of embarrassment and hand-screened sniggering, unless he was prepared to haul down his flag and practice elsewhere and somehow I couldn't see him doing that. He would be more likely to stay and brazen it out, but even a man like Morney-Sutcliffe was at a hopeless disadvantage in a community like ours. It made me gnash my teeth to think of how hopelessly Shapley had bungled matters.

It surprised me to discover, on reaching the lifeboat house, that there was still uncertainty regarding the identity of the vessel that had caused the coastguard to summon the lifeboat crew. Some said it was a Belgian collier stranded on the sandbar, others that the pilot boat had capsized on its way out to a coaster off Shelly Bay. I listened to their stupid chatter with the sour resentment of a man watching the world go by after playing a leading role in a personal tragedy. Their excited speculation irritated me.

The whole town seemed to be assembled outside the lifeboat shed, men and women jostling one another for places on the tow-ropes. I saw Bill Belcher and Her (now Mrs. Belcher), Dora Gorman from the Rainbow Café and her husband, Garfield Pyne, the undertaker, whom the wags said was there to apply the slide rule to any corpses washed ashore, Owen Rees and some of his boys, Cecil Trumper and even Linford Scott-Shawe, the bank manager, who was supplementing Commander Wheeler's stream of unnecessary directions. The general atmosphere was that of a popular wake.

I watched the boat shoot from its shed and go rumbling down the beach on its cumbersome caterpillar wheels and then I returned to the depot and looked around for someone who could give me accurate information. I knew that Ben Dagmar would expect me to cover the story in any case, but I had deliberately left my camera behind. The less publicized this wreck, I thought, the better for all concerned.

Syd Skinner, the pilot's brother, gave me the gist of the story, as far as he was aware of it. Just after six-thirty the Shelly Bay coastguard had telephoned to say that a small boat was awash on the eastern tip of the outer bar and was thought to be a derelict for it was dismasted and on its beam ends. No distress rockets had been fired from it and the coastguard had acted on his own initiative. On a flowing tide it would take the Redcliffe Bay lifeboat about an hour to reach and search her. As far as Syd knew no one had come ashore at Shelly Bay.

The information confirmed my gloomiest suspicions. Lorna's boat was single-masted and that was the direction in which they had been heading, south-east, with Shelly Bay on their port bow. In normal weather even an amateur could have cleared the tip of the sandbar and stood out to sea but I remembered that Lorna and Shapley had not been able to choose their time of departure and had sailed on an ebb tide. They had probably grounded as early as last evening and when I thought of the gusts that had kept Stump shop signs in motion during the night, I didn't give a great deal for their chances. Then I remembered something else. Their dinghy had been lost before they weighed anchor, in which case, unless washed overboard, they might be still aboard if the boat hadn't capsized when the tide began to flow again. In approximate circumstances there had been instances of amateur yachtsmen saving themselves by scrambling out onto the long sandbank, which remained uncovered for six or seven hours between tides, but I didn't think this could have been done in the pitch dark of a December night, with rather more than half a gale blowing. There was nothing to be gained by hanging around fending off the greetings and the speculations of acquaintances, so I hurried back to Ben Dagmar's yard, jumped into my car and made for the highest point of Coastguard Hill.

I kept a good pair of German binoculars in the glove recess and by the time I had parked, and crossed two soggy ploughed fields to the cliff edge, the light had improved and I could just see both wreck and lifeboat, the former awash on the extreme edge of the bar, the latter rising and falling on the heavy swell and making good progress in the fairway that extended as far as the cove. Beyond this point the sea looked menacing, a swirl of white horses already charging the seaward edge of the bar.

I stood there in the biting wind getting wet through in the spray and great gusts of sleet, waiting until the lifeboat had butted its way well beyond the wreck and then edged its way back until it seemed to be alongside. The coxswain then came at it from the starboard side but the squalls were so thick and so frequent that I had the greatest difficulty keeping them in view. At last I saw them cast off and work in a wide circle, to fetch up the landward side of the boat. As far as I could see they took nobody aboard.

I trudged back across the fields and drove down the Valley road to the Esplanade, where the crowd had thinned considerably. All the way I carried a burden of guilt as heavy and irksome as the sins of Bunyan's pilgrim. Somehow it seemed to be more my fault than anybody else's. If I hadn't rushed down on the Doctor like that he wouldn't have discharged the gun, and if he hadn't fired Shapley wouldn't have been panicked into leaving the anchorage in such a hurry. I had already made up my mind that both of them were dead for how could it be otherwise? My stampede, and the Doctor's involuntary shots, had even contributed to the loss of their dinghy in which, with luck, they might have got ashore.

I was standing just outside the shed awaiting the lifeboat's return when a perky voice at my elbow said, "Heard the latest, Pip?" and I turned and recognized the sou'westered figure of V[illegible] Marker, Shapley's chief salesgirl, the one whom I had obliged the previous day by driving the Morgan to Bedwell's garage. Her eyes danced with excitement and the wind had given her rather pudding-y face a rosy glow. She looked as if she had just won the Irish Sweepstake.

"Have they found out whose boat it is?" I asked, a ten-pound weight dragging at my belly, and she said, "Well, no, not exactly, but it certainly wasn't *his!* But neither was the cash he didn't take to the bank!"

"What cash was that?" I asked, stupidly, and she said, with a pretense of imparting a daring secret, "*Our* cash, silly! He's been hoarding it! He hasn't been near the bank since last Thursday week. They're reckoning up now, they say it's somewhere around seven hundred!"

I couldn't absorb any more shocks without some kind of support so I found a lifebelt locker, sat on it and held on to the edge with both hands.

"Shapley's taken the cash? Duckworth's cash?"

"That's why he left early. You remember me telling you it was funny! We had the area manager coming today and when His Nibs didn't turn up this morning the manager dived headfirst into the safe and then rang the bank. Of course, so far they only know about the week's gross, which he should have paid in every day. Some of the girls think he must have been at it a long time, but perhaps in driblets and not a lump sum. Then, to cap all, he tries to make a getaway by sea! It's better than a film, isn't it? It'll put Redcliffe Bay on the map, especially if he's drowned, like they say! Can you imagine him doing a crazy thing like that in this kind of weather? I mean, why on earth didn't he just drive somewhere, sell his car and skedaddle to South America? That's where people make for when they turn crook, isn't it?"

Her voice droned on and on like the rattling suck of the sea on loose shingle. I must have looked appalled for suddenly she said, "What's the matter with you? You look groggy!"

I said hastily that I had rushed out without any breakfast and had got soaked waiting to take pictures of the lifeboat when it returned.

"Well, go home, have some dinner and change your clothes,"

she said. "There won't be anything worth a picture unless they bring him ashore and if you ask me I don't think he's out there at all. He's deep, that one! Maybe he used the boat as a blind, doubled back, went by train and is now living it up at the Ritz." Her own cleverness amazed her. "*That's* it!" she almost screamed. "I bet that's *just* what he's done!" and she rushed off to unload her deductions on somebody else, just as Commander Wheeler came blundering down from the lookout platform shouting that everybody was to stand by to help haul the lifeboat carriage up the beach as soon as he gave the word.

I joined the crowd at the far end of the slipway. It wasn't as large as the crowd that had gathered for the launching. A launching was fun, with the lifeboat chasing the hauliers like a blue and white juggernaut, but rehousing was a heavy, laborious task and most of the onlookers suddenly remembered it was lunchtime.

The first person I saw as the boat nosed into the overspill was the Doctor, standing with feet wide apart and hands deep in the pockets of his overcoat that bellied in the wind. I went over and said, in a low voice, "Have you heard about Shapley?"

"What about him?" he said, without looking at me.

"He had about seven hundred pounds of Duckworth's money on him. He's been cooking the books over a period they say!"

He didn't react and before I could ask him what he thought of Lorna's chances of getting ashore, the coxswain stood up in the bows and called, in a booming voice, "Us 'ave got 'er, Doctor and 'er's cummin' round!" He turned and shouted to someone over his shoulder. " 'Er is, ain't 'er? 'Er's coughed up most of it, abben 'er?"

The Doctor still didn't move, not even when a swirl of gesticulating helpers rushed into the shallows and swarmed round the grounded boat. Every fresh wave wetted them to the waist and they all got in one another's way when the boat lifted on the swell and ground her keel deeper into the pebbles. The rush left us more or less isolated some ten yards up the slipway. He said, still without looking at me, "Keep your mouth shut and get to hell out of here!" and then, without any appearance of concern, he marched down to the water, everyone making way for him as though he really was the Emperor of Redcliffe Bay.

I remained where I was. It was like watching a scene at the Tivoli in one of the old silent epics, the kind that once featured Doug Fairbanks or Ramon Navarro. The force of the wind and the hiss of rain slurred everybody's voice, so that the sound effects might have been provided by the crash of Bruce Brayley's accompanist who was fired when talkies were installed. I saw a dozen hands reach up and a knot of oilskinned lifeboatmen lower something into them. There was a mere glimpse of red-gold hair as they cradled the limp bundle and began to edge towards the slipway. That was the last I ever saw of Lorna Morney-Sutcliffe.

[2]

I don't know how I got through that day and I don't think I should have done if I hadn't had the sense to get drunk on an empty stomach and come reeling home across Stump to Ben Dagmar, who had been looking for me all over the town. The moment he saw me he hustled me upstairs to the big living-room he occupied over the shop. There was a coal fire burning and he slammed the door on Thora Cottey, his daily help, and pulled off my wet clothes. Then he gave me a rub down with a rough towel, fetched some slacks and a sweater, and brewed some strong coffee. The coffee made me sick. After an hour or so, however, my head cleared and I felt better, well enough to admit that I hadn't taken a single picture of the launching or the rescue. He didn't seem surprised but said grimly that I had missed making a packet. No press photographer or freelance had shown up at the slipway, and I would have had a batch of exclusives for the daily papers.

"It's that big a story," he said, "the biggest we've had around here in a long time. I've already earned myself upwards of twenty pounds with the Central News Agency and some of the Fleet Street boys. It's got everything. Drama, crime and sex!"

I sat up so suddenly at this that his eyes narrowed and he began polishing his long nose with a finger and thumb, a habit he had when he was making a decision. He said, with an assumed carelessness that didn't fool me for a moment, "You heard about that chap Shapley, I suppose? Running off with the cash *and* Morney-Sutcliffe's wife?"

He didn't know it all but he obviously knew a lot more than he was prepared to admit. He seemed to be feeling his way round the rough edges of the story and weighing the pros and cons of some related problem of his own. He looked like an old, much-hunted dog fox, trying to make up his mind which line to take with hounds in the next field.

I looked up at the marble clock on the mantelshelf and saw that it was after five o'clock, more than four hours since the lifeboat had returned. A lot must have happened since then. News of Shapley's raid on the till, and his sensational involvement with the Doctor's wife, must be common currency on Stump by now. I said, cautiously, "How much do you know, Ben? How much does everybody know?"

"Let's put it this way," he said. "I know more than most!"

I thought this extremely likely. He had had me under close observation and he was a professional at the job of evaluating gossip. He was also one of the few in town in the confidence of Morney-Sutcliffe.

"I saw Mrs. Morney-Sutcliffe come ashore," I said. "Is she okay?"

"She's still unconscious," he said, "or was an hour ago, when I rang the hospital. They found her on the sandbank, with about as much water in her as there was in that cabin cruiser of hers! The Doctor is up there with her now but they aren't taking any more calls."

He said this without taking his eyes off me, and when I didn't say anything, he went on. "Shapley's still missing. I don't suppose we shall see anything of him for a week or two, and maybe not even then, dependent upon tides and the weather. The dinghy came ashore and there was a knapsack and other luggage in it. Duckworth's got most of its cash back. Lucky of them, don't you think?"

I was far too worried and depressed to fence with him and besides I still felt sick. He gave me another cup of coffee and I sipped it while he continued to sit there, still more obsessed with his own problem, whatever it was, than any comments I had to make on the biggest story that was ever likely to find its way into the *Redcliffe Bay Messenger.*

"You had better hear the real story," I said at last. "It'll break sooner or later and I wouldn't like you to get it the way the rest of Stump will, over the counter at Bill Belcher's or in one of the other clearing houses within spitting distance!"

He made his decision and it obviously cost him a great deal. "Whatever it is, let it simmer," he said. "It's been doing that long enough. Another few hours won't harm it."

"You don't want to hear my part in it?"

"No," he said, "or not from you! I'll leave it to the Doctor's discretion. This is where you get off, Sportyboy, but he can't, poor devil. Anyway, he wants you to get in touch with him. He'll be taking surgery as usual about six. Ring his home at about a quarter to and see if he's back!"

He got up then, muttering that he had to see to the rearrangement of his front page, and I remembered that it was a Thursday and his weekly deadline. It wasn't this, however, that got him out of my presence so much as a desire to remove himself from temptation. He had been collecting and printing local news for half a century and the pull of principle must have been very strong to make him turn his back on me at that moment. I knew why he did, however, and it wasn't solely out of consideration to me or the Doctor but in response to his conception of the ethics of a newspaper man. Whatever he knew he would have to print, regardless of loyalties. It was that much easier for him if he confined his story to the known facts, at least for the time being.

A long half-hour ticked by as I sat by the rustling fire, listening to the steady thuds of Ben's flatbed grinding out conjectures of the day's sensation in the printing office below. Sharp at five forty-five I rang the Doctor's house and he answered in a single, crisp, syllable that would have taken the bounce out of a professional beggar.

"*Yes?*"

"It's Stuart. Mr. Dagmar said you wanted me to call."

There was a longish silence and I could hear his controlled breathing. He said, "Hold the line a moment!" and went away, presumably to close a door.

"Where are you, now?"

"At Mr. Dagmar's."

"Have you spoken to anybody?"

"Only to Mr. Dagmar and he refused to discuss it until I had seen you."

Another long pause. "You had better come up here. There may be press picketing the front. Do you know your way in from the links?"

"Yes," I said, wondering if he had ever seen me use the letter-box in the wall dividing his garden from the rough.

"Right. I'll be expecting you. I'll leave the kitchen light on."

The phone clicked and I sat holding my end for several minutes. Ben had said that this was where I got off but I wasn't so sure. I had a wash, rinsed my mouth and went down the back way to the yard. The night was damp and mild, the gale having blown itself out, leaving a vacuum filled with cringing sea fog that made everything smell like steaming clothes. I drove up Frog Terrace, down the Esplanade and along it as far as Links Road, where I left my car near the sandpit and went across the seventh green by foot. The fog was thick here but I blessed it. For all I knew a good many people were keeping a casual watch on Morney-Sutcliffe's visitors that night.

I found the wall without using my torch and worked my way through the shrubbery to the vegetable garden, where I could see a yellow blob of light that was the kitchen. I looked through the window and saw that the room was empty. I lifted the back doorlatch and went in, bolting the door behind me. As I turned, blinking in the light, Morney-Sutcliffe entered from the hall. He looked the same, but from where I stood I could tell he had been drinking whisky.

"Anyone see you?"

"No," I said, "I'm quite sure they didn't!"

It was probably the only so-called American kitchen in Redcliffe Bay, with a number of red and white working surfaces and a variety of gleaming gadgets. There was the kind of stove you only saw in advertisements in glossy magazines, and a shining array of implements like a torturer's tool-kit fitted into a steel rack above the sink. It was all as clean and clinical as an operating theatre. He was right about Lorna having accustomed herself to creature comforts.

"It's all right," he said, "nobody will disturb us here. I can't hear the phone and I've sent the housekeeper up to her room. You heard about the dinghy, I suppose?"

"Mr. Dagmar told me it had come ashore and that the money was in it."

"Shapley's expectations," he said, but with no inflection of humor. "I told you he had some! Of course, we don't know if there was more on the cruiser, they haven't salvaged it!"

I wondered what he was getting at. Did he implicate Lorna in Shapley's clumsy attempt to finance the trip out of Duckworth's till? Then he gave me a professional glance, saying, "You look as if you had been washed ashore yourself!" I told him I had taken too much liquor on an empty stomach and been sick, also that I had eaten nothing since yesterday.

"Damn-fool way to carry on," he said, and opened the door of the refrigerator. A light came on inside. These kind of things were new to us in Redcliffe Bay and I watched with a certain amount of interest while he extracted some cold chicken, placed it onto the table and motioned to me to eat. He also boiled a kettle on the stove and in about two minutes had made coffee. My mind went back to the first meal Lorna had served me in the cabin of the vessel, now rolling to and fro on the spur of the bar, and the white meat nearly choked me. He cut some bread, poured two large cups of coffee and brought them to the table, placing one at my elbow, the other at the far end of the kitchen table. "Help yourself to butter," he said and sat down facing me.

I had the same impression that he was half-absorbed in a problem of his own in the way Ben Dagmar had been an hour or so ago, but he didn't take as long as Ben to resolve it.

"There was a box of Lorna's in the dinghy locker," he said, "a tin box, containing letters and photographs!" He dipped his hand in his pocket and took out a small bundle of letters and a spread of snapshots, secured by a thick rubber band. I stopped eating. It would have required a forcible feeding to make me finish the cold chicken. All night, as I had lain awake or dozed throughout the storm, I had been aware that the pattern was not quite complete, that one vital small piece was still missing. And yet, for the life of me, I couldn't put a name to it until he mentioned that tin box of souvenirs that she kept in the cavity under the floor of the shanty. It seemed strange that, in the midst of preparing to leave with Michael Shapley, she had the time and inclination to stow the rest of her scalps in the locker of the dinghy for shipment to the Hesperides.

"How did you get them?" I asked at length.

"I was able to prove they were my property!" he said and left it at that.

The letters lay on the table between us and presently I got up, took them over to the stove, lifted the lid and dropped the packet inside. The whiff of burning rubber crossed the kitchen like a red-nosed comedian stumbling into a cardinal's conference chamber. Morney-Sutcliffe's thin, high nostrils twitched as he said, "That's the only real link once people start digging! They will, of course, and not solely on account of the money. Sooner or later someone will start asking questions, but without some kind of lead the answers won't amount to much, not even if you were still around, waiting to be called as a witness. Did anyone see you chasing after me down to that cove?"

"Farmer Phillips's pigman, a man called Coates, but he isn't very bright."

"He's probably bright enough to make things uncomfortable when he reads the newspapers and reports of the inquest."

"The inquest won't be held until Shapley's body turns up and sometimes it doesn't happen for months."

He heaved himself up and crossed to the window, standing there with his back to me. I thought I would give him time to work that one out but he wasn't engaged in solving any problem now except how to break it to me. Finally he did it cleanly, like making a surgical incision.

"Lorna died two hours ago."

The light bulbs reflecting on so many metallic surfaces fused into a single winking flash as powerful as a lighthouse beam. I reached out and found the edge of the table, gripping its underside, so that the coffee in my cup slopped into the saucer. I didn't see him move but suddenly there he was standing over me and I was sitting, held in the chair by two rigid arms. His hands looked as big as hams and his wrists as thick as a child's thigh. I heard him say, "You've already had too much to drink so get that coffee down while I brew fresh!" and the cup was held to my mouth. I heard my teeth rattling against the rim.

Slowly the objects reverted to their normal size. The hard core of blinding light fractured any number of wavering points of light returning to various corners of the room, above the sink, beside the stove, inside the open door of the refrigerator, immediately above the table where I sat. I made shift to surface, to relate my presence here in this big, empty-seeming house to the chain of events that reached right back to the first time this man had ever addressed me as an individual on the night of the dance —"Ah, young Stuart, isn't it? Oblige me by giving my wife a turn or two—she hasn't danced with anyone under fifty all evening and is threatening to go home . . . !"

It was a million years ago and it was the day before yesterday; and now she had carried out her threat and he and I were left to make her excuses.

How did one set about inventing them? What could either of us say without stripping the other of the last vestiges of human dignity? And as I wondered this it occurred to me that I was not grappling with remorse or grief at all but something far less complicated. Fear that curdled the belly. Already I saw the events of yesterday and today front-paged across the country, and in the glare of publicity I heard the insistent voice of the coroner coaxing information from the walk-on players, like Farmer Phillips's pigman—"You saw the Doctor descend to the beach?" "You saw the witness Stuart follow him?" "What was the Doctor carrying?" "What time elapsed between their descent and reappearance?" Then the questions they were likely to put to me: "What was your relationship with the deceased?" "Was the Doctor aware of that relationship?" "Had you prior knowledge of deceased's relationship with Michael Shapley?" "How did you happen to be present when Shapley was confronted by deceased's husband?" So much for me, but what kind of impact would the public airing make upon Morney-Sutcliffe, cuckolded by a randy young local and then by a bottom-pinching picklock? How could he survive the weeks ahead of him? And unlike Shapley or me what, in the name of God, had he done to deserve them?

He was talking again now but there was no indication of panic in his voice. It was level and reasonable. In the appalling circumstances it was almost off-hand.

"Something you should know and think about—it was a miracle that she survived a night out there—she had a heart condition and anything of that nature would be enough to kill her—they'll all have to know that, of course—the way she wanted to live—she hadn't much time left and knew it—I can swear to that in any court . . . !"

I couldn't be sure whether he was addressing me or himself but I listened, weighing each word, for it seemed to me that what he was saying now went a long way towards explaining his monumental patience. Maybe it went all the way, from the first day he brought her here to the moment when he watched her hamfisted bid for the Hesperides. He set fresh coffee on the table and carefully refilled my cup. Then he lit his pipe and sat down at the far end of the table. The shock wave had passed but he still looked larger than life-size, sitting there puffing, his great bulk resting on his elbows.

"You once had it in mind to see the world, didn't you? Well, then, here's your chance. Maybe this is it, young Stuart. Give it time to blow over. Make it hard for them and moderately easy for me!"

Easy for him! Christ Almighty! How could anything ever be easy for him again?

Smoke rose from his bowl like vapor from a genie's bottle. "There is the *vox populi* and there's what I care to tell them. Time, that's what's needed! There will be another sensation tomorrow, and another the day after that. A vicar and a choirboy. A baronet's wife and her chauffeur. You have to get accustomed to false starts at your age. That's why I'm advising you to regard this as one and bolt. Before the town layabouts tie a tin can to your tail!"

I found my voice at last and it sounded as if I had laryngitis.

"You'll need someone to back your story. They could infer almost anything. That shot . . ."

He smiled at this. "Rubbish!" he said, "doctors have the edge on everyone in a witness box. I don't know why but they do and who am I to quarrel with witch-doctor mentality at this juncture?"

"But how could you even begin to make the truth sound credible?"

"I can make it credible," he said grimly. "Can you see any tinpot local coroner or police inspector bullying me in the witness box?"

I couldn't; neither could I envisage any set of circumstances to which he would fail to adjust, providing he gave his mind to it, but there were so many loose ends that no one line of argument presented itself.

"Do you suppose the whole truth ever emerges at any kind of public enquiry?" he suddenly demanded, with a touch of his old asperity. "Good God, boy, I am only required to tell them as much as they need to know! What's incredible about a woman under excessive mental strain playing the fool with a man in a boat? Is anyone going to believe that she helped Shapley empty that till? I don't even have to cloud the issue, it's already clouded enough. She knew she hadn't much time and once I tell them so I can see solicitude settling on me like a halo!"

"But there was the gun shot and there was Farmer Phillips's pigman. He saw me and I daresay he saw you . . ."

"I don't give a damn for fifty pigmen!" he said, filling the room with blue smoke. "Can't I threaten a man on the point of abducting my wife? I think I can and get away with it, so long as I don't have you on my back!"

Perhaps because he sounded so confident and reassuring, but

probably because, at bedrock, most of us look at every problem in the light of how it will affect us, the pincers of fear that had laid hold of me a moment before relaxed their grip and I was able, in that spasm of relief, to take a quick look at myself in the role of bereaved lover.

What I saw shamed me. Already I could think of Lorna as a dead person and therefore outside my calculations in terms of personal survival. After myself, it was Morney-Sutcliffe who concerned me, and this emotional abdication on my part absorbed the whole of my attention so that I failed to notice he had left the table and was now standing over by the window, looking beyond the blob of light that fell short of the vegetable garden. His stillness and solidity impressed me, but so did the fact that he was careful to keep his face turned away from me. And suddenly it occurred to me that her death in these circumstances, irrespective of any scandal that might follow, might have caused him far more pain and shock than it was causing me.

I wasn't sure about this. He was a master of detachment and, as Lorna had once pointed out, he was far more familiar than I with death in every form, yet there was something about the way he stood, hands pressed on the broad window ledge and face close to the glass, that indicated a degree of grief that I did not feel. The time would come when I did feel it, when I would catch myself, at odd and unexpected moments, remembering the scent of her perfume, the touch of her flesh under my hand, above all the leaping thrill that had always followed the sound of her voice over the telephone, but now I could not think of her in that way.

He began to speak again, without turning away from the window. "When you remember her," he said, "see that you do it kindly and realistically. It isn't easy for any one of us to know with absolute certainty that we'll never make old bones, but she managed it adequately. There are other allowances, you understand? She had the kind of upbringing one doesn't care to dwell upon. Her father wasn't really a painter, just some kind of meeting-point between a courier and a pimp, who fired a few damp squibs before dying friendless and broke. She never knew a damned thing about her mother, except that she was an unlucky drab. A person starting out with that kind of handicap has to build her own stage and if hers was a penny peepshow what gives luckier people the right to sneer? She made a fetish of her body because it was all she had and, when all is said and done, she was pretty convincing! She fooled you easily enough, and others older and more experienced than you. She even fooled me for a month or two and in a curious way I think she enjoyed herself most of the time. You won't have come across Philip Sydney's *Arcadia* I imagine?"

People like him and Ben Dagmar were always asking me questions like that, and remembering this makes me wonder a little about the standard of education in those days. I had never read much at all then but it would seem that many of the older generation of Redcliffians were very well-read indeed.

"No," I said, "I only remember him as the man who gave away his drink at Zutphen."

"He did rather more than that. He was a damned good poet and I remember thinking of Lorna when I came across a line that fitted her exactly when she had a new male on the lead. 'A happy couple, he joying in her, she joying in herself, but in herself because she enjoyed him!' Apt?"

He stopped talking but remained in the same rigid posture, hands still pressed to the sill, staring out at nothing. Then, with an effort, he straightened up and turned towards me, so that I noticed his eyes were moist. It was, I think, the moment I remember most vividly of all my years in Redcliffe Bay.

"I suppose one could argue that she made the best possible use of the time left to her," he went on, at length. "At least, insofar as she saw it, and if we don't belong to ourselves we might as well stop struggling, collectively and individually! I believe I told you yesterday she was a compulsive liar. That isn't the right noun. 'Borrower' would be fairer. She borrowed her personality from the nonfiction library and her emotions from novels of the last century. She even borrowed a name that appealed to her more than her own. She wasn't christened Lorna if, in fact, she was christened at all. Her real name was Ethel; Ethel Watkins."

And having said this he was done with the business of extenuation, shrugging off sentiment as though it were a coat in which he did not care to be seen.

"Well, young Stuart? What about it?" He might have been asking my advice on the best approach shot of the sandhills, where he already saw his bathing pool and miniature golf course.

"A decision like that must be up to you!" I told him.

"I rather think it is!" he said, quite the old Morney-Sutcliffe again, "so my advice to you is don't hang about. Pack the minimum and go tonight!"

I had thought about crossing the frontier for so long, and in such a variety of company, that it seemed fantastic the decision should be made for me by him and that I should be given no more than an hour's notice.

"Won't you at least want to know where I am?"

"Not on your life!" he said promptly. "You know where I am!"

"You mean you'll stay? After it's all over?"

"Of course I will. I've done all the travelling I intend to do!"

That was all. He opened the kitchen door and walked me out on to the concrete slab facing the vegetable garden. The night was still reeking with mist that swirled about our legs. You could smell the sea but you couldn't hear it. Perhaps, like me, it was exhausted by the bluster of the last forty-eight hours.

"Good luck, young Stuart!"

His hand enclosed mine. It really was about twice as big as most hands. I went up the short, flinty path, through the dripping shrubbery and over the wall alongside our letterbox.

[3]

There was only one thing I wanted to do apart from slip into Ben Dagmar's by the back way, pack a few things and say goodbye to Ben. At first I thought I would leave without seeing him and maybe write later, but I couldn't bring myself to do it now that I was certain he was in the secret.

I got in without anyone seeing me. The journeymen were all

in the printing office, churning out the most sensational edition of the *Messenger* Redcliffe Bay was likely to see in a couple of decades, and Ben was in his proof-littered office on the first landing. I packed my things and called in on the way down.

He was sitting in a little circle of light cast by an anglepoise lamp. In that light he looked his sixty-eight years and a few more. Then he saw it was me, and not his foreman with a pull of pages one and six, wet from the flatbed.

"I've had a long talk with the Doctor," I said. "He seems to think it better for everyone concerned if I leave now, without a forwarding address. I don't know how much he told you, or how much you've guessed, but you can still hear the rest if you care to. Do you, Ben?"

He polished his nose. Sitting there, his seamed face decorated with a fringe of whiskers thirty years out-of-date, he looked like Grumpy in Walt Disney's *Snow White and the Seven Dwarfs.* He said, finally, "Just one thing. I'd like to be sure neither you nor the Doctor laid hands on that Shapley fellow."

"We didn't," I said, "he just happened to be there when we went aboard. The Doctor's gun went off by accident when Shapley was way out of range and he panicked and rowed for the cabin cruiser like the very devil!"

He thought a moment. Then he said, "She was never worth it! My Hetty was, but not her! I've thought of telling him so often enough but you can never tell anybody anything important. Who's dead, who's married, who's broken his neck—that's about all! Nothing that helps. I could have told you too but what would have been the point? At your age a man doesn't look for anything else in a woman. It was no different with me, although I've been half a century telling myself the opposite!" He got up and shook hands. "Will you drop me a line some time?"

"Later, Ben, when the dust has settled!"

"Well then, that's it I suppose!"

In the embarrassed moment that followed I glanced over his shoulder at the uncorrected front-page pull of tomorrow's *Messenger*. Personal loyalties hadn't prevented the journalist in

Ben going to town. The headline, one of four, was in the heaviest type he had and it read, "TRAGEDY IN STORM-WHIPPED BAY." There was a picture of Lorna's head and shoulders, one I had taken back in June. I never ceased to wonder how and when he acquired it.

I drove out of town the Valley way, passing "Heatherdene" again and noting that two unlighted cars were parked outside the entrance so that Morney-Sutcliffe's suspicions seemed to be justified. Fleet Street, alerted by Ben, was on to a juicy story. I reached the crest, dimmed my lights and coasted down the slight incline to the hospital courtyard. It was close on nine and I knew hospital routine to a decimal point. At nine sharp the night staff took turns to pop into the kitchen for tea and a ten-minute break. They came in singly, helping themselves from a large enamel pot on the stove. The kitchen window was clear glass and the rubber curtains didn't meet. I got out of the car and waited, looking into the room and watching the plump, adenoidy nurse sip her tea. At ten past nine she left and almost immediately Esta came in. There was rarely anyone in authority about at this end of the building after the domestic staff had gone home. I slipped in the back door and closed it.

She didn't look startled, just glum and disapproving. Once again I had a feeling of vast distance between us, as though our association, even before it became a close one, belonged to another life and another century. All the sparkle had left her. She wasn't pretty and she wasn't plain but just Esta Wallace, youngest of the ironmonger's daughters, training to be a nurse and mooned over by the lumpish Cecil Trumper. She had no part in the black farce of the last few months and there seemed never to have been a time when we were friendly and loving.

She must have been as acutely aware of this as I was. There was a thinness in her voice as she said, "You again? I had an idea you had left town. Have you come up here to see her?"

It had never occurred to me that she would think I had called to see Lorna, now lying in the mortuary chapel. The only dead person I had ever seen up to that time was Birdie Boxall and it would have seemed a frivolous act on my part to "pay my last respects," as they said in Redcliffe Bay, before the undertaker moved in and took charge. I didn't point this out to Esta but said, "I'm leaving tonight and I couldn't go without telling you."

"Why not?" she asked, bitterly. "You did everything else without telling me. And why tonight? Hasn't that man Shapley let you out? Are you still mixed up in this awful business somehow?"

That was how she saw it, and how the vast majority of people who had known us would see it as soon as Ben's headlines were read in the morning. An awful business. An unpleasant, sleazy scandal, with half-comic undertones. A chain-store manager making off with the cash, a doctor's wife accompanying his melodramatic flight, and the certainty that someone, probably a lot of people, had at last succeeded in knocking Morney-Sutcliffe from his perch.

Yet it seemed to me that she should have read something more into it than that. She had respect for Morney-Sutcliffe now, not only as a surgeon but as a human being; and she had once been deeply in love with me.

I said lamely, "There's a lot more to it than most people think. Part of it will emerge when Morney-Sutcliffe has his say at the inquest but not all, Esta. That's one of the reasons why I'm going. The Doctor has advised me to, in case he isn't able to limit the amount of dirt stirred up. He doesn't want me involved. He says it will cramp his style."

That puzzled her but she tried not to show it, working hard to preserve her couldn't-care-less approach.

"If you really are going you'd better go," she said, and when I reached out to take hold of her wrist she skipped back as though from a snake. "*Don't touch me!*" she said, and then, "What do you mean, Morney-Sutcliffe 'advised' you? What can it matter to him whether you stay around town or go fishing? You can't play around with her any more!"

Gall on this scale was so alien to the Esta Wallace I had known since my schooldays that it had the power to inflict pain, like the jab of thorn under the nail. The smart was sharp enough to make me angry and I said, "For God's sake, Esta! How can you prejudge without knowing all there is to know? If Morney-Sutcliffe can wipe the slate clean, why can't you?"

The protest might have got through to her or she might, on her own initiative, have relented. At all events the compressed fury left her and her expression resumed the glumness I had noticed when I saw her enter the room a moment before.

"There's nothing on my slate against Lorna Morney-Sutcliffe," she said, "not any longer! I saw her die and I saw him watch her die. I don't even know what kind of woman she really was, or when she went off the rails and why! But *you* do! You once had a straight choice, Pip. Mind your own business, or go out of your way to spoil whatever chance existed of Morney-Sutcliffe and his wife making the best of it, and of you and I doing the same. You aren't another Michael Shapley just passing through. You belong here and owe everybody, including me, some kind of loyalty. What did it take to throw that to the wolves? A hitch of her skirt when her husband was busy. It's the shabbiness of it that sticks in my throat and always will, so why pile on the agony by coming here to say goodbye?"

"I didn't come to say goodbye," I said, "and I didn't come to see Lorna. I'm over it, Esta. It's like I said, there's still a lot you don't know about her and about her husband. He didn't hold it against me so why should you?"

I didn't care for the look of incredulity in her eyes. She said, "Are you asking me to start all over again? Just like that?"

"I'm asking if we could keep in touch. I'm not running because I want to but because I think it might help him."

She was silent for a moment. I was prepared to tell her everything in the hope that she would step outside the parochial circle and make some kind of definite effort to judge the thing as the Doctor had judged it, but this was neither the time nor the place for so much wearisome explanation.

"I thought I could write later and maybe, if you ever felt like it, we could meet somewhere."

She was looking at me now as if she had never seen me before, as if I was someone who had astonished her by some extraordinary feat of buffoonery performed in a public place, a park or a railway station.

"You can *make* a switch like that? With her lying dead just across the yard?"

What was the use? One had to be endowed with the wisdom and experience of a Morney-Sutcliffe or a Ben Dagmar to make a sane and balanced assessment of the situation and anyway, what had I done to deserve magnanimity from her? I said, "I'm sorry, Esta, forget it. I'll go now," and turned for the door but she said, sharply, "Wait!" and I stopped, not without hope.

"There's so much I don't know and don't understand but there's one thing you don't know either. Cecil Trumper and I are getting married in the New Year. I thought you may have heard but apparently you haven't and if you left here you never would. They don't sell the *Redcliffe Bay Messenger* on bookstalls and our engagement is announced in this week's paper."

I think I was more astonished than I had been by Morney-Sutcliffe's attitude towards me down in the cove. I stood there with my mouth open and she waited for the news to sink in, her lips so compressed that her mouth looked like a small gash.

"But you don't love Cecil!" I exclaimed, when I had ridden out most of the shock.

"No," she said, "but I might learn, providing I tried a bit harder than you did!"

She walked round me then in precisely the same way as she had on that warm June evening, when we had had our first and final quarrel in the kitchen behind the studio. I didn't make any attempt to stop her, or reason with her and I didn't offer my congratulations either. It wasn't the kind of engagement that called for congratulations, and that despite the certainty that Cecil would always be kind to her. I remember wondering, as her heel-taps died away in the corridor, whether she would learn to reciprocate, whether in fact it was within her power to give him the affection and constancy she might have given me. That was something I would never find out and neither would anyone else. Scatty Wallace had brought his mind to bear on many complex inventions, but his youngest daughter was by far the most unpredictable of his creations.

I turned up my coat collar and went out into the drizzle. There was a night breeze now and the ground mist was clearing rapidly. From the edge of the moor, where the byroad turned to rejoin the main highway and climbed the high ground that was Redcliffe Bay's backdrop, I could see the town lights routing the trailers of sea-fog. Beyond them lay the faintest phosphorescent glow that was the bay, nipped by its twin headlands. I stopped the car on the last crest and got out for a final look. This was the moment I had imagined for myself since I was rising fifteen, the leap over the wall, the great adventure, but there was precious little exhilaration about it now that it was here. More points of light began to show and the beam of a headlight from a car descending the Valley found and then lost a wet surface as a searchlight probes the sky for aircraft. Then it was gone and there was little else but blackness down there. The bowl of darkness enclosed everyone I had ever known and I thought about them, collectively and individually. Owen Rees and his Myfanwy; Rex Sweetland and Alison, delivered of a bouncing boy only that week; Scatty Wallace and his brood; the Gormans of Rainbow Café; and now Esta and the dogged Cecil Trumper, Redcliffe Bay's latest reassertion of the hare and tortoise fable. I wasn't even sure whether I envied them all or not. There they were, mostly paired off and likely to drown in their own complacency, and here I was, a kind of fugitive in what might prove a dismal swamp of loneliness. Of all the people down there only two had an inkling of my true situation and both had already been touched by tragedy. But Ben Dagmar had his newspaper, and Basil Morney-Sutcliffe his skill and his integrity. Neither was as far out on the limb as I was. Both could climb back if they felt like it.

The clock of All Souls' struck ten and I counted the strokes. I turned my back on the town, started the rackety little car and drove inland towards the junction.

RE-ENTRY

An hour before sunset I made my way down Frog Terrace and along the Esplanade to the crowded park where I had left the car. It was less congested now so that I could make some attempt to assess the tremendous physical changes that had taken place in this area since the Sunday I walked over the stretches of marram grass with Morney-Sutcliffe, taking photographs to support his development plan. Even he, Redcliffe Bay's midwife, could never have envisaged so much change, such a labyrinthine sprawl of concrete and roughcast, with beach chalets mushrooming all the way to the slopes of Coastguard Hill like the shanties of a goldrush town. I wondered whether, in fact, it had had his ultimate approval or if he, Ben Dagmar, Garfield Pyne and all the other progressives on the Council hadn't found themselves in the situation of the hard-pressed king who called on a neighboring state to help him fight a war and was at once swallowed by his ally.

There was no trace now of the "Peggoty" atmosphere that had once made me see David Copperfield's Yarmouth as my native heath. There were no nets drying, no longshoremen, no upturned boats. Instead there were airplane floats, short concrete piers with blackboards advertising shark-fishing and water-skiing, and a row of litter baskets that nobody used. Even the shape, size and nature of the visitors seemed to have changed. There were no sedate dads and mums, no scampering little girls with shrimping nets and skirts tucked into knickers. Everybody was either half-naked or dressed in jazzy garments of the kind that the comedians had once used to help a comic entrance in a concert party sketch. A woman about twenty-five came out of a chalet and went down the beach for an evening dip. She was wearing a bikini that would have stopped the clocks in Redcliffe Bay thirty years ago, but nobody gave her a second glance. Two ten-year-olds eating sundaes at a kiosk looked like half-grown Red Indian braves. A youth about nineteen slammed the door on a car, the size and design royalty might have used when I was his age. There was nothing specifically English about the scene. It might have been any one of a hundred resorts, from San Remo to San Sebastian.

I paid half a crown to the uniformed parking attendant (recalling how often I had parked there for nothing), drove the length of the Esplanade and over the extension of the front to the summit of Coastguard Hill. There was a network of new approaches out here but I had no chance to observe them closely, I was too busy avoiding the avalanche of cars pouring into the town from the east. It was only when I reached a three-lane highway heading in the direction of Shelly Bay that I had leisure to look around. The fields that had once stretched all the way from the Valley to the cliff were sliced into hundreds of rectangles and on every rectangle stood a caravan, ranked like squadrons of amphibious tanks awaiting orders to advance across the Channel.

Up here there was no smell of exhaust; it had been vanquished by the smell of fish and chips. Then the road dipped into what had been the goyle and I could pull on to the seaward grass verge and look down on the cove. I recognized it by the twin buttresses of sandstone. It was as full of boats as a Hong Kong backwater. Where Lorna's cabin had stood was a shop built of concrete blocks that looked exactly like a Foreign Legion outpost.

I turned off at the first crossroad and worked my way north and then west until I found the one readily recognizable road in the district, the Valley itself, still flanked on either side by big houses standing in their own grounds. Even these, however, were no longer private dwellings. Most of them had been converted into flats, with here and there a smaller house wedged into the garden. Four or five of the houses that, in my day, had sheltered retired admirals, major-generals and Indian civil servants, displayed hoardings announcing that they catered for the deaf and dumb or otherwise handicapped. Then, halfway down, I braked, for my eye caught a single name on a well-weathered shingle that I remembered. It was "Heatherdene" and it called to me like a despairing white man who runs against another in an African jungle. It didn't seem to have changed in any particular. It still had its tile-hung roof and cream front door, approached by a short, curving drive. The garden still had well-cared-for flower beds, lawns and clumps of hydrangea and laurel.

I saw all this as I coasted past and I saw something else too: a woman, kneeling or crouching beside one of the half-moon flower beds. She was wearing a lemon-colored overall and heavy gardening gloves and working away with a trowel or clippers.

About seventy yards down the slope I pulled into the kerb, just short of a freckled, snub-nosed young man, with the letters "R.B.U.D.C." on his cap. He was doing something to a fire hydrant and his bicycle was propped against the nearest tree. I asked him if he could tell me whether a Doctor Morney-Sutcliffe still lived in one of the houses on this side of the road. He looked up and gave me a friendly smile.

"Morney-Sutcliffe? Doc', you say?" and then, with more interest, "Owns a Triumph Herald? Hot-rod job?"

"No," I said, "he would be over seventy and if he still drives, it would be a Rolls-Bentley or a Daimler."

"Only one family on this block in that bracket," the young man said. He seemed to have taken a course in American paperbacks but he was genuinely anxious to help.

"Who would that be?"

"The Trumpers," he said.

"*Cecil* Trumper?"

"Sure. He was rolling in it. The Big White Chief around here for a long time. Chairman of the Council. Owned a lot of property. Aston-Martin too, but that was sold when he snuffed it. She makes do with a station wagon now."

"Cecil Trumper is dead?"

"About a year ago, maybe more. Cancer, they said it was, but don't quote me. I wasn't on speaking terms with him of course, but he was my boss in a manner of speaking." He pointed to the braided letters on his cap and grinned.

"Did he—does Mrs. Trumper still live at 'Heatherdene,' the big house up the road?"

"Yes, she's there now. Saw her gardening when I was checking Number Nine hydrant."

I realized then why I had stopped less than a hundred yards beyond the gate. There had been something familiar about the woman in the lemon overall as she crouched over the flower beds. Detectives and professional photographers have at least one thing in common—they look for recognition in a walk or posture rather than in features, for these are clues rarely mentioned in crime fiction. It was something about her posture that had made me instinctively slow the car and look inquisitively at the kneeling figure in the lemon-colored overall and gloves.

The young man was still trying to be helpful. "Morney-What-Was-it?" he asked.

"Sutcliffe," I said, "but it's not important. How long have the Trumpers lived in 'Heatherdene'?"

"Ever since I can remember." He looked about twenty-four and I don't know why his answer should have astonished me to that extent but it did, almost as much as his next remark.

"They gave him a handle," he said, with a grin. "*Sir* Cecil Trumper he was."

"They knighted him? Cecil Trumper?"

"You knew him then? You're from this neck of the woods?"

"A long time ago. Thirty years ago."

"Before my time," he said. Like all young men he was unable to conceive of anything of importance happening before he was about.

"What did they knight him for?"

"Search me. What do they knight anyone for? Making dough I suppose, and he made plenty. Land, building and what-not." The young man, however, was not really interested in Cecil Trumper, although the elusive Morney-Sutcliffe continued to bother him.

"Morney-Sutcliffe," he mused. "Rings a bell. You could look him up in the phone directory. There's a kiosk lower down the hill."

"Thank you," I said, "I'll do that," and was glad when he shouldered his crowbar, mounted his cycle and coasted down the incline towards the town.

The irony was superb. I remembered my reactions all those years ago when I tried and failed to patch things up between us, and Esta announced her engagement. I remembered thinking of it as a remarkable illustration of the hare and tortoise story but now it was even more of a fairy-tale. Cecil Trumper. *Sir* Cecil Trumper! Chairman of the Council. The man who had made his pile in land, building and what-not, and then set the seal on his achievements by moving into the headquarters of the biggest fish in the prewar pond. There hadn't been one of us in those days who hadn't been sorry for poor old Cecil, although this had never stopped us tormenting him at school. I wondered if he had finally cured his stutter and what part Esta had played, consciously or unconsciously, in his triumphs.

There was another twist, perhaps the drollest of them all. Cecil's father and uncle had been numbered among those who set their face against "development." I remembered old Rufus Trumper saying, at a Council Meeting, "Giddon, leave the town be, will'ee? Us dorn want forriners gallivanting yer out o' zeason as well as in zeason!" And then Cecil had crested in on the boom and made his packet.

I thought of it from Esta's viewpoint. How did it feel, I wondered, to be snipping flowers from beds that once filled the Doctor's expensive vases? Did it strike her as strange that her sons and daughters, if she had any, were the successors to the smart set of the twenties and early thirties, who had roared up and down this very avenue with their 'Varsity scarves flying in the wind and golf clubs protruding from the dickey-seats of Morris-Cowleys? What a turn-up for the book, as Cecil's bookie uncle might have said.

I wondered how she felt about Cecil dying in his early fifties and whether, in fact, it was possible to make a marriage work when you married on the rebound, as she had done. It wasn't vanity that made me so sure of this. If she had been drawn to Cecil Trumper, she must have shown it during the years we were growing up together, the months when he was hanging around as first reserve, grateful for a smile or a lift of the hand when the lights went up at the old Tivoli. I tried to remember him as something other than a butt but I couldn't. The only time I had seen him show a little spirit had been that night I was shadowing Mike Shapley in the saloon bar of the Lamb and Flag and I had urged him to reassert himself. He hadn't liked that, and it was probably the nearest he ever came to punching somebody on the nose. Even then, however, all he did was to slam the door on the way out.

I wanted to get clear of the place altogether but I couldn't. I stood beside my parked car eighty yards short of the gate, irresolute, and as dejected as an abandoned mongrel on a wet night. I looked for consolation in an attempt to measure my overall experience against the flatness of the lives lived by the stay-at-homes who had remained rooted in the wedge-shaped cleft between Mitre Head in the west and Coastguard Hill in the east, but this didn't work either. What was the use of reminding myself that this wasn't the town I remembered, or that development and expansion had destroyed any charm and taste and originality it had possessed when I was a boy? Cecil and Esta wouldn't see it that way. They had watched it grow and change, and had grown with it, not only financially but almost certainly in areas of tolerance and mutual understanding. At all events their marriage had lasted a very long time and even that was an achievement these days. It probably followed that they had sons, daughters and grandchildren who, for something approaching a quarter-century, had filled that big, impersonal house with noise, laughter and argument. What did I have to match all that? The knack of capturing moments of high drama with a camera and access to any number of hotel rooms in the corners of the world where those dramas took place. They had their memories and most of them would make mine look threadbare for who, in his senses, would trade a kid's first stumbling steps for a ringside seat at Gandhi's assassination, or a close-up of guides bringing broken bodies down the north face of the Eiger? I had been places and seen things but what places and what things? Decomposing bodies in Korean foxholes, mobs stoning steel-helmeted police in Continental towns, Negroes at Little Rock grappling with Alsatian dogs, burned-out tanks at Tobruk and the bloody debris of Omaha landing-beach. Hate, violence, persecution and disaster, against their slow unfolding of the years, starred with the tiny triumphs of passed examinations, family picnics, birthdays and civic occasions.

I took a step towards the car and then stopped, once more irresolute, as a two-seater sports car came zooming up from the town, its horn blaring and its cockpit dangerously overcrowded. I caught a glimpse of laughing girls and sunburned young men, of tennis racquets and headscarves, of uninhibited zest for life of the kind I had once had and somehow lost in the arms of a woman I still thought of as Lorna but whose real name was Ethel. "Ethel Watkins" he had said, and up the road, troweling away at her violas or zinnias or delphiniums, was Esta Wallace. It had never struck me before that the initials were identical. Now that it did the coincidence seemed significant.

The car shot across to the offside and stopped, still hooting, and as I watched a girl of about nineteen (daughter or daughter-in-law-elect?) leapt out and stood on the pavement shouting something into the driveway. Without even wishing it I found myself moving up the hill towards the open gate and was already halfway there when the woman in the lemon overall and gardening gloves came out and stood talking to the girl and the others in the overcrowded car. This time I got a good look at her. She had nicely-styled greying hair and there was a roundness about her figure that hadn't been there when she had walked out of my life all those years ago. But the roundness suited her. It was just enough to give her an air of repose that she had never had, not even as Water Queen in 1932. She stood with her sturdy legs slightly astride, hands dipped into the pockets of her overall. She looked at ease with the noisy, boisterous youngsters, and when the young man driving the car said something she threw up her head and laughed. The westering sun lit up her face. I saw that she was pretty again.

Then the girl who had climbed out of the car loaded her with racquets, which she accepted with counterfeit protests, and the girl kissed her and hopped onto the folded hood of the car. The engine let out a deep-throated roar and the car shot off like an electric hare, disappearing over the crest in a matter of seconds.

I was about ten yards below the gate now and Esta Trumper, widow of the local bigwig, was standing on the worn edge of the pavement, her arms full of tennis racquets and her face lifted to the sun. She was smiling and looking in the direction of the jet-propelled youngsters, and the smile still lurked about the corners of her mouth when she heard my step and turned.

She didn't recognize me. There was absolutely no doubt about that. For a second our eyes met, but in hers there was not the smallest flicker of recognition. All I got was a nod and that friendly, impersonal twitch of the lips that occasionally passes between people of an older generation in the presence of young people. Her almost imperceptible pleasantry had nothing to do with the girl I had known throughout the most impressionable years of my life. It was prompted by the orange glow of the sunset and her own sense of well-being. It came from a deep sense of peace and gratitude, from a quiet pride in one or more of the occupants of the sports car, from an assumption of shared experience in the ways of the young and their unquenchable high spirits. It said, in effect, "You're round about my age but wouldn't it be tiresome to have to racket about like that? It's fun watching them though!" I touched my hat and walked on up the hill. When I looked over my shoulder she had withdrawn into her garden.

I was breathing like a man who has walked up ten flights of stairs with a suitcase in each hand. I was trembling too, with a sense of monstrous injustice and exclusion, so that I stood at the crest of the avenue incline to cool off before nerving myself to walk down again to where I had left the car. When I drew level with "Heatherdene" I looked straight ahead. By now the sun had dipped beyond Mitre Head, and the vast new sprawl that choked the cleft was screened by a curtain of violet dusk. I was still doing my balance sheet, mine, Esta's and Cecil Trumper's, and I kept getting different answers because I couldn't check on most of the items. There was the town, and I could have looked for them down there, but if Esta Wallace didn't recognize me at two paces, who would? Myfanwy and Owen, Rex and Alison Sweetland, Bill Belcher and Her, Ken Pigeon and Greta, were almost certainly dead or scattered, and as I thought of this it occurred to me that here was part of an answer because I could only think of them all in couples. Whatever had happened to them, good or bad, had been a mutual matter. Not one of them would be required to do a sum like mine in solitude.

I understood then, and for the first time since breasting the edge of the moor and driving down into the cleft, precisely why I had returned. I was on the very edge of moral bankruptcy and something had to be attempted in the way of arriving at a profit and loss. It couldn't be put off any longer. Like the woman on the Island of Shalott I had to break through the web of my own isolation. This was where its first strands had been woven and this was where it would have to be completed or rejected. It was no good repeating my flight of December, 1932. Over the hill there was nothing awaiting me but more air terminals, more silent hotel rooms and more accounting. I was tired of looking for a place to scrape a hole in the ground and scramble inside. I could no longer support the role of Redcliffe Bay's Flying Dutchman.

I started the engine and drove down the hill into the dusk bowl, turning left, passing along the Esplanade and circling the new Frog Terrace roundabout to Stump. Earlier in the day I had noticed a small hotel occupying premises that were once filled by Applegarth's bookshop, one of Trumper's depositories, and the office of Cecil's bookmaker uncle. It was called the Bayview and it looked clean and comfortable. I was lucky. Someone had just phoned reception and cancelled. I got a second-floor room looking out over the enclosure, affording a view about fifty yards south of the one from the studio shop window. I changed, shaved, bathed and went down to dinner.

Awaiting it I had two large brandy-and-sodas, reflecting, as I sipped them, that I was sitting within a stone's throw of where I had once sipped brandy from the bottle Lorna brought me the day after Birdie Boxall died.

It might have been the spirit, or a memory more poignant than most, or the tune that came drifting over the piped radio doing duty for an orchestra. Someone—Mantovani, I imagine for it was his signature tune—was playing *Charmaine*, and although I did not associate this particular tune with Lorna or Esta it reminded me very sharply of the era, of all those simple melodies Lorna had played on her portable gramophone and all the later ones that came to us by courtesy of Bruce Brayley's talking-picture programmes at the Tivoli across the road. It succeeded in destroying what little appetite I had, and after playing with a couple of courses I had another brandy and went up to my room.

I didn't turn on the light. There was no moon but the Stump's street lighting had improved since my day and twenty-foot standards were spaced all the way from Frog Terrace to the bank, at the junction of Fore Street. From my window I could see the floodlit face of the gazing lifeboatman, the one symbol of the old town that nobody had dared to disturb. There he was, still staring southward across the bay, still watching for a wreck or, as the local wags had always preferred, a lady going to bed in one of the upper rooms on East Stump. The sight of him comforted me. Under his scrutiny and the mantle of summer darkness, the vast changes in the scene below were not as arresting as they had been in the sunshine.

I turned on the bedside light and opened the telephone directory, running my finger down the column of names beginning with "Tr" and finding "Trumper, Lady Cecil, Heatherdene, Valley Road" at the bottom. It was a five-letter dialing number and even this astonished me; in the old days our numbers only went up to about four hundred.

I don't know how long I sat there with my finger on the first number. It must have been five minutes at least, perhaps much longer. Traffic flowed up and down Stump, grinding and purring, and voices floated up from the pavement. Then a girl laughed and the sound of her laughter pushed me over the edge. I dialed carefully and deliberately. The double-purr of the phone synchronized with my heartbeats.

The purring stopped and a voice, her voice, said, "Heatherdene; Lady Trumper here."

"It's Pip," I said, "Pip Stuart."

The silence was the silence of the world that follows the roar of the last nuclear bomb. Every vehicle and passerby on Stump must have stopped dead.

Then she spoke again in a voice that I could just hear.

"Where are you, Pip?"

I had forgotten the name of the hotel so I said, "Where I used to read old Applegarth's second-hand books for nothing!"

"The Bayview?"

"That's it. Everything's changed its name."

"You were up here an hour or so ago."

I still did not believe that she had recognized me and nothing would have persuaded me that I was wrong. Before I could reply she confirmed this, saying, "I've been thinking about you ever since I came in from gardening. Someone came by but it didn't register, or not until I went into the house. Then I felt odd and it had something to do with you. How do you account for that?"

The timbre of her voice hadn't changed at all. She might have been asking my advice on how to solve the Sweetland problem, or whether it was permissible to bully Owen Rees into marrying Myfanwy. When I didn't reply immediately she went on, "But you recognized me?"

"No," I said, "not really, or only in the sense that you did. A Council workman filled in the blanks. He told me Cecil had died. Otherwise I wouldn't have rung. Do you believe that?"

"Yes, I believe it."

"Some youngsters loaded you with tennis racquets and then roared off in a Sunbeam Rapier."

"My younger daughter and some of her friends."

"How large a family have you got?"

"Three," she said, "one boy and two girls. Another boy was killed in the war."

"How is that possible?"

"A hit-and-run raid," she said, "the same bombs killed Ben Dagmar, Doctor Morney-Sutcliffe and Ken Pigeon and his wife, Greta."

I digested this. It accounted for some of the gaps on Stump and also, perhaps, why Cecil had been able to buy "Heatherdene." There didn't seem to be anything else to say unless she said it. I waited. The night breeze stirring the chintz curtains struck cold under my armpits.

"You're on your way somewhere?" she said, at last.

"No," I said, "nowhere at all."

"Then come up," she said. "The children won't be in until all hours and I'm alone. Would you like to do that, Pip?"

"Oh God, I can't think of anything I'd like more!" I said, with the fervour of Rex Sweetland launching one of his evangelistic campaigns.

"Then do it. I'll look out for you at the gate."

Her telephone clicked and I sat holding mine so tightly that I might have been attempting to crush it. It was the promise to wait at the gate that made the impact.

Suddenly I didn't give a damn about the rape of Redcliffe Bay. For all I cared they could build skyscrapers and Las Vegas casinos right along the front and all the way up Stump to Fore Street. I had the answer. It had finally got through to me that I had always been a Lilliputian.